MEANT TO BE

"Eden," he breathed, coming to life and moving a step closer to her.

"No!" she said frantically. "Don't come any closer. If—if you're going to stay here, then we'll have to keep away from each other. Not be alone—ever."

He knew all too well she was right. But his body was giving him a different message: it urged him to take her into his arms.

"How do you know what we feel is wrong?" he asked her, his voice husky. "Maybe it's not wrong at all."

He heard her indrawn breath.

"We don't even like each other! You think I'm a cold Yankee, and I—"

Jesse reached Eden, standing in front of the tree. He put his hands on the rough trunk on either side behind Eden's face, hemming her in. "Oh, no," he murmured, close to her ear. "I don't think you're cold. I don't think that at all."

His warm breath tickled her ear. She shivered. He was so close she could feel his body heat in the cool evening. She knew she should forget about her dignity and leave, get away from him, go back to the cabin.

Instead, she lifted her face to the shadowy outline of his.

Slowly he lowered his head. When his lips finally touched hers, he felt her shiver again. But she didn't try to move away. His mouth brushed over hers, lightly at first . . . then, as her lips parted a little, he shivered, too, deepening the kiss . . .

Advance praise for

Elizabeth Graham's

COURTING EDEN

*   *   *

"COURTING EDEN is a sensitive portrait of the post–Civil War South that will win the hearts of readers. Elizabeth Graham's compassion and eloquence make this a wonderful, memorable read."

—*Romantic Times*

"Americana romance readers will absolutely cherish Elizabeth Graham's latest novel."

—*Affaire de Cœur*

"COURTING EDEN is a lovely and heartfelt story of love and survival after a devastating war."

—*The Paperback Forum*

"A marvelous story from the very talented Elizabeth Graham. She never fails to entertain . . ."

—*The Literary Times*

*   *   *

Look for Elizabeth Graham's next historical romance, coming from Zebra Books in July 1997!

COURTING EDEN

ELIZABETH GRAHAM

ZEBRA BOOKS
KENSINGTON PUBLISHING CORP.

Chapter One

North Carolina
May 1865

"Damn it!" A sharp pain joined the constant ache in Jesse Bainbridge's wounded leg. He should have waited a few more days before starting home, as the kindly North Carolina farm woman who'd nursed him had urged. Jolting up these mountain trails on horseback wasn't helping any, either.

You don't have to do this, the sensible, critical part of his brain told him. *You could have gone straight home.*

But his conscience would give him no rest until he found Corporal Clayborne's cabin and delivered to his widow the man's personal effects. Why did he feel compelled to do it? He'd seen dozens, hundreds, of men die during the war. Why was this death different?

He knew why. Guilt twisted his gut again. As company commander, Jesse should have sent Clayborne back home when he'd showed up in North Carolina in February, coughing his head off, too sick to fight. But he hadn't.

Joe Johnston needed every man he could get, even though by that time, Jesse, as well as most of the troops left in the ragged, hungry army of Tennessee, knew the South was finished.

With no warning, a wave of dizziness swept over him, and he slumped in the saddle. Alarmed, he fought for control but realized it was no use. He reined Ranger in, sliding from the saddle onto the trail only a moment before blackness engulfed him.

"Mister, are you ailin'?"

The young, anxious voice penetrated the gray fog. He felt a light touch on his butternut coat. Jesse opened his eyes. He lay on his side on the trail, and a slim, barefoot girl in a faded calico dress, her flaxen hair in two thick braids, crouched beside him. Her bright blue eyes were as anxious as her voice had been. Her fingers loosened his shirt collar.

Jesse shook his head. "I'm all right." He'd managed to land on his good leg, barely missing a large, jagged rock, but the injured leg felt like someone had started a fire under it. He tried to pull himself upright and another wave of dizziness hit him. When it passed, he carefully eased to his back, then rose to a sitting position, bracing himself with his hands.

He hadn't missed the rock, after all. A gaping tear in his worn gray trousers showed blood oozing from his wound. Damnation!

He heard the girl draw in her breath in a shocked gasp. "Yore hurt! I knowed somethin' was wrong."

Jesse turned toward her, trying for a reassuring smile. "I'm all right," he said again. "I just need to rest for a few minutes."

"No, you ain't," the girl said, her voice very positive for one so young. "Yore leg is hurt bad. Did you git shot by a Yankee?"

The girl's forthrightness and complete lack of fear surprised him. But tucked up on this North Carolina ridge, her homestead probably hadn't been touched by marauders from either side. She hadn't learned to fear, as had so many in Georgia after Sherman had burned much of Atlanta and begun his rapacious march to Savannah.

Jesse's face tightened as he thought of his mother. His ruined plantation. Annabelle, his fiancée, who'd tried to keep things together.

He nodded. "Yes, and I only reopened the wound. I'll put a

new bandage on, and it'll be fine." The leg was far from fine, but he'd camp here for the night and find Mrs. Clayborne's cabin tomorrow. Then he'd head on home to Annabelle.

The girl got to her feet. "You need doctorin'. I'll take you to the cabin. Reckon you can stay on the horse if I help you back on?"

Jesse struggled to his feet, fighting off a new wave of blackness. He reluctantly admitted the girl was right: he needed help and didn't know if he could stay on Ranger. "I think I'd better walk. How far is the cabin?"

"A right smart piece. Maybe I ort to git Darcy and Pap." She frowned in thought, then her face brightened. "But Miz Hannah's ain't. We'll go there. Kin you lean on me?" She presented a slender shoulder.

"If you can find me a walking stick, that would work better," he told her.

" 'Course I kin." She vanished, reappearing a few moments later with a sturdy tree limb. From a pocket she produced a knife. She expertly whittled off a protruding knob and gave the stick to him. "Is this 'un all right?"

"It's fine," Jesse assured her, gratefully bracing himself with it. He glanced at Ranger, grazing a few feet away.

The girl followed his gaze. "Don't you worry none 'bout yore horse. I'll tether him and come back and git him later." She followed her words with swift action, securing Ranger to a tree in the shade.

Jesse felt warm blood trickling down his leg, accompanying the thrum of pain. He'd be a fool to argue further. A smart soldier knew when to quit. He'd learned that if nothing more from four years of war. "Lead the way."

"There's a path, but it's a ways. And you ain't in no shape to walk more'n you have to."

"You're right there," Jesse admitted. Sweat ran down his face, even though the May afternoon wasn't hot. He paused to remove his worn jacket and roll up his shirt sleeves. He guessed it was time they exchanged names.

"I'm—Jesse Bainbridge," he told her, barely stopping himself from adding "Major."

The Yankees had stripped the rebel buttons from his coat,

as well as his regimental insignia. His mouth twisted at those humiliating memories. But though he was back to being plain Jesse Bainbridge, that suited him fine. He was a planter—he'd never liked soldiering. He forced a smile. "What's your name?"

She glanced at him, smiling shyly back. "Willa Freeman."

"I'm happy to make your acquaintance, Miss Freeman," Jesse said.

Her eyes widened at his formality, but she bobbed her head in acknowledgment. "I'm real pleased to meet you, too," she said. "Are you lost, mister? We don't git many strangers up on the ridge."

This girl no doubt knew the location of the Clayborne cabin. He should ask her where it was, but he didn't feel up to it right now. And he certainly didn't feel up to talking to the widow. He'd wait until tomorrow. "No, I'm not lost," he told her. "I—have to take care of some business."

She nodded, asking no more questions. Staying close to him, she pushed aside the rank, tangled growth of laurel, sassafras, and sumac and held it back while he passed as they slowly made their way through a patch of woods.

They pressed through one more patch of underbrush and were in a clearing. A log cabin rose in the middle; behind it Jesse glimpsed outbuildings. A tall, black-haired woman stood on the cabin's small front porch, her hand shading her eyes against the sun as she looked toward them.

Jesse's muscles tightened. He dreaded the next few minutes. He didn't feel up to explaining why he was here to this woman, to anyone. He only wanted to get off his feet as quickly as possible. He forced a smile for the girl, then stepped forward again. Might as well get it over with.

Eden Clayborne's dark brows drew together as she watched the approaching pair. She'd heard a horse's whinny while inside the cabin but saw none with Willa and the stranger who walked beside her. Who was he?

Willa and the man came closer, and she now saw he was limping. Blood trickled down his leg from a gaping hole in his faded, worn gray trousers. A butternut-colored coat was slung over his arm. The tension eased, and she decided he posed no threat. He was only a soldier returning home, like thousands of others.

Her mouth tightened. *Her* husband would never come back . . .

The soldier reminded her of the mountain lions she'd occasionally seen during her four years here on this ridge. His thick, shaggy hair was a sunstreaked dark blond, and the sun caught glints off the hair on his well-muscled arms below the rolled-up sleeves of his coarse white shirt. His eyes, beneath blond brows, were another, deeper shade of yellow-brown. His nose was straight, his mustache and beard a slightly darker shade than his hair. His beard didn't conceal his well-molded facial structure.

Even though he limped, even though he wore only the sad, battered remnants of a Confederate uniform, she knew he'd been an officer. He still had an air of command showing clearly through his exhaustion.

And an inborn pride and arrogance. He was one of the planters. She lifted her head, her face tightening. Men such as he had started this senseless war which had destroyed so many lives. What was he doing here?

He and Willa had almost reached the porch. And he looked as if he'd never make it up the steps without more help. Eden swallowed, hurrying off the porch. It was possible her assumptions about him were wrong. Even if they weren't, no matter how she felt, she couldn't turn away anyone sick or injured.

"This here is Mister Bainbridge, Miz Eden. He's hurt right bad," Willa said. "I thought I'd better bring him here 'cause it's closer than Mam and Pap's."

Willa called him mister, Eden noted. So he'd not given her his rank. That was fine with her. She'd be glad to call him mister, too. She wanted no more reminders of the just-ended war.

"You did the right thing, Willa."

The woman stopped in front of Jesse. She gave him a tight, forced smile. "Can you make it up the porch steps?"

Surprise snaked through Jesse as he listened to her crisp words. This was no backwoods mountain woman. Her voice was cultivated and educated—and northern: a Yankee's. He felt his stomach muscles tighten. Her kind had conquered his people. *Defeated.* He hated the word. What in hell was she doing here, on this ridge, in this cabin?

The tall, striking woman wore a faded brown calico dress similar to Willa's. Glossy black braids wrapped around her head. Her skin was tanned a honey gold. But the gypsylike looks were broken by her deep blue eyes, fringed with thick black lashes and topped with arching black brows. As her dress moved with her steps, Jesse saw something else: she was pregnant.

He nodded, his face holding no return smile. "Of course. It's kind of you to offer your hospitality."

His voice was formal and cool, no friendlier than her own, Eden noted. The years she'd spent in these hills hadn't softened her speech, and she liked a Yankee woman no more than she did a southern gentleman. Good. That made things easier. No pretense would be necessary between them.

Jesse straightened his back and by sheer force of will limped up the steps. He wasn't at all sure he could make it to the cabin door, but he'd die trying. The two females hovered at his side, stopping before the open door. His leg throbbed like hell, and the dizziness had come back.

"Iffen you don't need me any more, I'll go fetch yore horse," Willa told him.

He nodded. "Thank you. He could use some water." He could hear his voice soften when he spoke to the girl. He had no quarrel with her. He'd fought alongside many a brave hill man, including the one whose family he was here to find. He set his face in rigid lines to keep from showing pain, but knew he had to get off his feet soon or collapse.

Another female voice called from inside the cabin. "Eden, who you got out there? Bring him in."

The woman led the way. In a moment, Jesse's eyes adjusted to the dimness after the sunwashed day outside. Light shone through gaps in the chinking between the logs, revealing one large room with a ladder to a sleeping loft at the far end. Two corners held beds. In one an old woman lay propped on pillows. Even though his vision was wavering, he could see the deep sadness in her dark eyes, in the downturned lines of her wrinkled face.

"Mother Clayborne, this is Mr. Bainbridge. He has an injured leg, and a fever, if I'm not mistaken," the younger woman said in her clear tones. "You may have this bed," she told him, indicating the empty one neatly covered with a bright patchwork quilt.

Clayborne. Shock spiraled through Jesse's tired body. He jerked his head up and stared at the tall woman. She stared back, dislike, almost hatred, blazing from her blue eyes. Was this Corporal Clayborne's wife, and the other woman his mother? One of them pregnant and the other sick or bedfast?

Jesus, he hoped not. Maybe they were just related to the Claybornes he sought. He closed his eyes as weakness spread through him. He couldn't find out anything more now. He was at the end of his endurance—he had to get off his feet, rest a while.

"Thank you, ma'am," he muttered. He managed to get to the bed, then everything went black.

"Oh, my land!" the older woman said, her voice trembling as Jesse sprawled across the bed. "He didn't up and die on us, did he?"

Eden pressed her hand against his forehead and her heart sank. As she'd thought, he burned with fever. And her mother-in-law sounded well on the way to a bad spell. "No, of course not. He only fainted. He'll be all right."

Tugging at his scuffed, worn-out boots, Eden hoped that was true. The sooner he was well and on his way, the better. Her instinctive feeling that he wasn't a hill man had been proved when he'd spoken. Her lips thinned. No, as she'd thought, he was a southern aristocrat.

She finally got the boots off. Both wool stockings had huge holes in the toes. She took them off, too, and carefully tugged up his ripped trouser leg to inspect the wound. At least it had stopped bleeding. It was a gunshot wound, she guessed, although she'd never seen one before. As she'd feared, the wound looked infected, pus oozing out from several places. It also looked as if it had been reinjured recently.

"He don't look all right to me," Hannah said. "Reckon you need to git the smellin' salts?"

Eden pulled a quilt that had been folded at the foot of the bed over him, rather than try to get his dead weight under the covers. The infected wound was probably causing the fever, she hoped, because he wasn't coughing and didn't sound hoarse, as if he had a respiratory ailment. Of course, any number of things could cause it. She wouldn't think about that possibility.

Turning to her mother-in-law, she forced a smile so the other woman wouldn't see her worry. She might despise his kind, but she didn't want him to die on her bed.

"I think he needs sleep and rest more than anything. But I'm going to make a poultice for his wound. What kind would be best?"

Hannah gave her a sad smile. "Gal, you know as well as I do. Better, now you and Willa are gatherin' all them wild plants to sell."

Eden didn't mind being caught out in her small deception, to draw Hannah into a discussion about remedies, because her mother-in-law had perked up a little and looked interested.

"I believe I'll use slippery elm bark. Comfrey tea later, when he wakes up." Without warning, nausea attacked, and she pressed a hand to her softly rounded abdomen.

The older woman hadn't missed her quick movement. "You need a cup o' peppermint tea yoreself. You work too hard fer a woman in the fambly way."

And who would do the work if she didn't? "I'm all right. Pennyroyal or crawley root for the fever?" she asked, hoping to distract Hannah.

Hannah frowned in thought. "Crawley root works faster," she finally pronounced.

Eden nodded. "I have plenty on hand."

Her dark eyes clouding, Hannah sighed deeply. "I wisht I was able to hep you."

Eden did, too, but knew urging her mother-in-law to get up and move about wouldn't get her out of bed. Only time could accomplish that. And maybe nothing would.

How they would manage later, when Eden grew heavy with this child, after it came . . . no, she wouldn't think about that.

She'd take one day at a time. At least a little money was coming in now, from the sale of the herbs and plants, especially the ginseng.

"I takened the horse to the barn, Miz Eden. Was that all right?" Willa's light, lilting voice asked from the doorway.

Eden flashed her a quick smile. "It's fine. I'm going to make up some medicines for Mr. Bainbridge." He looked to be in his middle thirties. Again, she wondered where he was going, why he was here on the ridge.

Willa glanced at the still figure in the bed and her eyes widened. "Is he real sick?"

"I don't think so," Eden reassured her, again hoping she was right.

"Reckon I had better go on home. Mam will git me with a switch iffen I'm late doin' my evenin' chores." Willa grinned at Eden. "*Get* me, I mean," she corrected herself. "Will you have time to give me a lesson tomorrow?"

Eden hated the way Willa's mother treated her, hated even more the casual way the girl accepted it. She forced a smile. "We'll find time. Come over in the afternoon. Goodbye, Willa."

She watched the girl walk down the steps with a natural grace and her lips tightened. In the boisterous Freeman household, Willa wasn't much valued. At thirteen, she was considered almost a woman. Eden knew in another year or two her parents would be finding her a husband.

"Not if I can help it," Eden muttered, searching through jars of dried herbs on a shelf. Of course, men were scarce now. The damnable war had taken a lot of them. Willa's two brothers had all miraculously escaped death, although the older one had lost a leg at Shiloh.

Eden shuddered. She hated even the names of the cursed battles! Hated remembering how she'd brought the newspapers from the settlement in the valley, read the rolls of dead and missing to Hannah and the Freemans.

Finally, the day she'd dreaded came. Alston's name leaped up at her from the newsprint. He'd died a few days before General Johnston had surrendered to Sherman. That was what she couldn't forget, couldn't stop blaming herself for. Last fall he'd come home to recuperate from pneumonia, and in January had gone back to the war. If only she'd told him about her suspected pregnancy and persuaded him to stay here, he'd be alive today. But her pride hadn't allowed her to beg.

Another, darker guilt gnawed at her. Her grief for Alston was only grief for a friend, not the bitter anguish of a wife who loved her husband deeply. She didn't know when her love had died, but die it had . . . long before Alston's physical death.

She found what she needed on the shelf and soon had the poultice ready to apply. Again approaching the bed where the man lay, she was relieved to see he'd regained consciousness.

His tawny lion's eyes stared straight at her. No, she thought, drawing a quick breath, *into* her. For a long moment, she felt as if her heart and soul were bared to this man, this stranger she'd never seen until a few minutes ago.

She stared back at him, realizing something even more startling. She felt, for a moment, as if she knew him, too, could read behind his disturbing eyes the pain that bracketed his well-shaped mouth.

His gaze shifted away and he asked, his voice weak, "May I have a drink of water?"

Eden laid her medical supplies on the chest of drawers near the bed. "Of course." She turned back toward the kitchen. Hannah was right—she needed more rest. Her mind was playing tricks on her.

"Well, I'm shore glad to hear you a-talkin," Hannah said. "Didn't know but what you might have left us fer good."

"Oh, I'll be around a while. I'm a tough bird. Take more than a wounded leg to do me in."

Eden, dipping water into a glass, spilled a little. He sounded very bitter, almost as if he was sorry he was still alive. Unbidden compassion filled her. He'd no doubt fought hard and bravely. Probably from the start, four long, agonizing years ago.

A vision of Alston lying somewhere under the North Carolina ground came to her. She also had no doubt her husband had been a brave soldier.

She finished filling the glass and took it to the man in the bed. She steadied his hand with her own as he drank thirstily. His hand was much too warm; she'd better get the crawley root into him. He drained the glass, then lay back on the pillow, closing his eyes. His long lashes swept his cheeks. Dark circles surrounded his eyes. He looked completely exhausted.

Eden fought another wave of pity. The sooner she could get him well enough to travel, the better. If his class of people had been willing to be reasonable on the slavery issue, there would have been no war for anyone to fight, to be wounded in. To die.

He didn't deserve her sympathy, no matter how bravely he'd fought.

Chapter Two

A girl's high, trilling laughter, followed by a woman's lower tones, came through the cabin doorway. Jesse's eyes snapped open and he was instantly awake. Four years of war had taught him that.

But for a few moments he couldn't remember where he was or what had happened. It gradually began coming back to him, in bits and pieces, dreamlike, with no continuity. He recalled being terribly thirsty and the woman giving him fresh, cool water, and putting a poultice on his wound that eased the pain.

She'd also given him some kind of herb tea to drink, which he hadn't wanted, but she'd insisted. He had vague memories of her tending him during the night. Renewing the poultice, giving him more tea and water.

Another dreamlike memory surfaced. The woman had looked at him, and he'd looked back at her, and for a moment he'd felt he knew everything there was to know about her—and she him. His mouth curved wryly at the fanciful thought. He was a practical man not given to such things. It must have been the fever, he decided. A fever dream.

He glanced around the neat cabin. A shelf of books was on the wall opposite his bed. He recognized the Bible and

Shakespeare's works, as well as several other volumes. A gleam of sunlight struck some cut glass pieces on another shelf in the kitchen, making them glitter like diamonds. A bowl of colorful wildflowers sat in the center of the oak table on a white table-cloth. The floor was of rough puncheon, but brightened with several colorful braided rugs. Altogether, it was a cheerful, pleasant room.

Another trill of laughter came from the porch, again followed by the woman's lower tones.

"Them two do have a good time together."

Jesse tensed at the unexpected voice and turned his head. The old woman sat up in the other bed, holding a pair of knitting needles and what looked like an unfinished stocking. In a rush he remembered everything else.

His stomach tightened as he looked at her. Was she Corporal Clayborne's mother? Was the younger woman his widow?

The old woman gave him a tremulous smile. "I declare, I don't know what Eden would do without that young'un. They're a heap o' company to each other. Eden's goin' to make a good mother."

He had to ask either her or the younger woman. But first he had to get out of this bed. He knew the hill people were clannish, that several related families often lived close together on the ridges. It was quite possible these weren't the Claybornes he sought.

"Where you from, Mr. Bainbridge?" the woman went on, without waiting for a comment on her statement. " 'Tain't here-abouts, I knowed that the minute I heared you talk yistidday evenin'."

Jesse managed a smile. "I'm a Georgian, ma'am. From near Savannah."

The woman sighed and shook her head. "Oh, the awful things that devil Sherman did to Georgee! Eden read us about it out of the papers, and Alston wrote us about it, too."

A muscle in Jesse's jaw jumped at her last words. He wasn't going to be lucky. This *was* the Clayborne family he was hunting. He tensed himself for her next questions. What unit was he in? What battles had he fought?

Instead, she gave a long sigh. "Oh, I jist don't see how the good Lord could be so cruel as to take Alston away from us, when we loved and needed him so much. With Eden in the fambly way—and the war jist about over, too."

Her words ended on a sob. The knitting needles dropped from her hands onto the quilt. Tears rolled down her wrinkled cheeks, and her features contorted into lines of deep sorrow.

Jesse's heart lurched as her words removed his last doubt. God, the damnable war! Guilt hit him anew. If only he'd sent Corporal Clayborne home. Or at least kept him from trying to fight in that last, futile battle before the surrender. What good had it done, to keep on fighting? None at all. And the worst of it was, the exhausted, hungry men had known it wouldn't.

Their damned southern pride had kept them going long past the time when they should have given in. Even now, he hated the idea of surrender, defeat. This was *his* land that had been invaded, defiled, destroyed. *His* way of life that was gone forever.

Should he tell this woman her son was in his regiment? His company? That he was Clayborne's commanding officer? Would it comfort her to talk about him? But how could he bring himself to do that when he felt such a load of guilt?

A loud honking came from the front porch. Jesse turned toward the door. A pair of large white geese peered inquisitively around the edge of the door frame. At their feet squatted three yellow goslings, peeping frantically.

His mother had kept geese. One old gander followed her around whenever she went into the barnyard, which was often. His mother came from a farm family. She liked to be outside. Pain sliced through him as he thought about the new grave he'd never seen. She was another casualty of the war, as much as if she'd fought in battle.

"Oh, my land, it's them pesky geese agin," the old woman said, her voice a little stronger. "Eden!" she called.

Another voice, firm and young, shooed the fowl from the doorway. The woman who'd tended him last night stood silhouetted there for a moment, the sun outlining her rounded figure.

The knot in Jesse's stomach hardened. He hadn't talked much to Corporal Clayborne, but the young man had many friends among the enlisted men. His harmonica playing around the campfires at night had cheered everyone during those last bleak weeks.

Jesse did some rapid mental calculations. The woman's pregnancy wasn't too far advanced, and Clayborne had been home recuperating a few months ago. But he felt sure Clayborne would have told his friends his wife was pregnant—if he'd known. Why hadn't he known?

She came inside, glancing toward the bed where Jesse now sat up. Her face tightened as she saw he was awake. "Good afternoon, Mr. Bainbridge. You're looking much better. I'm going to cook supper. Do you feel like eating?"

Supper? He must have slept around the clock. Like yesterday, her voice was crisply polite, but not friendly. That, and the tautness of her face, made him realize anew she didn't want him here.

Why? Was it only that she hated to be reminded of the war because of her loss? Did she resent the extra work he caused? Or was it personal, something about him she disliked?

Her shining black braids curved around her head, her winged black brows made a clean line over her blue eyes. She was a beautiful woman. He caught himself up short, surprised at his wayward thoughts. She was Corporal Clayborne's widow, pregnant with his child. A Yankee. Most important, he reminded himself, he was engaged to Annabelle.

But the woman had been very kind, and he was grateful. There were dark circles under her eyes, as if she'd not slept much last night. She couldn't have, since she'd tended him several times. And he must be in her bed. Surely she wasn't climbing the stairs to the sleeping loft in her condition.

"Yes, some food sounds good," he told her. "I appreciate all you've done for me." He tried to put warmth into his voice, but it sounded formal and polite, not much friendlier than hers had been. He didn't want to be here, either. He nodded toward the older Mrs. Clayborne to include her in his thanks. She'd wiped her tears away, he saw, but her dark eyes looked dull and blank, her face wrinkled and old.

Clayborne's widow inclined her head in acknowledgment. "We have ham and eggs and vegetables. Our homestead, and the ridge, weren't raided like so many in other parts of the country. But of course, we have no flour. Its price is outrageous, when it can be found at all."

She stared straight at him as she talked, and her voice sounded accusing, as if he were somehow responsible for the horrors the Yankees had laid upon the South, the shortages of everything, the terribly inflated prices.

A flash of understanding hit him. She was still a Yankee to the core, even if she had been married to a Confederate. That was why she didn't want him here. Like so many northerners, she blamed the southern planters for the war. And she rightly assumed he was of that class, because of his speech, he supposed.

Abruptly, she turned away toward the kitchen and the small iron cookstove. Jesse looked at her straight, firm back for a moment longer, smiling wryly at his thoughts. He was assuming a lot. But if he was right, if she disliked him now, as merely the representative of a class, she'd hate him if she knew the whole story of her husband's death.

Which he didn't plan to tell either her or Clayborne's mother. No, he would only tell them the man had fought and died bravely, like so many others. No point would be served by them learning his death wasn't necessary.

He had to get out of this bed.

He moved his leg experimentally. It hurt some, but nothing like yesterday. He slipped his hand under the quilt and gingerly touched the area around the wound. The poultice was gone, replaced with a bandage. His trousers were folded neatly at the foot of the bed, his shirt and stockings on top. Reaching for his pants, he saw his clothes were clean, the tears neatly mended.

"Young man, are you sure you ort to be a-gittin' up? You had a bad night."

Jesse glanced over at the older woman. She looked anxious, her brow furrowed. He pulled his pants under the quilt.

"Nature calls, ma'am." It sure as hell did. And it wasn't going to wait much longer. He looked toward the kitchen area to see if Clayborne's widow was also going to object to his leaving the bed.

She hadn't even turned her head. Her hands, quick and capable, stirred something in a bowl, then poured the mixture into an iron skillet and slid it into the oven.

Absurdly, he felt disappointed. She'd nursed him well. Shouldn't she be concerned about him reopening his injury? Especially since he was certain she wanted him out of here as soon as possible.

Frowning, he turned his attention to easing his trousers over the bandage without dislodging it, and also maintaining the precarious privacy afforded by the quilt and sheet.

Finally, he succeeded, then worked his stockings on, ignoring the twinges of pain the movement caused. This accomplished, he lifted his legs onto the rag rug by the bed. His haversack lay beside his boots. In it were Clayborne's harmonica, his book of poetry, and his letters from home.

Also one last letter he'd written just before he'd died.

Jesse felt a lump in his throat and quickly turned his attention to tugging on his boots. He got to his feet, relieved the pain was mild.

"You ort not to be on that leg this soon," the older woman scolded. "There's a chamberpot under yore bed and I'll turn my head away."

In spite of his bleak thoughts, Jesse felt his mouth curve at that idea. He again glanced toward Clayborne's widow. She still had her back turned, and from the stiff set of her shoulders, he didn't think she found her mother-in-law's suggestion amusing.

"I'll take it easy," he promised. He liked the older woman. She was forthright and down to earth and seemed genuinely concerned about him. She didn't blame him for anything concerning the war, as he suspected her daughter-in-law did. *She might, if she knew the whole story of how her son died . . .*

"The privy's out back of the cabin," the older woman told him, her voice resigned.

Jesse nodded. "Thank you." He walked toward the open doorway, not looking toward Eden Clayborne again, and out onto the big front porch.

It was another beautiful May day. Up here you could forget a bloody, agonizing war had just ended. Or would it ever end for the South? He turned off his dark thoughts, drawing in big breaths of the fresh mountain air.

The girl named Willa had apparently left, but the geese hadn't. The goslings, flanked by their parents, ate busily away at the grass. At his approach, the adult geese stuck out their long necks and hissed, raising their heavy wings to attack.

"I'm not going to hurt your babies, so don't take a chunk out of my leg when I turn my back," he told the fierce gander, his voice rough with suppressed emotion.

Annabelle had nursed his mother during her brief illness. His fiancée had written that she didn't suffer, but he wasn't at all sure Annabelle told the truth. She wouldn't want to worry him. She was kind and brave and loyal, and he was very lucky she'd waited for him all during the war.

After he found the privy and relieved himself, he looked around for Ranger. He soon spotted him grazing near a split-rail fence enclosing a field by the barnyard, along with two mules and a milk cow. Ranger was giving the mules a wide berth. Smart of him. Mules could be mean bastards.

Across from the barn and corn crib was a small orchard. Behind it he saw a cornfield and some other crops he couldn't identify at this distance. It was a pretty place, but showed signs of neglect. No wonder. It was too much for two women to tend. No, *one* woman, it appeared. And that one pregnant.

It wasn't any of his concern. Thousands of households were worse off than they were, including his own. And the Yankee woman could have stayed up North, safe and secure from the ravages of war. His heart hardened again as he thought of the beating the South had taken.

An unwanted thought entered his mind. *But she'd have a husband here now to take care of her, if you hadn't sent Clayborne out in that last battle.*

Jesse headed back to the house, testing his leg as he walked. The pain was increasing, he noted, the longer he walked. "Hell!" he swore. He hated the idea, but he knew he should stay here a few more days before he attempted the ride home.

A large, iron wash kettle stood in the side-yard, ashes and partly burned wood under it. He'd seen no pump, either inside or out. No evidence of a well, either. Probably a spring close by, which meant hauling water in buckets. A pregnant woman shouldn't have to do that. Especially in the later months.

And he was causing her more work. His jaw tightened. The only way he could remedy that was to leave today, and he'd be a fool to try to ride with his leg still not healed.

The geese had retreated to the far side of the yard. The gander hissed at him as he came back onto the porch, but in a half-hearted way, as if he knew Jesse posed no threat. The smell of frying ham drifted from inside, making his mouth water and his stomach rumble.

A washstand holding a wooden bucket of water and a basin stood beside the door. He washed his hands and face, deciding as soon as he got back home, he'd get rid of the beard. He dried on a cloth hanging from a peg on the log wall.

He stepped over the threshold again. The table had been set with only two places. Which must mean the older woman didn't get out of bed even to eat. Again he wondered what was wrong with her, if it was a chronic illness. The white plates and flatware glistened, he noticed. Out of the corner of his eye he saw his haversack by the bed.

When was he going to give Clayborne's things to these women? And how would it make them feel—comforted, or even more bereaved? He glanced over at the younger one, busy at the stove. Her dark head was turned away, her back straight as a ramrod. She must be a strong, capable woman to have adapted so well to this primitive way of life. Admiration for her courage stirred inside him, warring with his still smoldering resentment.

Resentment won out for the moment. She didn't have to come here!

Eden heard his step behind her and felt her shoulders tensing. She quickly bent to open the oven door and remove the pan of cornbread, setting it on the stove top. She slid the ham onto a plate and put vegetables left over from the noon dinner into bowls. She poured the milk gravy into another bowl and brought the food to the table.

He stood behind a cane-bottomed chair, his large hands with

their sprinkling of golden hairs resting on the back of it. She remembered how, when she'd removed his shirt, his ribs had stuck out as if he hadn't had a good meal for a long time. He'd have one now, no matter how she felt about him.

She tried to relax. He'd be here a few more days; no use in those days being any more unpleasant than they had to be. He didn't look relaxed, either, she noticed. She didn't think he liked her any more than she liked him. And why should he? He'd known she was a Yankee as soon as she'd spoken to him—and she'd seen him stiffen. He wouldn't be any more inclined to forgive her for the war than she was to exonerate him.

But for Hannah's sake, she'd do her best to hide her feelings, keep things pleasant. Again, she wondered why he was here on this ridge. If he wanted to tell them, fine. But she wouldn't ask.

"Sit down, Mr. Bainbridge." She motioned to the chair. "You shouldn't be on your leg any more than necessary for a few more days."

"You're right. I found that out a few minutes ago." He moved the chair out enough to slide onto it, sticking his injured leg stiffly out in front of him.

Absurdly, his deep, resonant voice with its southern cadences made the hair on her arms stand up. Today, he reminded her even more strongly of a fierce mountain cat. While he was outside, Hannah had told her he was from near Savannah. She wondered what battles he'd fought. Whatever else she thought about him, she instinctively felt he was no coward. She'd wager he'd made a good accounting of himself.

Eden filled a tray with food and took it to the bed. She propped up the pillows and smoothed the quilt, then set the tray across the other woman's lap.

"I declare, you jist take too good a care o' me. I hadn't ort to be in bed like this. I ort to be up helpin' you."

"Stop fretting," Eden said, her naturally crisp tones softened. "You'll soon be up, spry as ever."

Eden returned to the kitchen and sat down at the table. He'd waited for her, although he must be ravenous. His manners were perfect. Like most southerners, he was a gentleman to the core. And what difference did it make to her? She pulled a piece of cornbread apart and spooned gravy over it, wishing it was a biscuit. She'd learned to love southern cooking.

He cleared his throat. Eden glanced up to see him holding out the plate of ham. He'd served himself only one slice, she saw, even though she'd cooked an extra one for him. He was considerate, too.

"How did yore family and home fare durin' the war?" Hannah asked.

There was such a long silence that Eden glanced at him again. His hand gripped his fork so tightly she could see white across his knuckles.

"My family is gone," he finally replied, his voice hard. "My father and brothers were killed in battle and my mother died a few months ago."

Eden wished Hannah hadn't asked him that question. His losses were as great as theirs. Too, she didn't want her mother-in-law upset by terrible accounts of war atrocities.

"I'm sorry," she told him sincerely, knowing how inadequate the phrase was, but what else could she say?

"So am I," he answered, his voice still roughened and hard. "I do have a house standing—or at least, it was, the last I heard. But it's been gutted."

"My land," Hannah's quivering voice said from across the room. "Why, you poor soul. Ain't there no one left who keers fer you?"

Eden bit her lip, wishing Hannah would stop this. But she knew her mother-in-law well, knew the other woman wanted to know these things, had a genuine interest and concern in his life.

He lifted his head and half-smiled at the older woman. His gaze looked far away and full of pain, Eden saw, her heart contracting with pity.

"Oh, there's still someone who cares," he said, his voice under control again. "I've been engaged since before the war. Annabelle and I will be married when I get home."

"Well, that's a blessin'," Hannah said.

"Yes," Jesse agreed. "Annabelle has waited for me. She's a loyal, faithful woman."

He sounded as if he were talking about a friend or relative, not his sweetheart, Eden thought. His answer made her feel uncomfortable, and then she understood why. It was the same way she'd thought and felt about Alston for a long time before he died.

A scuffling noise on the porch brought her head up. Mattie Freeman, Willa's mother, stood in the open doorway. Behind her, almost hidden by Mattie's enormous bulk, was Darcy, her younger son. Darcy had been wounded in an early battle and come home. He hadn't gone back to the war even after he'd recovered.

Eden's heart sank as she rose from the table and forced a smile.

"Come in," she invited, motioning toward the interior of the cabin. As was the custom, she added, "Sit down and have supper with us."

Mattie waved a beefy arm as she entered, Darcy close behind her. "Don't git up. We done et. We'll jist visit with Hannie while you finish up."

Eden introduced Jesse to the pair.

Darcy's handshake was limp, Jesse thought, while Mattie's vigorous pumping left his hand numb. He braced himself for questions, but neither Mattie nor her son seemed interested in finding out anything about him or the last days of the war. He heaved a sigh of relief. He didn't want the Claybornes to find out why he was here now, like this, with these people here.

The young man gave Eden a half-sheepish, half-lovesick look, Jesse noticed, before sitting beside his mother in the other rocker. Jesse glanced at Eden and saw her dark brows draw together in a frown.

Apparently, whatever feelings Darcy held for her weren't returned. The knowledge pleased him, Jesse realized, a little disconcerted. Wasn't it a bit soon after her husband's death for someone to be trying to court her? Hell, it was none of his business, he reminded himself. He forced his glance away from her as she moved to the older Clayborne woman's bed.

Eden took Hannah's tray, concerned at the pallor and fatigue on her mother-in-law's face. Hannah wasn't up to one of Mattie's monologues. She'd have to try to cut the visit short. Which was easier said than done. Mattie was a generous woman, always there in an emergency, but she had the sensitivity of an ox. Eden decided she wouldn't try to use subtlety.

"Do you feel like visiting, Mother Clayborne?" she asked, not trying to keep the visitors from hearing. "Maybe you should rest."

Hannah looked scandalized at this breach of mountain etiquette. When someone came to "set a spell," you talked to them no matter how you felt. "Oh shore I do," she said, but her voice trembled.

The things Jesse Bainbridge had said had upset her, reminding her afresh of the loss she'd suffered, Eden realized.

I should feel that way, too, Eden told herself. But she didn't. She was deeply saddened by Alston's death—but she wasn't brokenhearted.

Mattie pushed back a wisp of graying blond hair that had slipped loose from its knot at the back of her head and arranged her bulk more comfortably in the rocker. It creaked alarmingly, and Eden held her breath. But the sturdy pine chair didn't collapse. After all, Mattie had sat in it many times before.

"Now, you jist settle back in bed," Mattie boomed. "We'll visit while the young folks talk." She nudged Darcy with her foot.

Eden feared her pasted-on smile would crack. She motioned to the table. "Sit down and talk to Mr. Bainbridge, Darcy, while I clear the table."

Jesse felt his mouth trying to curve upward. He took pity on Eden, who was ignoring both of them, while she deftly cleaned up the remnants of their meal.

He pushed back his chair and carefully rose to his feet. He'd even sacrifice a little of his precious ration of tobacco. "I'm going outside for a smoke," he told the younger man. "Do you want to join me?"

Darcy swallowed and his prominent Adam's apple bobbed in his thin neck. He darted a glance toward Eden, but she was filling a tea kettle with water from the bucket on the washstand.

Finally, he nodded. "I reckon so." He followed Jesse out on the porch.

Eden heaved a heartfelt sigh of relief as their backs disappeared from view. Her gaze collided with Mattie's. The older woman was struggling not to show her disappointment. Eden didn't know how to convince Mattie she had no intention of letting Darcy court her. Mattie, and probably most of the ridge folks, thought she should be grateful Darcy was interested.

A woman alone had a rough row to hoe up here, especially a pregnant woman, went their thinking. Any halfway decent man was better than none. Even Hannah shared this view. Although ravaged by grief for Alston, she was ridge born and bred. She knew how precarious their position was.

But the thought of Darcy kissing her, let alone bedding her, appalled Eden. Even if she was willing to marry him, their situation wouldn't be much improved. Darcy, though a good, decent man, wasn't very "work brickle," as Hannah would say. He'd be little help in trying to scrape a living off the rocky soil of this mountain.

Eden knew much of Mattie's promoting Darcy's courtship was motivated by self-interest. She'd caught the covetous glances Mattie had given the cabin, the homestead. The Freeman farm was smaller than this one, and due to poor farming practices, less productive.

When Mattie finally saw Eden had no interest in her son, relations between the two households would be strained at best. At worst, Mattie might decide if Eden thought herself too good for Darcy, the entire Freeman clan would have nothing further to do with her and Hannah. Which would mean the end of her and Willa's friendship.

Eden lifted a stove lid, added two sticks of wood, then put the filled tea kettle over the again lowered lid. She got down the jar of dried sassafras roots and enough cups for all. Several related families of Freemans lived on the ridge, Mattie's cabin the closest to the Claybornes.

People on the ridge depended on one another for help in time of need. But the Freemans could turn to their relatives. The only other family, the Lorimers, were the farthest away of all from her and Hannah.

She glanced up to see an inquiring expression on Mattie's face. Eden coaxed her smile back, but it felt stiffer than ever. "I'm sorry. Did you ask me something?"

"How long is Mr. Bainbridge goin' to stay?"

"Only a few more days, until his leg wound heals enough for him to ride."

"Willie said he told her he had business to tend to here on the ridge. I've been studyin' that. Since he's a stranger to us and our kinfolk and you and Hannah, reckon his business must be with the Lorimers."

Eden put some of the sassafras roots into a cracked old teapot and poured the boiling water over them, wondering if Mattie was right.

A small noise from the porch made her turn in that direction. Jesse Bainbridge's wide frame filled the doorway, the lowering sun outlining his muscled arms and legs, his flat stomach, gilding his tawny hair.

"Sassafras tea," he said, his unsmiling lion's eyes meeting hers. "I hope you made a cup for me. It's been a while since I've had any."

Eden nodded. "Of course."

He sat back down in the chair he'd occupied during supper. Darcy pulled out another one. Eden put their steaming cups in front of them, then gave Mattie and Hannah theirs.

Thank God Mattie seemed to have given up pushing Darcy on her for the moment, Eden thought.

Mattie sipped her tea, studying Jesse Bainbridge with her faded blue eyes. "We kin show you where the Lorimers' cabin is, iffen yore lookin' fer them," she said.

What was the woman talking about? Jesse wondered. "I beg your pardon, ma'am?"

Mattie set her cup and saucer down in her ample lap. "Willie said you had business on the ridge, and since none of us knowed you, we figured it had to be with the Lorimers, bein' as how they's the onliest other fambly up here."

He'd be damned if he was going to let this inquisitive female push him into a corner. No, the Clayborne women deserved to receive Alston's possessions in dignity and privacy. He drank deeply of the aromatic brew and set his cup down.

"No, I don't know the Lorimers," he said. "I guess Willa misunderstood me. All I meant was, I took the trail through the mountains because it was so beautiful."

Mattie stared at him, her eyes widening, as if she found what he'd said hard to believe. No wonder, Jesse chastised himself, but he couldn't think of anything else to explain his presence here. He felt as if everyone else was staring at him too. Especially Clayborne's widow.

"It *is* right purty up here," Hannah finally said, breaking the silence that had settled around the group.

"One of the most beautiful places I've ever seen," Jesse answered, relieved at her words.

"But weren't it a mite out o' yore way?" Mattie persisted, clearly not accepting his story. "Iffen you live on one o' them big plantations in Georgee?"

"Yes, it is, a bit. But it was worth it." He gave Mattie a smile, hoping he'd deflected the woman from her original line of questioning.

Behind him, he heard a chair scrape on the floor planks and out of the corner of his eye he saw Eden Clayborne rise.

"I'm sure Mister Bainbridge needed something like that after the last days of the war. Mother Clayborne, you need to rest now. You look very tired."

"Oh, I'm all right," the older woman protested, but her daughter-in-law was already across the room, removing the extra pillow behind her head, settling her down for sleep.

Mattie Freeman slowly raised herself from the rocking chair. "Well, I guess we ort to be a-gittin' home."

Her voice was definitely cool, Jesse noticed. She was offended by the other woman's words and actions. But at least she and her son were leaving. Jesse heaved a heartfelt sigh of relief as Mattie, followed by Darcy, left the cabin.

"You hadn't ort to a done that," Clayborne's mother said. "You know how easy Mattie gits her feelins hurt."

Eden smoothed her mother-in-law's bed coverings, then straightened, smiling. "I can't help that. You're exhausted. You need to rest."

She walked across the cabin, her expression changing into a cool mask as she approached Jesse. She went on by, then, after hanging her apron on a peg on the wall, picked up a woven basket and left the cabin.

Jesse got up, too, and followed her out. She'd defended him

a moment ago, but that didn't mean her feelings about him had changed.

He'd put it off long enough. He had to tell this woman why he was here.

Chapter Three

She walked rapidly and held her slim back very straight as she headed for the barnyard. Jesse didn't know if she heard him behind her. If so, she gave no indication and he couldn't catch up with her because of his injured leg. She vanished inside the barn, and when Jesse finally stood in the doorway, he saw her bending over, putting eggs into her basket from straw nests along one side.

The barn was dim and cool, smelling of hay and farm animals. A few chickens still sat on nests. Sharp homesickness and loss swept over Jesse as he remembered days back home. It would never be the same again for him or for thousands more like his family.

Jesse cleared his throat. "Mrs. Clayborne, I'd like to talk to you."

The sudden sound of his voice startled her and she dropped an egg. It broke on the hard-packed dirt floor. Eden turned her head sharply toward him.

He walked slowly across the big room to her, favoring his injured leg. "I'm sorry," he apologized, looking down at the mess. "I didn't mean to sneak up on you."

"What do you want? Why *are* you here on the ridge?" she

demanded, before she could stop herself. She'd meant to stay calm and cool, but his evasiveness with Mattie a few minutes before had upset her.

He sucked in his breath, then let it out. "That's what I want to talk to you about. I did come to the ridge for a specific reason. I came to see you and your mother-in-law."

The only possible reason a Confederate officer could have with them concerned the war—concerned Alston. Something cold slid down her spine. "Why?"

She wasn't going to make it easy for him, but he hadn't expected her to. No way he could lead up to this. He might as well plunge in and get it over with.

"I'm—I was a Confederate major—your husband's commanding officer when our regiment moved into North Carolina. I was looking for your cabin yesterday."

She sucked in her breath. "Why didn't you tell us then? Why wait until now?"

Jesse's jaw tightened. "I haven't had a chance before. I was out of it until a couple of hours ago. And after I discovered Mrs. Clayborne was ill, I wanted to talk to you alone first."

"Why?" she asked sharply. "Do you have something to say that would upset Hannah?"

He ran his hand across his beard. "No." He paused a moment, then continued. "I brought your husband's things—his harmonica and his book of poetry. And his last letter home. I thought you might want to show them to your mother-in-law after I've gone."

Sudden, unexpected tears filled her eyes. She turned away from him, began gathering eggs again. She felt his touch on her shoulder and blinked back the welling tears.

"Eden," he said quietly. "I didn't come here to cause you more grief."

It was the first time he'd used her given name. It sounded strangely intimate, coming from him now, here in this place, at this time.

She whirled around and Jesse drew in his breath. Tears starred her lashes above those vivid blue eyes. Her golden tanned skin seemed to be stretched tightly, emphasizing her high cheekbones.

She was the most beautiful woman he'd ever seen.

"Why *did* you come?" she demanded fiercely. "To make me feel even more guilty than I do already? I should have made Alston stay here. He was still sick, not fit to fight any more battles. He was *never* fit for war. He was a gentle man—a schoolteacher, not a soldier!"

The tears welled again and slid down her cheeks. "I didn't even tell him about the baby," she said bitterly. "He died not knowing, because I wouldn't try to keep him here because of my pregnancy. It's my fault he died. I'll never forgive myself."

Jesse moved back a step. The things she said echoed so strongly his own thoughts, his own guilt, her words hit him like blows. She was right—he didn't have to come here. He could have sent Clayborne's things.

And she must have loved her husband very much. Why did the knowledge give him a feeling of loss?

He moved forward, reaching for her free hand, knowing he had to say something to comfort her, to assuage her guilt. An unexpected warmth filled him as her slender hand was swallowed up in his own.

"There's no reason for you to blame yourself. If anyone's to blame, it's me. I knew your husband was a sick man when he came back to the unit. I knew I should send him home, but I didn't. I let him stay and I let him fight."

He felt her hand tense in his grasp, and then she slid it out, stepped back from him. Her blue eyes were enormous, her face pale beneath its tan. While he watched, disbelief, then anger, tightened her features.

"Why did you tell me that?" she cried. "So we could both feel guilty the rest of our lives? Do you know why Alston's mother is ill? What's wrong with her?"

Jesse stared at her, a muscle jerking in his jaw. Finally, he shook his head.

"She's slowly dying of grief." Her words dropped like stones. "Her husband died early in the war, and Alston was her only surviving child. Did you know that?"

Oh, Jesus. "No, I didn't. I'm sorry. Don't you think she'll get better in time?"

"No. I think she'll keep on getting weaker and weaker—and then she'll die."

"I'm sorry," Jesse said again, his voice full of pain. "I know how you feel. Many of us have lost our families in this accursed war."

Her blue eyes were as hard and cold as sapphires as she stared at him. "A war that didn't have to be fought if the rich plantation owners, *slave* owners, had been willing to listen to reason. To compromise."

His face went whiter than her own, his mouth tightening, his hands clenching into fists at his sides. But he didn't strike back at her with equally angry words.

A part of her was horrified at what she was saying to this man. Why was she doing this to him? Why was she trying to make him feel even more guilty? To try to ease her own guilt?

As he'd just reminded her, he'd lost his entire family. So had hundreds of other southerners. Even if she hated his kind because they'd caused this war, she didn't have to be this cruel.

But she couldn't find any forgiveness inside herself. Not for her, not for him.

She turned her back, gathered the rest of the eggs fast and furiously, then left him standing in the middle of the barn floor, staring after her.

Eden stretched her aching back, then leaned on the hoe handle, looking at the large unweeded section of garden still left to do. She shouldn't have started on the weeding this morning because she'd soon have to stop. Willa was coming over and they were going to dig ginseng.

But she'd had to stay out of the cabin, away from *Major* Bainbridge.

Her mouth twisted, anger flooding through her again. She still didn't understand why he'd told her those things about Alston. Did he honestly think it would make her feel better? Or was he merely trying to expunge his own guilt by diluting it with hers? Whatever he'd had in mind, as far as she was concerned, it hadn't worked.

After the scene in the barn, he'd come in last night, as she was heading for the sleeping loft. He'd opened his haversack and given her Alston's possessions. She couldn't stand to look at them. She'd put them in a wooden chest at the foot of her bed and changed the bandage on the major's leg all of it done quietly as possible, in order not to wake Hannah.

His injury had looked much better, the angry puffiness nearly gone. He'd be able to leave by tomorrow or the day after. Thank God.

The sweet morning song of a thrush broke into her thoughts, and in spite of her black mood, her mouth curved into a smile. She'd grown to love many things here in these southern hills, things she'd miss if she ever moved back to Connecticut.

She let her mind mull over that possibility for a few moments. She owed it to her parents to tell them about the baby. Deep inside, she knew only pride kept her from writing to them. They'd had four years to change their minds about the stand they'd taken. Obviously, they hadn't, or they'd have contacted her long since.

How could they have expected her to stay in Connecticut? Let Alston come back here alone? She knew their abolitionist feelings went deep. She'd shared them. She still did, for that matter.

But a wife had to stick by her husband. Along with their hatred of slavery, Rosalind and Norris Thornton had instilled a strong sense of responsibility and fortitude in their only child.

The fact that Alston had hated slavery, too, added a poignant irony to the situation. But he also loved the South and knew he could never take up arms against his own people, his homeland.

The only other choice was to fight for the Confederacy.

So he gave up his schoolteaching position and came home, back to these hills, and she'd come with him. He'd tried to prepare her, but the log cabin, the primitive way of life, astounded and appalled her. No wonder he'd left it to find a new life in the North.

Alston soon joined the southern forces and Eden spent many a sleepless night wondering if she'd been a fool to follow him here. If it hadn't been for Hannah . . .

Out of the corner of her eye, she glimpsed movement, and startled from her reveries, she lifted her head. She drew in her breath at the sight of the black-bearded, stocky man walking across the clearing toward her. Toby Varden! Oh, God, she didn't feel up to dealing with him now.

Eden glanced toward the cabin, but Toby, moving swiftly in spite of his size, had cut her off from that escape. She straightened her spine and kept her glance steady. She wouldn't let him know how much she loathed and feared him.

He came on until he was only a few feet away and stopped directly in front of her. A broad grin spread his thick red lips, surrounded by the bushy blackness of his beard. But no smile lit his beady black eyes. They raked Eden from head to foot, making her feel dirty.

"Well, now, you look as purty as a red-winged blackbird this mornin'," he said, moving a step closer.

Eden moved back as his pungent odor drifted across to her. She wondered if he'd ever bathed in his life. Certainly not recently. She ached to order him to get off the property and stay off, but Hannah had warned her about making an enemy of him.

The trapper, who lived in a shack deep in the woods, had a vindictive streak. People who'd gotten on his wrong side had found their livestock killed. There were rumors he was responsible for a couple of barns that had burned. Two women living alone couldn't afford to risk his anger, Hannah said, and Eden had to agree. She swallowed her disgust and forced a smile.

"Good morning, Toby. What brings you over so early?"

Trapping season was over, and Toby spent the late spring and summer hunting and fishing. Somehow, he'd managed to avoid fighting in the war. He'd been here several times now since Alston's death.

The smile became a smirk. He stepped closer again. "Why, to see you, purty lady. I'd walk ten miles through the snow fer that."

Eden's heart sank. He'd never before made it this clear he found her attractive. Or that he might be planning to do something about his feelings. She forced herself not to step back again. She wished Willa would appear. Or Darcy.

Even Major Bainbridge. The last thought gave her an idea. "I was just finishing up here. Let's go inside and visit with

Hannah." She was sure Toby wouldn't continue with his unwelcome advances if she could get him inside the cabin. Especially with the major in the other bed.

Toby's smirk widened. He shook his head of bristly black hair. "Now, why you reckon I'd crave to do that?" he asked softly, moving another step closer. "Talk to a sick old woman, when I got you out here all to myself?"

A wave of uneasiness went over her. How far would he dare to go? Her mind shied away from what he might plan to do. She had to show him she wasn't afraid. She drew her chin up and looked him firmly in the eye.

"Well, if you won't come in, I'm afraid I'll have to say goodbye. I have work to do inside." She half-turned to walk around him.

His heavily muscled arms shot out and grabbed her wrists. "What's yore hurry, purty Eden?" His voice was still low, but with a smirking undertone that made her shiver.

Despite the warnings she'd given herself, anger overrode her fear. This horrible man couldn't come onto Hannah's land and treat her like this! She glared at him. "Take your hands off me."

Toby's obsidian eyes shone; his grip tightened. "I like feisty gals," he growled, pulling her closer to his barrel chest.

His hard hands hurt, and his actions infuriated her further. She cried out, half in pain, half in outrage, and tried to jerk away from him. But he was much too strong. She couldn't dislodge his hands. The beginnings of panic struck her.

For the first time in years, she desperately longed for help. What was she going to do?

The geese, raising a ruckus outside, woke Jesse. As always, he was instantly alert. He lay there for a moment, then moved his leg experimentally under the covers. The pain was a good deal less than yesterday. By tomorrow he'd be able to saddle Ranger and head on.

The cabin was quiet. He glanced over at the other bed to see Hannah was still asleep. Eden was long up and about, he supposed. After all, she had to milk the cow, feed the pigs and chickens. All the regular morning chores of a farm would be on her back.

He frowned, feeling lazy that he'd slept while she'd worked, although he knew she wouldn't have let him help her if he'd been awake—especially not after what had happened between them yesterday. He also knew he should rest his leg as much as possible today and tonight, so he'd be fit to leave. Give her that much less work to do.

But, by damn, it galled a man to let a pregnant woman do heavy work while he lay abed.

Why had he come here? He should have listened to the sensible voice inside him instead of to his conscience. He should have sent Alston's things.

What the hell had he been trying to do?

All he'd accomplished by confessing his own guilt was make the Yankee woman despise him further. He'd sensed she loathed his class, that in spite of being married to a rebel, her sympathies were with the North. Yesterday, she'd told him that in so many words.

Jesse flung back the covers, and then, forgetful of his injury, swung his legs over the side of the bed. Pain shot up his leg as his feet made contact with the hard floor.

Under his breath he swore again at his heedlessness and reached for his pants. He pulled them over his legs, then put on his stockings and boots. He walked to the cabin door and eased it open, not wanting to wake Hannah, and went out on the porch.

A woman's voice, raised in anger and pain, came sharply through the early morning air. Jesse stiffened. It was Eden's voice.

And she was in trouble.

Forgetting his leg, he hurried down the porch steps. Rounding the end of the cabin, he saw her by the garden patch. She was struggling with a big bruiser of a man who held her wrists and tried to pull her toward him.

She looked angry—and also afraid. Fury exploded in Jesse's brain. Ignoring the pain in his leg, he walked swiftly across the yard. "Let go of her!" he ordered.

Toby glanced at him in hostile surprise, not releasing his hold on Eden. "Who the hell are you?"

"You don't listen well." Jesse planted a hand on Toby's shoulder and shoved backward.

The move caught Toby off guard. He staggered, letting go of Eden's wrists. Before the other man could recover his balance, Jesse drove his fist into Toby's midsection, his other fist coming up and under Toby's chin.

Toby fell like a wounded ox, bellowing like an animal, too. Jesse, his amber eyes blazing, stood over him. "Get up and get out of here," he ordered.

His voice was low, but something in its timbre made Eden's nape prickle. It was the voice of a soldier who'd been through a bloody war. Who had killed men and who would kill again if he had to.

From Toby's face she knew he'd heard it, too, and decided not to continue the fight. Like most bullies, he was a coward at heart. He stared sullenly up at Jesse from under his heavy black brows, then lumbered to his feet.

He looked at Eden, his eyes angry and hostile, then turned and walked away, toward the woods. Jesse Bainbridge had gotten rid of him only temporarily. He'd be back. And he'd be meaner next time, because the other man had bested him.

Eden's heart pounded heavily; her breathing was shallow. She turned to Jesse. "Thank you," she said shakily, her resentment toward him momentarily forgotten.

If he hadn't come when he had, Toby would have kissed her, and she'd have been powerless to stop him. She shuddered at the thought of his wet, red mouth on hers, his smelly body pressed against her own.

He might have tried to do more than kiss her.

"Has he bothered you before?" Jesse asked.

Eden quickly shook her head. She didn't want this to go any further. This man would be gone in another day or two. He wouldn't be here to protect her next time. "He's Toby Varden, a trapper who lives in the woods. He just had too much to drink. He's harmless."

The man had smelled rank and dirty, but there was no whiskey odor on his breath. For some reason, Eden was playing this incident down. Jesse's glance traveled over her, stopping at her wrists. His mouth tightened as he saw the angry red marks on her honey-colored skin. He reached over and gently touched the marks.

"That bas—" He cut his angry word off and looked up at her. "I ought to go after him and beat him senseless."

Eden shook her head. "No! It's all right. He didn't hurt me." Her skin warmed where his fingers touched her. She moved back, and his hand dropped away. "I'm fine."

Her skin had felt like warm satin under his fingers, Jesse thought, as he watched her. And her hair would feel like silk if he reached over and released it from its heavy braids. All of her would be warm and smooth to his touch.

He felt a sudden, intense urge to unfasten the row of tiny buttons down the front of her dress. Pull it apart, expose her full breasts, her rounded stomach . . .

The last thought brought him back to his senses.

He felt himself reddening beneath his battlefield tan. What kind of man was he to think such thoughts of a pregnant widow? Who wouldn't be a widow if Jesse had sent her husband home.

And he was long betrothed to Annabelle.

Jesse stepped back, away from her, his face hardening in disgust at himself and his lustful thoughts.

"Your breakfast is keeping warm on the back of the stove," Eden told him. Her voice had lost its fear—and its gratitude. It again sounded crisp and cool. "I see Willa coming. We're going to hunt for ginseng. Would you give Mother Clayborne a tray when she wakes?"

Jesse knew she wanted to get away from him. He wondered if she'd somehow sensed his thoughts. No, he decided, she'd probably have slapped him if she had. She just didn't like him. And now, after what he'd told her yesterday, her dislike had deepened.

"Of course. But you're not going the way that animal did, are you?" He didn't care how she felt about him; he wouldn't let her do that.

She shook her head. "No, we'll go down in the hollow. That's where the best plants grow."

Willa came running up, her fair skin flushed, her smile wide. "Mornin' Mr. Jesse. Yore lookin' a heap better than you was."

Jesse smiled at her. "I'm feeling much better, too. I'm glad you came along when you did."

The girl grinned. "Me, too. You shore needed help, but you didn't want to ask fer it."

Any more than Eden liked to accept help, he thought. They were akin in the stubborn pride both had in full measure.

His leg was throbbing with pain again, from the activities of the last few minutes, but to hell with it. The longer he stayed, the more enmeshed he'd get in her life. This Yankee woman who despised all he and his kind stood for.

Maybe he should tell her how he felt about what the North had done to his homeland, his people. No, he wouldn't. He needed to get out of here. Get home to salvage what he could from the life he used to have. The life that was gone forever.

And Annabelle was waiting for him. Why did he keep forgetting that?

He'd leave tomorrow if he had to crawl.

Chapter Four

"Look, thar's a painter's tracks!" Willa stopped at the stream's edge, and Eden moved up beside her. They'd walked down the ridge to this small hollow where the ginseng grew thickest.

Eden had seen mountain lion tracks before, but these were huge. The thought of the fierce-eyed, tawny beast reminded her of Jesse Bainbridge again.

Major Bainbridge. She tried to curl her lip, tried to feel the anger and resentment of yesterday when he'd told her about Alston. But she couldn't summon those same intense feelings.

He had saved her from Toby, and she was exhausted. Last night, after she'd changed his bandage and climbed to the sleeping loft, she'd lain awake most of the night. Trying to sort things out, and not succeeding.

A few minutes ago, he'd touched her wrist and looked at her in such a strange way.

As if he found her beautiful. As if he desired her.

Heat flooded her skin again, as it had then, leaving her confused. Guilt soon followed. She had imagined the look, she told herself firmly. He didn't like her any more than she liked him, and what difference did it make, anyway? He'd soon be gone, and she'd never see him again.

She forced these disturbing thoughts out of her mind and looked at the panther tracks again. "I don't guess we'll have to worry about it getting the livestock this time of year. Should be plenty of food in the woods."

Willa nodded in agreement. "And this 'un could most likely ketch anythin' he wanted to. Winter's time to fret 'bout painters. Game's scarce then."

"Yes." Eden turned away, not wanting to think about either man or beast. "Do you see any ginseng beds?"

The girl's blue eyes sparkled. "Yessum, I shore—sure do," she corrected herself, grinning at Eden. She pointed. "Right over yonder's a big old bed o' three-prongers. I even seen a few four-prongers."

In a few moments they were kneeling beside the dark green, glossy-leaved plants. The sharp smell of leaf mold filled Eden's nostrils as she broke off the tops of the ginseng and put the roots into the burlap sack she carried.

Without warning, she felt something feather-light touch her hair and smooth down it. She froze, her heart giving a big thump.

"So soft, jist like a baby's," a high-pitched voice crooned in her ear, as the stroking continued.

Willa whirled, the alarm on her face fading as she saw the newcomer. "It's jist crazy Sadie," she told Eden.

Eden got to her feet and smiled shakily at the apparition standing close beside them. The middle-aged woman, her wildly tangled gray-brown hair streaming down her back, didn't return the smile. She wore a ragged dress which had once been brown calico, and her dirty bare feet were as callused and silent as any Indian's.

Hannah had told her the story when Sadie had come to their door. One of the Freeman clan, Sadie had lost her first baby years ago, and it had driven her mad. Husband long gone, she roamed the woods, searching for her dead infant. People sometimes gave her meals and a bed in their barns. Often, though, she slept under a tree and lived on what she found in the woods.

She stepped closer to Eden again. Her hand darted out and smoothed down over Eden's rounded abdomen. "A leetle 'un's in thar," she crooned softly. She looked up at Eden, her vacant stare changing into a stern expression. "You take good keer o' that leetle 'un when it comes. Don't you let it out o' yore sight fer a minute."

Eden had never been afraid of the woman before, but now, Sadie's words and actions made a shiver go down her spine. *Humor her,* Eden told herself. "I will. Don't worry about that."

Sadie stared at Eden a moment longer, then nodded, apparently satisfied with her answer. She tilted her head, putting a hand to her ear. "Hark," she said. "Was that my baby cryin'?" Her empty eyes lit up as she listened to sounds no one else could hear.

An aching pity welled up inside Eden. This poor woman. Spending her life searching for the baby she'd never find. Eden stepped closer and squeezed the woman's shoulder. "Would you like to come home with us and eat something?"

Sadie shied away from Eden's touch like a woods animal. She shook her head, her unkempt hair flying around her face. "No, no," she mumbled. "I cain't take the time. I have to foller the cry."

She silently made her way into the underbrush and it swallowed her up.

Eden's knees trembled so hard she feared her legs would hold her up no longer. The encounter with Toby, and now this, had finally taken their toll. She found a patch of moss under a tree and shakily lowered herself to it.

Willa squatted beside her, worry on her young face. "Air you ailin', Miz Eden? Want me to go fetch Mam? Or Mister Bainbridge?"

"No!" Eden shook her head. She didn't want anyone to see her like this. Especially Jesse Bainbridge. "I—I'll be all right. Sadie just startled me. She's been to the cabin, but she wouldn't come in, or talk to us."

"I ain't been close to her often. Mam says she's got the evil eye."

Eden took a deep breath and got to her feet, brushing at her skirt to rid it of leaves and dirt. "There's no such thing as an evil eye. It's only silly superstition." Even while she spoke, something inside told her she wasn't being completely honest with the girl. There *was* something frightening about Sadie.

"Let's get this ginseng bed finished; I have to be getting back. It's washday." At the thought of carrying the buckets of water, heating the big iron kettle, boiling the clothes, and scrubbing them on the washboard, her spirit quailed. She was bone tired. She didn't want to go home and do the wash.

Most of all, she admitted, she didn't want to face *him* again. She'd have to change his bandage today. She'd have to be close to him . . . touch him . . .

But as her mother had told her often during her growing-up years, in life you have to do all kinds of things you'd rather not. She ignored her aching back and concentrated on digging the ginseng plants from their bed.

"Many thanks, ma'am, for your hospitality and your nursing care." Jesse's voice was formal and polite. He stood at the bottom of the cabin steps, looking up at Eden on the porch. The early morning air smelled of honeysuckle, its sweet, almost drugging scent filling his nostrils.

A premonition hit him. For the rest of his life, whenever he smelled honeysuckle, he'd remember this moment. He'd remember exactly how she looked. Her shining black braids wrapped around her head. Her fine-boned, honey-tanned face. Her pink, full, unsmiling mouth. Her vivid blue eyes steadily on his own. Her proud, straight-backed stance.

"I've done nothing any other woman hereabouts wouldn't have done," she said, her crisp northern tones as steady as her gaze.

He'd been talking to Hannah when Eden had returned from her ginseng gathering yesterday. She seemed surprised he'd cleaned up the kitchen after his and Hannah's breakfast. She thanked him politely and distantly, then went back outside to start the wash.

Jesse couldn't watch her hauling water from the spring to fill the big kettle and not help. Over her protests, he went with her (each of them carrying a bucket) knowing he shouldn't tax his still painful leg to save her work today. Tomorrow he'd be gone and she'd have it all to do. He found himself picturing her even heavier with child, carrying water, scrubbing the clothes on the washboard.

By the time the kettle was full, he was cursing himself for a fool. His leg ached painfully. Sitting on a horse tomorrow would be sheer hell.

Eden saw his discomfort and refused to let him help her further. He knew she was right and retreated to the cabin porch. Hannah was asleep, and anyway, he didn't feel comfortable talking with her, since she still didn't know the things he'd told Eden about Alston. He doubted if she'd ever know.

The rest of the day Eden avoided him. She fixed the noon meal and they ate in silence, then she went back to the wash. That evening she changed his bandage, trying not to touch him any more than necessary, it seemed to him. He told her he'd leave in the morning, and she'd made no reply. She'd retired to the sleeping loft soon after dark, leaving him to lie awake, staring into the darkness far into the night.

Now, as he looked at her, knowing he'd never see her again, he felt a strange urgency to find out more about her. "How on earth did you end up in these mountains?" he asked her baldly.

For a moment he thought she'd turn and go back inside and not answer him. Then she shrugged, as if it didn't matter.

"I married Alston in Connecticut. He was a schoolteacher there. When the war started, he came back here and I came with him."

He felt instinctively her brief statements left a lot unsaid. "Do you have family up north?"

She shrugged again. "I don't know. I haven't heard from my parents in four years."

In spite of her neutral tone, he felt the pain behind her words. "They didn't approve of your marriage?"

Her mouth curved into a wry smile. "They didn't mind my marriage. What they disapproved of was my coming south when the war started." She looked at him. "Why do you care?" she asked, as baldly as he had.

"I feel responsible for you," he said quietly. "I should have sent Alston home."

Her eyes flashed blue fire. She moved back a step.

"You're right. And I should have kept him here. We're both responsible for his death. But hundreds, thousands of men, died in this war. What difference does one more life make? I shouldn't think it would bother you at all."

Her cruel words hit him like a physical blow, tightening the knot in his stomach which had been there for days. He wanted to turn and gallop out of here, but he forced himself to finish what he'd started.

"Don't you think I'm human? Of course it disturbs me, like every man I've seen die."

She stared at him. "I think you southern gentlemen should have realized what you were starting. But all you cared about was riding around on your blooded horses, in your fine uniforms, talking about how you'd whip the Yankees the first week. Do you know how many men like Alston fought your war to help you keep a way of life that had nothing to do with them?"

Jesse checked his anger because there was more than a grain of truth in her words. But there was more that she didn't understand, too. "You're wrong," he told her quietly. "Men like your husband were fighting for something too. Their land. Their country."

"Their land wouldn't have been in jeopardy if people like you had been willing to give up slave holding," she told him bitterly.

He sucked in his breath. "It wasn't, isn't, that simple, and I think if you'll be honest, you know it."

"Eden, what are you two quarrelin' about out there?" Hannah called from inside.

All the fire left Eden. Her blue eyes dulled. She slumped a little and sighed wearily. "Nothing, Mother Clayborne," she answered, then looked at him again.

"What difference does it make now? The war is over. We'll all have to live with our mistakes."

Would she end up marrying Darcy, or someone like him? What if the trapper came back?

Jesse met her gaze. "You should tell your parents about the baby. You're going to need help. Don't let your pride keep you from asking for it. If you won't think of yourself, think of your child."

Ranger, tethered to a tree, raised his head and nickered his readiness for them to be on their way. Jesse took a deep breath and let it out. None of this was his concern.

It was time he left. Past time.

He turned away and walked across the clearing to his horse. He checked his gear—canteen, bedroll, haversack. His Colt revolver. A bitter memory flashed into his mind. Watching his men file by, stacking their rifles. Their weary, gaunt, defeated faces.

He stuck his foot in the stirrup and swung himself into the saddle, wincing as his injured leg jarred against the hard leather. He didn't know if Eden still stood on the porch or not. He didn't intend to find out.

"Wait a minute," he heard her call. He looked up to see her hurrying across the clearing carrying a cloth-wrapped bundle.

"You forgot the food I packed for you."

He looked down at her, surprised she'd do this after the bitter words they'd exchanged. But of course she would. She'd think it her duty. And he knew by now she was a woman who would never shirk what she considered her duty.

A lock of black hair had escaped her braid and curled alongside her ear. It gave her a soft, vulnerable look. Jesse reached for the package and their fingers touched for an instant.

Fire seemed to leap from her slim fingers to his hand. Startled, Jesse glanced at her. Had she felt that momentary flash, too? For an instant, he thought her eyes said she had.

Jesse felt a sudden, insane urge to sweep her up into his arms in the saddle. Take her away with him. Protect her. Care for her. Love her. Without thinking, he leaned toward her in a yearning stance, his gaze searching hers.

Stunned by his glance and the heat that had passed between them when their hands touched, Eden instinctively moved backward a step. But her eyes remained held by his.

The morning sun gilded Jesse's tawny hair, turning it to gold. She felt an intense desire to step forward again, run her hands through that shaggy golden mane. She forced herself to stand rigidly still.

Abruptly, he turned away. She watched as he stowed the food in his haversack. Then, again, he looked down at her, his strong back very straight, his amber eyes burning fiercely as he held her gaze.

Without warning, just as it had the first night in the cabin, that other kind of connection—a connection of the soul, or heart or spirit—happened. Eden saw Jesse's eyes widen, then darken, and knew he felt it, too.

Crazily, something inside urged her to throw herself into his arms, beg him to stay, not leave her. She swallowed hard.

Were her feelings on her face, plain for him to see? She drew herself up as tall as possible, tilted her chin upward.

And, much to her own surprise, smiled at him.

Jesse drew in his breath as Eden's smile transformed her face, removed the hardness, gentled it.

This is how she'd look at you if she loved you, a voice inside told him. *After you'd made love to her . . .*

He leaned down from the saddle toward her. Eden moved a step nearer. Jesse slid all the way to the ground and stood there looking at her for a moment. Then, he pulled her against his hard chest and kissed her.

For a moment she was rigid, then her body softened and her lips moved under his, either from surprise or passion like that burning through his veins.

And as he'd known it would, her body felt as if it belonged pressed tightly against his own.

Jesse released her and swung back up onto his horse. He pushed his booted feet into Ranger's sides and rode away toward the trail beyond the stretch of woods, not looking back.

Eden watched until he disappeared from view. Her heart pounded against her ribs, her mouth felt hot and tender from his kiss. She walked slowly back to the cabin, fighting the absurd feeling of loss threatening to overwhelm her. The cabin was dim and cool after the brightness outside.

"Well, did he git on his way?" Hannah asked.

"Yes." She was surprised her voice sounded so normal. Why had she let him kiss her? Why had she kissed him back? When she hated him. When she couldn't wait to get him out of her life.

Hated him?

Eden pressed her lips together, shame flooding over her. She wouldn't think about it. He was gone; she'd never see him again. She firmly pushed down the strange, lost feeling welling up once more.

She'd be fine. She was strong and healthy and could take care of Hannah and the coming baby. She picked up the almost empty water bucket and headed out the door again, to the spring.

She didn't need him—not in any way.

Chapter Five

Jesse slowed Ranger to a walk along the rutted wagon path, telling himself the mount needed the rest. But he knew that wasn't the real reason. Their nearly month-long journey was ending. He was almost home, and the scenes of devastation he'd encountered from Atlanta southward had made him physically sick.

Hardest to accept was the bitter knowledge that so much of it wasn't necessary. The hard-fought war had ended by turning people into avengers and scavengers.

His bitterness, softened a little during his few days stay in the Clayborne cabin, had returned full force. He didn't, couldn't, accept Sherman's conviction that to end the war, the South had to be brought to her knees.

No, worse than that. She had to be pushed flat on her back, then trampled into the red Georgia soil. In the end, both North and South seemed to actually enjoy destruction for its own sake.

Several times, by taking to the woods, he'd narrowly avoided being set upon by marauding bands of both Yankees and Rebs. Others weren't so lucky. He'd encountered more than one murdered man—and some women and children, too.

Just a few hundred more feet down this road, then he'd come to the tree-lined lane leading to Riverview. He could feel his stomach muscles tightening painfully at that thought. He knew what to expect—Annabelle had prepared him well.

But that wasn't the same as actually seeing it. He also knew he should be grateful the house still stood. Many others along the way had been burned.

Including Morgan Hall, which belonged to his aunt and uncle. Uncle Ezra had been killed in one of the later battles, and his widow, Viola, with no one left except her young son and daughter, had abandoned the plantation and moved to Alabama to stay with her sister.

Needing water for himself and Ranger, Jesse stopped there, dreading what he might see. His bitterness and hopeless despair increased. Only the foundation stones and the brick chimney rising toward the uncaring summer sky was left of the once majestic house.

The well had been spared, though. He'd drawn sweet, cool water from its depths and slaked his and his mount's thirst, then filled his canteen.

Reaching the lane entrance at last, Jesse reined Ranger in, then stopped. He could see a distance down the lane before it curved, and the normalness of what he saw gave him a sudden rush of hope. Maybe it wasn't so bad after all. Maybe . . .

"Fool," he muttered, urging Ranger forward again. His injured leg throbbed dully from the contact with the hard saddle, but it was almost well now. Of course the lane looked normal. Even the Yankees wouldn't have taken the time to hack down all the trees.

From one of them a mockingbird trilled. If Jesse closed his eyes he could imagine that nothing was changed, that he'd round the last bend and find the house as it always was, his mother running out to meet him . . .

His jaw tightened. "Double fool!" He wouldn't do that. He'd keep his eyes wide open and face whatever waited for him. A trickle of perspiration ran down the side of his sunbronzed face, stinging his eye in passing. Savagely, he swiped at it with the back of his hand.

Suddenly, the house loomed before him, and he sucked in

his breath. At first glance, it didn't look any different. But riding closer, he saw how wrong that impression was. The once white paint peeled in dozens of places. Windows were broken—some boarded over, others staring at him blackly like blinded eyes.

What had been a lush, green lawn was now crisscrossed with deep wagon ruts, torn up by horses' hooves. His mother's carefully tended flowerbeds trampled into the ground.

He dismounted, tying Ranger to a still beautiful magnolia. The bottom two porch steps were gone. He leaped to the next remaining one, jarring his leg again, making him wince. Whole boards were missing from the floor, used for firewood, no doubt.

The roiling in his stomach increased, and he leaned against a once pristinely white pillar and closed his eyes.

When he opened them again, he saw the pillar was further marred with deeply carved initials. *M.G.* Bitterness welled up inside him. What Yankee soldier had done that, and why? Idly, out of boredom? Or had it been a deliberate act, to show in one more way the disdain he felt for the South? Had he lived to go home to a house still standing, a family still intact?

"Stop it," Jesse told himself sternly. "You're not going to change anything by your maudlin anger."

He forced himself to walk to the massive front door, which was firmly closed but not locked, he discovered. It creaked on rusty hinges, but opened, revealing a barren foyer, the once beautiful floors filthy and scuffed.

Not a stick of furniture was left, and the walls were bare. Holes in the dirtied wallpaper, spilling plaster around them, attested to pictures yanked off. He glanced to rooms on either side to discover the same devastation.

Another vision filled his mind: the house as it had been. Filled with the carefully maintained rosewood and mahogany furniture in which his mother had taken such pride. The smell of flowers and polish, the sound of laughter floating on the soft summer breeze . . .

A wry smile curved his mouth. No, not much need for locking the door now. He didn't want, couldn't bear, to see any more. He walked to the back of the house and outside. The separate kitchen building was still standing, too, he saw, dully surprised, walking around it.

Where the bountiful vegetable gardens had been there lay barren fields. A rank new growth of weeds mingled with last year's plant stalks which were still in the ground, withered and black from winter frost.

Tension hit him, tightening his jaw muscles. A small patch of garden had been dug up and planted. Uneven lines of green plants met his eyes.

But that wasn't what caused the rush of mixed emotions flooding over him.

In the middle of the patch a woman knelt, pulling weeds. A neat stack lay beside her. Her small frame was clothed in a dark cotton gown, her head covered with a faded sunbonnet, but he recognized her.

Annabelle.

Her fingers froze on the weed she clutched. For a moment she was immobile. Then, she jerked upright and whirled to face him, a hoe clutched in her hand like a weapon, fear stamped on the delicate features of her face.

Again, bitterness and hatred overshadowed Jesse's other feelings. A black haze dimmed his sight. To think that the women of the South were reduced to this cowering fear . . .

Then the haze lifted and he realized Annabelle might be afraid, but she was far from cringing.

No, her small, well-shaped head was lifted proudly, her back ramrod straight. The moment passed swiftly and then a look of dawning recognition replaced the fear. Her brown eyes widened and an incredulous smile curved her mouth.

"Jesse! Oh, Jesse, is it really you?" She rushed forward and he held out his arms to her. She half fell against his chest and he closed his arms around her, wincing as he felt her ribs beneath the thin cotton of her gown.

He felt a rush of affection for the woman he'd known all his life and tenderly ran his hand down her hair. She'd been like a sister to him for so many years . . .

Shocked, he pulled his thoughts up short. Why had he thought that now? He was engaged to her, had been for all the years of the war. It was no longer brotherly affection he felt for her . . . was it?

For a long moment, she stayed with her face pressed tightly

against the breadth of his chest. When she finally raised her head, Jesse saw tears trickling down her fair-skinned face. Impulsively, he lowered his head and kissed the tears away, then his lips sought hers.

Without warning a vivid flash of memory invaded his mind: that last moment before he'd left North Carolina . . .

Eden, in his arms just this way. No, not just this way, he corrected himself. Even though Eden's body had been stiff against his at first, her mouth was hot and sweet, yielding and eager.

Annabelle's mouth was cool, its firm contours remaining closed. As did his own, he realized. This wasn't the first kiss of two people who loved each other, who planned to be married, after a four year absence. He pushed that errant thought aside, along with the others. Of course they were shy with each other after such a long time.

Gently he withdrew his mouth from hers and pulled back a little to look at her. Her pretty face was thinner, the cheekbones more prominent than he remembered. But her skin was still pink and white and delicate, no doubt due to the sunbonnet she wore, now fallen back on her neck. Her chestnut-brown hair was pulled into a neat bun.

Another picture appeared unbidden in his mind's eye. Eden's golden-hued skin, her shining black hair, her tall, erect figure.

Her pregnancy.

Her widowed state, due largely to his own decisions regarding her husband.

The old guilt hit him anew and he forced the thoughts far back into his mind.

"Annabelle," he said, his voice rough. "How are you?"

She pulled herself out of his arms. "I'm all right," she said wryly. "Still alive and fairly healthy. That's all that can be expected now, I suppose."

"Why are you here alone? Where are Tucker and Cilla?"

Her mouth tightened. "Cilla died of fever a few weeks ago. And Tucker was killed by a Union soldier while trying to defend me. But he managed to shoot the soldier before he died."

Jesse's eyes darkened. She hadn't mentioned any of this in her letters. The two slaves had been all that was left of dozens on the plantation when the war began. The others had died or drifted off over the years. "How long have you been alone here?"

"Only since Cilla died." She forced her mouth into another smile as her eyes fell to his leg. "How is your injury?"

He looked at her strained face. Obviously, she didn't want to talk about her ordeal. He wouldn't push it. Thank God he was back. She'd never have to be alone again.

"Almost healed," he told her. He paused a moment, then continued. "A widow of one of my men poulticed it on my way here. She did a good job."

That brief statement didn't begin to cover what had happened on that North Carolina ridge, but he knew he wouldn't tell his fiancée more.

Silence grew between them, an awkward silence such as he could never remember having with Annabelle before. It was to be expected, he told himself again. After all, it had been four long years of hell since they'd been together.

And he'd put off the final thing he'd dreaded long enough. He raised his head. The Yankees had burned the stables and barn, but the iron fence surrounding the family cemetery looked intact, the old graveyard undisturbed. He guessed that was one place they hadn't dared vandalize.

Annabelle had followed his gaze, he saw. Her face tightened again, sadness mixing with anger, and it seemed to him some other emotion he couldn't name. "Do you want to see your mother's grave?" she asked, her voice as tight as her expression.

He nodded, following her as she turned and walked that way, the knot in his stomach returning, intensified a dozen times. *Want to see your mother's grave?* No, he didn't want to; but he knew he must.

Annabelle opened the gate before he could, surprising him a little. She'd never have done that before the war. But then, a lot of gentle-born southern women had gotten used to doing many unaccustomed things during these last years.

His mother had died in late autumn, and by now soft new grass covered the stark outlines of her grave. A crude wooden cross stood at the head. He wondered if Annabelle had fashioned it.

She lay alone, which somehow hurt more than anything. His father was buried in some unmarked grave, as were his two brothers.

He reached over to Annabelle, enfolding her small hand in his. "Thank you for taking care of her." Her hand was cold, even though the June day was hot.

"Mother Livia was all I had left," Annabelle said simply. Her parents had died several years before, and her only brother had been killed in the war. Her home, like so many others, had been destroyed.

Living on the plantation nearest to Riverview, Annabelle and her brother had grown up with his family. She'd been like a younger sister to him until one day, a year or so before the war, he'd realized she was no longer a child, but a very pretty woman. They had drifted into an engagement.

Then the war had come. They had talked about getting married before he left, but he hadn't wanted to take the chance of leaving a widow behind—possibly with a child to raise alone.

A loud hissing came from outside the iron cemetery fence. Jesse tensed, knowing what it was, yet half-disbelieving. Slowly, he turned his head to see the old gander, Henry, his mother's pet, standing in the open gateway. His fierce blue eyes were fixed on Jesse as if he were an intruder, and he hissed again, raising his huge wings and flapping them.

That was Jesse's undoing. This creature, which had somehow survived the carnage, was too painful a reminder of days gone forever. Tears came to his eyes. He turned back around. He couldn't stand to see the gander.

Annabelle's hand squeezed his in understanding. Her small palm was rough with calluses. A flood of memories threatened to overwhelm him. "I wish that damned bullet had finished me off!" he said savagely.

Her hand stilled in his.

Compunction filled him. He'd survived the war and stood hand-in-hand with his lovely, faithful fiancée, voicing such a thought. He glanced at her, new guilt in his eyes, and the churning emotions inside him stilled at the expression in her brown eyes.

She didn't look offended or horrified—or even upset. She

looked as if she completely understood what made him say such a thing. Somehow, he knew her understanding wasn't based on her own feelings of loss.

No, it went beyond that—to something he didn't know about. With a sense of shock, he realized Annabelle had changed in more than merely superficial ways. Of course she had. Just as he had. War did that to people. She'd had experiences she didn't want to discuss now, might never want to talk about.

"I'm sorry," he told her. "I shouldn't have said that."

She nodded gravely. "It's all right. You must be hungry and exhausted. Let's go inside."

He followed her out of the graveyard, closing the rusty gate behind him. The gander had retreated to the kitchen building, still glaring and hissing. Annabelle made her way there, too. She opened the door and went inside, and Jesse followed.

Looking around the large room, he saw she was living here now. A small cot sat in one corner, neatly made up with a bright quilt. With another shock of loss, he recognized it as one his mother had made. Quilting had been one of her passions. She'd made some beautiful creations.

"There's no coffee, of course," Annabelle told him, "but I do have some sassafras. Would you like a cup?"

Another memory shot through him as he sat down at the crude wooden table. Eden's slender hand giving him a steaming cup of sassafras tea.

He started to shake his head, then checked the motion. He was being a fool. He smiled at her. "Of course. Thank you."

She returned his smile, but it seemed somehow distant and strained. She turned back around to the hearth, adding kindling to a tiny heap of ashes. The pile of wood near the hearth was composed mostly of what looked to be fallen tree branches. She must have combed the woods for them.

He couldn't begin to know what she'd suffered, what she still was enduring. "Is there any food?" he asked, prepared for a negative answer, ready to tell her he'd hunt some game.

Instead, she nodded. "Yes, there was some food left in the cellar. The Yankees didn't take it all."

Surprise widened his eyes. "That's amazing. From the stories I've heard, Sherman's troops looted or destroyed everything."

Annabelle kept her back turned and didn't at once answer. Finally she faced him again. "We were spared because the Yankees used the house as a headquarters for a while."

Surprise jolted through him. "Why didn't you or Mother write me about all this?" he asked.

"We didn't want to worry you. You had enough to deal with, fighting the war."

Her voice sounded odd and stilted, Jesse thought. "I'm sorry you had to put up with that, too," he said gently. "I'm still amazed they didn't burn it to the ground when they left."

Her gaze slid away from his. She lowered her head, picking at something on her skirt. "Some of them were decent people," she said, her voice clipped. She lifted her head again. "Not the monsters the entire South wants to believe."

Jesse stared at her, surprised again at her defensive tone. "Of course that's true," he said in a moment. Eden's image came into his mind once more. He remembered his first feeling of anger and dislike toward her merely because she was a northerner.

"There's stewed apples and some fish I cooked this morning," she told him, still with that edge to her voice.

He guessed he shouldn't be surprised at all the things she'd learned to do—cooking among them. "That sounds wonderful, after what I've been eating. I haven't had anything approaching a real meal for . . ."

His voice faltered. Not since that last breakfast Eden had cooked for him. The morning he'd left.

As if it had happened only a moment ago, he could feel her warm mouth, her soft body pressed against his own. His body, incredibly, stirred in response to the erotic memory. Resolutely, he pushed it away and managed a small smile.

"You never could stand to bait a hook. Don't tell me you learned how to fish and caught them yourself," he teased, trying to lighten the atmosphere.

Color came into Annabelle's pale cheeks. "Yes, I did," she said quickly, then turned back to the small fire now crackling on the hearth. She dipped water into an iron pot and hung it on a crane suspended from inside the fireplace.

Jesse looked at her slender back, frowning. Something was

wrong with Annabelle, other than the horrors of the war she'd had to endure. The Yankees who'd occupied the house couldn't have hurt her—she'd been too quick to defend them.

Had the soldier Tucker had killed abused her? Was that why she'd not wanted to talk about the experience? Anger surged through him, making him clench his fists. He forced himself to calm down, think this through.

That conclusion didn't seem quite right, either. She had almost a guilty air. Had she done something she was afraid to tell him about?

As he'd also done.

Did he plan to tell her about the passionate embrace and kiss he and Eden had exchanged? No, of course he didn't. That confession, even if it relieved his conscience, would only give her pain.

Was it possible Annabelle had had some passing encounter with a rebel soldier? The thought jolted him, and his first instinct was to deny it. But of course it was possible. War, and its aftermath, did strange things to people. Made them do things they'd never think of doing in peacetime.

As it had made him slide off his mount and pull Eden into his arms when he'd had no intention of doing such a thing a minute before it happened. He resolutely pushed down the sure knowledge that the war had had nothing to do with that incident.

If Annabelle had been involved in something like that, it didn't matter. All that was in the past, and they had to try to pick up the pieces of their shattered lives and go on.

He got up and walked toward her. Her bent head, her slender neck, looked fragile, vulnerable. He put his hand on her shoulder and gently squeezed it. "Can I help you do something? You must be tired."

Her shoulder jerked, and she moved away a little, enough so that his hand dropped. "You're the one who should be tired. You've been on horseback for weeks." She kept her face averted and there was still something strange in her voice.

Her words made him remember his horse. "I'm all right. But I'd better get Ranger. He's tied up out front. Is there any pasture land with intact fences left?"

She shook her head, her back still turned. "No. You'll have to tether him out."

Jesse stared at her for a moment longer. "I'll be right back."

She didn't answer and he shrugged and left the kitchen. Maybe nothing was wrong. Probably she just felt ill-at-ease because they hadn't been together for so long.

And then there was the matter of where he'd sleep.

He walked around the side of the house, trying to ignore the evidence of ruin everywhere. In the old days, the Negroes had kept the place in perfect condition.

But those days were gone forever, he reminded himself, untying Ranger and leading him toward the back. And he couldn't bring himself to be sorry slavery had ended. He'd never liked the idea of one person being able to own another. Their slaves had been well treated, but they hadn't been free.

Jesse led Ranger to the field next to the burned barn. He loosened the girth strap and removed the saddle, then the bridle, replacing it with a rope halter. He took another coil of rope from his saddlebags, attached it to the halter, then tied it to one of his tent pegs and pushed it into the ground.

He found himself strangely reluctant to go back into the kitchen with Annabelle. For the first time in their lives, he felt awkward around her. And whatever the reason, he'd rather stay outside than go in and try to make conversation.

But he wouldn't. Jesse gathered up his haversack, saddle, and bedroll from the ground and headed back to the kitchen.

Annabelle still stood with her back turned toward the fire. The spicy smell of cooked apples tantalized the air, mixed with the aroma of fried fish. His mouth watered. It had been a long time since he'd had anything that could be called a meal.

Not since he'd left the cabin on the ridge, he thought again. He quickly pushed the memory away. Annabelle had set the table with two old, cracked plates, but he saw that the utensils were some of the silver from the house.

"How did you manage to save that?" he asked, amazement in his voice. "Did you hide it?"

She shook her head, her back still turned. "No. I didn't have to."

Jesse sat down in the chair he'd occupied a few minutes ago.

"Do you mean your decent Yankees actually left the silver?"
He heard the sarcasm, the disbelief in his hard voice.

"Yes," she answered, her voice tight.

"I'm sorry," Jesse said. "I know what a rough time you must
have had. No matter how decent you say they were."

Without answering, Annabelle whirled toward him. Her chin
was lifted defiantly, her brown eyes blazed. She reached out
to grasp the back of a chair with her hands, her knuckles
whitening with the force of her grip.

"I thought I could go on as if nothing had happened," she
told him, her voice trembling. "That we could marry and I'd
never have to tell you anything. But I was wrong." Her last
words ended on a sob.

Jesse got to his feet, staring at her. He walked toward her.
"Annabelle, what are you talking about?" His eyes glinted, his
face hardened. "Did that bastard hurt you before Tucker killed
him?" he demanded. "Rape you?" He gripped her shoulders.

"No!" she said quickly, her voice horrified. "No," she said
again. "That's not it at all."

Jesse dropped his hands and moved back. "Then what is it?"

She took a deep breath and met his angry and puzzled gaze
with a steady look.

"One of the Yankee officers who lived in the house was a
very nice man. He protected me. He managed to keep anyone
from bothering me."

He nodded tightly, still not knowing what she was leading
up to. His voice was clipped as he answered her. "I agreed not
all the Yankees were as bad as Sherman."

She shook her head. "You don't understand what I'm trying
to say. He was—different." Her voice faltered a little.

Jesse felt impatience sweep over him, adding to his anger
and puzzlement with Annabelle's strange behavior. "We're all
different from each other," he said, his voice even tighter.
"What are you trying to tell me?"

She nervously wet her lips with her tongue. "He wasn't
destructive. He hated what the war had done to the South."
She raised her chin a little more. "He loved this house. It was
because of him it wasn't burned to the ground when they left!"

Jesse's impatience grew. He knew he should feel gratitude

to this unknown Yankee officer she kept talking about, but he couldn't summon any at the moment. He was dead tired, angry, bewildered at his fiancée's words and behavior.

He shrugged wearily. "All right, your Yankee officer was a saint. What do you want me to do, write him a letter expressing my undying thanks he so kindly left me the ruined shell of this house? And what has all this got to do with our marrying?"

Her steady gaze faltered, turned into a stricken look. "Of course I don't want you to do anything like that. That's not at all what I'm trying to tell you. And what I'm saying has everything to do with us. You and me."

She took a deep breath and let it out. "I—we talked, Colonel Hastings and me. We found our ideas, beliefs, were very similar. I never thought I could like a northerner again after what they did to our country, but I . . ." Her voice trailed off as if she didn't know how to continue.

Jesse clenched his hands into fists, feeling himself sway a little on his feet. He let out a gusty sigh. "Annabelle, could all this soul-searching wait until tomorrow?"

"No! I can't live with this another minute longer. You don't understand," she said again, her voice trembling. "How could you? I don't understand it myself."

She gave him a look filled with despair. "He fell in love with me, Jesse—and I love him, too! So you see, I can't marry you!"

Chapter Six

Jesse lifted a rail and fitted it in place, then paused to wipe the sweat trickling down his face. The late June morning was hot and humid, and his bandanna came away streaked with dust and dirt. Sticking the bandanna back in his pocket, he looked out over the field.

The split rails he'd salvaged weren't the best. Hell, they were old, half-rotten ones. But at least Ranger had a fenced field to graze in. Or would, after he'd put the last few rails in place.

He turned and picked up another rail from the dwindling stack, then paused as he caught a glimpse of someone through the trees. Someone on a horse. Jesse stiffened, his glance hunting his Colt revolver, laid on a nearby stump. Someone stopping by didn't automatically mean a neighbor come to pay a visit, as it once had.

More often than not these days it meant trouble.

The horse and rider, moving toward the house disappeared from view. Jesse dropped the rail back on the pile, picked up his gun, and headed for the house himself. He'd reached the kitchen when the back door opened. A tall, light-haired man stood framed in the doorway.

Jesse stopped, his hand tightening on his gun. Was the man

alone? Or the scout for a marauding band behind him? He didn't seem to have a gun. He'd probably left it with his horse.

"What do you want?" Jesse asked, his voice clipped and cool. He brought up his revolver a little, so the man could see it.

"Cousin Jesse?" the man asked, tentatively. He left the doorway, came down the back steps toward him, his hand outstretched.

Jesse frowned, still holding the gun level. Who was this? He didn't have any kin left around here now. As the man drew closer, a small shock went through Jesse. This wasn't a man—only a boy of fifteen or sixteen. And there was something familiar about him—he *did* look like family.

The boy stopped a few feet away, his smile faltering. "Don't you know me?" he asked. "I'm your cousin, Cade Morgan."

Another shock, of recognition this time, swept over Jesse. "My God, Cade! I'd never have known you. You've grown up since I saw you last." The boy's clothes were worn and ragged, and he had a large bruise on his cheek and a black eye.

The boy shrugged. "I guess so. It's been almost four years. I was only eleven."

"What are you doing here? Are Aunt Viola and Belinda with you?"

Cade shook his head. "No, they're still with Aunt Eulalie in Alabama. We left when Sherman started this way." He gave an apologetic shrug, his young face tightening. "I wanted to stay, not let the Yankees take everything—but you know Mama. She was about to fall apart, and she made us go."

"That was the smartest thing she could have done." Jesse paused. "Have you been by your place yet?" he asked cautiously.

The boy's face tightened more, until his cheekbones stood out white against his tanned face. "Yes. Everything's gone." His voice cracked on the last words.

He was trying not to cry, Jesse saw, his own jaw hardening. Cade's father had died before the war and his older brother had been killed early on, leaving his widow with only Cade and his younger sister, Belinda. Damn this war to hell! Damn Sherman and his rapacious army!

Belatedly, Jesse realized the boy was so tired he swayed on his feet. He stuck the gun in his waistband and held out his hand. "I know. I saw it." His voice was rough with anger for Cade's loss—for his own. For all that the entire South had suffered.

Cade took his hand. Jesse felt the tremble in his thin hand. He was thin all over. "Did you come all this way by yourself?"

"Yes. Mama didn't want me to come, but I had to see what was left, now that they say the war is over. So I left her a note and took my horse and some food and came anyway."

"What happened to you? Did you run into trouble?"

Cade firmed his young chin and shrugged. "Yep. A bunch of drunk Rebs jumped me." He gave Jesse an incredulous look. "Can you believe that? Our own people!"

"You can't trust anyone these days. I'm surprised you still have your mount." Jesse's anger settled into the constant aching burn he felt all the time now.

The boy gave him a sly grin. "Oh, they took Duke. I walked ahead a mile or so, then doubled back and waited until they went to sleep and got him."

"Good for you," Jesse clapped Cade on the shoulder, even while he winced inside for what could have happened to his young kinsman. "You look like you could use some food and a good sleep."

"I haven't slept for two nights and I ran out of food yesterday. They took my rifle and I couldn't get that back."

"Come on," Jesse said, leading the way to the kitchen building. "I've got some squirrel stew and cornpone. You can bunk with me in the kitchen."

Cade threw a glance over his shoulder. "I'd better go get Duke." His young voice trembled with exhaustion.

"I'll get him. You go on in there and find something to eat."

"All right," Cade agreed.

The horse stood where Cade had left him, tied to the same magnolia Jesse had used the day he'd arrived. Duke, eagerly eating what grass he could reach, was gaunt, as exhausted looking as his owner.

Only a battered canteen hung from the saddle. The Rebs must have taken everything else. Jesse tethered Duke not far from Ranger. He should be able to finish the fence this afternoon, and both horses could be turned into the field.

When Jesse entered the kitchen, he saw Cade had found the stew. He hadn't bothered to warm it up, but ate hunched over the bowl as if he were starving. It was a miracle the boy had come this distance without more misadventures. He had grit, though. Not many youngsters his age would have dared steal their horse back from a drunken bunch of ex-soldiers, hardened by war and death until they didn't care for much of anything.

He sat down by Cade and tore off a piece of cornpone.

The boy, his hunger satisfied a little, looked up. "I'm sorry about Aunt Livia. Annabelle took good care of her, but she was just too sick." His eyes widened. "Where is Annabelle? Nothing's happened to her, has it?"

Plenty had happened to his ex-fiancée, but not what Cade meant. Jesse shook his head, feeling himself tense. "She's fine. She's living in Savannah." His voice sounded taut.

Surprise widened Cade's eyes more. "In Savannah? Why? Aren't you two going to get married?"

"She's getting married, but not to me." Jesse paused, wondering how much to tell the boy. Hell, why not all? It was over and done with now. "She's marrying a Yankee officer."

Cade dropped his piece of cornpone in the almost empty bowl, his face darkening with anger. "Annabelle's marrying a *Yankee?*" His voice broke, somewhat spoiling the indignant tone of his words.

A wry smile turned up Jesse's mouth. His cousin sounded much as he must have when Annabelle had told him a week ago. "Yes. And it's all right, Cade."

The boy's mouth hung open, then he closed it, a frown drawing his brows together. "How can it be all right? Don't you want to kill them both?"

"No," Jesse answered truthfully. He'd never felt as strongly about Annabelle's defection as Cade apparently did. He'd been stunned, angry. But not outraged. Or broken-hearted.

"But you *love* her!" Cade insisted, still scowling.

"We grew up together. We were more like brother and sister than sweethearts, but we didn't know it. When Annabelle truly fell in love, she knew the difference."

"But what about you?" Cade persisted. "Doesn't it bother you at all?" He shook his head. "Annabelle, marrying a *Yankee?*"

Jesse's tension grew. He didn't want to talk about his feelings. They were too complex, and Cade would never understand. "It hurt my pride," he admitted tightly. "And yes, it bothered me she'd fallen in love with a Yankee."

But not as much as it should have. And now, a week later, he let himself recognize why.

Because of Eden. Because he couldn't get her out of his mind . . . Had she also managed to invade his heart?

No! he denied silently.

Undeniably, she attracted him physically. That was the only reason he still remembered the feel of her soft, warm mouth against his own, her rounded body . . .

Her rounded, *pregnant* body.

And let's not forget, he reminded himself, that she's widowed because of your decisions regarding her husband.

"I *hate* the Yankees," Cade said, his voice hard. "They killed my pa and my brothers! They burned our house! For no reason—just burned it." His voice began to lose its hardness, trembled.

In another moment he'd be crying, and he wouldn't want Jesse to see that. Jesse pushed back his chair and stood. He took Cade's empty bowl and the remainder of the cornpone off the table, putting the bowl in a dishpan and the pone on a shelf.

He heard Cade's chair scrape on the floor, too. "I don't see how you can take it so calmly. Don't you even *care* about all we've lost?"

Jesse's held-back tension finally erupted into fierce anger. He whirled on Cade. "Don't say those things to me," he warned. "Of course I care."

The boy backed up a little, staring at Jesse. "All right," he said in a minute. "I'm sorry. But I don't see how you can let Annabelle go—"

"I don't want to talk about Annabelle anymore," Jesse interrupted, his voice rigid. "Leave it alone."

Cade nodded, thoroughly chastened now. "All right," he said again. His thin shoulders sagged as he leaned against the wooden table.

Jesse took a deep breath and let it out in a whooshing sigh. "You're tired to death. Get in the bed and go to sleep."

"I don't have to go to bed like a child," Cade protested. "I can take care of myself."

The fierceness drained from Jesse's anger, leaving him with the usual dull ache. "I know that. In fact, you've handled yourself on this crazy trip better than most men could have. But you don't have to *prove* anything to me. Go to bed."

Cade threw a longing glance at the bed in the corner, spread with the quilt Jesse's mother had made. He nodded. "All right, but only for a little while."

His cousin would sleep around the clock, Jesse thought, and he needed to. Cade stumbled to the bed and fumbled with his worn boots, finally getting them off. This accomplished, he stretched out on top of the quilt and his eyes fluttered closed. Within seconds he was sound asleep.

He'd go finish the fence, Jesse decided, so the horses could have the freedom they needed. He might as well do something constructive. God knew there wasn't much else he could do here.

He had no money to buy seeds. With no promise of a crop, only the battered house and land for collateral, and with the Yankees in control, he'd already discovered how nearly impossible it was to borrow money. Besides, it was too late in the season to plant.

The now-familiar frustration rising in him, he left the kitchen door open to let passing breezes in to cool the room and headed back to his pile of posts.

He put his revolver back on the stump and again picked up the rail he'd been ready to lay when Cade had arrived. He'd told Cade he didn't want to talk about Annabelle, and he didn't. But the boy's anger and hurt had brought all that to the surface again.

He'd met Annabelle's Yankee. As she'd said, the man was decent. And Jesse owed him a debt of gratitude for keeping the plantation house from being burned to the ground. Jesse had managed to express his thanks, but his simmering resentment of the North showed.

But he didn't hate either of them. What he mostly felt was

envy. Annabelle was obviously in love, and so was her Union colonel. Their faces glowed with it.

Would *he* ever feel that way for a woman? Be certain he wanted to spend the rest of his life with her?

Maybe he already had, something deep in his mind suggested.

Savagely, Jesse heaved the rail in place, so hard it bounced out against his knee on the recently injured leg. A sharp pain shot up his leg.

God damn it to hell! How long were thoughts of Eden going to torture him? No matter how hard he tried, he couldn't keep her vivid face, her tall, lush body out of his mind's eye.

Over a month had passed since he'd left North Carolina. How was she doing by now? Of course, she'd be bigger, more awkward. All the work she must do would be harder for her, more tiring. She shouldn't have to do it! What if she fell, got hurt? Who would be there to help her? No one except Hannah, and, bedfast as she was, what could she do?

She might not even know about any emergencies until it was too late.

Jesse began to sweat, even more than the hot day called for. Pictures filled his mind: of Eden lying hurt in the woods, of that bastard Varden bothering her again. Of the neighbor, Darcy, coming courting, finally persuading her that she'd be better off to marry him.

He turned in a tight arc, picking up another rail, hoisting it as if it weighed nothing, and fitting it into place.

Eden's life, her problems, were none of his concern, he tried to convince himself. He'd have to endure the guilt he felt because of her husband's death; he'd have to somehow come to terms with it.

Because she wouldn't accept his help, even if he tried to offer it to her. Her damned Yankee pride was far too stiff for that.

Like his own damned southern pride wouldn't let him forget what he owed her.

He slammed the rail down and grabbed another, grimly determined to work himself into exhaustion so that he'd go straight to sleep tonight. With no black-haired, blue-eyed, honey-skinned woman haunting his dreams.

Chapter Seven

Eden stood by the kitchen stove, rubbing bacon grease into her roughened hands. It was evening, and she'd just finished doing the supper dishes.

Unbidden, her mind flashed back to when she was a girl in Connecticut, before she'd met and married Alston. Standing by her mahogany fourposter bed, smoothing fragrant glycerine and rosewater into her smooth, white hands.

A wry smile curved her mouth at the memory. Those days were gone forever, and despite all that had happened since, she didn't wish them back. She could never be that protected, useless girl again.

She *would* like to have some of that lotion, though.

She glanced over at Hannah. Her mother-in-law's eyes were closed. Her chest rose and fell at regular intervals. She was truly asleep, not the feigned sleep she increasingly put on to keep from talking. Or eating.

A worried frown creased Eden's brow. Hannah wasn't getting any better. In fact, she grew weaker with each passing day. Eden tried to make tempting meals from her limited food supplies, but nothing seemed to interest the older woman now.

Not since Jesse Bainbridge had left two months ago.

Without warning, she remembered that day. How he'd slid off his horse and stood there looking at her for a moment, then taken her into his arms. How his mouth had burned against hers! For days afterward, she'd still felt his kiss on her lips.

And now, just with the memory, she felt it again. Appalled, she scrubbed at her mouth with the back of her hand to erase the phantom touch. "Oh, you're a fool, Eden Clayborne," she muttered. "A true fool!"

She hadn't realized how much Jesse's stay had improved Hannah's spirits until he'd gone. She didn't quite know why, either. She supposed it was because he was someone new and different for Hannah to talk with.

Willa, as well as Mattie Freeman, usually accompanied by Darcy, made regular visits. Some of the other ridge dwellers, too, occasionally.

Darcy still wasn't openly trying to court Eden—she doubted if he had it in him to court any woman. But the day would arrive when he'd propose, Eden was sure. She dreaded it. Refusing him would put a rift between the two families, which could very well have serious consequences for her and Hannah.

Mattie's company only seemed to tire Hannah. No wonder. The woman's conversation consisted of monologues of who was sick, who'd died, and how many sons and husbands wouldn't be coming back to the ridge—or the settlement in the valley— all of it reminding Hannah afresh of her own losses. Too, Mattie seemed to accept the fact that Hannah would never leave her bed—to even relish her decline in a morbid way.

Until Hannah took to her bed after Alston's death, no one could have made Eden believe it was possible for a healthy, able-bodied woman to literally die by inches from grief. Hannah was no longer interested even in the coming baby. Eden feared she knew the reason for that, too.

Hannah didn't expect to be alive when the baby came.

Eden forced the thought away, denied it. No! She wouldn't let that happen. She'd think of something, *do* something, to help her mother-in-law get well again.

The cabin felt hot and stuffy. She'd closed the door at night-fall, but now she felt if she didn't get some fresh air, she'd suffocate. Her hands went to her rounded abdomen, curving protectively over it. The baby growing inside her caused this, she guessed.

She quietly eased the door open and walked out on the porch. A full moon and thousands of glittering stars filled the clear night sky. Walking to the edge of the porch, she leaned against a post and breathed deeply of the fresh mountain air.

The clearing was bathed in moonlight, magical in its beauty. Quick tears came to her eyes. A night like this was made to be shared with someone you loved. Impatiently she brushed the tears away.

"Getting sentimental about the full moon is about the silliest thing you could think of," she admonished herself.

But just the same, she wanted to walk across that illumined expanse. She stepped down from the porch and moved out into the clearing, tilting her head up to the sky. Sadness washed over her.

Oh, she was lonely. So lonely! An intense longing for her family joined the piercing ache. Why did she miss them so much now, after all these years? Memories of her life in Connecticut, her childhood, swarmed up from inside her.

. . . Her father, his blue eyes so much like Eden's own, auburn hair disheveled as he pushed Eden in a rope swing, his laughter joining with his daughter's joyous shrieks.

. . . Her mother, close beside Eden on her small white bed, black hair falling across her cheeks, reading to Eden from one of her beloved storybooks.

. . . Her wedding day, when she'd thought she'd found her one true love. That she and Alston would share a long, happy life together, complete with several children. She'd been lonely as a child, wishing for brothers and sisters.

Now all that life was gone, swept away as if it had never existed. All that remained of it, of all her dreams, was the baby to come. . . .

She had no one now except Hannah. And maybe she wouldn't have Hannah for long. She tried to push the thought away again, but it persisted.

She would have the baby in a few more months, she told herself again, trying to gather courage. She heard a small sound from the stretch of woods leading to the trail, alerting her and shattering her pensive mood.

A figure came out of the woods, as silently as any wild animal, and walked toward her. In a few moments, she saw it was Sadie. Eden stood still, fighting an irrational urge to flee. In spite of the superstitious ridge talk, Eden told herself firmly, she'd never heard of Sadie doing anything harmful to anyone.

"Hello, Sadie," Eden said as the older woman approached. "It's a beautiful night, isn't it?"

Sadie came steadily on, not responding to Eden's words. The moon glinted on her rough, brown-gray hair, and when she at last stood in front of Eden, the rays turned her eyes to silver.

In spite of herself, Eden moved back a step, feeling the hairs on the nape of her neck stand up. "What are you doing out tonight, Sadie?" she babbled, still hoping to elicit some rational response. "Do you want to sleep in our barn?"

Sadie's thin brown arm reached out, as it had that day when Eden and Willa had been digging ginseng. Her hand curved over Eden's rounded abdomen. "Yore leetle 'un is still in thar. But not too much longer and it'll be out."

Eden froze at her touch, desperately wanting to push the thin, clawlike hand away from her and turn and run as fast as she could back to the cabin. She forced herself to stand her ground. "Yes, that's true," she said, hearing the small wobble in her voice.

The other woman caressed Eden a moment longer, then moved her hand away. Her eyes met Eden's and they were clear and focused, as sane as anyone's.

"What are you doin' outside by yoreself in the night?" she asked accusingly. "You got to think o' the babe! You git back to the cabin!"

"I will," Eden said soothingly, stepping back again. "But it's a warm night, nothing out here to hurt—"

Another noise traveled through the clear night air. An unexpected noise—like something hard striking against a stone on the trail. Instinctively, she turned her head toward the sound. She saw nothing at all.

When she turned back, Sadie was gone, melted away into the night like a wraith. Eden breathed a sigh of relief.

That had been a real sound she'd heard. She tilted her head, listening, hearing nothing else.

But Sadie was right. She'd better get back to the cabin. It could have been a wild animal. Possibly the huge panther. She and Willa had seen its tracks several times since that first day at the stream.

She'd taken only two steps when she heard the sound again. Closer this time, and now she could identify it: a horse's shoe, hitting a stone. Bushes rustled as if the unseen rider slowly and carefully made his way along the path through the woods toward the clearing.

She froze. Who could it be this late in the evening?

Toby Varden? The trapper hadn't been back since the day Jesse had knocked him down. But she still believed he would. Toby wouldn't forget the humiliation he'd suffered at Jesse's hands. Sooner or later, he'd be back to make Eden pay for it.

For the second time that night, someone emerged from the woods—and, as she'd thought, on horseback. Eden's breath caught in her throat. Her heart began thumping wildly as she stared in disbelief. She had to be wrong, it couldn't be the man who'd haunted her dreams since he'd left all those weeks ago.

But a deeper part of her knew it was. Her senses could pick him out of a crowd at midnight on a pitch-dark night. And even across the distance, she was sure his tawny eyes were fixed on hers, holding her captive in their gaze. Heat suffused her body as her memories of those last moments before he left swept over her again.

How could he be here? Why was he here?

As he approached, she saw it was Jesse, all right, but he wasn't alone. Another man, slighter of build, rode behind him.

The two men reined their horses, then dismounted, standing side by side, facing her. Jesse still wore his gray Confederate trousers, a worn white shirt. The moonlight gleamed on his sunstreaked hair, his strange lion's eyes. He'd shaved his beard, revealing a strong jaw and chin. She took a deep breath and held it for a moment, trying to calm her racing heart.

The other man had similar coloring, but as she'd thought, he was slighter of build, probably because he was still only a boy. He couldn't be more than fifteen or sixteen. Had he, too, fought in this horrible war?

"Hello, Eden," Jesse said at last.

The rich, deep timbre of his voice caused goosebumps to rise on her arms. She'd forgotten what a wonderful voice he had . . .

She took herself in hand sharply. "What are you doing here?" she demanded.

Jesse swallowed. Her voice was as crisp and firm as he'd remembered it. And as unfriendly. What had he expected her to do—fall into his arms? If so, he'd been a fool.

The moonlight made her black hair glossy as a raven's wing, her blue eyes deep as sapphires. He felt his body stirring to life at the sight of her.

Then, his gaze traveled farther down her body in the simple dark dress. In spite of the gathered front, he could see she was much more rounded than when he'd left.

And that's why you're here, he reminded himself desperately.

His peripheral vision told him his cousin's eyes were also riveted upon Eden. Jesse felt his mouth turn up in a wry grin.

Even very much pregnant, she was enough to make any man forget he'd ever thought another woman beautiful.

The silence was drawing out—he had to say something. Would she accept the truth? That he'd come to see her through these last months of her pregnancy? Would she demand he turn right around and go home? Probably.

"This is my cousin, Cade Morgan," he said instead, turning to nod at the youth beside him. "Cade, this is Mrs. Eden Clayborne."

Eden stared at him, then reluctantly turned to Cade. Jesse saw her face soften as she looked at the boy. She smiled and nodded. "How do you do?"

Cade visibly swallowed, then bowed in acknowledgment. "I'm honored to make your acquaintance, ma'am," he answered, his still reedy boy's voice cracking a little.

Encountering Eden in the clearing wasn't what Jesse had planned, but this last leg of the trip had taken longer than he'd expected. He'd thought to ride up to the cabin and have their first meeting take place in Hannah's presence.

Although he'd anticipated Eden's probable hostility, he'd also known she'd temper it if her mother-in-law was there. Once the first awkwardness was past he could ease into his real reason for being here.

"We've ridden a long way. Would it be all right if we stayed in your barn tonight?"

The question came out easily enough, since this was the arrangement he'd intended to suggest anyway. Hell, he certainly couldn't expect Eden to put them up in the small cabin. Now that his injury was healed, it wouldn't even be decent.

Eden pressed her lips together. Her first shock at Jesse's unexpected appearance was fading, but not her awareness of him. She hoped he hadn't noticed. She had no idea why he was here, and apparently, he didn't intend to tell her tonight, either.

But she couldn't refuse them shelter. It went against all the manners instilled in her as a child and certainly against the welcoming hill code. Finally, she nodded. "Of course you may shelter in the barn."

Jesse stared at her straight back as she walked away, then glanced at Cade. The boy's mouth was open as he looked after Eden.

"Let's lead the horses," he told his cousin.

Cade nodded, grabbing Duke's reins.

"It's bad enough that she's a Yankee," Cade said in a low tone. "I was getting used to that idea. But why didn't you tell me she didn't want us here?"

A good question. Jesse decided to answer it honestly. "Because I knew you wouldn't come with me if I did. I couldn't spare the time to go with you back to Alabama and I sure as hell wasn't going to let you go alone."

"I could have gone by myself," Cade said a little stiffly. "I did it once."

"Yes, and you were lucky to escape with your life," Jesse told him. "Of course, when Aunt Viola gets my letter, she'll probably disown me for bringing you here."

"I don't want to go back there," Cade admitted. "I'd rather be here with you. But will *she* let us stay?"

Another good question, one Jesse didn't know the answer

to yet. "I don't know," he admitted. "But I'm going to make it as hard as I can for her to send us away."

His gaze followed Eden's retreating figure. And that would be no easy task. She wasn't even waiting to walk with them.

Eden felt a frisson slide down her back. She seemed to feel Jesse's eyes boring through her. She picked up her pace. She wanted nothing more than to get them settled in the hayloft, then go to bed. She hoped they'd be quiet, not awaken Hannah. When she reached the barnyard, she stopped and turned, watching the two men lead their mounts. Jesse's leg had healed completely. He walked straight and tall, with no trace of a limp.

He still looked too lean for his big frame, though. She guessed he probably hadn't found many good meals in Georgia. The boy was also too thin, painfully so. She could soon take care of that. They had enough food, even if it wasn't fancy.

She drew in her breath sharply. Why was she thinking this way? Of course she'd give them a good breakfast tomorrow. But after that, they'd be on their way to wherever they were going.

What if they've already reached their destination? her mind asked. Why would they be here on this ridge otherwise?

Impatiently, she pushed that ridiculous thought aside as the two men reached her.

"There's hay in the loft," she told them, letting her gaze rest somewhere between their faces. "And you can put your horses in the stalls."

"Thank you, ma'am," Jesse said, his voice as impersonal as her own had been.

She hesitated, knowing she should offer them food. "Have you eaten? Hannah's asleep, but I could bring you some corn-bread and molasses."

Jesse quickly shook his head. "No, that's fine. We had our supper."

"Goodnight, then," she said. "Come to the cabin in the morning and I'll fix you breakfast before you leave."

She didn't miss the disconcerted look Cade gave Jesse, as

if he hadn't been expecting that remark. She ignored it and turned to go.

"That's kind of you," Jesse said to her back. "We'll do that."

Her back felt warm; she was sure his eyes were on her as she walked. It made her feel self-conscious in a way she hadn't for years. A new thought entered her mind. Did Jesse, like her, still remember the kiss they'd exchanged when he'd left before?

Did he, too, lie awake at night, unable to sleep?

Oh, stop it! she told herself furiously. Of course he didn't. He had more sense. Whatever he was here for, it had nothing to do with those intoxicating moments when he'd held her in his arms. It had nothing to do with *her!*

As Eden disappeared around the corner of the cabin, Cade looked at Jesse again. "*Now* what do we do?" the boy asked. "Head back to Georgia tomorrow?" He sounded exhausted, as if he'd be asleep the instant he closed his eyes.

Guilt hit Jesse. He'd pushed his cousin hard this trip. The horses, too. Animals and people needed rest. And he wasn't going to give up his plan without a fight. He shook his head.

"No. I came here to help Eden, and that's what we're going to do." He grinned at Cade. "How long has it been since you've done farm work?"

Cade looked at him, then grinned back. "I did it every day in Alabama."

"Good," Jesse said with satisfaction. "We're going to have a busy day tomorrow. Now let's get these animals tended and go to bed."

Chapter Eight

Moving quietly to not disturb Hannah, Eden dressed and started the morning fire in the kitchen range. She gave silent thanks that Alston had insisted on buying this stove for her before he'd left to join the Confederate forces. If she'd had to cook on the huge fireplace, she didn't know how she'd have managed.

As always, the thought of Alston sent guilt coursing through her.

She heated enough water to make herself a cup of peppermint tea, then eased open the door onto the front porch. She was later than usual. But no wonder she'd overslept. She'd lain awake for a long time last night, trying to forget Jesse Bainbridge was asleep in the hayloft.

In vain she'd tried to convince herself it didn't matter. He'd be gone in the morning and she'd never see him again. She'd told herself these same things almost two months ago—and here he was, back on the ridge. And she wouldn't even speculate on his reasons for being here this time. When she finally dozed off, her sleep had been restless.

So by all rights she should feel dreadful this morning. She didn't, though. Instead, she felt alert and exhilarated, a tingling anticipation singing in her veins. She ignored the implications of that and turned to the peg where the milk bucket hung.

It was gone. Eden stared in disbelief at the empty peg. She knew she'd put the bucket there after washing it last night. Frowning, she looked around the porch, even out in the clearing, thinking it must have somehow fallen off the peg and rolled away. But it hadn't.

She must have left it inside, then. She went back in and looked around the kitchen. No bucket. Maybe it had fallen off the peg and some wild animal had dragged it away. That explanation seemed farfetched, but she had to get to the milking and not worry about it. She found the other bucket in the corner, and after glancing at Hannah to see she still slept, she returned to the porch.

She'd try to be as quiet as possible while she was doing the morning chores. Jesse and his cousin had looked exhausted last night. They might as well sleep until they woke naturally before they started on their way again. She'd cut some of the remaining bacon, which had been stored in a crock of fat, for breakfast. And she'd cook a few of the precious eggs and make john-nycakes and gravy.

The milk bucket swinging against her skirt, Eden entered the barnyard. Her eyes widened in surprise. Jesse's cousin stood inside the fenced field, currying his mount.

Jesse must be awake and up, too, then. She tried to ignore the way her heart fluttered at the prospect of seeing him again and finished her journey to the barn. She walked into the dim interior and down to Bossie's stall, then stopped short.

The mystery of the missing bucket was solved. Jesse sat on the stool beside the placid Guernsey, his shirt sleeves rolled up, exposing his muscled forearms, milking as if he'd done it all his life.

Hearing her, he turned and smiled. Eden's eyes traced the contours of his mouth, remembering when those lips had been pressed ardently against her own. She felt her face warming and quickly moved her gaze to his eyes. That was a mistake. Their glances met and held and Eden sucked in her breath at the emotions rioting inside her.

She moved her glance again, a few inches to the side of his face. "Why are you doing the milking?" she asked.

He shrugged. "Why not?" he countered, turning back to his task.

Eden watched the movements of his hands, his strong fingers, as he pulled rich streams into the pail.

"Well?" Jesse whipped his head around again.

She frowned in irritation at herself. He'd caught her staring like a lovesick schoolgirl. "That's my job," she said stiffly. "I'm used to doing it."

"I was, once upon a time," Jesse answered, his voice muffled as he leaned his head against the cow's warm flanks.

"You?" Eden asked. "With all those slaves to do the work? I thought all planters' sons did was ride around on their thoroughbred horses and go to balls."

Jesse finished stripping the cow of the last bit of milk, then moved the stool back and carefully eased the almost full pail from under the animal. He turned to face her, his face expressionless.

But Eden could see a muscle moving in his jaw. She knew she'd angered him, but she didn't care. Somehow, he'd learned to milk a cow, but that didn't mean he knew anything about real work—hard, dirty, physical work such as she'd been doing for the last four years.

"It's—it was the custom in Georgia for the planters' sons to spend time working in the fields alongside the hands. I've planted and hoed and picked cotton until my hands were blistered. My father taught me how to milk a cow and tend to farm animals."

The flat, blunt tones of his deep voice rang with conviction. She believed him and felt genuine astonishment at his words. And also ashamed of herself for her unthinking remarks. Not only unthinking, but apparently ignorant, too.

Her face burned again. That last thought was unbearable to her. She lifted her dark head and gave him a firm, straight look. "I'm sorry," she said stiffly. "There was no call for me to say those things."

Surprise swept over Jesse's strong-featured face. He stared

at her as if he couldn't believe what he'd just heard. Then his face relaxed and a wry smile curved his mouth upward.

"It's a common misconception among northerners," he said dryly. "As we tend to think of northern women as prim, homely Puritan types." His golden gaze swept over her from head to foot.

Touché. Eden felt the warmth of his glance as if it were a physical touch. This had gone on long enough. She extended her hand. "Thank you for doing the milking. I'll take the pail back to the house."

He shook his head. "No, I'll do it. Since you promised Cade and me breakfast, I'll go along to the cabin."

"All right," she conceded. "But I need to give the chickens some grain."

"Cade did that," he said, his voice a little smug. "Is there anything else that needs doing?"

Irritation rose again. "No, except to slop the hogs. But I'll do that after breakfast."

"Fine," Jesse said agreeably, following along with her as she left the barn and started back to the cabin.

Cade had finished currying his mount and was now doing Jesse's, Eden saw. If what Jesse had said was true, this boy, too, must not be afraid of hard work. She turned away and began walking faster.

Jesse easily kept up with her. "How is Hannah?" he asked. "Better, I hope."

She shook her head. "No. She's weaker. She's not eating well now." Why had she told him that? It was none of his business.

"I'm sorry to hear that," he said in a moment. "I like Hannah. She's a good woman."

"Yes," Eden briefly agreed. Somehow, he'd gotten closer to her. Her skirt brushed against his trousers. She moved to the left. When they reached the porch, she again reached for the milk pail and this time Jesse let her take it.

"Breakfast will be ready in about half an hour," she told him briskly. "You can wash up and wait out here." She indicated the three cane-bottomed rockers lined up along one side.

"I'd like to talk to Hannah, if you don't mind," he said instead.

Eden stiffened. She didn't want him in the cabin any longer than necessary. She didn't want him talking to Hannah, upsetting her. "I'm afraid you can't. She's still asleep."

"Who're you talkin' to out there, Eden?" Hannah's voice came from inside, belying Eden's last words.

Eden let out her breath in exasperation as she opened the door and left it open for Jesse to follow her in.

The cabin looked the same as it had a few weeks ago, Jesse saw. Neat and clean, inviting and friendly. Hannah lay flat on her pillow, and she *did* look thinner. Eden took the bucket of milk into the kitchen and he walked across the room to Hannah's bedside.

"Hello, Mrs. Clayborne," he said, his voice soft.

Her head jerked around and she stared at him in amazement. "Major Bainbridge?" she asked. "What are you doin' here?"

A good question, Jesse thought, the same one Eden had asked. He guessed this time he'd have to answer it. "It's plain Jesse, and I'm here to . . ." He hesitated a moment and then went on, "Pay you a visit."

Hannah was struggling to sit upright and Jesse helped her, easing another pillow behind her head and steadying her. When she was situated, she gave him another confounded look. "It's a right far piece to come to pay us a visit, ain't it?" she asked.

He nodded, sitting down in the rocker beside the bed. "Yes, it is."

He glanced across the room at Eden. She was straining the milk through a white cloth into two big bowls, her profile turned to him, her mouth very firm. Because of what he'd said? A wisp of her black hair had come loose from its braid, curling on her forehead, giving her a vulnerable look. His heart softened and he forgave her for her sharp words in the barn.

He turned back around to Hannah to find her studying him, her sunken dark eyes holding a spark of interest that hadn't been there a few moments ago.

"I want to thank ye fer bringin' Alston's things to us," she said. "It were mighty thoughty o' you."

"I wanted to do it," he answered, knowing that wasn't a

truthful answer. The guilt he'd carried for months prodded him again.

"How did you find yore homestead?" Hannah asked in a moment. "I hope it weren't as bad as you thought it'd be."

He considered what to say. He didn't want to upset her, but he also knew she was accustomed to blunt truth and probably nothing could shock her. "The house is still standing, but everything else is gone."

She shook her head sadly. "Oh, that is sorry news. But leastwise yore woman was there, so you didn't lose everythin'. Didn't she keer that you left her agin so soon?"

He'd forgotten Hannah knew about Annabelle. As he'd told Cade, he didn't want to talk about it, but he didn't see how to avoid doing so.

"No, Annabelle didn't care that I left," he said after the silence had drawn out. "She's going to marry someone else." His voice sounded stiff.

His side vision caught a flash of movement and he glanced over in time to see Eden staring at him, long strips of bacon suspended from her hands. As their glances met, she quickly turned her head away, dropping the slices into a black iron skillet on the stove.

He returned his attention to Hannah, who also stared at him. She, too, looked shocked.

"Oh, my, that is awful," she said. "No wonder you didn't crave to stay there fer a while."

He couldn't leave Hannah with the impression he was devastated by Annabelle's defection. "We realized we didn't love each other."

Again he caught that flash of movement across the room, but this time he didn't turn toward it. Hannah? Was it really the older woman he wanted to make sure knew the truth?

The surprise and sorrow left Hannah's eyes, replaced by an expression he couldn't read. "Well, then," she said, "I reckon it's best you parted."

Jesse nodded, smiling at her. "Yes."

A scuffling of feet at the open door made Jesse turn that way. Cade stood in the doorway, looking a little unsure of himself. Jesse cursed himself for forgetting the boy. He rose and smiled at Cade, then turned back to Hannah. "This is my cousin, Mrs. Clayborne, Cade Morgan."

Hannah looked over at him, too. "Well, come on in, boy," she invited, her voice warm. "Don't be bashful." She smiled at him.

Cade smiled back, his discomfort obviously eased by her open friendliness, and walked a few steps into the room.

"Set down in t'other rocker," Hannah said.

He did as she asked, and Hannah studied him. "You look like yore cousin, that's a fact," she proclaimed in a minute.

"Thank you, ma'am," Cade said. "I take that as a compliment." He turned to give Jesse an impudent grin.

Jesse grinned back, glad to see Cade's normal high spirits returning. "Be sure that you do," he answered in kind.

Eden turned a johnnycake, listening to the conversation across the room. She tried hard to feel disapproving, but couldn't as she glanced at Hannah. Her mother-in-law's eyes were bright with interest. Her voice even sounded a little stronger. It was clear the two unexpected male visitors weren't doing her any harm.

She tried not to think about the implications of what Jesse had said about the woman he'd planned to marry. That was none of her concern.

What *was* her concern was his statement that he and his cousin were here on the ridge for no other reason than to visit her and Hannah.

He was clever, she'd give him that. No wonder he'd wanted to talk to Hannah. He'd known she wouldn't tell him to leave, as he must have realized Eden would. Now, what was she to do? Send them packing after breakfast, as she'd planned?

A sound from across the room made her freeze. A small, weak chuckle. But still a laugh.

Hannah's laughter. She hadn't heard that for weeks. Unexpected tears filled her eyes, and she blinked them away. No, she couldn't make them leave today. Cade seemed like a nice boy. He'd be no problem. And she could cope with Jesse a few days, for Hannah's sake.

She finished the meal and put it on the table, then fixed a tray for Hannah before she called the men over.

"My land, girl, you shorely don't expect me to eat all them vittles, do you?" Hannah looked at her plate with amazement.

Eden had cooked her an egg just as she liked it, soft and pink on top from being basted with bacon fat, and given her a golden brown johnnycake with gravy. As well as a crisply fried piece of bacon. "You can try," Eden told her, smiling. She hoped Hannah's perked-up mood would extend to her appetite.

When she turned back, Jesse stood behind his chair, his hands on the back, waiting for her, as he had the first time he'd been here. Cade did likewise. Eden slipped into her place and the men sat, too. She picked up the platter of bacon and, smiling, handed it to Cade.

She was startled at the hunger on his face. As if he hadn't had a good meal in weeks. Her conscience smote her. Maybe he hadn't. She knew things were very bad over most of the South, especially Georgia, from Atlanta to Savannah.

They'd been lucky, here on the ridge. North Carolina in general had fared better than any other southern state. It was the only one to escape widespread invasion.

Cade took one piece of bacon and put it on his plate. "Take two," Eden urged. There wasn't much bacon left in the crock, but never mind. She'd fatten these two up a little while they were here. She couldn't stand the thought of man or beast being hungry if she could help it.

"Thank you, ma'am," Cade said, taking another slice.

Eden noticed his voice sounded a little reserved. The warmth that had been in it when he'd talked to Hannah was missing. Wondering why, she felt her heart contract as she saw how he tried to control his eagerness to get at the food.

She passed the plate across the table to Jesse, making sure their fingers didn't touch in the exchange. She remembered too well the last time his flesh had touched hers.

Jesse, without being urged, took two pieces. As he handed the plate back, their gazes met and held. Eden found herself staring into his golden eyes as if mesmerized. Was he, too, remembering those other times they'd been together?

Was that why he'd returned?

The thought slipped into her mind as if it had been waiting

for an opportunity. She at once tried to deny it. No, of course that couldn't be the reason. How absurd!

What other reason could he have?

She gave Jesse a cool smile, helped herself, then passed the platter of eggs. The most likely reason Jesse was here was the one Hannah had voiced.

He couldn't stand to be in Georgia because his fiancée was marrying another man. Because he'd said he no longer loved Annabelle didn't make it true. His pride wouldn't let him admit otherwise.

"Ma'am, I haven't seen eggs like these in years," Cade said, his voice almost reverent as he slid one onto his plate.

His appreciation for the food didn't quite cover the touch of reserve still in his voice, Eden noticed. She smiled at him, placing the crock of golden butter by his plate. "Here, try some of this with the plum preserves."

After a moment, he smiled back, a little hesitantly.

"You two eat hearty," Hannah said from across the room. "There's plenty o' vittles here."

Eden threw her a glance. Her mother-in-law had a stricken look on her face, as if she also realized these two hadn't eaten well in a long time. Except, perhaps, for those few days Jesse had been here before. Eden noticed something else: Hannah was eating.

The knot of tension that seemed to stay in her stomach all the time eased a little. If Jesse and his cousin could have this good an effect on Hannah, she'd encourage them to stay the rest of the summer!

Instantly appalled at her thoughts, she repudiated them. Of course she wouldn't. No matter how Jesse felt about being jilted, he'd certainly have to get back to his home soon. She'd stop thinking about it. She'd talk to the boy, try to loosen him up a little.

"Is your home near Mr. Bainbridge's?" Eden asked Cade, knowing the question was fraught with peril. But she didn't know any other way to start.

"It *was,* ma'am," he answered politely, but not looking at her. "Sherman burned it and everything we had." His young voice broke at the end.

Eden swallowed, her heart softening with pity. Whatever quarrel she had with landed southerners, it didn't extend to the youngsters. She only felt grief and sorrow for what they'd had to endure.

"I'm sorry," she said softly. "I shouldn't have asked."

He gave her a quick glance, something in his eyes making her realize with a jolt he was surprised by her sympathy.

"It's all right," he finally said. "My mother and sister are in Alabama. I'll go there when—" He glanced over at Jesse, as if not sure how to finish. "When we leave here."

"Your family will come back to Georgia eventually," Jesse said.

"Why?" Cade demanded. "We haven't got the money to rebuild. Or to plant new crops or even pay taxes on the land." His voice broke again and Eden saw tears come to his eyes.

"Of course you and Belinda and Aunt Viola can stay with me," Jesse said, his voice tight. "We'll survive."

He sounded as if he thought that was all they'd do. Eden was furious with herself for starting this. But it wasn't possible to have a pleasant, ordinary conversation these days. Any question asked about family or home was likely to bring on these sad stories of loss and grief.

She picked up the empty johnnycake plate and pushed back her chair. And she'd realized what was wrong with Cade. He resented her for being a Yankee.

"There's more of these," she said. "And they're no good cold." By the time she returned to the table with the refilled plate, Cade had himself under control again. He politely took another cake, smiling stiffly at her. Jesse's face had relaxed a little, too.

Still standing, Eden glanced across to Hannah. She'd been quiet for a while. Hannah's eyes were riveted on Cade, and even from this distance, Eden could see the tears glistening in them.

Oh, no. The lump in Eden's stomach grew again. But then Hannah drew a handkerchief from under her pillow and wiped her eyes and pulled herself up a little higher in the bed.

"Eden," she said. "Could I have another cup o' that peppermint tea? It shorely did taste good."

"You surely can." Eden walked across the room with a light step and removed Hannah's half-empty plate. Hannah hadn't eaten this much for several weeks. She brought her a fresh cup of tea, her heart feeling lighter than in weeks, too.

A sound from the doorway made her turn. Willa stood, silhouetted, the sun haloing her flaxen hair. The girl saw Jesse and a delighted smile broke over her face. "Oh, Mr. Bainbridge! I didn't know you was back." Her gaze moved to Cade and stopped. Shyness faded the smile. She backed up a step.

Both men rose politely. "How have you been, Willa?" Jesse asked, affection in his deep voice. He turned to Cade. "This girl practically saved my life when I was here before."

Willa turned red. She looked as if she might take off at any moment. "Oh, I didn't do any such thing!" she said. "I jist helped you to the cabin."

Jesse shot a quick glance at Eden. He'd put his foot in his mouth. If anyone had saved his life, and he knew that was stretching things, it had been Eden. If he was going to praise anyone to his cousin, it should have been her. And long before.

She didn't look offended, though. In fact, she wasn't looking at him at all. Her glance was on Cade, a startled expression on her beautiful face. Jesse returned his gaze to his cousin.

Cade's mouth hung slightly open as he stared at Willa. Startled himself, Jesse looked at the girl with new eyes. She was more grown up than he'd realized. The bodice of her faded calico dress curved over her chest, and her face was beginning to lose the roundness of childhood. She had good bone structure—in a few more years she'd be a lovely young woman.

"I reckon I'd better be gittin' on back home," Willa said in a rush. She turned and vanished.

"Wait," Eden called after her. "We were going to dig ginseng this morning, remember?" Eden hurried across the room and also vanished out the door.

Cade looked at Jesse, his young face bemused. He cleared his throat.

"Who on earth is *she?*"

Chapter Nine

Jesse checked the smile trying to turn up his lips. He'd never have thought anyone could make open, friendly Willa turn bashful. Cade was old enough to show an interest in attractive females—he'd proved that last night when he'd reacted so strongly to Eden. But Willa? The two were worlds apart in background, upbringing . . .

And those things no longer mattered, Jesse reminded himself. Not that they ever should have. Eden had married Alston, hadn't she? And she'd loved him deeply, too. He remembered that day in the barn when she'd revealed that. She probably still loved him.

Besides, no one was talking about marriage. He was jumping the gun. The two weren't even full grown, and they'd just met. He guessed he'd better answer Cade's question. "Her name is Willa Freeman. She's a neighbor of the Claybornes."

"And a sweeter, smarter little gal ye'll never hope to see," Hannah put in. "I declare, Eden and her seem more like sisters than many true sisters I've knowed."

Jesse turned toward the older woman. "She is a very nice girl," he agreed.

Talking of Willa made him think of Darcy, her brother. He

wondered if Darcy was still trying to court Eden. The thought made his stomach tense, even while he told himself it was none of his business. He was here to help Eden and Hannah until after the baby was born and that was all.

"And how are the rest of the Freemans?" he heard himself asking Hannah.

"Oh, they's all right. They're havin' a hard time now, though. Hollis ain't a very good farmer, and his older boy Oran come home from th' war with one leg gone."

She hadn't mentioned Darcy, he noted.

A sound from the doorway made Jesse turn. Eden entered. Behind her on the porch, he glimpsed Willa's blond head. But the girl moved out of sight, her shyness still with her, he guessed. He glanced at Cade, to see the boy's gaze turning toward the porch, too.

Eden walked to the kitchen area and hurriedly started clearing the table. Jesse remembered her calling to Willa something about digging ginseng. He began stacking plates and flatware. Cade, taking his cue, did the same.

"You don't have to do that," Eden said, her voice crisp. "It'll only take me a few minutes."

Jesse kept stacking, but Cade took Eden at her word. "Thank you for a wonderful breakfast." His smile a little warmer now, he ambled casually to the doorway.

Eden's gaze followed him, a frown between her eyes.

"Will Willa bolt again?" Jesse asked, setting a pile of dishes at the edge of the table. He felt another smile tug at his mouth and wondered at it. He'd had little enough to smile at for a long time now. He guessed it wouldn't hurt to try a few out.

"I don't know. I've never known her to be shy around anyone." She echoed Jesse's thoughts of a few moments ago.

She was so surprised at Cade's obvious interest in Willa, she'd forgotten to keep her voice crisp and cool, he noticed.

But he dreaded the moment they were alone. She'd for sure light into him about his revelation to Hannah they planned to stay a while. What would she say when he told her for how long? He'd worry about that when the time came, he decided.

He glanced at his cousin. Cade had stopped in the doorway and was looking toward Willa. The girl was perched on the rail, throwing grass to some geese honking below. The boy looked as if he didn't know what to do, speak to her, or come back inside. Suppressing a grin, Jesse turned away, picking up another plate and adding it to his stack.

Cade stepped onto the porch, his heart beating faster as he gazed at Willa's profile. Gosh, but she was a pretty girl! About the prettiest one he'd ever seen. Her hair was pretty, too, even if it was skinned back in those braids.

He edged out a few more steps, trying to be quiet, but she heard him and whipped her head around. When she saw who it was, her face reddened as it had in the kitchen. She slid down from the rail and stood against it, looking cornered.

Cade wished he hadn't sneaked up on her like that. He stopped where he was, a few feet away.

"Hello," he said, desperately hoping he could finish a sentence without his voice breaking. "I'm Cade Morgan, Jesse's cousin. Mrs. Clayborne said you're Willa Freeman."

He heaved a sigh of relief. His voice sounded too high, but at least it had remained steady. He saw her swallow, then a shy smile lit up her face. Cade drew in his breath. She was even prettier when she smiled.

"Yes. So what are you and Jesse doin' here on the ridge?"

For the first time in her life Willa was struck, like the force of a blow, with how different her speech sounded from that of this boy who looked something like Mister Jesse. She felt like a fool for running away from him. She didn't know what had got into her.

Becoming aware of her bare, brown feet, she edged them backward, under her dress as far as she could.

He shrugged, uncomfortable at her question. He didn't know how much Jesse wanted him to say. Last night, his cousin had admitted he'd have a hard time getting Miss Eden to agree to let them stay until after . . .

He felt his face reddening. Men didn't talk about such things. And he'd better be careful what he said. "We're only here for a visit." He knew that sounded dumb, too. Men also didn't just up and come to visit two women living alone.

She stared at him for a minute, then a sly smile curved her mouth. "I betcha Mister Jesse likes Miz Eden," she said, her voice low, as she cast a look toward the open doorway. "My brother likes her, too. He's a-tryin' to court her."

Cade didn't know how to answer either of her surprising statements. He thought she was right about Jesse, but he figured his cousin would skin him alive if he admitted it to this girl he'd just met. He decided he'd better change the subject. "Have you always lived here?" he asked her.

She nodded. "This ridge is full o' Freemans. I got me so many kinfolk I don't rightly know which is which."

He felt his mouth curving upward at her quaint speech. It sounded a little like that of the Negroes who used to work his family's plantation, yet different, with a lilting, musical quality. It enchanted him.

Seeing his half-smile, Willa blushed again. She knew he was amused at the way she spoke. She vowed to try harder at her daily lessons with Miz Eden. "What about you? Is your homestead close by Mr. Bainbridge's?"

He wondered how long it would be before he could talk about his destroyed home without wanting to cry. He forced back the tears. He was a man now. "Yes, real close. But our house was burned down." He was relieved his voice hadn't trembled, well, at least not much.

The girl's face sobered. She looked at him as if she knew just how he felt and didn't think him unmanly at all. "I'm dreadful sorry 'bout that," she said. She paused, then went on. "Did you fight in the war?"

He looked at her a minute, bursting with pride that she thought him old enough for that. He wanted badly to tell her yes, he'd killed many a damned Yankee. But sure as anything he'd get caught out if he tried it. She'd probably want to know details about what battles he'd fought in. So he shook his head.

"No. I'm not as old as I look. I'll be sixteen in December."

She looked surprised—as if she'd indeed thought him older, boosting his pride even higher—then concerned again. "Are your folks all gone? Is that why you're here with Mr. Bainbridge?"

He shook his head and told her about his family. "I came

back to Georgia to see how bad our place was damaged. I'll
go back there in—a little while, I guess."

"Willa, are you ready to go?" Eden walked out on the porch.
Jesse came behind her, a bucket in his hands.

"Yes'm, Miz Eden, I shore—sure am," the girl said. She
gave Cade a warm smile and followed Eden off the porch.

"Want to go with me to feed the hogs and do some weeding?"
Jesse asked Cade.

The boy, watching Willa's light, graceful walk as the two
moved across the clearing, started. Looking a little shamefaced,
he turned toward Jesse, then reached for the slop bucket. "Sure.
I'll take that."

Jesse relinquished the bucket with no reluctance. "Let's go
see how much we can get done before she gets back and stops
us."

"Fine with me," Cade answered. He hated weeding, but he
could do it. Like Jesse, he'd grown up learning all there was to
know about farm work. He followed his cousin to the barnyard,
handling the bucket gingerly in order not to spill its contents
on himself.

He realized he felt better inside than he had in a long time.
Some of the pain and fear he'd carried for years had lessened.
Dimly, he knew it was somehow connected to the hill girl,
Willa. But he didn't understand why. Nor did he want to pursue
it right now.

It was enough to know she'd likely be around often and he'd
get to see her while they were here. Miss Eden wasn't bad,
either—for a Yankee. She sure could cook. For the first time
since he'd left Georgia with Jesse, he hoped they *would* stay
here for months.

"Can we have my lesson now?" Willa asked Eden, as they
came back up on the cabin porch, her voice eager. Both carried
burlap bags filled with ginseng roots. It had been a fruitful
morning.

Frowning, Eden dropped her bag by the door. She'd glimpsed
Jesse and Cade a few moments ago weeding the garden, and
she was fuming. What did Jesse think he was doing?

Barging in here uninvited last night, doing her chores this morning, telling Hannah he was staying for a visit, and now, weeding her garden! Not that she wasn't grateful for the help. If it had been anyone but him . . .

She had to talk to him, the sooner the better. "If you'll wait a few minutes, Willa, that would be fine," she told the girl. "I need to talk to Mr. Bainbridge first. You could go in and sit with Hannah."

Willa glanced toward the garden, even though it wasn't visible from this part of the porch, a slightly crestfallen look on her face. She quickly turned back to Eden. "All right, Miz Eden. I'll do that."

The girl had wanted to go with her, to talk to Cade, Eden realized, her frown deepening. The two young people were obviously attracted to each other. They were too young for such ideas! Aside from that, no good could come of Willa taking a fancy to Jesse's cousin. She'd have to try to keep them apart.

"I'll be back in a few minutes," Eden said, smoothing her frown out and smiling at Willa.

The girl smiled back, but her face still looked a little wistful. "All right." She went on inside the cabin and Eden heard her greet Hannah.

Stiffening her spine, Eden headed for the garden. When she reached it, Jesse and Cade were throwing armloads of weeds onto an already huge pile at the garden's edge. Her eyes followed Jesse, noticing how the smooth muscles of his arms rippled with his movements.

Aware of what she was doing, she quickly looked away toward the garden, then her eyes widened. They'd weeded the entire expanse.

She whipped her head back around. Jesse was standing by the pile of weeds, his gaze fixed on her. Cade stood beside him. Both looked tired and hot, smears of grime on their faces where they'd wiped perspiration away with their dirt-smudged hands.

To her dismay, her indignation with Jesse's high-handed ways began to melt. They'd put in a hard morning's work, doing a job that would have taken her the better part of a week. How could she jump all over him now? But she had to, she reminded herself desperately. This couldn't go on.

She took a deep breath and let it out. "Thanks for doing all this," she told them. "You saved me a lot of work, but you shouldn't have done it."

"Why not?" Jesse asked reasonably enough, as he had earlier, when she'd said the same thing about his milking Bossie. "You helped me when I needed it."

He momentarily stopped her with that remark because it was true.

"We wanted to, Mrs. Clayborne," Cade said earnestly. "It wasn't anything."

Eden smiled at the boy, liking him better all the time. "It was a hard job."

She felt herself softening even more, and, alarmed, pulled herself up as tall as she could. She turned to Jesse, her smile fading. "I'd like to talk to you," she told him, forcing her voice to sound firm and no-nonsense.

His face changed at her words, became wary. After a moment he nodded. "Of course."

"I'll go up to the cabin," Cade said quickly.

Eden let out another frustrated breath as she watched Cade hurry off. *This* was a good start to her plans to keep him and Willa apart!

"Can we sit down somewhere?" Jesse asked.

"Of course," Eden answered, her frown back. He stood straight and tall, but his leg injury wasn't that far in the past. It might very well be paining him. She cast her mind about where to go. Not the cabin or the porch, because she wanted to talk with him frankly, not worry about any of the others hearing.

There was no place else here or in the barnyard. She could see them perched up in the hayloft! Then an idea came to her. "Let's walk to the spring," she suggested.

Jesse felt some of the tension leave his body at her words. He had at least a few minutes' reprieve. And maybe she'd be reasonable about the plan he intended to present. He nodded. "All right, that sounds fine."

There was no use starting this now, Eden decided. But neither

did she want to begin a pleasant conversation. That would
certainly give him the wrong idea. Maybe walking to the spring
had, anyway.

Alarmed, she glanced at him. Could he think she'd suggested
this so she could be alone with him? Did he believe his parting
kiss had meant something to her? That she wanted to build on
it?

His head was turned away, presenting her his profile. His face
was rugged and strong, and even a side view again reminded her
of a mountain lion in its strength and coloring. It also gave her
no indication of what he thought.

But she couldn't walk beside him without speaking at all,
she decided. She glanced at him again. Her heart skipped a
beat. He was looking directly at her. She jerked her head back
around. "You shouldn't have done all that work," she said again,
primly.

Jesse clamped his lips together, barely keeping himself from
swearing. The woman had a one-track mind. Why was he doing
this? Why had he ridden all this way to try to help a stiff-
necked Yankee woman who didn't want his help in any way,
shape, or manner?

He knew why—because of his damn guilt. It wouldn't leave
him alone in Georgia, night or day. He'd kept picturing her in
all kinds of bad situations, afraid, alone. Instead, she was fine
and healthy looking, and he doubted if she ever felt fear. Except
the day when he'd knocked that trapper down. He'd seen fear
in her eyes then.

And she needed his help, even if she wouldn't admit it. He
didn't know how she was keeping up with everything. Hell,
she wasn't. The garden had been neglected, weedy.

There had been a short rain during the night and he'd discovered the barn roof leaked. Fortunately, rain had missed the
hayloft, but it was close. A loft of moldy, ruined hay could be
a disaster. They couldn't have much money. Who did, since
the war?

He heard her sigh of relief when they reached the trees
surrounding the spring. They walked between two willows and
reached the banks.

It was cool and dim under the trees, with a mossy, pleasant

smell. The sparkling water gurgled and almost sang as it swiftly made its way over the rocks in the bed.

Jesse looked around in appreciation. "I'd forgotten what a beautiful place this is."

"Yes, it is," she answered quickly, trying to make her voice cool. *She'd* forgotten he'd helped her carry water from the spring the day before he'd left to go home.

The day before he'd kissed her.

Her face warmed at that thought which persisted in remaining in her mind. Eden sat down on the wooden bench. It felt cool, even through her layers of clothing. "It's always pleasant here," she added inanely.

Jesse sat down beside her, determined to stay calm, no matter how Eden riled him, and to employ every bit of persuasion he owned. Since the bench was small, he had to sit close, and then he was faced with a new problem.

He tried to force his body not to react to her nearness. But her warmth, the clean smell of her shining hair, drifted across to him. No matter how he tried to deny it, he wanted to curve his hands around her honey-hued face, draw her into his arms . . .

The shortness of the bench was a problem she hadn't considered when she'd suggested this. Maybe Jesse *would* think she wanted to be with him. She moved as close to the end of the seat as she could get, then turned to face him.

His shaggy lion's mane was appealingly disordered. She wanted to run her fingers through it, feel the texture on her skin. Was it soft, or as rough as it appeared? Appalled at her errant thoughts, she made her gaze straight, her face serious. She cleared her throat. "We came here to talk," she reminded him.

"Yes," Jesse agreed. Here it comes, he thought. He braced himself, sure her first words would be to tell him he had to leave. Convincing her she badly needed his help, even though both of them knew it did, would be a formidable task.

"You told Hannah you came for a visit. Is that the only reason you're here on the ridge?" she asked bluntly.

He considered how to answer, finally deciding the truth was the only thing she'd believe. Or at least, a part of the truth.

"Yes, it is. I worried about you, Eden. I feel responsible for Alston's death, and nothing you can say will change that."

Guilt swept over her at his unexpected words. Oh, God, she didn't need to be reminded they were both to blame for that.

"I'm not going to try," she said in a moment. "But we can't change the fact he's dead, either."

"No, but there's one thing I *can* do—help you until the child is born," he said, making his voice as neutral as possible.

Shock pushed the guilt away. She stared at him, her blue eyes wide. "You can't mean you want to stay here for months!"

"Yes, that's exactly what I mean," he answered, still calmly, although his heart pounded and his palms sweated.

Her eyes were still filled with shocked disbelief. "That's impossible. Surely you realize that!"

"No, it isn't. Cade and I will sleep in the barn, if you're worried about how it will look to your neighbors."

"I'm not worried about that."

Jesse felt a little hopeful. She'd conceded a point, if he wasn't mistaken. "Then what other problem is there?"

"Are you crazy? A dozen!"

"Name one," he answered, still calmly.

She couldn't tell him the true reason he mustn't stay was because his presence disturbed her so greatly, in so many different ways. "You and your cousin are strangers, for one thing."

He smiled wryly. "How can you say that when you've poulticed my injured leg, washed my clothes, cooked for me?"

And that's exactly why! she wanted to shout at him. Everything he said threw her off, left her almost sputtering.

"I merely helped you as any woman would have done," she answered, trying to make her voice as calm and under control as his own.

"Maybe so, but after that, how can you say we're strangers?"

She decided to abandon that line of argument. "How can you stay gone from your home so long? Surely you must need to start rebuilding your life."

He felt a bit more hopeful. She hadn't refuted his last statement.

"That can wait. It's too late in the season to plant a crop. And no one can do any more damage to the house, except burn it. I don't think that will happen now. And whether or not you'll admit it, you *do* need help."

"No, I don't," she insisted. "I can manage fine."

He wouldn't mention the work she could no longer keep up with, like the weeding, he decided. There were stronger arguments he could use.

"Maybe you can now, but what about when the baby comes? Who's going to help you? Hannah isn't able."

"Fern Willard, the valley midwife," she answered quickly. "Darcy has said he'll go for her."

His eyes narrowed at the mention of Freeman's name. It seemed as if the hill man was becoming more firmly entrenched in her life.

"What if it comes at night?" he countered. "Or there isn't time to send for the midwife?"

She gave him a confident smile, even though his last words sent a flash of fear through her.

"Darcy can go at night. He can ride these trails blindfolded. And first babies never come fast. There'll be plenty of time."

"Things don't always work out as you think they will." Didn't he know that well? His entire life was in a shambles. Maybe forever. "You're taking a lot for granted."

Fear again hit her. She pushed it down. Jesse was right: worry about all these possibilities kept her awake often. But she couldn't allow him to be the one to solve her problems. She couldn't let him stay!

"I can manage fine," she repeated stubbornly, her gaze steady on his.

"No, you can't," he answered, his gaze as firm and stubborn as her own. He wasn't surprised she hadn't given an inch, although unable to refute him. "And you know it."

Eden felt trapped. All right; she didn't have to continue with this argument. She only had to tell him to leave.

"We don't like each other, and you know it," she said, spacing her words so that each one came out firm and distinct. "I don't want you here."

Even though he'd wondered how long it would take her to get to that, her last statements strangely jolted him. But he had one last weapon in his arsenal, one he didn't think she'd brush aside.

"I believe Hannah likes me and wouldn't mind my staying," he answered slowly, watching her face.

She swallowed. He'd unerringly found her weakness. He, too, must have realized how glad Hannah was to see him. Of course he had, or he wouldn't be saying this. But he couldn't stay here for two months!

Perhaps, though, even a short stay would help put Hannah on the road to recovery . . .

No, she was grasping at straws, that was an absurd notion. But this morning Hannah had talked with animation, eaten better than she had in weeks. And Eden had done everything she knew to do to help her. If letting Jesse stay for a little while would help, then of course she'd have to allow it.

"Yes," she answered reluctantly, "you're right. She does. If I . . . if I allow you to stay for a short visit—say, two weeks— will you leave with no more arguments?"

Two weeks wasn't very long. She could keep away from Jesse, be sure they weren't alone together. *Like now?* her mind asked slyly. *You can't deny you wish he'd hold you, kiss you like he did that other time.*

She'd neatly turned his argument on its head. He admired her skill even while he tried to find a way around her proposal. "What about if we let Hannah decide?" he countered.

"No," she said quickly, emphatically. "Hannah's sick. I have to make these decisions." Of course, Hannah would want him to stay. She'd see how much work he could take off Eden's shoulders. *And Hannah would also enjoy his company? Maybe continue to improve?* She wouldn't think about that, because he couldn't stay!

Jesse saw her mind was made up. It would do no good to argue further. But he wasn't giving up his plan this easily, either.

"All right," he said. "But how about if you wait until after the two weeks to make a final decision."

"I already have! I just told you."

"Maybe you'll change your mind." He'd use this short time

to do everything in his power to make her see how much he was needed here.

Eden firmly shook her head.

"No, I won't," she said, her words as firm as the gesture.

Already she regretted her decision to let him stay for even one more day. Looking into Jesse's golden eyes, she knew the strange attraction between them, the force that was trying to pull them together, was as strong as before.

Despite her dislike for Jesse's kind, her angry resentment because he hadn't sent Alston home.

Even now, she wanted nothing more than to move into his arms as she had the day he'd left, feel his warm, seeking mouth on hers . . .

Appalled at her thoughts, she quickly rose from the bench.

"Will you agree to let me try to persuade you?" Jesse persisted, rising too. "You need my help—and I need to do this to try to atone for my part in your husband's death."

His last words touched her to the quick. She, too, needed that atonement. She had no way to obtain it for herself, but how could she coldly refuse him? Yet she must, because letting him stay was too dangerous—for both of them.

Even if Jesse didn't know this.

"I don't often change my mind once it's made up," she said crisply.

"I can believe that, but stranger things have happened," Jesse answered. "I take that as an agreement. Shall we shake on it?"

Eden looked at his arm, covered with that golden hair, his extended hand. No! She didn't want to have his big, bronzed hand enfolding hers. She didn't want to touch him!

"That's the way men handle these things," she said. "We both agreed, that's good enough for me. Now, I have to go back to the cabin to give Willa her lesson." She turned and started walking up the path.

He stared after her for a minute, wondering at her reaction. Unwillingly he felt an answer came to him, one he didn't want to accept.

She was afraid to touch him.

Like him, she still remembered what had happened between them the day he left.

The need to help Eden wasn't the only reason he'd come back to this mountain ridge, he finally admitted. He also wanted to see her again, be with her. And maybe he was God's biggest fool for that decision. Because there could never be anything between them. They were worlds apart in every way that counted.

He blamed Eden personally for nothing, but his resentment of the Yankees who'd destroyed his way of life was still strong. And she belonged to those people. Would forever, no matter how long she lived in the South.

In return, her resentment of his kind was even stronger than his.

That wasn't the worst of it. Alston's death would always stand between them like a granite wall.

Alston's death—and their mutual guilt.

Chapter Ten

Eden hurried away from the spring. This was never going to work, even for two weeks! How could she let Jesse stay, when she feared what the mere touch of his hand would do to her?

She'd been a fool to agree!

She continued her fast pace for a few moments, then slowed down. Jesse was not trying to catch up. She pushed down what felt disturbingly like a twinge of disappointment. Of course it wasn't! She didn't want him anywhere near her.

But the baby inside her was getting too heavy for her to keep that pace up for any length of time. Besides, it was a hot day and it might not be good for him, either.

Him? With a small shock, she realized that, for the first time, she'd thought about the coming child as either a boy or girl. *Him.*

Her hand smoothed down her rounded abdomen, and in spite of her inner turmoil, a smile curved her mouth upward. Why had she thought that? True, Hannah kept telling her she would have a boy—because she was carrying the baby completely in front. Anyone seeing her from behind would never know she was pregnant. But Eden had dismissed this as superstition.

Him. A small human being would soon be here in this world. She'd be his mother. To care for him. To love and protect him. That is, if all went well.

Another kind of fear swept over her, and her other hand also went protectively over her abdomen. So many things could go wrong. There was no one to help except the settlement midwife.

And Cherry Creek was too far away for her to count on getting word to Fern in time if her labor should go fast. Most first births didn't, of course, as she'd told Jesse, but she couldn't count on that, either. She couldn't count on anything!

Hannah had birthed all the ridge babies over the years. Until she'd taken to her bed. Oh, how she wished Hannah was well! Not only for her own sake, but for that of Hannah's soon-to-be-born grandson.

Or granddaughter, Eden hastily added. She didn't care whether the baby was a boy or girl. All she prayed for was that it be healthy and its birth be normal.

A sudden, intense homesickness for Connecticut swept over her. Vivid pictures of her parents' gracious white-painted clapboard house in Hartford, near the big brick building that housed her father's very successful insurance business, filled her mind's eye.

As busy as he was, Norris Thornton had found time to be with his wife and daughter, take them on trips to visit both sets of grandparents in Bridgeport.

Eden blinked back a tear. Only Gramma Landers, her mother's mother, was left when she came here with Alston four years ago. Now, in all probability, that sole remaining grandparent was gone, too.

She'd loved her life in the attractive city in the Connecticut Valley during her growing up years. She'd felt safe and secure, loved and nurtured by both her parents.

There, she would have no worries about anything except the actual birth. Her parents would see to it she had the best doctors, the best care . . .

But Hartford might as well be on the moon, for all the good it would do her now. She'd chosen to follow Alston here, against her parents' urgent pleas. It was her own decision. As Hannah would say, she'd made her bed.

Now she had to lie in it.

Eden resolutely pushed back the clamoring fears, as she'd learned to do over these last seven months. She was healthy, she was young, she'd had no problems with the pregnancy, she repeated like a litany to calm herself. Mattie would help her, if it came to it, she knew. And she'd make Mattie scrub her hands, keep everything as clean as possible, even if the ridge woman scoffed at such "foolishment."

Passing the now weed-free garden, Eden couldn't help giving a sigh of relief. Jesse and Cade had saved her hours of work, work that tired her greatly these days, even if she wouldn't admit it to Jesse.

In some ways, it *would* be wonderful to have them here until after the baby's birth. Jesse could ride down to the settlement to get Fern, she wouldn't have to walk to the Freemans' for Darcy . . .

She brought herself up short. It was true, Jesse had presented her with realistic, compelling reasons for him to stay—both for his sake and hers. But there were equally compelling reasons for her to send him back to Georgia.

The strong physical attraction she felt for Jesse, a former plantation master, a southern aristocrat, disturbed and frightened her.

She'd never felt this way before, she admitted. Not even about Alston.

Maybe Jesse, too, felt that attraction. Otherwise, why would he have given her that fiery kiss when he'd left the ridge weeks ago? Maybe that even figured into his return. But if so, he must also know there could never be anything between them. They were playing with fire to be close to each other.

Her philosophy of life was as different from Jesse's as night is day's opposite. She didn't like his kind, she didn't like *him!*

And even if all that hadn't been true, the searing guilt they both felt for Alston's death would always be between them.

Will you agree to let me try to persuade you? Eden stopped dead as she remembered Jesse's words. What could be more persuasive than doing most of the heavy work? As he'd done today with the weeding. If he couldn't convince her with words, he'd *show* her.

Didn't he think she could figure that out?

Her peripheral vision caught a glimpse of his white shirt behind her. She stiffened. She didn't want to talk to him again. But he turned and walked toward the barn, again leaving her with that strange, almost disappointed feeling.

The cabin door was open to any passing breeze, and the geese were up on the porch, almost to the doorway. "Go on, shoo," Eden said briskly, clapping her hands at them.

Willa and Cade sat by Hannah's bedside. As Eden walked over the threshold, the older woman chuckled at something Cade had said, as she'd laughed with Jesse earlier today. Oh, that sounded so good! It had been far too long since Hannah had laughed.

But she didn't like the way Cade and Willa had their heads so close together. Of course, they could be friendly with each other, but . . .

Hannah glanced over at Eden, her laugh fading to a warm smile. "Come in and rest yoreself, Eden. You ain't set down since sun-up."

Eden's emotions did another flip-flop. She was still amazed at the improvement in Hannah's spirits. For Hannah's sake, she couldn't be sorry she'd agreed to let Jesse and Cade stay for a little while.

She could keep away from Jesse. It shouldn't be hard not to be alone with him, with Cade around. And she was flattering herself. So far, he showed no indication he wanted to be alone with her.

"I'd better start dinner," she said, smiling back at Hannah.

Willa quickly got up from her chair. "Do you want me to fetch some garden stuff?"

"Yes," Eden agreed. "Get some of the corn, and there should be green beans ready. And dig some of the new potatoes, if you will."

"I'll help, too," Cade said.

With the ease of familiarity, Willa got a woven basket from a shelf and she and Cade walked out the door together.

Eden watched them go, a frown between her brows. With Willa here almost every day, keeping those two youngsters apart would be almost impossible, without it becoming obvious. She didn't want to hurt the feelings of either of them.

"That Cade is a nice young 'un," Hannah said. "And I shore never seen Willa take a shine like that to a boy afore." Her voice sounded totally approving.

"I've never seen her *with* a boy before," Eden said, trying to make her voice light. "Besides, they've just met. And look at their backgrounds. They're completely unsuited to each other."

Hannah gave Eden a searching look. "You and Alston was unsuited, too, I reckon. But you made a match of it."

There had been an odd note in Hannah's voice. What was she insinuating? That she knew Eden hadn't loved Alston for a long time before he died? Eden tried to dismiss these unsettling thoughts. Her guilt over that fact was making her oversensitive.

"Yes," she finally said. "We did. But I wasn't fourteen, and Alston wasn't Cade's age, either."

"Young 'uns grow up fast in the hills. But I guess them two need to do a mite more of it afore they begin sparkin'."

Relief swept over Eden. Her nerves were on edge. She was imagining things. Hannah hadn't meant anything like that, thank God. "Yes," she said lightly. "And now I'm going to cook dinner, and I expect you to eat as well as you did at breakfast."

"I believe I jist might be able to eat a few vittles. It does a body good to have company once in a while, don't it?"

"Yes, I suppose so," Eden answered, pleased at Hannah's first sentence, troubled by the second. After Jesse and Cade left, she'd ask Willa to visit with Hannah more often. The girl's lively company would lift anyone's spirits.

"Jesse is a good man," Hannah said with conviction. "He's had a mighty bad time of it, and he ain't complainin' a bit. That woman of his was a downright idjit to give him up."

Eden, shaking down ashes from the breakfast fire, gave her mother-in-law a quick glance. Why had she brought that up? Hannah was looking straight at her. Eden concentrated on laying kindling in the firebox, then added bigger logs.

"Shoo, go on now," Jesse's vibrant voice suddenly said from the doorway, a strange note in it.

Eden quickly looked up. He was chasing the geese away, his face set in tense lines, as if the sight of the birds was painful to him. His sunstreaked, tawny hair was damp, slicked back from his bronzed face. He must have washed at the stand on the porch.

Their glances met and held, and her heart lurched. Finally, Jesse's face smoothed out, and he nodded to her. Eden jerked her attention back to starting another fire.

"Cade says you know how to tell a story better than anyone he ever talked to," Jesse told Hannah.

Eden's head came up again, surprise in her eyes this time.

An equally surprised look came over Hannah's wrinkled old face, then changed into a self-conscious, but pleased expression. "Alston used to say that same thing to me. He said I ort to write them down." She gave a self-deprecating shrug. "Course, he knowed I couldn't do that."

Jesse's head turned toward Eden. "*You* could," he suggested.

Jolted by his words, Eden stared back. Something in his eyes made her realize he knew exactly how much good his and Cade's presence were having on Hannah.

"Yes," she heard herself answer. "That's a good idea." And it was, she admitted silently. Her mother-in-law had been a spellbinding storyteller before she had taken to her bed. Back in the days before her son had died, when Hannah still hoped he'd return safely from the war. If she could keep this spark of interest going, growing, Eden vowed, she'd write until her hands cramped!

A tingle of excitement stirred inside her at the thought. There was paper left over from the schoolteaching supplies Alston had brought with him when they'd moved here from Connecticut.

"Oh, pshaw!" Hannah said, embarrassment replacing her smile. "That's jist foolishment. You ain't got time to waste on sich as that."

Jesse gave Hannah a wide smile. "Eden will have more free time now, at least while Cade and I are here. We'll be helping with the work."

"That will be a real blessin'," Hannah said fervently. "Lord knows she has a heap o' work on her shoulders."

Eden glared at his back. She'd been right about Jesse's campaign to change her mind about letting him and Cade stay. And he was clever, too. Mentioning his intentions in front of Hannah, getting her on his side right from the start.

Footsteps and Willa's merry laughter came from the porch. Roses blooming on her cheeks, she walked through the doorway, Cade behind her, carrying the basket, now heaped with garden vegetables. "Is that enough, Miz Eden?" Willa asked, indicating the basket.

Eden took a deep breath and let it out. Two could play at this game Jesse had instigated.

"Yes, it's plenty. Thank you, Willa. Of course you'll stay for dinner."

The girl frowned, then her face cleared. "Mam will likely be mad and give me a switchin', but I'll chance it."

Cade gave her an astonished look, as if he couldn't believe her words. "Your mother *switches* you?" he asked, incredulous.

Willa's roses deepened to an embarrassed flush. "Not much anymore." She darted a quick look at Cade, and her lips pressed together. She turned back to Eden. "Reckon I better git on home," she said in a subdued voice. She brushed by Cade, and hurried out the door.

He looked after her, his face distressed. "Wait, Willa!" He quickly went after her.

"What was that all about?" Jesse asked, surprise in his voice.

Didn't he know? Couldn't he figure out that the huge, unbridgeable gap between Willa's and Cade's backgrounds had been painfully brought home to the hill girl?

Eden picked up the basket and began removing the vegetables. She hated to see Willa hurt, but it was better it happened now than later, when her feelings were more deeply involved.

Her hands stilled on the ear of shucked corn she held. What was she thinking? Of course Willa's feelings for Cade wouldn't be growing, deepening. No matter what Hannah and the ridge folk thought, Willa and Cade were far too young for a serious involvement. He and Jesse would soon be gone, but maybe she needed to talk to Jesse. . . .

She put the ear of corn into the pan of water on the stove, then glanced back at Jesse. He still looked at her, as if waiting for an answer. Eden's irritation grew. How could he be so blind?

"My land," Hannah's also surprised voice came from the bed. "I never knowed Willa to act like that afore. I guess she figgers she's a'gittin' too old fer the switch. Reckon she is. Mattie allus was one to lick a young 'un too much fer ever' little thing."

"Yes," Eden agreed, her mouth tightening. She'd seen welts on Willa's arms more than once. She placed more corn in the pan, not looking at Jesse.

A sound from the door made her look that way. Cade stood there, frowning. "I don't know what happened to Willa. She ran off home, wouldn't even talk to me."

"She's a mite shy," Hannah said. "Never been around no boys much but her brothers and other kinfolk. But she'll be back. Eden gives her a lesson most ever' day. And they dig herbs together."

Yes, Willa would be back tomorrow, Eden had no doubt. For the first time since she'd met the hill girl, Eden wished she'd stay away during these next two weeks while Jesse and Cade were here.

She'd fight Mattie for Willa's future in any way possible. She'd try to see the girl had a chance for some education, a life off this ridge.

But that chance didn't include an involvement with a boy such as Cade, no matter how likable.

A boy who was essentially the same as his cousin, Jesse, with all the aristocratic, *wrong* attitudes. Who was from the southern planter class who'd caused all the horrors of war that the South had endured. Was still enduring. That had killed so many of her own people.

No, that wasn't what she wanted for Willa. Never in a million years.

With dinner over and the dishes washed, Eden headed for the barn, her arms full of bedding. She didn't know what Cade and Jesse had with them but was pretty sure they hadn't brought pillows. Or maybe even an extra blanket to put down on the hay to sleep on. No matter how much she wished they were back in Georgia, she couldn't rest easy at night knowing they might be cold or uncomfortable.

Hannah had again eaten fairly well. She'd joined in the dinner table conversation from her bed with apparent enjoyment. Eden had left it to the three of them, only saying something when it would have been awkward not to.

For Hannah's sake, she'd be polite for these two weeks, but she didn't have to be overly friendly. Well, she didn't want to hurt Cade's feelings—he wasn't to blame for any of what was between her and Jesse.

But Cade hadn't seemed to notice Eden's near silence. He'd chatted and joked with Hannah, as he'd done earlier, but he'd seemed subdued, Eden noticed. And he kept glancing toward the door as if he expected to see someone.

Willa, she would bet. Cade had all the earmarks of being smitten with the girl, even if they had met only today. Eden realized she could be anticipating trouble that would never come, but better that than be sorry later.

Jesse hadn't said much. He'd given Eden a few glances, but not ones that held. It appeared he had no more desire to pursue anything personal between them than she did.

His reasons for being here were only what he'd said at the spring: he wanted to help her because of his guilt for Alston's death. It was obvious he was also trying to improve Hannah's health. She was deeply relieved at this knowledge. Why couldn't she get rid of that tiny, disappointed feeling?

She was no young girl hungry for a man's admiration. Eden gave a short laugh at that absurd thought. No, she was a seven-months-pregnant widow.

She and Jesse didn't even *like* each other. They hadn't from the moment they met.

And that moment out of time when he'd swept her into his arms and given her that soul-shattering kiss meant nothing. Sometimes she was sure she must have imagined it.

Nearing the barn, she frowned to see Jesse on the roof, a hammer in his hand. He wasn't wasting any time proving his point.

The hot afternoon sun glinted on his shaggy head, the golden hair on his arms. He'd taken off his shirt, she saw, drawing in her breath. His back and chest were bronzed, like his arms. He lifted the hammer and brought it down, and the movement made muscles in his shoulders, his upper arms, flex and ripple.

She hastily moved her glance away, down across the barnyard to the cornfield. Cade stood amid the waist-high stalks, a hoe in his hands, weeding again, after all he'd already done this morning. Cade must approve of Jesse's plan, and the boy was a hard worker, she had to admit.

So was Jesse, despite their privileged plantation background. She heard the sound of Jesse's hammer pounding in another nail and fought the urge to glance toward him again.

Damn! Jesse's mouth tightened as, from his perch on the roof, he saw Eden coming, her arms heaped with what looked like pillows and blankets. She shouldn't be carrying that heavy load. Her black braids shone in the sunlight, her carriage was erect and graceful.

She was still utterly beautiful and desirable.

He still wanted her.

Shame washed over him at his wayward thoughts.

But he couldn't deny them.

Eden lifted her head, her glance meeting his. Even at this distance, he saw a blue flash from her eyes before she quickly looked away, toward the cornfield.

"Damn it!" He didn't want to have any more confrontations with her today. After their argument at the spring, he thought they'd had quite enough interaction already.

She'd been cool and remote during dinner. Maybe because he'd suggested she write down Hannah's stories. She could have considered that none of his business, which it wasn't. But he liked the old woman. And Hannah had shown a definite spark of interest at that idea. He'd enjoy trying to help improve her health, maybe get her out of that bed. That would be one more reason for him to stay here. Would Eden acknowledge that?

He didn't think that was Eden's problem, though. She was devoted to her mother-in-law and would do anything to help her. It was likely just his presence in the house, at the dinner table. More than once she'd made it clear she didn't want to be around him.

He couldn't let her carry that big load.

He put the hammer down and quickly descended the ancient ladder he'd found in the barn, then strode across the barnyard to intercept her.

"Let me take that," he said, half-expecting her to protest and insist on carrying it all the way herself.

But she didn't. She relinquished the bundle as if relieved to be rid of it, affirming his suspicion that it was too heavy, that she routinely did all kinds of work she shouldn't be doing now.

He noticed she was careful not to let her hands touch his during the exchange.

"Is this for Cade and me?" he asked, sure it was, but merely for something to say since she was silent.

"Yes." Eden let her glance meet his.

It was cool. Her mouth was unsmiling. Her glance moved to the barn roof.

"I found some cedar shingles inside," Jesse hastened to say, before she had a chance to object. He started walking toward the barn again. "Several leaks barely miss the hayloft. You could lose a whole winter's worth of hay."

He heard her sharp intake of breath, as if she'd been unaware of this. He felt her closeness and tried to ignore it. He wasn't very successful.

"Thank you," she said. "I didn't know. Did you find any nails?"

"I used the ones in the old shakes and found some inside. There's a lot of leaks in the roof. And not enough shakes to cover all of them. Cade and I will have to fell a cedar tree to make more."

She gave him a quick, startled glance. "You know how to do that, too?"

Her insistence on believing he was only a useless southern gentleman was in her voice. The same as this morning when he'd been milking—it riled him. He gave her an ironic glance.

"Yes, Mrs. Clayborne, I know how to do that, too. So does Cade. As hard as it is for you to accept, we have quite a few practical skills."

His voice sounded irritated and challenging. Damn it! He hadn't meant to say that. He hadn't meant to say or do anything that might make Eden retract her promise to let them stay for the next two weeks.

They'd reached the barn by now. Jesse walked inside and put the bundle of bedding in the part of the loft where he and Cade had slept last night. There were two pillows, he saw. They'd appreciate that. And an extra quilt each.

He walked back to where she stood. "Thank you for being so considerate," he said formally, his mouth as unsmiling as her own.

"You're welcome," she answered, her voice as reserved as his had been. She gave a quick look toward where Cade still worked in the cornfield, then went on, "I want to talk to you about Cade—and Willa."

His irritation increased. He knew exactly what she was getting at. "Oh?" he asked, feigning a total ignorance of her meaning. "I hadn't noticed anything amiss. They seem to be getting along very well."

Her full, pink lips pressed together. Most women's faces would have taken on a pinched, unattractive look, but it only made him aware of the fire she kept banked inside her.

"They're getting along *too* well. I want you to help me make sure they're not left alone together."

Jesse moved back a step, leaning against the barn doorway. "Are you suggesting something improper might happen if they are?" he asked lazily.

Damn it! He heard the mockery in his voice, knew he was digging his own grave, but he couldn't seem to help it. She was being so infuriatingly self-righteous!

"Yes!" she answered, blue fire flashing from her eyes. "Willa's not quite fourteen. She's a complete innocent! I *won't* have that innocence taken away from her by a—"

"By another member," Jesse cut in, his voice hard now, "of the idle, aristocratic planter class you so despise?"

He straightened his tall, strong frame, and moved away from the wall. This was no longer amusing in any way.

Eden's eyes darkened as she backed up a step. She really hadn't meant to say those last things, but Jesse had acted so obtuse, as if not aware how volatile feelings could run among young people. And now that she'd gone this far, there was nothing to do but finish.

"I wasn't going to say that," she said evenly, "but since you've brought it up, yes. Why do you think chaperones were invented? Willa isn't equipped to handle someone as different from her own background as Cade."

Jesse advanced until he was standing only a foot away from her. Eden saw, uneasily, that he'd gone white around the mouth.

"Lady, I don't care about your opinion of me," he said, his voice as even as her own, "but I do care what you think about my cousin—and what you say to him. He's a good boy. He's trustworthy and honest. I'd trust my life to him, if need be."

Eden swallowed. This was getting out of hand. She'd thought it would be so simple, and that Jesse would agree with her. "I didn't mean anything like that. I only meant—"

"I think you meant every word," he interrupted again, his voice even harder. "Your innocent little hill girl seduced by the indulged plantation youth."

She drew in her breath in shock at his harsh, angry words. She didn't know what to say next.

He didn't give her the chance to say anything. "You're too intelligent to be so prejudiced, Eden," he said coldly.

Her eyes widened. "Me? *Prejudiced?*" Her voice was full of genuine amazement. "Oh, that's not true!" she said furiously.

"Yes, it is. You show as much ignorant prejudice against my kind of people as any ever shown against the Negroes."

She backed up a little, anger mixing with confusion in her face, creating an uncertainty Jesse had never seen in her beautiful features before. Then she stopped retreating and drew herself up tall and straight. She looked him in the eye.

"And have you quite forgiven the Yankees who devastated your homeland? Who laid waste to everything you hold dear? Do you think them justified? Or do you resent and hate them for what they did—and are still doing?"

Jesse's tall frame tensed, his jaw hardened. He stared back at her. He guessed he deserved that, and she'd unerringly homed in on his deepest feelings, as he had hers. Now all was out in the open—their hates and fears, their darkest, most unattractive emotions.

"How could I ever have thought to have the last word with an opinionated Yankee?" he drawled. "If your people hadn't won the war on the battlefield, you would have by sheer talk."

"You've been holding your own very well, I think," she said coolly. "And you didn't answer my last question. Could that mean you have a bit of the prejudice you assign to me?"

They stared at each other for an endless heartbeat of time.

Then she turned and walked back toward the house, her proud head of black, shining braids held high.

Jesse watched her go, his anger fading. She was right. Both of them carried a heavy load of resentment and bitterness. It hurt each of them much more than it could ever hurt their self-avowed enemies.

The entire country was divided by this kind of hostility. Maybe it would never be whole again.

"What in the world were you and Miz Eden arguing about?" Cade's voice held amazement.

Jesse shook his head. He'd forgotten about Cade, the very subject of their argument. He let out a deep sigh and managed a smile for the boy. "Nothing important."

"Nothing important? Why, she looked like she wanted to bite your head off! And *you* didn't look much better."

"True. I imagine we'll be asked to leave very shortly," Jesse answered. And he had no one to blame but himself. He was the one who'd escalated the argument.

Hell, he mostly agreed with her. Although he'd defended his cousin strongly, he knew Cade was attracted to Willa and that young blood could run hot in the veins. If Willa and Cade were alone together for extended periods, things might well get out of hand.

What he'd objected to was Eden's attitude about Cade's background and his own. But he should go after her and apologize. Maybe he'd be able to salvage the situation. He considered it for a moment, then discarded the idea.

It wouldn't do any good. He'd have to leave it up to her. If he stayed here, they were bound to clash at regular intervals, being the kind of people they were.

Anger was closely related to desire, in some inexplicable way. Even while he'd been the maddest at Eden, when he'd liked to have shaken some sense into her, he'd wanted her.

Hell, he *still* wanted her! Even seven months pregnant with another man's child. A man he'd sent off to fight and die.

His passions cooled. He looked at Cade. "I've got to get the worst of the leaks covered. We may have more rain tonight." And maybe he'd be out of here tomorrow, riding back to Georgia, with no chance to finish the job.

Cade nodded, giving Jesse a slightly wary look. "I'll help you." They walked back to the barn.

Eden reached the cool, shaded porch and sat down on a rocker. She hoped Hannah was sleeping, because she didn't want to talk with her now. She wouldn't be able to keep from showing her agitation, and then Hannah would probably get the entire story out of her.

Leaning her head against the back of the chair, she tried to relax. She was hot and tired, her emotions in such turmoil she didn't know how she felt.

She wasn't prejudiced! She'd been raised to be fair and open-minded, and she'd always prided herself on being so. But in a few moments, doubt crept into her mind. It was true, as Jesse had so tauntingly told her, that she had a rigid view of the southern aristocracy of which he was a part.

Or at least, had been a part. There wasn't much left of that class now, and there never would be again. Not with the slaves freed. That whole way of life was gone for good.

Jesse was only a farmer now—if that. He owned an empty shell of a house that had no doubt once been a grand mansion. And some land, she didn't know how much. She thought he had very little money. He still wore the worn uniform trousers with the rip she'd mended, and his white shirt looked like the one she'd washed.

Sympathy for his plight, for that of the entire South, swept over her. He should be in Georgia, trying to get his life back together.

Instead, he'd chosen to come here. He wanted to stay here

for months. To help *her*, the Yankee who wanted nothing to do with him or his people. He'd admitted his guilt had pushed him into this decision. But had there been more to it than guilt?

Was he devastated over his broken engagement, no matter if he had denied it this morning to Hannah? Had he wanted to get away from there for a while? After all, he'd said his fiancée was marrying someone else. That indicated she was the one who'd defected. When he was here the first time, he'd talked confidently about going home to her . . .

"Eden, are ye all right?" Hannah's trembly voice came from inside the cabin. "Didn't git too hot, did you? It's a miserable hot day."

"I'm fine," she called back. "Just resting here on the porch. Do you need anything?"

"Nary a thing. You jist git yoreself a little rest."

"I will."

She wasn't fine. She was unhappy and lonely—and scared of the future. The baby moved within her, reminding her of her responsibility to this unborn life. Taking deep breaths, she tried to blank out her turmoil, for the baby's sake. Surely, she could think of something pleasant . . .

The day hadn't been all bad. One thing had been wonderful— Hannah's lifted spirits. And for the first time in her life, Eden realized she'd questioned her fundamental beliefs and convictions. Maybe that was good, too.

Jesse had been the catalyst for these things, she realized. He was refreshing and vigorous. She couldn't deny that.

But he was also deeply disturbing to her. His presence was dangerous for both of them. He couldn't stay! And he planned to do everything in his power to change her mind about that.

He'd already started. Doing her chores this morning, weeding the garden. Fixing the barn roof. She could fight that. She could be as wily as he.

But he also planned to make Hannah *want* him to stay. He'd also already started that aspect of his campaign. That would be a much harder thing to fight. Jesse knew that, too.

However, that was before their argument, she reminded herself. Maybe he wouldn't want to stay now. Maybe he was preparing to leave right this minute.

No, she could hear him nailing shingles to the barn roof. And something told her it would take more than one argument to get Jesse off the ridge. More than several arguments. She didn't understand why he was so stubbornly determined to stay in spite of her objections. Even if he *did* feel guilt for Alston's death.

She'd made an agreement with him. She wouldn't renege on that and order him off until the two weeks were up. Her head was beginning to pound fiercely. She'd had all she could take for one day.

And she still somehow had to get through supper with Jesse.

Chapter Eleven

The meal wasn't as bad as she'd expected, mainly because she and Jesse spoke to each other only when absolutely necessary, leaving Cade and Hannah to keep the conversation going.

Eden caught Hannah's speculative gaze on her a couple of times and expected her mother-in-law to question her when Cade and Jesse left, which they did as soon as supper was over. But the older woman, who'd eaten a very small meal—but at least finished it—picked up her knitting, which she hadn't touched for weeks.

After Eden finished the dishes, she headed out to do the evening chores—and met Jesse at the door, bringing in the pail of milk.

"We already fed the stock," he said, setting the pail on the table.

His voice was plainly audible to Hannah.

"Thank you," Eden said stiffly, annoyed with herself for not anticipating this.

"You're welcome."

Jesse knew his voice was wary. His expression, too, he imagined. He'd kept an eye out for Eden all the rest of the afternoon, expecting to see her marching to the barn to tell him to head back to Georgia tomorrow.

When she hadn't appeared by suppertime, he'd relaxed a little. He didn't think she'd bring up the subject during the meal. He very much doubted if she'd mentioned anything to Hannah.

But now, he and Cade had done all the evening chores, as they had the morning ones. He was challenging her, and clearly she didn't like it. The question was, what would she do about it?

He wasn't going to wait around to find out.

He turned to Hannah. "Goodnight, Mrs. Clayborne," he said, smiling warmly at her. It seemed to him she looked better than she had this morning. At least she wasn't lying flat in bed, but was occupying herself with her knitting.

Hannah's return smile was just as warm. "Goodnight, Jesse. You and Cade did a powerful lot o' work today."

Jesse turned to Eden. "Goodnight," he said politely. "I'll see you in the morning."

"Goodnight," she returned crisply. She'd been right. Their bitter argument hadn't made Jesse decide to leave. She tried to ignore some part of her that was happy to realize that.

Tomorrow would be no repeat of today, she vowed, watching Jesse's strong back as he left the cabin. She'd get things under control again.

He'd no sooner gone than Cade appeared. "Chores all done. Thought I'd sit with Miss Hannah a little," he told Eden, his voice tentative.

Yes, she well knew the chores were all done! Eden glanced at Hannah. "Do you want to go to sleep now?"

Hannah shook her head. "Not for a little while." She smiled at Cade. "Come and set down here, boy. And visit with me."

Cade sat with alacrity. "Will you tell me some more of those stories, like you did this morning?"

"Why, I reckon so," Hannah agreed.

Eden heard the satisfaction in her mother-in-law's voice, and a small shock went through her. Could Hannah be starved for attention? Of course all her physical needs were taken care of.

But this was different. Cade didn't look at her as an old, sick woman he should talk to for kindness' sake, as Mattie did, and the other occasional ridge neighbors. No, it was plain he found her an interesting person who he enjoyed listening to.

Of course Hannah needed stimulation, this easy kind of give-and-take. Everybody did. No wonder she seemed in better spirits, had eaten a little better.

Eden felt guilt sweep through her. She'd thought she was doing everything she could to try to get Hannah over this sickness. Now she saw that wasn't true.

But from now on it would be! She'd take care to provide this special attention after Jesse and Cade left. She could certainly show an interest as well or better than a couple of strangers!

And she'd start with the stories. Eden tried to memorize what Hannah said. Later tonight, she'd look in the chest and get out some of Alston's paper to write the stories down.

Cade stayed for an hour, reluctantly leaving when Hannah began to yawn, and after extracting a promise for more tales tomorrow.

When he'd gone, Hannah gave her another of those reflective glances and Eden braced herself for fending off questions she didn't want to answer.

"You don't look as wearied out as usual, Eden, honey," Hannah said instead, her voice approving. "Jesse and Cade did a lot o' work today. I'm glad they'll be here fer a while. You shore need to git more rest than you do."

"I don't work too hard," Eden said firmly, giving her mother-in-law a warm smile that she hoped didn't reveal her inner uneasiness.

By the end of the two weeks, Hannah would think she was crazy to refuse to let Jesse stay until after the baby's birth. However, she reminded herself, pushing down the feeling, tomorrow she was going to change all that.

Eden was relieved when Hannah went promptly to sleep. She intended to get some paper, but she wanted to be as unobtrusive about it as possible. If Hannah knew what she was doing, she'd most likely freeze up and be unable to tell the stories in her spontaneous, natural way.

Kneeling by the cedar chest at the foot of her bed, Eden traced the carvings in the lid before opening it. Alston had made this chest before he'd moved to Connecticut. It was beautiful, the carvings simple, yet wonderfully done.

She quietly lifted the lid. Alston's harmonica and book of poetry lay on top, along with his last letter to them, never mailed. She'd shown the items to Hannah the day after Jesse'd left, apprehensive about how the older woman would react.

Hannah had wept bitterly when Eden had read the letter. Alston had said he was sure this was the last battle. That soon he'd be coming home to stay. His cough was better, not to worry about him.

To the very end, he was trying to spare their feelings, not cause them any worry.

The familiar, but no less bearable, guilt swept over Eden. Would she ever be able to stop blaming herself for Alston's death?

And blaming Jesse for his part in it?

Resolutely, she put the items to one side and unwrapped the cloth bundle containing the blank paper. Her hands stilled on the cloth. Alston's letter wasn't the only one in the chest. She'd forgotten this one, written to her parents soon after she arrived here.

She'd been so homesick for Connecticut, for the familiar, pleasant life she'd known there, the letter had been blotched with tears by the time she finished it. She could still see the stains.

That's why she'd never sent it. She *wouldn't* appeal to her parents' sympathy by sending them a tearstained letter.

If they loved her and wanted to end the estrangement— caused by their ultimatum that if she left, gave her support to the southern slaveholders, they could no longer consider her their daughter—they'd have to write to her first.

Now, looking at the paper, her certainty of the rightness of that long-ago decision wavered.

Maybe her parents were the ones who'd been right.

Even Alston had tried to get her to stay in Connecticut, but she hadn't listened. A wife's place was with her husband, she'd insisted. Even if Alston went off to war as soon as he got her settled into this primitive cabin on this isolated ridge.

If not for Hannah's goodness and courage, she could never have stood it.

Hannah, and Eden's flinty New England pride, kept her from going home, her tail between her legs. No, she couldn't be sorry she'd come here—and stayed here.

Who would be here for Hannah now, if she hadn't stayed? She loved Hannah like her own mother, and she knew the feelings were reciprocated.

But didn't her own parents deserve to know about the coming baby? She was an only child. This infant would be their first grandchild—perhaps the only one they'd ever have.

She didn't even know if they were still alive. Both had been in excellent health when she'd left, but that didn't mean anything. Illness and disease could strike at any time. So could accidents.

She'd think about it. And one thing for certain: she didn't need to keep this letter any longer. Crumpling the page, Eden took it and the bundle of paper out and silently closed the chest.

Hannah still slept deeply. Eden took the paper to the table and laid it down. She went to the stove and lifted a lid and thrust the letter into the coals from the supper fire.

She watched as it smoked for a moment, then flared up and in a few seconds was reduced to ash.

She went back to the table and wrote busily for half an hour, trying to capture the essence of two of Hannah's stories about her childhood. Finished, she slipped the sheets into the cloth-wrapped bundle and put it into the top drawer of the chest.

Somehow she felt better. Whatever she decided to do, it would be as an adult. She was no longer that frightened, lonely, out-of-her-element girl.

And now she'd better get to sleep, because tomorrow was going to be a busy day.

Eden slipped quietly out of bed, throwing a glance at Hannah. Good. The older woman still slept soundly. She quickly dressed, brushed and rebraided her hair, then looked longingly toward the stove. She'd love to build up the fire and have a cup of herb tea, but she couldn't take the time.

She eased open the heavy door, then closed it behind her, relieved when its inevitable creaks didn't make Hannah stir. Glancing toward the eastern horizon, she smiled at the still low-lying globe of the sun. It hadn't been up half an hour yet.

Turning toward the washstand, she thought about the day ahead of her. She'd wash, do the milking, feed the stock, then—

She stiffened. Alongside the water bucket and the washbasin stood her milk pail. Moving closer, she saw the pail was half full of rich milk, still warm from Bossie. She drew in her breath, then let it out in a whoosh.

Here she'd gotten up an hour early so she could get out to the barn and do the chores before Jesse and Cade awoke.

But she hadn't been early enough.

Jesse must have anticipated her actions. She was quite sure it would do no good to go on to the barn. The stock would be fed, turned out of the barn, and back in the field. The chickens and geese would have their grain.

She had to see, though. Maybe she'd been wrong about his intentions. Maybe he'd done these chores so early because he planned to leave this morning. Eden left the porch and walked to the barnyard. Cade's and Jesse's mounts placidly ate grass in the fenced field, alongside Bossie and Oscar, the mule.

Cade and Jesse were already out in the cornfield.

It certainly looked as if they planned to stay—even after the bitter argument she and Jesse'd had yesterday. She denied the relief that coursed through her. No, she wasn't relieved—she was annoyed!

If she went out to the barn at daybreak tomorrow, she'd probably have to wrestle the milk pail out of Jesse's hands!

Jesse and Cade had weeded the entire garden yesterday. Now they were hoeing the cornfield, after doing all her morning chores.

Her mouth tightened. All right. She'd go ahead and do the wash, even though she didn't need to for several days yet. But she had to prove to Jesse that she didn't need his help.

Hannah, awake now, gave her a smile as she entered the cabin again. Ten minutes later, she'd helped Hannah to a chair while she changed her sheets, pulled the sheets off her own bed, and gathered up the dirty clothes.

"Why are ye warshin' today?" Hannah asked, after Eden had settled her back down on fresh bedding. "Ye jist warshed a few days ago."

Eden, sorting through the clothes, glanced at her mother-in-law. If she told Hannah the true reason, the other woman would be shocked and think Eden was behaving childishly. Her jaw set.

Childish or not, it seemed the best, the *only* way she could think of right now of proving to Jesse she was strong and capable of doing the work of the homestead without his aid.

"It's going to be a nice, sunny day. I just felt like it."

Hannah looked toward the open doorway and nodded as if satisfied with Eden's answer. "Yes, 'tis."

"I'll be in to fix breakfast in a little while, unless you're hungry now."

"Go ahead, don't worry about me. I'll jist take me another nap. It's still awful early."

There was a definite question in Hannah's voice. "Yes, but I'd like to get this started." Carrying the woven basket of soiled laundry, Eden headed for the door.

"Why don't ye ask Jesse or Cade to fetch the water?" Hannah said. "You hadn't ort to be totin' them heavy buckets as far along as you are."

Eden straightened her back and gave Hannah a forced smile. It certainly hadn't taken Hannah long to get used to the idea of Jesse and Cade's help. "I'm fine. I don't mind doing it at all."

Hannah looked at her for a moment. "Don't fergit to gather up Cade and Jesse's clothes."

Eden nodded, her face turned away so that Hannah couldn't see her dismay at that suggestion. She hadn't even thought about that, but of course she must.

"I won't." She went on outside, planning. She'd hurry up and carry the water and get the fire started before Jesse noticed what she was doing and came to help. Then, she'd go ask the two males what garments of theirs needed washing.

She left the clothes on the porch and found two empty buckets. Rounding the corner, she glanced toward the cornfield. Jesse and Cade had their backs turned to her.

Heaving a sigh of relief, she hurried toward the spring. She was out of breath by the time she reached the pleasant spot and sat down for a moment on the bench to rest. That was a mistake, she knew at once, because it made her think of yesterday, when she and Jesse had sat here so close together.

She got up and, carefully bending over the spring, dipped first one bucket in, then the other, awkwardly pushing herself back upright. Oh, it was hard to do things now! And it would be even harder in another month. Then another, before the baby arrived. Doggedly she pushed those thoughts aside— she'd managed so far, she could manage all the way. Picking up a bucket in either hand she left the shelter of the trees.

Jesse walked toward her, his long strides eating up the distance. He wore his old white shirt today, but she remembered when she'd watched him nailing the shakes to the roof yesterday, the way his bare-muscled, bronzed back and chest had glistened in the sun.

Eden pressed her lips together and kept walking, her head high. When they reached each other, she'd keep going, she *wouldn't* let him take her load!

Almost before she'd formed the thoughts in her head, Jesse was there, stopping directly in front of her, so that she had to stop, too, or run into him.

"Here, let me have those," he said, trying to keep the irritation out of his voice.

He'd lifted his head from his hoe in time to see her hightailing it to the spring. Carrying two big, heavy buckets to fill with water and make even heavier. Damn it!

He knew why she was in such a hurry, too.

The War between the States might be over, but their own private war had only started.

His big hand closed over one of hers on the pail's handle. Her hand felt small under his, too small to be carrying this load. It also felt warm, and as if it belonged under his own hand, and he wouldn't think about that. He tugged at the handle. Eden held on.

"I can carry this. I was doing fine."

Her clear voice sounded even more northern than usual. He

could picture her as a schoolmarm, having no trouble handling
a roomful of rowdy students. He gave her a straight look.

"Eden, let go."

She wouldn't, she thought, stubbornly, returning his look
with a matching one. She'd stand here and hang on until sunset,
if necessary. Then, as happened frequently these days, a fierce
pain attacked her back, making her gasp and loosen her hold
on the buckets.

Jesse caught them before they overturned. He set them down
on the path, then turned back to her, his face concerned. "Are
you all right?"

Eden nodded, taking deep breaths to try to ease the pain.
Her hand slipped to her back, massaging the lower part from
where the pain originated. Oh, why did this have to happen
now, when she was proving to Jesse that she didn't need him
at all?

She should sit down, give the spasms time to go away. That
was the only thing that worked. But she *wouldn't* give in to
this weakness in front of Jesse! She wouldn't help him prove
he should stay here!

Despite her fierce determination, she swayed on her feet.
Before she knew what he planned, Jesse scooped her up in his
arms as if she weighed nothing at all and strode back toward
the spring.

Eden was too stunned at his actions to react for a moment.
Jesse's enclosing arms felt so good holding her, carrying her.
She fought an intense urge to snuggle against his chest, surren-
der herself to him, to his care.

Horrified at her wayward thoughts, she tried to jerk herself
out of his arms, back onto her feet. She was a strong woman,
but she might as well have pushed against steel as to try to
escape him. Jesse ignored her struggles and kept walking.

"Let me down!" she commanded loudly and firmly. Maybe
words would work, if her actions couldn't.

He'd reached the bench. "All right." He set her gently down
on the seat, his face only inches from her own. She gazed into
his golden eyes as if mesmerized. They seemed to be drawing
her into him, deeper and deeper . . .

Jesse sucked in his breath. He'd never seen any other eyes

such a shade. A deep, impossibly deep, blue. And her full, pink lips were parted. He remembered that other time when her lips had opened for him. When he'd taken the sweetness she had made no effort to withhold . . .

She moved a little on the bench. She gasped again as if in pain. Abruptly the spell snapped. Jesse straightened and moved back. "Are you all right?"

Eden nodded, not looking directly at him. "Yes. I—I get these pains in my back sometimes. They're nothing."

She knew she should sit for a few more minutes, massage her back, but she wouldn't do either of these things with Jesse standing in front of her! She tried to struggle to her feet, but Jesse's big, strong hands grasped her shoulders, gently restrained her.

"You need to rest," he said, his voice brisk and impersonal. "If I let go of you, will you promise to sit there while I carry the water to the wash kettle?"

Oh, she shouldn't agree to that! It would be defeating her purpose completely. But the thought of being alone, to gather herself together, get over this annoying hurt, was too tempting.

She nodded. "Yes."

"I won't be long." He turned and left the shelter of the trees.

Eden let her head rest against the seat for a long moment, her eyes closed, her hands rubbing the small of her back, until the pain eased a little. She was furious with herself for giving in to this. Even more angry because she knew she'd had no other choice.

Her plan wasn't going to work.

It was all too obvious, even to her, that she did need help. And she'd welcome it from anyone but Jesse. Well, maybe not welcome it, but she could at least accept it as she couldn't accept it from him. From somewhere deep inside, she gathered determination.

She'd *make* it work; she had to. And right now she was going to get up from here, go back to the cabin, and do the wash. She got to her feet, cautiously, relieved when no new twinges of pain hit her. She moved out into the clearing.

Jesse came toward her with his long strides, carrying an

empty pail in either hand. The memory of his arms holding her, carrying her, a few minutes ago swept over her.

She shouldn't have enjoyed it! But she couldn't deny that she had. She braced herself for his scolding words because she wasn't meekly waiting at the spring, as he'd ordered her to.

He paused beside her, his face expressionless. "I've built the fire under the kettle. How many pails of water do you need?"

She blinked in surprise at his unexpected words. He was always doing that, throwing her off balance when he didn't do what she'd expected.

"Six will be enough to start," she answered, knowing she was conceding this skirmish to him. How could she do otherwise? She couldn't physically wrench the buckets out of his hands, and she was certain that's what it would take to make him give them up.

He nodded and went on by.

Eden forced herself not to turn and watch him. She started walking again, but more slowly this time. She wanted no repeat of her humiliating weakness in his presence. He caught up with her and passed her without a word when she was only halfway there.

Before she reached the wash area, he'd passed her again, heading back to the spring for his third and final trip. He'd also built a good fire under the heavy iron kettle.

She supposed he'd had a lot of practice building campfires during the years of war. Even yesterday, she'd have been surprised at his skill, thinking that only the lower-ranked men did such menial jobs.

But not now; she'd never think that again.

She retrieved the basket of clothes from the porch, reaching the wash area again just as Jesse brought the last two pails of water and poured them into the kettle.

She knew her expression was challenging. He gave her a sharp glance but didn't comment as she set the basket down and began sorting the clothes.

Eden felt his eyes on her bent head. Why was he still standing there? Surely he didn't intend to stay here and help her with the entire washing! She added some shaved lye soap to the water, stirred it with the stick she kept there for that purpose, then dumped an armful of white clothes into the kettle.

Finally, unable to stand the felt but unseen gaze any longer, she turned toward him. "I can manage fine now," she said crisply.

"All right." Jesse forced his face to hold its bland look. Damn! But that was hard. How could he appear indifferent when his body still felt the soft contours of her own?

"I'll have to fell a cedar tree to make more shakes for the barn roof," he told her, relieved at the even tone of his voice. "Do you want to help me pick one out?"

"No, that's fine. I'm sure you can do it," she said hastily, relieved he planned to leave her alone.

He nodded. "If you need more water, let Cade or me know. You shouldn't be carrying those heavy buckets."

Why was he wasting his breath? If she needed more water, she'd go after it. He'd have to try to keep an eye on her.

But now, he'd get Cade out of the cornfield and pick up the crosscut saw from the barn and cut down the tree. His stomach rumbled with hunger. He'd like to eat before he did any more work, but he had a feeling breakfast was going to be late this morning. He turned and headed back toward the barnyard.

Watching him go, Eden heaved a relieved sigh. Then a shock went through her. Oh, she'd done it again! Why hadn't she told him she didn't want him cutting any cedar trees? That she didn't want him to do any more work on the barn roof? Because it would be nice to have a barn roof that didn't leak, she answered herself. She tried to ignore the other reason.

And because she was still so unsettled by that interlude at the spring.

She drew her dark brows together and went back to the porch for the big copper kettle she rinsed the clothes in, surprised Jesse hadn't thought of that, too. By the time she got it to the wash area, her back was hurting again, and she set it down with a hard *thump*.

The thought of carrying another half dozen pails of water was dismaying. She didn't think she could do it. Yes, she could!

There was no use getting used to Jesse's help when she'd only have it for a little while.

And that's entirely your own decision, her mind told her. *One word from you and he'll be here for two more months— maybe more. Wouldn't that be wonderful?*

No! It *wouldn't,* she told herself fiercely. It wouldn't be wonderful at all. Every minute of that time would be nerve-wracking and tension filled. And she wasn't going to let herself think about it any more.

She punched down the clothes in the kettle, then stirred them. It would be a while before they boiled, before she needed rinse water. She'd cook breakfast now—if Hannah hadn't gone back to sleep. Which was likely.

Eden stopped in the cabin doorway, her eyes widening. Hannah sat up in bed, knitting. "I expected you to be taking another nap," Eden said, going to the kitchen.

Finishing her stitch, Hannah looked up, smiling. "I was a-fixin' to, but that yaller sun jist streamed in the door so purty, I decided not to waste any more time sleepin'."

Eden's hands stilled on the kindling she was arranging in the stove. How long had it been since she'd heard Hannah say anything as life-affirming as the words she'd just spoken?

She glanced over at her mother-in-law. The older woman had gone back to her knitting, a small smile lingering on her mouth. Something positive was happening to Hannah. Eden didn't understand it. Maybe it wouldn't be permanent.

She'd not get her hopes up yet, then. But she'd do everything in her power to coax it along.

Everything? that traitorous part of her mind asked her. *Does that include letting Jesse Bainbridge stay here for two more months?*

Chapter Twelve

Eden transferred the wooden bucket, filled to a third with water, to her other arm. She entered the barnyard, where Cade and Jesse were making cedar shakes.

Breakfast was over and so was the washing, clothes hung out to dry in the hot, bright sunshine.

As she'd expected, Jesse had intercepted her first trip to the spring for rinse water. She'd let him carry it all, with no more arguing. What was the use? He'd do it anyway, and she wanted no repeat of the episode at the spring.

While washing the breakfast dishes, she'd made a decision. She'd stop trying to show Jesse that she didn't need his help with the homestead work. He'd made it painfully clear yesterday and today, even to her, that she did.

She didn't want this battle of wills to become obvious to Hannah.

So she'd go along with him, let him do the outside chores, carry the water and wood. And do extra things—such as making the shingles and repairing the barn roof.

But when Jesse's allotted time was over, she'd send him on his way back to Georgia.

Two weeks' rest from the heavy work should get her in fine

shape to handle the remaining time until the baby came. She smiled wryly. And Jesse's conscience should be somewhat eased, even if he wouldn't get to stay the full time he'd wanted. Her smile faltered.

Of course, there was Hannah to contend with. Eden had no doubt at all her mother-in-law would protest strongly when Jesse and Cade left if she knew this was solely Eden's decision. Sighing, she told herself she'd worry about that when the time came.

She'd decided something else—to be friendly as she could manage with Jesse and Cade for this short time. After all, she wanted Hannah to get as much out of the visit as possible. Besides, she liked Cade. Offering him her friendship would be no problem.

Eden stopped a little distance away, watching them work.

They'd trimmed the limbs and sawed the tree into chunks, and the aromatic smell of fresh-cut cedar hung strong in the summer air. Cade held a chunk in place. Jesse, using a wooden maul, hammered a wedge-shaped tool at an angle against it, splitting the wood. He made it look easy, as if he'd done it for years.

They both glanced up at her arrival, the dipper jiggling cheerfully against the bucket as she walked.

"Thought you might like some cool water," she said pleasantly, setting the pail down on the ground.

Jesse finished the shingle he was cutting, then laid his tools down. He pulled a red bandanna out of a back pocket and wiped his forehead. "It is hot today."

He gave her a cautious smile, wondering what else she had planned to prove how she didn't need him here, that she could do all the work herself.

"Wash all finished?"

"Yes, it is."

Eden's return smile was as pleasant as her voice had been. She gave the filled dipper to Cade, who eagerly drank the water, then refilled it. "Dinner will be ready in about an hour."

"I can't wait!" Cade said, grinning as he handed the dipper to Jesse. "You sure are a good cook, Miss Eden!"

Her smile warmed even more as she turned it on the boy.

His first stiffness with her seemed to have disappeared. "Thank you, Cade. It's nice to have one's efforts appreciated!"

Listening to her words, she felt uncomfortable. Of course it was, and she'd shown no appreciation at all for Jesse's help.

Cade got up and stretched widely. He glanced at Jesse. "I'll be back in a few minutes."

Jesse nodded. "All right." Why was Eden so friendly all of a sudden? He finished his dipper of water and gave her another wary look. She was watching Cade head toward the woods, her usual assured expression replaced with uncertainty.

What was she up to?

Eden felt Jesse's gaze, even as her own followed Cade. Why had he left? Surely not to give Jesse and her a chance to be alone together. Heat warmed her face at that thought.

This wasn't what she'd had in mind when she'd walked out here. No, she'd only intended to declare a truce. And let Jesse see this. She'd planned to talk for a little while, so she wouldn't leave now just because Cade had. She took a deep breath and smiled at Jesse.

Jesse returned the smile in spite of his reservations. Then, feeling self-conscious, he turned back to the block of wood he'd been working on. Steadying it against the large chopping block, he neatly split off another shingle.

He glanced up to see Eden's eyes on his hands, as if she was fascinated by his work.

"You do that very well," she said, deciding to act as she would with any other person with whom she was having a casual conversation. "Did your father teach you that skill, too?"

"No," Jesse answered, surprised again by her interest. "Our plantation carpenter did. Rufe was the best carpenter I ever knew. He made beautiful cabinets and furniture."

"Was he a slave?"

Jesse tensed. Had her friendly show of interest been only a prelude to another condemnation of slavery and plantation life? "No. He was a free Negro. He worked for us for wages."

"Was that common practice?" she asked.

Jesse could hear surprise in her voice, but that was all. His tension eased. Maybe she wasn't looking for a fight. "On some plantations, yes. We employed several freemen."

"Oh." She was silent for a moment, as if thinking, then went on. "I've always thought of plantation work being done completely by slaves."

His irritation began rising, but he reminded himself to keep his feelings in check. He wanted no repeat of yesterday's senseless argument. "That's another common misconception among northerners," he said, but his voice was mild, not challenging.

"I suppose it is," Eden said, surprised but relieved at his calm answer. She reminded herself she was merely attempting to have a normal conversation with him for a change. "Did you like having slaves?"

Her voice sounded genuinely curious. He gave her a quick look. Her blue eyes looked inquiringly at him. He thought for a minute. "When I was a child I took it for granted," he finally said. "As I grew up, no, I didn't like it."

"What about your parents?" She tried hard to keep her voice pleasant, as if they were discussing the weather or something else equally innocuous, not the subject that always ended up making them furious with each other.

"They saw nothing wrong with it. We always treated our slaves well. They had a better life than many free, white manual laborers."

Eden nodded. "Yes, I've heard that argument before. And it may be true," she conceded. "But it's wrong for one person to own another."

"I agree with you," Jesse said evenly. "When my father retired and I took over the plantation, I intended to free all our slaves." He felt satisfaction as she again looked surprised.

"But you didn't get a chance to do it?"

"No. The war killed my father and took me away. And then Lincoln freed all the Negroes."

"That shouldn't have bothered you, if you feel as you do."

He wondered if Eden was deliberately trying to keep herself in check, as he was. How long could they keep this up without it turning into an argument? He shook his head. "No, it didn't. What I couldn't deal with was losing the only kind of life I'd ever known."

She gave him a long, level look. "I felt the same way when I came here from Connecticut." She lifted her head and looked around her. "Everything here was so strange. So completely different."

"I imagine it was." He smiled at her, and she smiled back. He realized, with a small shock, that for the first time, they were talking to each other only as people. As if they had no wide gulf of differences separating them.

But he knew that it was only an illusion. The same things were still between them, driving a wedge that split them apart, just as he'd split the cedar shingles.

They resented each other's people, because of what the war had cost each side. They shared a mutual guilt.

His smile died, killed by his somber thoughts.

So did Eden's. At this moment, Jesse seemed far removed from the arrogant southern plantation master she'd thought him. His words of yesterday came back to her, accusing her of prejudice, of narrow-mindedness. She felt oddly shaken and moved her glance away from Jesse's to hide it.

Jesse suddenly turned away. He propped the cedar on the work block again and raised the maul. Before he could bring it down on the froe, the block slipped. The maul barely missed smashing his fingers.

Damn it! He should have waited for Cade's return.

"Here, let me steady that for you." Eden reached out and held the block as she'd seen Cade do.

"All right." Jesse kept his gaze straight ahead. He didn't want her to see the amazement in his eyes at her unexpected offer. He didn't want to spoil this unusual moment of harmony between them.

But she made him nervous. Sweating, he took careful aim with the maul. What if it slipped? Her slim, tanned hands held the block very steadily. He guessed it was the first time he'd ever seen them not in motion. Her fingernails were short, and there was a scratch across her right thumb.

Steadily, carefully, he brought the maul down on the froe. After several repetitions, the shingle, cleanly cut, fell away from the block.

Eden looked away from his golden, muscled arms, his tawny,

intent face. A small shiver slid down her spine. Quickly she picked up the shingle, turning it over in her hands, examining it from every angle.

"Beautiful," she said, her voice a little husky. She was talking about more than the shingle in her hand, but she pushed that knowledge aside. It *was* a beautiful piece of work, something only a skilled craftsman could produce. She looked up at him. "Is there anything you *don't* know how to do?"

"Lots of things," he said finally. "Plantation life is all I know." He paused, then went on, tension back in his voice now. "And soldiering. But that's nothing I want to remember."

"I don't imagine most ex-soldiers do," she said, after a moment.

He gazed at her upturned face, her blue eyes framed with jet-black lashes, and at her shining, dark head, the white part down the middle even and straight.

Her voice was softened, softer than he'd ever heard it. He reached out a tentative hand. He yearned to run his hand over her smooth, shining hair. To draw her up from her crouching posture, enfold her in his arms.

He wanted much more than that. He wanted all of her. Not only her body, but her heart and soul, too.

Their look held, deepened, as if they were somehow seeing into each other's innermost being . . .

She moved her hand a little and the afternoon sun flashed off her wedding ring.

The ring her husband, now dead, had placed on her finger.

With part of his mind, he heard a whistle behind him, then, in a moment, Cade's youthful voice. "Hey, I guess we'd better get these finished."

Eden got to her feet. So did Jesse. They avoided each other's eyes.

"I'd better leave you two to your work," she said. "Don't forget—dinner will be ready soon." She picked up her depleted pail of water and walked away, her back very straight.

"What's wrong?" Cade asked Jesse. "Did you two have another fight?"

Jesse shook his head. "No." He picked up his tools again. "Ready?"

"Sure." Cade crouched and steadied the block. "Well, she left in a hurry. Do you think she'll let us stay for the two weeks?"

"I believe so."

"You know, she isn't *really* a Yankee. Her husband was a southerner. Why wasn't she as friendly when she left?"

"Leave it alone, Cade," Jesse said, tersely.

"Sure," Cade said again. He held the block steady, watching Jesse's strong hands. "Do you think Willa's going to come back after dinner?"

Jesse took a deep breath and let it out. He tried to relax the tense muscles of his jaw. "I don't know." He brought the maul down in a sure, steady move.

"She said Miss Eden gave her lessons every day. So that should mean she will."

Frowning, Jesse gave the froe another hard blow. His cousin seemed mighty interested in the hill girl. Again he conceded that maybe Eden was right to be concerned about the two youngsters. "You don't want to start something . . ."

His voice trailed off as he saw swift embarrassment come to Cade's face.

"I'm not starting anything," the boy protested. "I just like her, that's all. She's interesting. I never knew a girl like her before."

Jesse decided he'd said enough. "Willa is a nice, pretty girl," he agreed. "I like her, too."

He clenched his jaws against the strong urge to turn and look after Eden's departing form. No! He wouldn't, he told himself, his fingers tightening on the maul until the knuckles stood out starkly white against the dark wood.

Eden glanced behind to see if Jesse was watching and would come running to grab her bucket. No, he seemed intent on cutting another shingle. She veered off toward the spring. No use going back to the cabin with an empty pail.

At the spring, she knelt and dipped the bucket in, filled it two-thirds full, then rinsed off the dipper in the clear, cold water.

What had happened back there? It was another of those moments that she'd experienced twice before with Jesse.

That day, when he'd come to the cabin hurt, he had lost consciousness on her bed . . . he'd looked at her . . . and she'd looked at him . . . and it had seemed as if something in their souls had touched for an instant . . .

And then, when he was leaving . . . right before he'd kissed her . . .

There had never been a moment like that between her and Alston, not in all the years of their marriage. She'd loved him—at first, anyway—as a wife is supposed to love her husband. But it hadn't lasted long.

Within a few months she'd realized a large part of her feeling for Alston was based on nothing more than the idea of being loved, being married, having her own home.

She guessed she'd unconsciously assumed their marriage would be like her parents'. A union of two strong-willed people who flared up at each other occasionally, but shared their deepest feelings and thoughts, and wanted a similar kind of life.

But Alston wanted nothing more than to be left alone most of the time to pursue his studies, to read voraciously, as if to make up for the lack of it during his childhood. If one of his schoolmasters hadn't taken an interest in him, paid for his higher education, then persuaded him to return with him to Connecticut, he'd still be on this ridge, with no more future than the other ridge dwellers, he'd often told her.

Alston had lived with the schoolmaster's family for a while, until he'd found a position teaching in a small private academy. Eden's father had been on the board of trustees. He'd met Alston, liked the gentle, transplanted southerner, and invited him to their home.

He'd been so different from the young men Eden had known. He'd fascinated her with his soft, slow drawl and his uncommon diffidence.

Within six months they were married. Within another half year, Eden knew it had been a mistake. But she never, by so much as a word or glance, let Alston know this. She'd chosen him and married him, and now, somehow, she'd make the marriage work.

But that first young love was gone forever; only affection remained . . . and tolerance. Sometimes Eden felt as if Alston were her child, he was so dreamy and absentminded, so uninterested in the realities of daily life. So averse to planning for their future.

If only she'd gotten pregnant then, before the war had changed all their lives, ruined everything! Maybe that would have made a difference, made Alston the kind of husband she wanted, and needed.

But she hadn't, and now he was gone and she had to live her life as well as she could. She had to think of the coming baby and what was best for both of them.

Any involvement with Jesse Bainbridge couldn't possibly come under that heading.

What was this strange thing between her and the Confederate officer who'd sent her husband out to die, whose way of life was so totally foreign to her and so impossible to imagine? Who embodied all the things she hated about the South?

Or did he?

Why was she repeating these things to herself, almost desperately? As if she had to say them over and over in her mind to keep on believing them.

Slowly, Eden got to her feet and picked up the nearly full pail. Returning to the cabin, her back was straight as always, but her walk was slow. Nearing the barn, she was relieved to see both Cade's and Jesse's backs turned to her.

Dinner, she said to herself, hurrying her pace. Yes, go back to the cabin and talk to Hannah, and get dinner and do all the ordinary, prosaic household things. Forget these foolish fancies that make no sense. Remember your vow not to be alone with Jesse.

He'll be gone in less than two weeks.

This time, for good and all.

Chapter Thirteen

The trail through the woods ended in a clearing. In the clearing stood a cabin. Cade hoped it was the Freemans'. Willa had told him vaguely where she lived and yesterday he'd seen her take this trail.

Trouble was, the trail branched off several times. He stayed on the main one, figuring, rightly, he hoped, that from what Willa had said, she and her family were the most frequent visitors at the Clayborne cabin.

He stopped at the edge of the woods. The cabin looked a lot like the Claybornes'. Several people sat on the front porch. They'd finished their work for the day, he supposed. He couldn't tell from this distance if any of them was Willa, but he didn't think so.

He and Jesse had finished cutting the shingles the past afternoon. Tomorrow, if it was a fair day, they'd try to finish patching the barn roof. He'd helped with the evening chores.

Miss Eden hadn't come out at all. He guessed she was glad he and Jesse were taking the heavy work off her hands. At least, he hoped so. That might mean she'd agree to let them stay longer than two weeks. The way he felt about Yankees in general, he was still surprised that he liked her.

Cade straightened up as tall as he could and walked toward the cabin. Halfway there, he saw all heads turn to look in his direction, and embarrassment swept over him. Why should he feel like this?

He knew why, though, and that made him feel even worse. He'd come to see Willa and he'd never gone calling on a girl before. He didn't know how her family would react to him. He was close enough now to see that Willa wasn't on the porch, only three men and a very large woman.

Disappointment took the place of his embarrassment. One of the men got up from his seat and walked out to meet him. The man had a weatherbeaten face and grizzled gray hair. He wasn't smiling.

Cade stopped a few feet away. He extended his hand. "I'm Cade Morgan," he said. "My cousin Jesse and I are visiting at the Claybornes'." He knew his words were plainly audible to the other people.

The man hesitated, throwing a look over his shoulder at the big woman behind him. She nodded, and the man turned back around and stuck out his hand. "Hollis Freeman's m' name," he said. "Come on up on the porch and set a spell."

Cade followed Hollis. One of the men got up from his chair and sat on the porch's top step. Willa was nowhere in sight. He wished he hadn't come. How was he going to make conversation with this bunch of strangers?

Hollis sat down by the woman on a wooden settee at one end of the porch. She waved her hand at the empty chair against the cabin wall. "Set down and rest yore feet." Her faded but sharp blue eyes looked him over thoroughly before giving him a warm smile.

He sat down in the crude chair. One of its legs was shorter than the others and the chair tilted, throwing him off balance a little. The man who'd given Cade his seat hid a grin behind his raised hand.

Cade's self-consciousness grew. A lean hound that had been sprawled out in front of the other man, at the far end of the porch, ambled over and sniffed at Cade's trousers.

"Roy, git back over here," the man said, and the dog obeyed.

Cade turned to smile at the man, then was shocked to see he was missing a leg, one trouser leg pinned up.

"I'm Mattie Freeman, and that's Darcy," the woman said. She pointed at the man on the step. "And t'other one's Oran." She indicated the one-legged man.

Cade nodded at everyone. "I'm glad to make your acquaintance," he said politely. The two men nodded back, but said nothing.

"Willie told us you and yore cousin was visitin' Hannie and Eden," Mattie said. "Are ye from Georgee, too?"

"Yes, I am," Cade said, his voice breaking a little. He felt red creeping up his neck as Darcy again hid a grin with his hand.

"Seems a far piece to come a-visitin'," she commented. "Ye ain't no kinfolk to the Claybornes, are ye?"

"No," Cade said. "We're not related." He was relieved his voice held steady.

Mattie leaned back in her seat, the wood creaking under her bulk. "Yes, it shore is a far piece to come a-visitin'. 'Pears to me there's likely some other reason to make sich a journey. Maybe there's a leetle courtin' goin' on over at the Claybornes'."

She gave Darcy a frowning, almost accusing look.

Darcy returned it with a guilty, abashed one.

Cade stared at Mattie, amazed at her frankness. There was no mistaking her meaning. She was talking about his cousin Jesse. His discomfort increased. He suddenly remembered Willa saying her brother Darcy was courting Miss Eden. No, she'd said "trying to." He must not be getting very far, either, and that's why his mother had given him that look.

He had to get out of here! He started to get up from his chair and Willa came through the open doorway. Cade sat back down. "Hello, Willa," he said, giving her a warm smile.

She stared at him, a shocked expression on her pretty face. She had on the same faded blue calico dress she'd worn yesterday, and her feet were again bare. Finally, she nodded, then turned as if to go back inside.

"Where are yore manners, Willie?" Mattie asked. "Iffen you finished in the kitchen, come on out here and set."

Her mother didn't mean that as a request, Willa well knew.

It was a command. Ducking her head, she walked across the porch and sat down on the top step beside Darcy.

"I b'lieve this young man has done come all the way from the Claybornes' to see ye," Hollis Freeman suddenly said, a jocular note in his voice. "What do ye think o' that?"

Willa raised her head, her eyes wide with shock. She gave Cade a stricken, humiliated look then, and in one fluid motion, got to her feet and ran down the steps and off into the woods.

Hollis yelled with mirth at the results of his joking words, and slapped his hand on his knee. His two sons wore wide grins. But Cade saw that Mattie wasn't amused. Her frown was back.

In a moment, the three men noticed her silence. Hollis's noisy laugh died in his throat. His sons' grins faded.

Mattie tilted her head in a parody of a coquettish look and gave Cade a girlish smile. "Now, that wasn't perlite of my menfolks. I'm plumb 'shamed o' them. I don't know what got into Willie. She gits shy once in a while like that."

Cade could never remember being so uncomfortable in his life. The men might have been merely teasing, but Willa's mother obviously thought that, like his cousin Jesse, he, too, planned to do a little courting. Just as obviously she approved of it in this instance.

He got up so suddenly that the chair overturned. Cade righted it, his embarrassment growing. "I have to go now," he mumbled.

Enough of his upbringing remained even in the midst of his misery to make him throw over his shoulder as he hurried off the porch, "I'm very glad to have made your acquaintance."

He heard Darcy's snicker behind him, and Mattie's fierce shushing of it. He increased his speed, so that by the time he was halfway across their clearing, he was almost running. He felt a great relief as the woods swallowed him up, and he slowed his pace a little.

"Damn it!" he said. He aimed his worn boots at a rock on the path ahead of him and kicked it with enough force to send it flying.

* * *

Ahead and off to the side, hidden behind a big oak tree, Willa watched. Oh, Pap had ruined everything, she mourned. It was bad enough, what had happened yesterday. But now she'd never be able to look Cade in the eye again.

She had to get away before he saw her. Carefully, she began to ease out from the tree's shelter.

Cade slowed his steps a little more, his head down, thinking. Kicking the rock had eased some of his anger and chagrin. He lifted his head just before he came to Willa's tree and caught a glimpse of her blue dress and flaxen hair. His eyes widening, he walked toward the tree.

Her startled blue eyes gave him a quick glance, then she turned to flee. But her skirt caught on a brier, holding her fast. Cade saw her frantic movements to free herself before he reached her. She didn't make it.

"Willa, I'll help you get loose—if you promise not to run away again," Cade said. "Please."

She swallowed the lump in her throat. Finally, she raised her head to look at him, then quickly down again. "All right," she answered, her voice low and a little trembly.

Cade knelt and carefully worked the fabric loose from the brier, then looked up at her averted face. "It tore a little. I'm sorry."

"That's no matter," Willa said hastily. " 'Twas my fault."

Cade looked at her until the silence drew out. "Can't we sit down somewhere?" he asked, finally. "I want to talk to you, Willa."

He didn't sound mad at her, she noted. He didn't sound any different than he had yesterday, when they'd talked and talked. Except a little worried that she wouldn't agree to his suggestion.

She raised her head. As she'd surmised from his voice, Cade's brows were drawn together in a worried frown. Amazement swept over her. After the way her family had acted, he still wanted to be with her!

"They's a bed o' moss over there," she said, pointing, "where we could set."

Cade followed her to where the dark green moss spread its

velvet. He waited politely until she sat down, then sat across from her.

They looked at each other without speaking for such a long time that Willa lost her embarrassment; her natural openness and joy in life returned.

She grinned at him, drawing her legs up under her skirts and sitting crosslegged. "Well, I reckon if we're here to talk one of us ort—ought to do some talkin'!"

Cade watched her movements, realizing that none of the girls he knew would ever dream of sitting like that. But Willa had done it so unselfconsciously and with such a natural modesty, how could anyone object?

He'd also noticed how she'd corrected her speech. Was she doing that for him? The thought pleased him at the same time it startled him.

"Why didn't you come to the cabin today?" he asked, deciding to get right to the point. He paused and then added, "Are you mad at me?"

Her cheeks pinkened. She started to look down, then checked her movement, giving him an open, frank gaze instead.

"No, 'course not. It's jist I ain't the kind of gal you're used to. I don't live in a fancy house, on a big plantation. I don't talk right—and my folks ain't got no money. We got nothin'."

Cade stared at her. "Was that why you ran away yesterday? Why you ran away from your cabin a few minutes ago?"

Willa nodded. "Reckon so. And I cain—can't stand to be funned like that!"

"I *did* come to see *you,* Willa," Cade said in a moment. "Didn't you know that?"

Her face burned hotter. "I guess I did. But that ain't what I meant. Pap was a-funnin' about us sparkin'."

He felt as uncomfortable as she did about that idea. He shook his head. "No, that's not why I came to see you. I just wanted to be with you. I like to talk to you."

"I like to talk to you, too," Willa admitted.

"And I don't care about your family or how they live. My family doesn't have anything now, either. We don't have a fancy, big house. We don't have *any* house!" His voice broke at the end, but he didn't even notice. He looked away from her, off in the distance.

In a moment, he felt a feather-light touch on his shoulder and looked back around. Willa's small, tanned hand lay on his old white shirt. Somehow, as soft as it was, her touch was comforting. He tried to swallow the hurts and fears and smiled at her.

She smiled back. "That may be the case now," she said earnestly. "But yore folks still have all that land. You kin build 'nother house like you had before. 'Tain't like we have to do here on the ridge. Jist scrape a livin' off the rocks, like Pap allus says."

He realized that to her, and he guessed all the hill people, ownership of many acres of fertile farmland spelled riches. She couldn't share his deep despair at all their losses because she'd never had much of anything to lose.

Part of his sorrow lifted as he thought this over.

There was something to be said for her point of view. "I guess you're right. We *do* still have the land." Then his face fell. "But Mama doesn't want to come back. She wants to stay in Alabama with my aunt and sell our plantation in Georgia."

Willa patted his shoulder, then removed her hand. She squirmed a little, getting more comfortable. "Do you want to live in Alabama?"

He shook his head vehemently. "No! I want to go home. But I'm not old enough yet to do anything about it. By the time I am, Mama will have the plantation sold."

"That is a sorry mess yore in," she said in a moment. "Would yore Mam be willin' to build you 'nother house if you had the money for it?"

Cade shrugged. "I don't know. Maybe. But we're not likely to *have* any money unless we can get started planting again. And that takes money, too."

"Don't reckon you could borry from the aunt in Alabama?" she asked.

"No. Aunt Eulalie's a widow, too. She lives in Selma, they don't have any land or much money. And Selma was about destroyed by the Yankees."

"Yes, we heard that were true." After a moment, she went

on. "But iffen you *could* git—get some money somewheres, then you could stay in your cousin Jesse's house for a while, couldn't you?"

Cade nodded. "I suppose so. Jesse keeps saying we can."

Willa smiled at him again. " 'Pears like the biggest problem is talkin' yore Mam into movin' back to Georgee and tryin' to find some money fer you to start over. That ain't as bad as you were a-thinkin', now, is it?"

No, it wasn't, Cade realized, his spirits lifting more. Willa had taken what he considered a hopeless situation and cut it down to size. Maybe it *wasn't* hopeless. Only difficult. He gave her a wide smile. "How did you figure all that out?"

She shrugged. "Iffen us ridge people had all that land, they'd think they was in hog heaven," she said. "Land is all that really matters. You can build the rest back."

"How old are you, Willa?" he suddenly asked.

Her eyes widened at his unexpected question. "I'll be fourteen next month."

"How did you get so smart so young?" he asked her, his voice half-teasing, half-serious, but wholly admiring.

Willa blushed again. She unscrambled her legs and got to her feet. "I ain't smart. I never got past the second reader in school. That's why Miz Eden is a-tryin' to teach me some book learnin'."

He couldn't believe that. "Why not?" he asked, getting up himself.

"Oh, there was allus too much work to do around the place. Mam needed me. And when the boys went off to the war, I had to help Pap in the fields, too."

Cade knew the gentle-born women he'd grown up among, his mother and sister included, had learned to do all kinds of work they'd never have dreamed they could. But he doubted if any of them had worked as hard as what this hill girl took for granted as a way of life.

He reached out and clasped one of Willa's small hands in his. He felt the calluses on her palms. "Book learning isn't the only kind of smart there is," he told her. "You're just naturally smart."

She gave him a surprised look as if she'd never considered

anything like that before. "But I don't talk right," she said. "Not like you and Mister Jesse and Miz Eden do."

He gave her another grin. "I like the way you talk just fine. But if you want to change, I know you can learn that, too."

She grinned back at him, a surprised, delighted grin. "Reckon I kin?"

He nodded. "I *know* you can."

Willa's grin faded as their glances met and held. She looked into Cade's yellow-brown eyes and felt something go over her, some kind of feeling she'd never had before. It was nice, but at the same time, it scared her. She pulled her hand out of Cade's and moved back a little.

"It'll soon be black dark," she said, her voice a little breathless. "I got to be gittin' home. Mam is goin' to be fierce riled at me."

Cade felt a little dazed. He looked around and saw that dusk was indeed falling. But he didn't want Willa to leave. He wanted to stay here and talk to her for hours. He'd enjoyed the feel of her hand, too. He wished she hadn't taken it away.

"I'll walk you home," he told her.

"No!" Willa said quickly. "I know the way. You'd best hurry on back to Miz Hannah's cabin whilst you can still see the trail." She gave him a quick, slightly tremulous smile and hurried away.

"Wait!" Cade called, hurrying after her. "Are you coming to the cabin tomorrow?"

For a moment she hesitated, then she said, over her shoulder, "I reckon so. If Mam will let me."

Cade watched as she broke into a run and vanished from sight. His spirits rose. He'd see her tomorrow. They could talk and listen to more of Miss Hannah's stories.

He hurried in the opposite direction. Jesse would wonder where he'd gone, maybe be worried about him. He should have told him where he was going.

His spirits were higher than they'd been since he'd made the journey from Alabama to Georgia and seen his family's burned house, the desolate plantation. Willa had made him see that maybe things weren't hopeless.

When they left here, whether it was in two weeks or two

months, he'd head back to Aunt Eulalie's and talk his mother into returning to Georgia. He knew Jesse wouldn't mind them staying in his big, empty house. They could all help each other get started again.

Only one thing bothered him. He was sure going to miss Willa when he left here.

He was going to miss her a lot.

Chapter Fourteen

"These here flowers are right purty—pretty, ain—aren't they?" Willa, on her knees by a ginseng bed, held up a big plant with a cluster of small, greenish yellow flowers amid its leaves.

"Yes, they are," Eden agreed, trying to find a comfortable position. She finally tucked her skirts under her and sat on the cool, mossy ground. Crouching was almost impossible for her now. She felt so heavy and awkward.

The two weeks of Jesse's visit had passed.

Today, she had to tell him he couldn't stay. She'd thought of little else since she'd arisen this morning.

As she'd decided, she'd continued to let Jesse and Cade do the heavy work of the homestead. Eden spent the time keeping up with the inside work and finishing her preparations for the baby's birth. From the bolt of flannel she'd bought at the general store in Cherry Creek months ago, she'd made tiny gowns and wrappers and diapers.

Hannah insisted on helping, even though her eyes weren't good enough to do much of the fine hand stitching.

Cade sat by her bed every evening after the work was done, listening to stories of her childhood and folk tales that went

back a century or more. Sometimes, Jesse joined him. And
Eden wrote the stories down, no longer trying to hide what she
was doing. Hannah seemed pleased.

Eden was cautiously optimistic at the continued improvement
in Hannah's spirits. True, even though she was eating better,
she didn't seem to be much if any stronger. But possibly that
would come in time.

Even when Cade and Jesse left? her mind asked her. Yes!
Maybe Hannah's improvement had nothing to do with Jesse
and Cade. Maybe her grief had run its course and she was
finally recovering from Alston's death.

And as for the stories, Eden would coax Hannah into continu-
ing with the nightly ritual. Even if that wasn't the secret of
Hannah's improvement, it wouldn't stop.

Since that day by the barn, when Eden and Jesse had again
experienced one of those strange moments together, Eden had
taken care not to be alone with him. It hadn't been too difficult.
Jesse didn't try to seek her out. He didn't seem to want to be
with her, either.

The days had passed. Now they added up to two weeks.

Eden put another ginseng root in her burlap sack, a frown
drawing her dark brows together. Jesse had said nothing about
leaving. Did he still retain the hope she'd change her mind and
let him stay?

"It's so pitiful that Cade don't—doesn't have a home to go
back to," Willa said into their busy silence. "I keep a-thinkin'
'bout it, wonderin' what it'd be like not to have a home."

Willa broke a flower-covered top from a root, her pretty face
pensive. The girl had returned to the cabin two days after she'd
run away so upset. And she'd been back every day of these
two weeks.

Eden was surprised at the girl's new attentiveness to her
lessons. Willa made sure Cade wasn't around at these times,
and Eden realized she was making a conscious effort to speak
more correctly—especially to Cade.

The two obviously enjoyed each other's company, and their
friendship deepened day by day. That they were aware of each
other in a more than friendly way, Eden couldn't help but

notice. But she was relieved they made no attempt to try to be alone together.

And tomorrow Cade and Jesse would leave.

"Yes, to be homeless is very sad," Eden answered Willa. "But Cade's family still owns the land. Someday, they can rebuild." She knew, even as she said the words, how far in the future that time might be—maybe it would never happen.

Willa sighed. "I reckon so, but Cade says his Mam wants to stay in Alabama with her sister. She don't—doesn't want to go back to Georgee."

Eden's frown deepened. "Willa, you know Jesse and Cade will be leaving soon. We probably won't see them again." She winced at her blunt words, but it was better Willa was prepared.

The girl gave her a wide-eyed, startled look, then turned quickly back to dig at another root. "I thought maybe they wouldn't. Cade said he figgered they might stay a while longer."

So Jesse hadn't given up his plan to stay here until after the baby's birth! Why wasn't she more surprised to find that out? And why did something deep inside her come to life at that thought?

"No, that won't be possible," she said firmly. "They have their own life to return to, and I can't let them stay."

Of course she'd miss them for purely practical reasons. She chided herself for the way her spirit quailed at the thought of having to again pick up the burden of the work they'd taken off her shoulders these past weeks.

Willa sighed again, deeper this time. "I reckon not. Mam says it's a scandal fer them to be here. Even if they are a-sleepin' in the barn."

Irritation swept through Eden. Mattie was a terrible gossip. She'd probably repeated her biased opinion to everyone on the ridge. Maybe in the settlement, too. And Eden knew she was being ridiculous. She wanted the two gone, more than anyone.

Didn't she? Of course she did. But still, she intensely disliked the idea of Mattie gossiping about the situation.

"There's nothing scandalous about Jesse and Cade staying here," Eden said firmly. "That's not the reason they have to leave."

"Then what is?" Willa blurted. "Cade says you need him

and Jesse to help you, and they do a heap o' work. Mam says no use sendin' Darcy over to help no more long as Jesse and Cade are here."

Oh, so *that* was what lurked behind Mattie's objections! Now that she thought about it, Eden realized Darcy hadn't been around since Jesse had arrived. She hadn't even noticed, probably because he didn't help much when he came.

But of course Willa's mother would feel that Darcy's suit was being threatened. Even if there *was* no suit. Mattie refused to recognize Eden's lack of interest in Darcy. That was another thing she had to settle, and soon. She dreaded it.

She pondered how to explain to Willa the impossibility of letting Cade and Jesse stay and found she couldn't come up with a good reason for sending them away. And she couldn't tell the girl the truth—that the real basis for her decision was her feelings about Jesse.

She pressed her lips together and reached for another plant, then heard a rustling in the bushes behind her.

Her hands froze on the ginseng plant. Was it Sadie again? She hadn't seen the woman since the night of their encounter in the clearing. Slowly, she turned her head, dreading the sight of Sadie's vacant eyes, her avid interest in the coming baby.

But Sadie didn't come out of the underbrush toward them. Eden sucked in her breath and struggled to her feet, realizing Willa did the same. If she'd dreaded encountering Sadie, a much stronger emotion now coursed through her veins.

Toby Varden, a leer on his thick lips, pushed aside the wide leaves of a mountain laurel and walked toward them. "Well, now, if you two ain't a purty sight. Don't know when I seed a purtier one."

Eden felt her heart pounding and tried to calm herself. There were, as Toby had noted, two of them. Surely, even a man like him wouldn't try anything. But they were a distance from the cabin.

Even though they'd only started on the bed, they'd better go back. She picked up her small spade and burlap sack, motioned for Willa to do the same, then drew herself up as tall as possible.

"We're finished—we're leaving," she said, trying to make her voice calm, not show her fear.

Toby moved closer to Eden, his leering grin still in place. "No call to go runnin' off, 'specially since I jist got here." He gave her a bold head-to-toe inspection. "Yore a mite heavy on yore feet jist now, but 'fore too long you'll be a right handsome woman agin."

"You git yore ugly self out o' here and leave Miz Eden alone," Willa said, indignant anger in her voice. She moved closer to Eden. "My Mam says you're a no-'count piece o' trash."

Eden sucked in her breath. Why did Willa have to say that? Did the girl have no idea how truly dangerous this man could be?

Toby's big, shaggy dark head slowly turned to take in the girl. His black eyes raked over her young body with an even more insolent look than he'd given Eden. His tongue came out and ran around his upper lip.

"Yore Mam is that fat old cow Mattie Freeman, ain't she? Cain't keep her mouth shut nohow." He moved away from Eden, toward Willa.

Oh, God, what could she do? Eden looked around for a stick, a rock, anything with which to defend Willa and herself. To her despair, she saw nothing close enough to grab before Toby could prevent her, except her puny spade.

She took a step toward him, her fingers sliding down into her sack, fastening over the tool. "Go on home, Toby, and leave us alone. You don't want to start anything—"

His head swung around to face her again. "Anythin' that I cain't finish?" he drawled. "Don't you worry, I aim to finish this."

He turned back to Willa. Both of his big, dirty hands, the backs covered with coarse black hair, reached out, falling heavily onto Willa's thin shoulders. "You ever been kissed by a real man, Miss High-and-Mighty?" he taunted her.

Willa jerked her wiry body backward, anger flashing from her blue eyes. "You leave go o' me!"

There was still no fear in her voice, only indignation. Eden moved up behind Toby, the spade lifted over her head, praying it would stun Toby enough for them to get away.

Catching him by surprise, Willa managed to get one shoulder

free, but his remaining hand squeezed her other shoulder like a vise, halting her escape. "It ain't gonna be that easy, leetle gal," he said, his voice soft but deadly.

With all her strength, Eden brought the flat side of the spade down on the back of Toby's head. He let out an angry bellow, then pushed Willa backward and turned toward Eden. He jerked the spade out of her hand and threw it into the underbrush, then caught her wrist in a punishing grip.

"You owe me somethin' fer that time yore boyfriend jumped on me," he said, his voice still deadly soft. "I b'lieve I'll jist collect a little on the debt."

Her wrist felt as if he were snapping the bones. Eden pressed her lips together to keep from crying out and tried to tug her hand away, but he pulled her toward him, then let go of her hand so suddenly, she staggered and almost fell.

Willa had regained her feet and was about to launch herself on Toby. Before she could, Toby savagely backhanded Eden across the face.

She fell heavily. Everything went black, and white points of light danced inside her skull. She heard Toby's satisfied laugh and Willa's enraged cry, then her vision cleared.

Toby had hold of the collar of Willa's high-necked calico dress. He yanked downward. The soft, old fabric ripped, exposing Willa's thin cotton chemise, her budding breasts half visible beneath it. Toby's avid stare fixed on them. "Ain't them little titties a sight to behold," he said, gloating.

"You let me go, you nasty varmint! You better not have hurt Miz Eden," Willa screamed, twisting and jerking to get out of his grasp.

Toby held fast, his free hand cupping one small breast, the gloating leer widening.

Fighting dizziness, Eden tried to struggle to her feet, then she gasped.

Cade was suddenly there, the sounds of his arrival gone unnoticed, his young face white with fury. "You bastard! I'll kill you!" he yelled at Toby.

"Cade! Oh, Cade," Willa said, relief and fear in her voice.

Toby released Willa and stood facing Cade. The boy was so angry his golden brown eyes glowed, giving him that same lionlike look Jesse had. But in his case, it was a lion cub. Oh, God, Toby would kill him!

"What's that you said, boy?" Toby asked, that sneering grin on his face again. "You think a puny young 'un like you is gonna scare me?"

Blind fury in his eyes, Cade threw a wild punch at Toby's chin. Toby sidestepped and the blow glanced off, landing harmlessly on his shoulder.

Toby laughed. "You'll have to do better'n that." He hit Cade a swift, punishing blow in the stomach that doubled the boy up, then smashed his fist into his face.

Cade went down. Toby stood over him for a minute, then kicked him brutally in the ribs. Cade moaned, rolling over on his stomach to protect himself.

Willa launched herself on Toby's back like a small wildcat. Her fingers were curved, and the nails raked down his face like claws. Bellowing with rage, Toby threw her off. Willa landed on her tailbone, giving a small yelp of pain.

The scratches Willa had inflicted dripping blood into his black beard, Toby sneered at the three people on the ground. "I guess I've had 'nuff fun fer one day."

His black gaze found Eden's, his eyes narrowing. "But I don't b'lieve I've collected all my debt from you. You better keep a good watch on yore barn and cabin, *Miz* Eden. There jist might be a accident some dark night. Lightnin' strikes been knowed to cause bad fires. Sometimes when they ain't even no lightnin'."

He swaggered away, disappearing into the woods.

Willa got to her feet, looking at Eden, then at Cade. "Are you all right, Miz Eden? Did that low-down varmint hurt you?"

Eden shook her head, slowing rising. Her head felt as if it were twice its size, and reaching to her cheek, she felt the imprints of Toby's hand beginning to raise welts. Another fear slammed into her.

Was the baby all right?

Willa, seeing Eden wasn't badly injured, was already kneeling by Cade. Her dress gaped open, but she wasn't even aware of it. "Cade," she half sobbed, "what did he do to you?" She gently turned him over, then gasped.

Toby's blow had caught the boy in the mouth. Both his lips were split, blood trickling down his chin, a dark bruise already starting to form. Cade's eyes fluttered open. He took a deep breath, then winced at the pain that struck his ribs.

Then, his gaze riveted on Willa's torn dress, his eyes widening, darkening. He struggled to his feet, crying out at the new pain hitting him. "Where did the bastard go? I'm going after him!"

He staggered and almost fell again. Willa quickly supported him with her arm and shoulder. "You ain't in no shape to do anythin' right now. We got to get you back to the cabin."

"Yes," Eden said, moving over to support him from the other side. Relief swept over her. Nothing in her abdominal region hurt.

Cade looked at Eden's face, and his eyes darkened even more. "Jesse and I'll go after him," he said, his young voice hardening.

He tried to straighten, even though Eden could see it hurt him badly. "I'm all right. I can walk by myself. I shouldn't have let him do that! I should have protected both of you!"

Pity and admiration filled Eden. She had no doubt he would, without hesitation, risk his life for either of them. "You did fine," she told him, smiling warmly. "You came along just in time."

Cade's jaw tightened. "I didn't do anything," he mumbled, "except make a fool out of myself."

"Yes, you did," Eden insisted. "You made him leave. Now, let's get back to the cabin." She gathered up the burlap sacks, found her spade and put it inside again.

Cade struggled to stay erect, even though he was weaving on his feet. Thank God the cabin wasn't too far, because she could see he wasn't going to accept any help from them.

He wouldn't be in good enough shape to ride tomorrow. He might even have some broken ribs. He and Jesse couldn't leave now. And she had to figure some way to keep Jesse from searching out the trapper's cabin.

Of course Jesse would go after Toby. He'd wanted to that other time, and she'd managed to talk him out of it. But that

wouldn't work now. Not with her swollen face. Cade's injuries.
Willa's torn dress.

Jesse would go after him and would try to kill him. But it
would be anyone's guess who came out of that encounter alive.
She didn't want him to kill Toby. The man deserved it, but she
didn't know what repercussions with the law would arise if
that happened.

And she didn't want Jesse to die.

Oh, no, she didn't want that!

"Where is everyone?" Jesse asked, entering the cabin. He
smiled at Hannah, who sat propped up in bed, knitting something that looked like infants' wear. As always, the cabin seemed
dim and cool after the midsummer sun beating down outside.
But compared to Georgia's stifling summer heat and humidity,
this was nothing.

Hannah smiled back, setting the knitting needles aside. "Eden
and Willa went a-sangin'. Cade went to find them."

"Good. I don't like them to go off alone like that."

"I don't, either," Hannah said, her face puckering in a frown.
" 'Specially not with Eden gittin' so big. But when she takes
a notion to do somethin', ain't no way o' stoppin' her."

Jesse's smile turned wry. "I know." And when Eden made a
decision about anything, he didn't think she was likely to change
her mind.

He and Cade had been here two weeks today.

It was time for Eden to decide if they stayed for the remainder
of her pregnancy—or left. He was sure Eden hadn't forgotten
that fact, even though they hadn't discussed it again.

Since that strangely intimate moment in the barnyard, they
hadn't been alone together. Eden was deliberately avoiding
him, and he'd made no attempts to catch her by herself.

That wouldn't help his campaign. He knew Eden deeply
feared whatever was between them, trying to draw them
together. Sometimes he wondered if that wasn't a big part of
why she was so adamant that he couldn't stay. Maybe she was
right about that—but not the rest of it.

This was the first time he'd been alone with Hannah, too.

Should he seize this opportunity to try to convince her he should stay, so that maybe she could influence Eden? He didn't think it would take much convincing. Hannah knew how much work he and Cade had done these weeks. She had to know Eden would need even more help as her time neared. Afterward, too. His mouth tightened.

Hell, she'd need help from now on. And there was nothing he could do about it. Many times during these two weeks he'd wondered if he was a fool to fight so hard against her stubborn insistence he leave. No, he answered himself. He could be as stubborn as Eden and he knew he should stay.

The geese started making a ruckus out front, as they always did when someone approached. He hoped it wasn't Mattie Freeman and Darcy. They hadn't visited since he'd come back to the ridge and he had no desire to see either of them.

Especially Darcy.

And why was that? he asked himself, already knowing the answer. He couldn't stand to think about the other man being close to Eden, maybe eventually talking her into marrying him.

"That must be Eden and them comin' back now," Hannah said.

Jesse rose. He hoped so, even though his chance to talk to Hannah was ruined. "I'll go see."

He walked to the open doorway. Eden, Willa, and Cade were walking toward the cabin. He frowned and tensed. Something was wrong. Cade walked bent over, as if he was in pain. Willa and Eden walked close by on either side of him.

He tensed, frowning. Too close. They looked ready to catch him if he collapsed. He smoothed out his frown, turning to Hannah. "I'll go meet them." No use getting Hannah alarmed until he knew what had happened.

"All right." She smiled and picked up her knitting again.

Jesse kept himself from running down the steps in case Hannah was watching. But once off the porch, his long legs ate up the distance. As he and the group neared each other, alarm hit him. Cade's lips were split and bleeding, his face bruised, and it was obvious he was in pain.

That wasn't all. The neck of Willa's dress was torn, and one side of Eden's face was red and swollen.

"What in hell happened to all of you?" Jesse demanded.

There was no way they could keep this from him, Eden thought despairingly. No way at all.

"That no-good Toby Varden was after me and Miz Eden!" Willa burst out, her anger still high. She glanced at Cade, pride in her look. "And Cade got there jist in time to stop him."

Cade's young face twisted. "I didn't do much stopping," he mumbled, throwing a look full of self-disgust toward Jesse.

A red rage filled Jesse's head, blocked his vision. His hands clenched together at his sides. When his sight cleared, he looked at Eden again. What had that bastard done? If he'd hurt her . . .

"I'm all right," she quickly said. Her hand went to her cheek. "He only slapped me." The blow had been much harder than a slap, but she'd try to downplay this as much as possible.

Jesse moved forward, the muscles of his face tight and hard. He reached out to touch the angry red welts on her face. "God damn him," he said savagely. It was all he could do to not sweep her into his arms, hold her, comfort her.

Instead, he moved back a little, glancing at Willa. When he realized the significance of the torn dress, he became even more rigid. "He didn't . . ."

Willa quickly shook her head. "No, he didn't do nothin' to me! Cade wouldn't let him!" Her voice was full of pride and anger.

"Damn it! Will you stop acting like I did something great?" Cade said. "I didn't do anything except let him knock me down."

Jesse touched his cousin's face, feeling for broken bones, relieved when he found none. "What's wrong with your side?" he asked tightly, his rage still building.

Cade tried to shrug, but the movement turned into a grimace. "He kicked me," he mumbled, shamefacedly. "I let him knock me down, then kick me!"

The boy must have badly bruised ribs. Maybe a cracked one, Jesse decided. He gave Eden a swift glance. "Do you know where the son-of-a-bitch lives?"

She'd known this was coming. She swallowed. Her throat felt dry as a milkweed boll. "No. Somewhere deep in the woods." At least she could answer him honestly. She wasn't sure if anyone on the ridge knew exactly where Toby lived. She could see Jesse didn't believe her.

"Does Hannah or anyone else know?"

"Hannah doesn't," Eden quickly answered. "Jesse, we don't want to get Hannah upset!"

Jesse gave her a cold look. "Don't you think she's going to be upset when she sees all of you? What are you planning to do—hide for a week?"

Eden shook her head. "No, of course not." He was right. There was no way Hannah could be spared this.

Jesse looked at Willa. "Do you or your family know where this animal lives?"

Willa shook her head. "No, Mister Jesse. All the ridge folk stay away from him. Ain't nobody tried to find him."

"Don't you think your father and brothers will want to when they see what he did to you?"

Willa looked at him for a moment, then bit her lip. "I don't rightly know."

Jesse stared at her, shocked at her reply. What kind of family did she have that she wasn't sure they'd care she'd been attacked?

He turned back to Eden. "You told me when I was here before that he was just drunk and no threat to anyone. That wasn't the truth, was it?" His words were like chips of ice.

Eden stared back at him. "No," she finally said.

"Has he done anything like this before? Has he struck and tried to rape women and the ridge people ignored him?"

"No, he ain't!" Willa said. "Nobody knows for certain but folks think he's burned some barns, and sich as that."

"He threatened Miss Eden!" Cade said. "He said he wasn't finished with her. That she still owed him for—" Cade's voice broke off. "I guess he meant when you knocked him down before."

The red film of rage blocked out Jesse's sight again. When it dissipated, he took a deep breath. He was getting nowhere. He wanted nothing more than to go back to the barn, grab his revolver and take off into the woods to find Toby.

But he couldn't do that. Not right now, anyway.

"Let's get back to the cabin," he said. "Then, I'm going down to the town in the valley. Find the sheriff. See if we can't get this man locked up."

"Jesse . . ." Eden began, then stopped. Jesse's anger was barely under control. It wouldn't take much more to send him into such a rage that he'd take off after Toby alone, just as she'd feared.

"All right," she agreed, "but let me tell Hannah."

Chapter Fifteen

Jesse walked in the cabin first, the others behind him. Smiling, Hannah put down her knitting and glanced toward the door. Her smile died as she saw the look on Jesse's face. "What's wrong?" she asked, her voice quavering.

"Mrs. Clayborne, there's been some trouble, but everyone's all right," Jesse said quickly.

Eden stepped out beside him, giving Hannah what she hoped was a reassuring smile. "Don't get upset, Mother Clayborne."

Hannah's eyes widened in shock as she saw Eden's welted face. "Oh, my land, what happened? Did ye have a fall? Is the babe all right?"

"The baby's fine," Eden hastened to assure her. She took a deep breath. Might as well tell her now. "Toby Varden came upon Willa and me in the woods. He hurt us a little. Cade, too."

She moved aside and Cade and Willa came into the room. Willa had tried to tuck her torn neckline up, but it was still plain someone had ripped it. Cade, a white line of pain around his bleeding mouth, shakily sat down on the nearest chair.

The shock on Hannah's face deepened. "How bad hurt are ye all?" Her voice trembled.

Eden hurried to the bed. She sat down on it, taking Hannah's hand in hers. "Not bad. He only slapped my face. Cade's mouth is cut, and some ribs are bruised." She gave Hannah another smile, then turned to Willa, still smiling. "Willa isn't really hurt at all."

At least physically, she added to herself. She hoped the girl's spirit hadn't been damaged.

Willa took the cue. She walked to the bed, managing a smile. "Miz Eden's right. I ain't hurt a-tall."

Hannah's eyes fastened on Willa's torn bodice and her face whitened. "Oh, Lord," she said, shakily. "I allus knowed some-day that man would do somethin' truly bad."

"Willa, will you sit with Mother Clayborne?" Eden asked. "I want to make up a comfrey poultice for Cade."

"O' course I will." Willa took Eden's place on the bed.

Eden handed the girl Hannah's black shawl from the foot of the bed, then hurried to her herb shelf.

Hannah's eyes found Jesse's grim face. "Then ye didn't catch him whilst he was a-doin' his meanness?" she asked tremulously.

"No. But he'll not get away with it. I'm going over and see the Freemans. Then we'll all go down to Cherry Creek and talk to the sheriff."

"Ye prob'ly won't git much help out o' ole Sheriff Taylor," Hannah said. "Nobody pays much heed to what goes on up on the ridges."

Jesse's grim look deepened. "Someone's going to this time."

Eden glanced at Cade. He looked as if he might lose consciousness any second. "Jesse, help Cade to my bed," she said.

God, yes, Jesse saw. He hurried to Cade's side. Cade rose, his mouth pressed together. "I don't need help," he said shakily. He walked stiff-legged to the bed and carefully lowered himself to a sitting position again.

Eden brought over the poultice and some strips of clean cloth, placing them on the chest. "You need to lie down," she told the boy gently.

Cade stiffly obeyed. He removed his boots and lay on his back, staring at the ceiling. It was plain he still felt humiliated, convinced he'd let Eden and Willa down.

"You'll have to take your shirt off," Eden said. "Do you want me to help?"

"No! I can do it," Cade insisted. By the time his shirt was unbuttoned and removed, his face was pasty and perspiration bathed his forehead, but he still hadn't uttered a moan or groan.

Eden's mouth tightened with anger as she saw the scraped, bleeding skin on Cade's side, the dark bruises. Everyone in the room silently watched as she cleansed the area. She looked up at Jesse, standing by the bed, his face still taut with angry frustration.

"Jesse, will you look at him? I don't know much about this kind of thing."

She got up and Jesse took her place, gently feeling along Cade's ribs. In a few moments, he glanced at her. "I think it's only bruises, but it's hard to tell if a rib's cracked or not. All we can do is bind him up, anyway."

Eden nodded. "Yes, and apply the poultice." She picked up her supplies and sat beside Cade again.

"I guess I'd best be gittin' home," Willa said. "Mam told me not to stay gone long today."

Her voice sounded unsure and wobbly to Eden. She glanced at Jesse to suggest he escort her, and found him looking at the girl.

"I'll walk home with you, Willa."

Willa quickly shook her head, her eyes widening. "That's thoughtful o' you, but I'm all right. You don't have to do that."

"Yes, I do. I want to talk to your family about what happened today."

Willa swallowed visibly. "I ain't sure if Pap's around. Might be off squirrel huntin'."

Jesse finally saw that the girl didn't want him to talk to her parents. Why? Was she just embarrassed about what had happened today? Or was it something else?

He pushed down as much of his still raging anger as he could, forcing a smile. "I'll go see."

"Wait a minute, Willa," Eden said quickly. "I'll mend that tear in your dress."

Relief filled Willa's eyes. "I'd 'preciate that, Miz Eden."

Damn it! Jesse swore to himself. Why did Eden have to say

that? Of course Willa didn't want to go home with her dress
torn. But she must.

"We'd better leave Willa's dress as it is," Jesse said. "So
that her parents will understand what took place today and what
we have to do about it."

Eden looked chagrined. She smiled at Willa apologetically.
"Jesse's right, honey. You can wear Hannah's shawl. Are you
sure you'll be all right?"

Willa nodded, pulling the shawl close, her face wooden.
"Don't worry 'bout me." She walked to Eden's bed and stood
looking down at Cade. "Goodbye, Cade," she said, her face
softening. "Don't you fret over what went on today. You done
jist fine."

He looked up at her, then tensely nodded. "Goodbye, Willa."

She turned to Jesse, her face expressionless again. "Reckon
we better go."

She was making a valiant effort to hide her feelings, Eden
saw, as the two left the cabin. Uneasiness went over her as she
realized more than just the aftermath of Toby's attack bothered
her.

Why was Willa afraid to go home? Why didn't she want
Jesse to go with her?

Willa and Jesse came out of the woods into the clearing
where her family's cabin stood.

"There 'tis," Willa said, tension in her voice. She turned to
Jesse. "I'd druther you didn't talk to Pap or Mam today, Mister
Jesse."

The girl had been silent during the trip through the woods,
and now Jesse saw the fear and dread in her clear blue eyes.
He didn't know what was wrong here, but he had to do this.

He patted her shoulder. "I'm sorry, Willa, but I must. Can't
you see we have to get that beast put behind bars so he can't
hurt anyone again?"

Finally, she nodded reluctantly. "I guess so. Well, then, come
on with me."

Jesse walked beside her across the clearing and up onto the

cabin's cluttered porch. The cabin was much like the Claybornes', except not so well built, and it needed repairs.

"Come on in," Willa said. Her voice sounded stiff, as if she
were trying to keep it from trembling. Jesse followed her into
the big room. As his eyes adjusted to the dimness, he saw a
man lying across an unmade bed in one corner.

Willa's mother, Mattie, sat in a rocking chair, slowly rocking
back and forth.

He'd forgotten how big a woman she was. Her brown calico
dress was soiled, her hair messy. This room didn't have the
clean, welcoming feel of the Claybornes' cabin. Dirty dishes
littered the rough wood table. Another unmade bed sat in the
far corner, and clutter was everywhere.

Mattie stared at Jesse, her eyes unfriendly, as the rocker
slowly stopped its motion.

He might as well get right to it, Jesse decided. "Mrs. Freeman,
a terrible thing almost happened to Willa a little while ago. I
have to talk to you and your husband about it."

Mattie turned her gaze on her daughter, then back to Jesse.
"What are ye a-talkin' about?" she demanded. "Willie looks
all right to me."

Jesse smiled at the girl, dismayed to see she looked more
fearful than ever. "Willa, show your mother your dress," he
told her gently.

Willa slowly pulled the shawl aside, exposing her ripped
bodice.

Jesse heard Mattie's intake of breath, then her glance flew
back to him.

"What is the idee o' bringin' my gal home with her dress
tore half offen her?" she asked indignantly. Her angry gaze
stayed on Jesse, and he realized she'd already been angry with
him before he'd walked in the door.

"That's what I'm trying to tell you," Jesse said, barely holding
onto his temper. His anger with Toby still simmered, ready to
burst through. Willa was shrinking with embarrassment beside
him.

"Then you better git to tellin' afore I yell fer Hollis to come
with the rifle!" Mattie slowly raised her ponderous bulk from
the chair.

"Mam!" Willa suddenly came to life. "Mister Jesse didn't do anythin'. It was that Toby Varden!"

"You hesh yore mouth, or I'll slap it shet," Mattie warned, giving Willa a cold look. "I ain't a-talkin' to you."

The girl shrank back as if she fully expected a blow.

Jesse's anger increased. "Mrs. Freeman," he said, his words clipped, "Toby attacked Willa and Eden and my cousin Cade. We have to go down to the village and talk to the sheriff."

Mattie's pale blue gaze inspected her daughter again, then came back to Jesse. "Are you a-sayin' that woods varmint tore her dress? What else did he do to her?"

"Nothin, Mam!" Willa said, a note of desperation in her voice. "Cade came and stopped him."

Mattie's eyes narrowed as she swung around to stare at Willa again. "Are you shore that boy didn't do that to ye? And yore tryin' to pass it off on Toby?"

Jesse heard Willa draw in her breath. He was so shocked and angry himself he could have struck the woman. He took a step toward her.

"Mrs. Freeman, Varden hit Mrs. Clayborne in the face. He may have broken my cousin's ribs."

Jesse heard noises on the porch, and then a lean hound bounded into the house. Looking toward the doorway, Jesse saw a tall, stooped man holding a rifle filling it, another male behind him.

"Git that dawg out o' here!" Mattie demanded. She lifted her foot and kicked at the animal. "Go on, git!"

The hound slunk under the table and lay still. The man on the porch disappeared from view. The one in front came on into the room. He propped his gun up against the wall, then approached the group, his expression cautious.

He looked from one to the other, then extended his hand to Jesse. "Howdy. I'm Hollis Freeman. You must be t'other feller stayin' at the Claybornes."

Jesse took a deep breath and let it out, extending his hand. This man seemed reasonable. Maybe now they could get the conversation on a rational basis. "Yes, Mister Freeman, I'm Jesse Bainbridge."

"Jist look at Willie," Mattie shrilled, pointing at the girl, the flesh hanging down from under her arm quivering like jelly. "He's a-sayin' Toby Varden tore her dress like that!"

Hollis slowly turned his head and inspected his daughter. Then he turned back around to his wife. "What did he do that fer?" he asked. "Never knowed Toby to do anythin' like that."

A wave of fresh anger swept over Jesse. He'd been wrong. He'd get no help from this man, but he had to try. "Mister Freeman," he said quickly, before Mattie, who had her mouth open again, could start a new tirade. "The man is dangerous. He should be locked up. He hurt my cousin and Mrs. Clayborne today, too."

Hollis turned and looked at Jesse, his blue eyes blank. Then he looked at his wife again, as if for guidance.

She glared at him. "Did you ever hear of sich a bunch of foolishment?"

Her husband quickly nodded. "Reckon it do sound foolish." His voice was relieved. "Never heared tell o' Toby doin' nothin' like this."

Jesse clenched his hands into fists at his sides. What was wrong with these people? he raged inwardly. He glanced at Willa to see her looking at him, fearfully but with resignation, as if this lack of concern from her parents was what she'd expected, as if it didn't surprise her at all.

No wonder she hadn't wanted him to come with her. If he hadn't, and Eden had mended her dress, she'd probably never have told her parents anything.

"Are you saying that I'm lying to you?" he demanded.

Mattie looked at him, her eyes still narrowed. "What we're a-sayin', *Mister* Bainbridge, is that we ain't never had no trouble like this up on the ridge afore you and your cousin come here."

She paused a moment, then turned her gaze on her husband. "Hollis, it 'pears to me you need to have a talk with that boy Cade. And you better take along yore gun."

Hollis's mouth fell open. "Well, now, Mattie," he said placatingly, "maybe we better study over this a spell afore we do anythin'. That boy seemed like a right nice 'un to me."

Willa let out a strangled sob. Turning, she ran for the door and outside, headed for the woods.

"Willa, wait!" Jesse went after her, but stopped on the porch, realizing he'd never catch up with her. The other male had disappeared.

Jesse stood on the porch for a moment, taking a few deep breaths, then came back inside. He was so angry with Mattie Freeman he'd have to leave before he said something that would make the situation hopeless.

Hollis was completely under Mattie's thumb. No use trying to appeal to him to be sensible. Jesse looked at Mattie, his jaw clenched.

"Listen to me! Varden is dangerous. I'm going to Cherry Creek to get the sheriff to arrest him. If you care anything about your daughter's welfare, you'll come with me."

Jesse wondered if she'd launch into a new harangue against Cade and him. Or perhaps Willa. God, he hadn't known what a strange household the girl lived in. No wonder she stayed at Eden's all she could.

Mattie stared at him for a long time. Then she looked at her husband. "Hollis, why don't you tell *Mister* Bainbridge we ain't a-gonna do any sich thing?"

The man quickly nodded. He glanced at Jesse, then looked away. "I b'lieve Mattie's right. We cain't go a-doin' that. We cain't take a chance on havin' our barn burnt."

"If Varden is locked up in jail, he won't be burning any barns," Jesse said evenly. "Or anything else."

Mattie snorted. "Ain't nobody in the settlement goin' to worry about anythin' up on this ridge."

"That's right," Hollis quickly put in. "We 'uns has to take keer o' ourselfs."

Jesse gave up. "It doesn't look as if you're doing a very good job of it. Don't you know if you let him get away with this, there's no telling what he'll do next?"

"We done tole you we ain't shore Toby did anythin'," Mattie said. "I b'lieve we better take a visit over to Hannie's. Need to see fer ourselfs jist who's hurt and who ain't."

"Yes, why don't you do that? I'd be glad to escort you, but I haven't time today. I'm going down to Cherry Creek to see the sheriff."

He turned and walked out of the unkempt cabin and down the porch steps. Willa was nowhere in sight. There was no use trying to find her in the woods. She knew them like one of the wild animals who lived there, knew all the hiding places.

He wished now he'd let Eden sew up Willa's dress. The girl would have said nothing to her parents. And he couldn't blame her for that. If he could get the sheriff up here, Cade's injuries and Eden's would be evidence enough against Toby.

What kind of hornet's nest had he unintentionally stirred up by coming here? Would Mattie calm down, realize how foolish her talk had been? Or would her anger keep on building, make her go over to the Claybornes' cabin, cause more trouble there?

Hollis might go with her, but Jesse didn't think he'd take his gun along, even with Mattie egging him on. He remembered suddenly his impression that Mattie had already been angry with him before he'd told her anything, before she'd noticed Willa's torn dress.

Why was that? Then, he remembered something else—the other man who'd been behind Hollis, who'd quickly disappeared.

Darcy. Eden's would-be suitor.

Neither Mattie nor Darcy had visited the Claybornes' cabin since he and Cade had arrived. And he'd gathered from Hannah that they usually did on a regular basis.

Could it be that Mattie considered Jesse a rival for Eden's affections, her hand in marriage? Could that be why she'd so quickly and venomously accused Cade of molesting Willa?

Jesse gave a short, mirthless bark of laughter. If she only knew how far from the truth her fears were! That this was to be his last day on the ridge if he couldn't persuade Eden otherwise.

Of course, things had changed now. Cade wasn't fit to travel for a while. They'd have to stay here another week or two, in any case.

And if he couldn't get the sheriff to do anything about Varden, he was going to stay here, look after these two women, no matter how much Eden protested.

Even if he had to put up a tent in the woods.

Chapter Sixteen

Jesse wearily rode into the clearing at dusk. Ranger was as tired as he. It had taken him so long to make his trip down to Cherry Creek and back that he knew Eden must have done the evening chores by now. Cade was in no shape to help her. He hated to have left them for her, especially since he'd accomplished nothing.

His raging anger had cooled into a simmer.

As Hannah and Mattie had predicted, he'd had no luck with Sheriff Taylor.

The man had a dozen reasons why he couldn't do anything about Varden's actions. He had only one deputy. Since the war had ended, both he and his deputy were kept busy sending war stragglers on, making sure they didn't rob and pillage the communities they passed through on their way home. And times were bad; law and order was hard to maintain.

He couldn't spend days up on the ridge trying to find the trapper's cabin in the woods. And he knew these hill folk. Sufficiently riled, they might go after Varden on their own, but they'd never let one of their girls admit to attempted rape and all that would involve. Even if he found Varden and brought him in, he doubted he could hold him.

Taylor hinted strongly that if Jesse and the other ridge dwellers wanted to take the law into their own hands, a blind eye would be turned. Then, he'd gotten up from his rickety chair in his equally battered office and escorted Jesse to the door.

The urge to hunt Varden down and dispense his own justice still ran strong in Jesse's veins. He'd been fighting it all the way back from Cherry Creek. Even now, he was tempted to put the horse up and strike off into the woods.

But that would be pure stupidity. If the ridge dwellers hadn't been able to find Varden's cabin, he couldn't expect to. Especially at night. But, damn it, how could he let the man get away with what he'd done? And even if he found him and gave him a good beating, that wouldn't solve things. Beating Varden up would only make him more determined on revenge.

If not now, later—when Jesse was gone. The man had shown he could wait. The episode today was at least partly in retaliation for the blows Jesse had administered nearly three months ago.

And he couldn't cold-bloodedly kill Varden, the only other choice, even though at the moment putting a bullet into the man wouldn't bother him at all.

He could and would stay here until after the baby came to protect Eden and Hannah. That solution didn't suit him, either. Hell, it wasn't even a solution, only a stop-gap measure. He *hated* a situation that needed resolving when he was not able to do anything about it.

He dismounted in the barnyard, removed Ranger's saddle and bridle, and put the animal into the barn stall, then gave him some hay.

The heat of the day had given way to a cool, pleasant evening. The half moon, already high in the sky, was showing its brightness as the day faded, the stars beginning to reveal their own kind of sparkle. Jesse took deep breaths of the fresh mountain air, wanting to present as calm a demeanor as possible when he entered the cabin.

The door was still open to catch evening breezes. Jesse frowned at that, then decided no one, even himself, expected Varden to do anything else now. Jesse walked across the threshold and glanced around the room.

Cade lay on Eden's bed, face pale, eyes closed. Hannah also

lay in her bed, apparently asleep. Jesse's frown deepened. She'd been sitting up in bed knitting every evening lately. Had the incident today upset her that much?

At last he let his eyes travel to Eden, sitting at the table, a stack of papers before her. She was looking at him, he saw, her gaze intent. She'd lit a candle and its warm glow made her black hair gleam; it darkened her eyes, highlighted and shadowed her facial contours.

The welts on her face were swollen and red, and he pushed down a wave of fresh anger as he looked at them. He didn't know if he could keep himself from going after Varden.

Her eyes were questioning, but she put a finger to her lips, then motioned to the door as she quietly rose. Jesse understood she wanted to talk to him, but outside, so as not to disturb Hannah and Cade.

She moved past him and he followed her, quietly closing the door behind him. Eden looked dubiously at the closed door, then at him. "Let's go out in the yard," she said.

"All right," Jesse agreed. He followed her a little distance from the cabin, near a huge old walnut tree. Twilight was fast turning into dark. Soon, they'd have a hard time seeing each other.

Eden turned to him, the questioning look still in her eyes. "You didn't have any luck, did you?"

Jesse's jaw clenched. "No," he admitted. "Everyone was right. No one down in the valley gives a damn what happens on this ridge."

"Everyone?" Eden questioned.

After leaving the Freemans' cabin, he'd gone straight to the field, saddled Ranger, and headed for the valley. He'd been too angry to talk to Eden or Hannah.

His mouth twisted. "Mattie and Hollis told me the same thing as Hannah, among other things. Did they come here today?"

Eden's gaze was intent on his. "No. Did you have a run-in with Mattie?"

Thank God Mattie hadn't made good on her threat . . . yet. But he'd better tell Eden what had happened in case she did.

"I guess you could call it that. She not only didn't believe me when I told her what Varden did, but she accused Cade of being the one who'd attacked Willa."

Eden drew in her breath, her eyes widening. "Oh, my God! Did Hollis believe that, too?"

"Who knows? He went along with whatever Mattie said."

"Yes, he would. And Willa? How is she?"

Jesse let out his breath in a sigh. "She ran off into the woods right in the middle of everything. I didn't try to find her. I knew I probably couldn't."

Eden bit her lip. "She didn't come here. Oh, I hate for her to be treated that way! I *wish* there were some way I could get her away from them!"

"I've been thinking the same thing all day," Jesse said grimly. "But I don't suppose there is."

"No. They're her parents. They have rights."

"You know Mattie better than I do. What do you think she'll do? She threatened to come here and see if you and Cade were actually hurt."

Eden looked physically sick. "She usually flies off the handle, then calms down. She's a good neighbor, will help anyone, unless she decides you're her enemy. According to Willa, she's at odds with at least half her kinfolk here on the ridge most of the time."

"I feel sorry for the girl, but I won't let Mattie come over here and browbeat Cade."

"Neither will I," Eden said quickly. "I can't imagine what made her say that. She's not usually that unreasonable."

"I still think I should go after Varden and half kill him," Jesse said, his voice hard.

She sucked in her breath. "No!" she said quickly. "You'd never be able to find him. And even if you did—"

"He might kill me instead?" Jesse asked, his voice still hard. "I don't think so." He glanced at her, saw her widened eyes. He took in a breath, let it out. "Don't worry. I'm not going to do that. But we do have to be prepared for anything Varden might do."

Eden gave him a quick look. He'd said "we" as if he planned to be around for any eventuality. As if he was sure she planned to let the two of them stay. She felt her heart begin beating faster. She might as well get this over with.

"Jesse, of course Cade won't be able to travel for a while. But you know your two weeks are up today."

Had he really expected her to change her mind? Jesse asked himself. No matter how much she needed him to stay? And even after today's events? No, deep inside, he guessed he hadn't. So he'd be as direct as her.

"I'm not leaving, Eden," he said flatly. "And I don't mean until Cade is all right. We're staying until after your baby is born."

"You can't," she said quickly. "I've already made up my mind—"

"Yes, I remember that statement," Jesse interrupted, his temper, not long banked, beginning to rise again. It had been a long, disturbing day. His eyes hard, he challenged her.

"After what happened today, no power on earth will make me leave you and Hannah alone with Varden still loose. If you kick us out of the barn, we'll set up a tent in the woods. I doubt Sheriff Taylor would bother to come up and run us in for trespassing."

For a long moment their gazes held. Eden's dropped first. He was as determined to stay as she was to have him leave. She had no doubt whatever that he meant every word he'd said.

He *would* put a tent in the woods if she made him leave the barn. And he was right—Sheriff Taylor would probably laugh in her face if she lodged a trespassing complaint. Not that she'd consider such a thing after all Jesse and Cade had done for her and Hannah. She might as well give in gracefully.

"All right. You and Cade may stay—for a while."

Jesse's eyes narrowed. "Until after your baby is born," he said firmly. "I don't intend to argue about this anymore."

She swallowed, then finally nodded. "Until after the baby's born."

Relief went through him. He'd been ready to get their things from the barn tonight and head for the woods, if necessary, to prove to Eden that he meant what he said. He was surprised she'd given in so easily. But maybe . . .

"You're afraid of Varden, aren't you?" he asked her.

It had been a long, bad day for Eden, too. Toby's attack had left her shaky and half-sick. And after two weeks of not doing the outside chores, she'd been exhausted when she'd finished them this evening.

"Of course I'm afraid of him!" she flared. "Any sane person would be!"

She still stood erect and tall, but Jesse saw how she trembled with weariness.

She was so beautiful.

And desirable.

The moonlight cast shadows on her face, her blue eyes flashed fire at him. He moved a step closer to her. "Then why do you want me to leave?"

His voice had gone so soft, so suddenly. A frisson moved down her spine. She backed up a few steps. How could she tell him the true reason she wanted him gone without betraying how she felt?

Jesse could barely make out her features, now that she'd moved under the walnut tree's spreading branches. But he recognized what her retreat meant.

She was as intensely aware of him as he was of her. He stepped forward again.

"Why, Eden?" he repeated, his voice even softer.

Again she retreated, until she was against the tree's huge old trunk. It was dark under here and Jesse was only a darker shadow, but she saw him move again, come closer. She pressed her lips together, angry at herself for retreating.

She *wouldn't* turn and flee into the cabin like some frightened schoolgirl! She'd tell him the truth. Once and for all, they'd face this and settle it.

"You know why as well as I do! There—there's something between us that shouldn't be. I don't know what it is. But we can't let it continue. It's not right!"

From the tree, a mockingbird began singing a night song. Somewhere across the clearing, another one joined in. The harmony was achingly beautiful. An evening breeze drifted under the tree, bringing with it a tantalizing scent of honeysuckle.

Jesse stood still as a stone, remembering the day he'd left here to go back to Georgia. Remembering the smell of honeysuckle. The unforgettable kiss they'd exchanged.

He couldn't believe what she'd just said. She'd acknowledged she, too, felt the compelling force between them ... admitted that was the real reason she didn't want him here.

"Eden," he breathed, coming to life and moving a step closer to her.

"No!" she said frantically. "Don't come any closer. If—if you're going to stay here, then we'll have to keep away from each other. Not be alone—ever."

In his mind, he knew all too well she was right. But his body was giving him a different message: it urged him to take her into his arms.

"How do you know what we feel is wrong?" he asked her, his voice husky. "Maybe it's not wrong at all."

He heard her indrawn breath.

"We don't even like each other! You think I'm a cold Yankee, and I—"

Jesse reached the tree. He put his hands on the rough trunk on either side of Eden's face, hemming her in. "Oh, no," he murmured, close to her ear. "I don't think you're cold. I don't think that at all."

His warm breath tickled her ear. She shivered. He was so close she could feel his body heat in the cool evening air. She knew she should forget about her dignity and leave, get away from him, go back to the cabin.

Instead, she lifted her face to the shadowy outline of his.

Slowly he lowered his head. When his lips finally touched hers, he felt her shiver again. But she didn't try to move away. His mouth brushed over hers, lightly at first. Then, as her lips parted a little, he shivered, too, deepening the kiss.

Eden kissed him back, almost desperately. Oh, how she wanted this, no matter how often she'd denied it. She lifted a hand to his shadowy face, finding his cheek and caressing it.

Jesse drew in his breath at her touch. "You are so sweet," he whispered as their mouths explored each other. "So very sweet."

His hands left the tree trunk, moving to her shoulders, drawing her close to him. Her full breasts pressed against his chest, and her rounded stomach against his.

Her rounded stomach. Big with another man's child.

The husband who would be with her now, if not for decisions Jesse had made . . .

She hadn't mentioned the most compelling reason they could never be together.

Jesse felt his heated body cooling. His mouth left hers, his hands dropped from her shoulders, and he moved back, away from her. "I shouldn't have done that," he said, his voice stiff.

Eden slowly came out of the sensual spell that had held her. She couldn't see Jesse, but she could feel his complete withdrawal. His sudden coolness. Hurt mingled with relief and consternation. Oh, she'd been right to try to prevent him from staying. She'd known this would happen.

"This is what I was talking about," she answered, her voice as stiff as his. "We can't let it happen again!"

"No, we can't," Jesse agreed gravely. "Come on, let's go back to the cabin. I want to see how Cade's doing."

They walked back to the cabin in silence, both of them careful to stay far enough away from each other that not even their clothes brushed. Jesse saw shadowy movements of Eden's hands as she patted at her hair, adjusted her dress.

Both Cade and Hannah were awake when they got inside. Cade sat on the edge of the bed, his head down. He looked up when they entered, relief coming over his face. "Where have you two been?" he asked.

"Just outside." Eden smiled at him, feeling red creeping up her neck and into her face. She hurried to Hannah's bed. "How are you feeling, Mother Clayborne?" she asked.

Hannah looked at her, then at Jesse, then managed a weak smile. "Tolerable, honey. Did you give Jesse his supper?"

She'd forgotten all about that! Eden turned to him. "I'm sorry. I kept your supper warm on the back of the stove." She carefully kept her eyes from meeting his.

"Thanks," he said.

"I don't guess ye had any luck with that Taylor feller," Hannah said.

"No," Jesse said, feeling his anger rise again. "I didn't. But

Cade and I are going to stay here until after the baby's born," he said firmly, just in case Eden had decided to renege on her promise after the kiss they'd exchanged.

Hannah's faded blue eyes lit up. "Oh, that's jist th' best news I ever heared!"

Jesse turned to Cade. His cousin's eyes were wide with surprise. "I'm going to eat, and then it's time we got settled down in the barn for tonight."

Eden set a plate of food on the table. She looked up at him, still not quite meeting his eyes. "Cade is going to stay in here for a few days," she said firmly. "I'll sleep in the loft."

"I can't take your bed, Miss Eden!" Cade protested.

"Yes, you can," she said, her voice still very firm. "And you will. I don't want to hear anything else about it."

Jesse decided that since she'd given in on the important issue between them, he wouldn't argue with her about this. He didn't like for her to climb the ladder to the loft bed, but it would be a good idea for Cade to stay in here for a while.

He sat down at the table and picked up his fork. Even though he hadn't had dinner, either, he wasn't hungry. His mind and body were in a turmoil after what had happened outside. But he had to eat. Everyone expected him to. Well, maybe not Eden, he amended.

Yes, they'd have to make sure they weren't alone together. Because every time they were, they couldn't seem to stay out of each other's arms.

There was, indeed, something between them. Something as ancient and powerful as time itself.

But, as Eden had said, it wasn't right.

And it never could be.

Chapter Seventeen

"Right hot day, ain't it?"

Darcy's voice came out of nowhere, startling Eden. She dropped a juicy red tomato on the ground. It broke open, splattering seeds and juice. Eden frowned at the waste.

Pushing a hand against the garden earth for leverage, she rose from her crouching position and warily faced him. She certainly didn't expect to see Darcy after what had happened between Mattie and Jesse yesterday.

His usual uncertain smile was on his face, but that was all.

"Yes, it is hot," Eden answered, still waiting cautiously to find out why he was here.

"Thought I might do some hay cuttin' fer you, but I see someone else done beat me to it." He waved a hand at a lower field where Jesse wielded the big scythe.

He apparently didn't even want to use Jesse's name, even though she was certain he hadn't forgotten it. She took a deep breath and let it out. She might as well tell him now and get it over with.

"Yes. Mr. Bainbridge is helping me out with the chores until after the baby's born."

Darcy's pale blue eyes widened. "You mean he's a-goin' to stay here all that time?"

"It's only six weeks now," Eden said crisply. "But yes, he is. Along with his cousin, of course."

Darcy swallowed, his Adam's apple bobbing up and down. "Well, uh, is there anythin' else you need done?"

Eden looked around as if seeing the homestead for the first time. Jesse and Cade had done a lot of work in a short while. And Jesse wasn't letting Cade's temporary inability to help slow him down. The garden was freshly weeded—the corn patch, too. Jesse had started cutting wood for the winter to come.

The winter to come. She didn't want to think about that cold, fearsome time.

She shook her head, giving him a small smile. "I don't believe so." Now, go on back home and leave me alone, she told him silently.

Darcy turned and glanced toward the cabin, a little nervously, Eden thought. Turning back, he shifted from one foot to the other, but made no move to leave. Or to let her know why he was here.

Eden sighed. Darcy wasn't a talker. Having to say more than a dozen words at a time about did him in. She'd have to help him along, she guessed. "Was there something else?"

He nodded, then looked even more ill-at-ease. "Wal, yes, thar was somethin' I been aimin' to talk to you 'bout."

She tensed, belatedly wondering if Mattie had sent him over here to inspect her and Cade, as she'd threatened to do herself. To see if they'd actually been hurt.

That idea mightily annoyed her. She straightened, turning her right cheek, bruised and welted, toward him. "My face is better," she said, her voice cool, "but you can see Toby hit me pretty hard."

Darcy swallowed again, looking as if he wished the earth would rise up and swallow him. "I ain't a-doubtin' yore word a bit on that," he said earnestly. "Mam gits upset real easy. But that ain't . . ." He hesitated again.

Relief replaced her irritation. Darcy meant well, she supposed. "What is it, Darcy?" she asked, as patiently as possible.

He glanced all about him, as if eager to look anywhere but at her, then looked down at his feet, pushing one brogan-clad foot into the soft earth of the garden.

Eden's relief began to edge into impatience. "Darcy, I have to finish gathering these vegetables."

His narrow chest rose and fell. Finally, he turned back around. He swallowed again, a pleading expression in his eyes. "Eden, would you take me fer yore man?" he asked, his words tumbling over themselves in his hurry to get them said.

She stared at him for a moment, not understanding what he meant. When she did, her heart sank. He was proposing to her! Oh, Lord. She'd known this moment was coming, but she hadn't expected it to happen now, out in her sunny garden patch!

Her first instinct was to blurt out "no" as fast and emphatically as she could say the word, but she stopped herself. She didn't dislike Darcy, had no wish to hurt his feelings or his masculine pride. She'd have to soften her refusal, break it to him gently, she decided, forcing a smile.

"Darcy, let's walk to the spring." She glanced down at her abandoned basket, her half-picked vegetables for the noon meal. That would have to wait a while.

His eyes brightened and he smiled back. "Why, I reckon that's a right nice idea."

At once Eden realized the mistake she'd made. Now he'd think she planned to accept him, but wanted a more private place. And there was no way out, since she was the one who'd suggested this.

Together they walked out of the garden and onto the path leading to the spring.

Jesse, catching a blur of movement in his peripheral vision, let the scythe finish its swing, then rested it on the ground while he turned for a full look. His hand clenched the smooth wooden handle.

Eden walked toward the spring, Darcy beside her.

Why in hell was she doing that? He flung down the scythe and took a couple of long strides toward the pair before realizing what he was doing. With an effort he checked himself and stood scowling after them. It wasn't any of his business who Eden walked with.

He had no claim on her. Never would have.

So why did he want to race after them, catch up with Darcy and knock him to the ground?

Jesse stood until they disappeared from view, into the trees by the spring, battling with his anger and another feeling he didn't want to recognize.

But as he was an honest man, he was forced to. That raging emotion he felt was jealousy. Jealousy? Why in God's name should he feel that about Eden? True, he was strongly drawn to her physically. Hell, he was *obsessed* with her. A hundred times today he'd relived that achingly bittersweet kiss they'd shared under the walnut tree.

He accepted the fact that he wanted her and that she wanted him. He also accepted that they'd never have each other. Why should he care that she was with Darcy? Why should jealousy rage through him?

Because in order to feel that emotion you had to feel more than passion and desire, no matter how strong.

You had to feel love.

Appalled, he instantly tried to deny that conclusion. Oh, no, Jesus, no! He didn't love that stubborn Yankee woman! He wanted her as she wanted him. He felt guilt because of her husband's death. He felt responsible for her and Hannah's welfare. That's all he felt.

It *had* to be all.

Because, as he'd so often told himself, and as Eden had made clear yesterday evening, a relationship between them was impossible. And always would be.

Eden sat down on the bench by the spring, as far to the end as she could get, remembering when she'd sat here with Jesse, and worried about being too close to him.

She was worrying about the same thing now, she thought, as Darcy sat down gingerly beside her. But her reasons for the concern were entirely different.

He cast her an adoring look and inched a little closer.

Eden closed her eyes, chiding herself again for this stupidly wrong move of coming here. She tried to gather strength for what she must do. Darcy said not a word, but his eager face told her how he felt. What his expectations were. He thought she was going to accept him.

Finally, she made herself face him with a forced smile. "Darcy," she began, "I always hope to count you as a good friend and neighbor, but—" she hesitated, then hurried on. "I can't marry you."

He stared at her, all his happy expectations dashed, his long face visibly drooping at her words. "Why cain't you?" he asked mournfully.

"Because I don't love you," Eden said, as gently and patiently as she could manage.

Instantly his eager look returned. "Oh, if that's all that's a-botherin' you, don't worry none."

With a sudden burst of bravado, he reached for her hand, covering it with his own and squeezing. "I don't 'spect you to keer fer me now, bein' as how Alston's only been gone fer a leetle while."

Eden froze, dismayed at his reaction, his words, his sudden unexpected move. She couldn't stand the feel of his hand on hers! She pulled her hand out from under his and quickly stood up.

"I can *never* marry you, Darcy. And I don't want to talk about it again."

He stood, too, all his awkwardness back. "I didn't noways mean to git you all lathered," he said humbly.

At once, her heart softened. Darcy was good-hearted and decent. She hadn't wanted to sound cold and hard. "Darcy, you don't understand, it's—"

"Mam was wrong," he went on, not looking at her now, not even seeming to hear her. "She told me if I didn't git over here and ask you to marry up with me, then that Jesse feller would beat my time. Looks like he has."

Eden's softened feelings evaporated, embarrassed anger replacing them. She should have known this was all Mattie's idea. Darcy didn't have the gumption to do it on his own. It was a wonder he didn't bring his mother along to coach him.

As for the rest of what Darcy had said, she hastily pushed that aside. What a ridiculous idea that Jesse would ever ask her to marry him!

She drew herself up as straight as she could. "I have to get back to the garden," she said coolly. "I need to finish picking vegetables and cook dinner." She turned and walked away. In a moment, Darcy was beside her.

She wouldn't say another word to him, she decided, her anger still simmering. Catching a blur of movement out of the corner of her eye, she turned toward the field where Jesse worked.

He wielded the scythe fast and furiously, as if he were in some kind of a race, she saw, frowning. It was too hot to be working like that. He'd taken off his shirt, and even from this distance his bronzed back gleamed in the sun.

And although she knew there could never be anything between the two of them, something inside her ached with longing. She wanted to hurry across the fields, walk up behind him, put her arms around his lean waist, his taut belly. Then he'd throw down his scythe, turn, pull her into his arms, and kiss her long and deeply, as he had last night . . .

Appalled, Eden turned off those thoughts, trying to hurry her pace. It seemed to take forever, with Darcy walking silently beside her, before she reached the garden again.

She turned to face him. "Goodbye, Darcy," she said firmly. Normally, she'd tell him to give her regards to his family, but not today. She was furious at the entire Freeman clan—except Willa, of course. She wouldn't care if she never saw any of them but the girl again.

He looked solemnly at her, blinking. "Are ye shore you won't change yore mind?" he asked hesitantly. "I'd try to be a good man to you."

"I'm sure, Darcy," she answered, her voice softening a little again.

He nodded, apparently accepting this as final. "Goodbye, Eden. Mam is shore goin' to take on when I tell her."

Eden's eyes flashed. She had no doubt with Mattie pushing

him every step of the way, he'd eventually find a wife. Whether he wanted one or not. "That's really a shame, isn't it?" she said, able to hide her irritation no longer.

Darcy turned and left without another word. Eden looked after him for a minute, then went back inside the garden. She jerked a tomato off a vine, plopped it in her basket, then another, and moved on to the squash.

And all the while she was very conscious that behind her, in the far field, Jesse still swung his heavy scythe. Or did he? Had he, perhaps, stopped? Was he looking at her as she'd looked at him a few minutes ago?

"Don't be such a fool," she muttered to herself. She quickly finished gathering the vegetables and left the garden, not looking back.

When she reached the clothesline, she took down the white cloth pinned to the line and tied it to the end of the pole. It fluttered in the tiny breeze, the signal to Jesse to come in for dinner. The meal wasn't ready yet, but he'd done enough work for one morning. He needed a little rest before he ate.

Cade sat in one of the porch rockers, his young face unsmiling. He wasn't alone. Willa sat beside him.

Surprise swept over Eden. Willa, here today? After the terrible things Mattie had said to Jesse about Cade yesterday? She'd have thought Willa would be far too humiliated to face Cade this soon.

The girl, who'd been saying something to Cade in a low tone, looked up as Eden approached. Her face broke into a warm smile.

"I was goin' to help you in the garden, but when I walked out there, you was—were gone. Then, jist now I saw Darcy a-walkin' home like he'd lost his favoritist hound dog."

Eden smiled back, amused at Willa's colorful description, and surprised and relieved at the girl's tone. She sounded as if nothing at all had happened yesterday. Eden tried to think how to answer without revealing what had gone on at the spring, finally deciding to ignore everything Willa had said concerning Darcy.

"That's all right, Willa," she said instead. "I didn't have that much to do."

Willa half rose. "Do you want me to help fix dinner?"

"No. Go ahead and talk to Cade. Can you stay for the meal?"

Willa bit her lip, then shook her head. "No, I better git on back home in a little while. Mam's kindly upset today. But I had to come and see how you and Cade were doin'."

Her head turned away from Cade, she gave Eden a pleading look.

Eden gazed at her, forgetting her own troubles. Now she understood. Willa was silently asking her not to tell Cade of what her mother had accused him. As if she would! Eden smiled at her reassuringly and nodded. "Are you all right, Willa?"

The girl's relief was painfully evident. She threw a glance at Cade. The boy gazed straight ahead of him, his face totally expressionless. "I'm fine, Miz Eden. Don't you worry 'bout me."

Was Willa only pretending because she didn't want Cade to feel any more guilt at what he perceived as his lack of manly courage yesterday? Eden didn't know, but she'd try to talk to Willa alone as soon as possible.

Eden hesitated, then decided no matter how much unneeded blame Cade was heaping on his own shoulders, she wouldn't act unconcerned about his injuries.

"Do your ribs hurt much today, Cade?"

He shook his head, not turning it toward her. "I'm fine," he said shortly.

"I'll put another poultice on after dinner."

Cade jumped up from the chair so suddenly the rockers moved violently back and forth, and the chair back hit the cabin wall with a thump. He winced, and Eden knew the movement had caused him pain.

"I'm all right!" He glared at Eden. "Don't keep acting like I need all this babying! I didn't do anything to deserve it!"

"What is goin' on out thar, Eden?" Hannah's anxious voice came from inside the cabin. "Is somethin' wrong?"

"No, Mother Clayborne, everything's all right," Eden called. She turned back to Cade and gave him a firm, straight look.

"You did fine yesterday," she said, her voice pitched low so that Hannah couldn't hear. "But I know you're not going to believe me for a while. So for now, all I'm asking is that you remember Mrs. Clayborne is a sick woman and try not to do anything to get her upset."

Cade's angry-at-himself expression changed into an abashed look. "I'm sorry," he mumbled. "I'm going for a walk."

He turned and went down the porch steps, carefully now, Eden was relieved to see. She knew he shouldn't be walking yet, but she also knew she'd never be able to convince him of that.

"Wait, Cade, I'll go with you." Willa threw an apologetic smile at Eden and went after the boy.

Eden took her basket of vegetables inside the cabin. Hannah sat propped up in bed as Eden had left her, but her knitting was cast aside. She still looked pale, as she had yesterday. She hadn't eaten much breakfast, either.

"Well, are you ready for a big dinner?" Eden set the basket down on the table, forcing her voice to sound cheerful.

Hannah looked at her, then her eyes filled with tears. "Oh, ever'time I look at yore pore face, I jist wish that varmint would fall in a holler and never git out!"

Eden blinked in surprise at Hannah's vehement language. Her mother-in-law was normally the gentlest of souls. Eden went over to the bed and gave Hannah a hug, then kissed her wrinkled cheek.

"I'm perfectly all right. All I have are a few bruises."

Hannah found her handkerchief under a pillow and wiped her eyes. "I jist keep thinkin' what are we a-goin' to do when Jesse leaves? We'll be here all by ourselves and with a new leetle babe to worry 'bout."

"We'll be *fine*," Eden said, making her voice very positive, even though Hannah's words had conjured up visions she didn't want to dwell on. "Haven't we managed all right so far?"

Hannah's look was steady on hers. Finally, she shook her white head. "No, we ain't," she said, flatly. "You might as well stop makin' out like we could have done without Jesse."

"Of course we could," Eden said, just as firmly. "I admit it's nice to have Jesse and Cade do the heavy work, but I'd have managed. Lots of other women do. And have done."

"Most of them other women have got some kind of kinfolk to hep out," Hannah insisted. "We ain't got nobody."

Her bleak words sent a cold shiver down Eden's back. She forced another smile as she retreated to the table and began sorting vegetables. "We have each other."

But this time Hannah wasn't going to be lulled with Eden's comforting words.

"You know I love you like you was my own gal. But that ain't enough. Eden, you need to write yore folks and tell them about the babe. It ain't right not to tell them. They need you, and you shore are a-goin' to need them."

Eden jerked her head up and stared at her mother-in-law. These feelings must have been with Hannah for a while, but never before had she voiced them. A cold chill went over her. Why was Hannah saying this now? Did she think she wouldn't be around much longer? Wasn't she getting any better, after all?

Or had Toby's attack brought it on? Made her see how vulnerable they were to such things? For a moment she considered telling Hannah she'd thought about writing her parents for weeks now, but she couldn't bring herself to do it.

They were the ones who'd broken with her, not the other way around.

Stubborn determination in her old face, Hannah still held her gaze. "It ain't right, Eden," she repeated.

Eden couldn't seem to look away, until a sudden noise from the doorway made her turn her head that way.

Jesse stood on the threshold. He'd put his shirt back on, and his tawny hair glistened wetly. He must have washed up on the porch and she and Hannah had been so intent on their own problems, she hadn't heard him.

Had he heard what *they'd* said? She hoped not. Whatever she decided to do about her parents, she had to make the decision alone. She didn't want Hannah—and possibly Jesse— trying to talk her into it.

"I see dinner's not ready yet," Jesse said, looking at Eden. "I'll wait on the porch." He gave Hannah a smile. "How are you doing, Mrs. Clayborne?"

Hannah smiled back, but it was a feeble effort. "I reckon I've done better many a day."

"Yesterday was hard on everyone," Jesse said. "We all need to forget it."

There was something strange in his husky voice, Eden realized. Something almost angry and accusing in his golden eyes as they swept over her. She watched, puzzled, as he gave Hannah another smile and went back out on the porch.

A new thought occurred to her. Had he seen her and Darcy walk to the spring together? It certainly was possible, even probable. Could that be bothering him?

Last night, Jesse had admitted he was physically drawn to her, as she was to him. He'd agreed with her that they should make sure they weren't alone together any more. But neither of them had admitted to any stronger feelings. Of course they hadn't, because they didn't have any.

Are you so sure of that? Something inside her asked. Yes! she answered, pushing down a panicky feeling that her continued denials of any serious feelings for Jesse were becoming desperate attempts to deny the truth.

Eden made up the fire, then went ahead with dinner preparations. Glancing across at Hannah to find the older woman's eyes again closed, she frowned. She'd talk to Cade, see if he wouldn't coax Hannah into telling a story or two this evening. That would be good for both of them.

If Cade was thinking about Hannah, he wouldn't be brooding over his self-perceived failures. Maybe she also should talk to Hannah. If Hannah was trying to lift Cade's spirits, she'd not be fretting over her own troubles.

And if *she* kept on with her daily tasks, Eden told herself, even more firmly, concentrating on getting through the days until the baby arrived, then she'd be all right, too.

She'd thought if she stayed away from Jesse, then this arrangement would have a chance of succeeding for these few weeks. And she could do that. It wouldn't be all that hard not to be alone with him. Especially since he seemed prepared to cooperate with her.

But she hadn't taken into consideration her wayward thoughts—and feelings. Those weren't going to be so easy to ignore, push aside. She firmed her resolve. Not easy, maybe, but she'd do it. Somehow, she'd find a way to get through these next few weeks until the baby was born.

And Jesse left.

She bit her lip to stop the bitter rush of sorrow and loss that swept over her at that thought.

This time, oh, yes, this time when he left it *would* be for good and all.

Chapter Eighteen

"What happens if it rains?" Jesse looked at Eden over his side of the bedsheet they were spreading on a sunwashed section of the side yard, to lay peaches on to dry for the winter.

He burned to ask what had gone on between her and Darcy yesterday. It's none of your business, he told himself for the dozenth time. None whatsoever.

He tried to ignore how the sun shot glints off Eden's thick black braid, how his heart beat faster because of her nearness. He tried not to remember how her soft mouth had felt pressed against his own.

Eden smiled and shrugged. She tugged at her side of the sheet until it was smooth, forcing down her awareness of him. Thank God, he was at least wearing a shirt, but he'd rolled up the sleeves, so that his golden-tanned arms were exposed. Those strong arms had held her not long ago. That well-shaped mouth had kissed her.

And a hundred times since that had happened, she'd told herself she wouldn't think about those magical moments under the walnut tree.

"Today, we watch for clouds and put everything on the porch if it looks like rain. Tonight, we bring it inside, and pray for hot sunshine tomorrow and in the next few days."

Even though she knew she shouldn't, she enjoyed Jesse's help. She'd asked him to pick some of the early peaches this morning, not even attempting it herself. Mainly because she knew he'd be there to intercept her the instant she propped the ladder against the old tree.

"Now what?" Jesse asked.

Eden raised her brows. "Do you mean you don't know how this is done? I thought you knew everything about farm life."

Her voice was light, almost teasing. Jesse knew he should be relieved. If they were going to spend the next six weeks in close proximity, that was certainly the tack to take. And if he could stop wondering what she and Darcy were talking about yesterday, maybe he could reciprocate.

Damn it, he would anyway! "Terrible thing for me to admit, isn't it?" he agreed, giving her a friendly smile. "I'm sure we dried a lot of foods, but I never got much involved with household things."

"It's very simple. We put the peaches on the sheet and let the sun do its work. I imagine your family didn't use such a primitive method."

Eden sat down on the grass, settling the skirts of her brown calico print dress around her. She lifted a handful of peach halves out of the bucket next to her and arranged them on the sheet.

"I don't remember." Jesse, after a glance to see how she was placing the fruit, did the same with his bucket of peaches. He forced his eyes away from the movements of her slender tanned hands.

"I'm still surprised you know so much about farm life. Were Georgia plantation owners the only ones who raised their sons that way?"

He gave her a quick glance. She sounded genuinely interested. "I'm afraid I don't know that, either."

"Since you've been here and we've talked, I realize I know very little about the South. Or southern plantations. When I was growing up in Connecticut, all these issues seemed so simple." Eden kept her eyes on her work. "Slavery was wrong, the plantation system was wrong, the entire *South* was wrong. After I came here to the ridge, saw these hill men going off to fight a war most of them didn't understand or sympathize with, I felt that way even more strongly."

"And you no longer do?" Jesse asked. He realized he was holding his breath, waiting for her reply. Why was it that important?

She glanced over at him, her deep blue eyes, framed with those fringes of thick black lashes, steady and frank on his. Finally, she shook her head.

"No, I don't suppose so. I never knew or talked with a plantation owner before I met you. You're not at all like my mental image of the aristocratic southerner."

Jesse stared at her. "I guess you meant that as a compliment."

Eden nodded. "Yes." His eyes revealed his surprise at her words. She felt better after this admission. She'd mulled over all these things since she and Jesse had talked in the barnyard the day he and Cade were making shakes.

"I know I told you I don't often change my mind once it's made up. But I think I'm fair-minded. If I see I've been wrong, I can admit it."

"So can I. And I must concede I'm also mightily impressed with your abilities. You're not at all like I'd pictured Yankee women. Could you do all these things when you moved here from Connecticut?"

Eden laughed at the absurdity of that idea. Low, throaty laughter.

Jesse stared at her. "That's the first time I've ever heard you laugh."

Surprise went over her face, then she lifted out another handful of peach halves and gave him a quick glance. "Maybe I could say the same thing about you."

He shook his head. "No, I've laughed at Hannah's stories."

"Yes," she said again, remembering his laughter. Of course, she'd smiled, along with Jesse and Cade. But a real laugh, such as that one she'd just uttered? Maybe she hadn't. The thought startled her.

"You should do it more often. You have a wonderful laugh." He shouldn't have said that, he knew at once, hearing the warm, almost caressing tone of his voice.

Eden took a quick breath, her amusement fading. She forced

herself not to glance at him. There had been something disturbing in the way he'd made that last remark. She didn't reply to it.

"Well?" he asked, with an effort again making his voice bland. "You didn't answer my question."

"No, I couldn't do any of these things when we moved here. Hannah taught me everything. I grew up in a town." Now, he'd no doubt ask her about the kind of life she lived growing up. About her parents. She didn't want to talk about them.

"No one would ever know it. You're very good at all these farm chores."

Relief filled her, and to keep the conversation on this casual level, she said, her head lowered, "I'll probably forget how to do them, with you and Cade taking everything over for all these weeks."

She managed to keep her voice as bland as his had been, but anxiety, never far from the surface, seized her as she inadvertently gave voice to worries haunting her night and day.

Frowning, Jesse looked at her bent head. That pose made her look so vulnerable.

She *was* vulnerable.

He tried not to think about what would happen when he and Cade left, because frustration tied him in knots whenever he did. How could he leave her and Hannah alone on this ridge with no help, no protection?

"Eden." He paused, knowing he should stay out of this. But he also knew he wouldn't. He'd do anything within his power to try to improve the situation. "This isn't any of my affair, but are you planning to tell your parents about the baby?"

Her hands full of peaches, Eden jerked her head up and stared at him. Either he remembered what she'd told him about her parents when he left the first time, or he'd overheard her and Hannah yesterday. Whatever, he'd been unable to resist talking about it, after all.

"You're right, it *isn't* your affair."

Eden laid the handful of peaches down, lifted another, the last, from the bucket, quickly arranged them, and got to her feet. "It's a good thing we locked the geese up for the time being," she said. "Can you imagine what they'd do to these?"

She'd tried to make her words sound offhanded, but Jesse heard shaky undertones that she hadn't been able to prevent. He, too, spread the rest of his fruit on the sheet and stood.

And she was going to ignore his question. All right, he'd started this, he'd push a little more. He didn't want them back to coldness or hostility, but it was a risk he must take if it might force her into making this decision.

"Are you planning to tell them?" he persisted. "You'll badly need their help. This work has been hard enough on you, but with a baby to tend it will be twice as hard."

Eden picked up her pail without answering, trying to calm her suddenly chaotic emotions. First Hannah, now Jesse.

"I'm well aware how much work there'll be. Do you think my parents would *move* here to help me? Leave me alone," she said, her voice trembling. "This is something I have to decide on my own." She turned and walked back to the porch, where more peaches waited their turn to be washed and halved.

His jaw tightening, Jesse looked at her straight back, the lovely curve of her neck. He'd pushed enough—and gotten nowhere. He'd leave it alone for now.

Settling down beside her in a rocker, he picked up a peach, sliced it in half, then pried out and discarded the pit. Its sweet, summery fragrance rose to his nostrils and the thick juice ran down his hands. From inside the cabin, he heard Hannah's voice, a little weaker and more shaky than it had been up until the incident with Toby. In a moment, Cade's low chuckle followed.

"I'm glad Cade's laughing again," he said, hoping his insistence a few moments ago hadn't driven her back inside her hard shell.

"So am I," she answered in a moment, relaxing a little. She'd forget what Jesse had said, let it go, because six weeks was a long time. She didn't want to spend those weeks arguing with him. She put the two halves of the peach in her empty pail and picked up another.

"They're good for each other," Jesse said in a moment. "While Cade's listening to Hannah's stories, he's not worrying about how he thinks he failed you and Willa. And when Hannah's trying to entertain him, she's not fretting."

A surprised, warm feeling spread through Eden at his words. He had picked up so quickly on her own thoughts, her own wishes. "Yes," she agreed, her voice soft. "That's what I was hoping."

She smiled at him, the pleasant feelings increasing. Despite their near-argument, it felt nice to be sitting here with Jesse. She and Alston had never done anything like this together. He'd spent long hours after the school days were over grading papers, planning the next day's classes.

Of course, he *had* recited poetry to her. And at eighteen, she'd thought it terribly romantic to lie with her head in Alston's lap, listening to his dreamy voice intoning Byron or Shelley . . .

But this was how she imagined a happily married couple might spend time together, contentedly sharing some simple, homey task . . .

Eden's hands stilled on her knife. Her smile faded and she quickly looked down at her work. What on earth had made her think something so preposterous? She felt red stain her cheeks and hoped Jesse wouldn't notice.

The smile Jesse had given Eden in return also faded as he looked at her suddenly lowered head. He felt bereft. For an instant he'd felt so close to her, happiness springing up inside him. But whatever its cause, such a moment between them couldn't last.

They were too different in every way. She was a Yankee in her thinking, and she still resented him and all the planter class for the war just ended. And he still felt bitterness against the North for the destruction they'd brought to his homeland.

Strongest of all, their mutual feelings of guilt for Clayborne's death still haunted them, maybe always would.

As he went over the litany of obstacles between them, his mind came to a halt.

Was he so sure about all of them? Hadn't Eden just admitted she'd changed her mind about many of her preconceived ideas concerning the South?

And since he'd been on the ridge, away from the horrible destruction the war had wrought, he'd begun to heal, he realized, surprised. Spending his days doing simple physical tasks had sped that process along. The bitterness that had been a part of him for so long had begun to lessen, too.

He looked over at Eden again. Her head still turned away from him, her slim fingers reached for another peach and quickly cut it in half, popped the seed out, then dropped it into the fast-filling bucket.

Jesse forced his gaze to leave the high-cheekboned beauty of her face and drop lower, to her pregnant body. Maybe he was right about the other things—perhaps their North-South differences had been more or less resolved . . . or could be in time.

But Eden's love for her dead husband was tied inextricably to the guilt she felt for Clayborne's death. And his own guilt was still strong. No amount of rational discussion or argument could remove this barrier. It might as well be made of stone. Only the passage of time had a chance of breaking it down.

Time was what he didn't have much of.

Six weeks.

He could probably stretch that into a few more after Eden's baby was born. But that was all.

And he still didn't know what she and Darcy had been talking about yesterday. Why she'd taken that walk with him. He'd never know, either, if he didn't ask her. Did he want to risk getting her upset again so soon?

No, he didn't. But he had to know.

"Why did you walk with Darcy to the spring yesterday?" he asked bluntly, still looking toward her.

Her head jerked up and she stared at him. So he *had* seen them. And was that why he'd so fiercely attacked the hay with the scythe? Obviously, something about that bothered him or he wouldn't be asking her this question.

"He proposed to me," she answered just as bluntly. "I wanted to make my refusal as gentle as possible, so I suggested we go there."

Relief swept over Jesse. At least, now when he had to leave, he wouldn't worry about her ending up marrying Darcy. Or would he?

"Was that a final refusal? Or do you think you'll reconsider later?"

Her mouth tightened. "It was definitely final." She gave him a cool look. "Not that it's any of your business."

"No," he agreed, smiling at her. "It isn't. I'm sorry." That was a lie. He wasn't a bit sorry he'd asked, for now he felt infinitely better.

Eden looked at him a moment longer, then nodded. "Let's just forget it." Her pail filled, she stood.

Jesse realized he held an unhalved peach in his hands and his own pail was only half full. He rose. "I'm not as fast as you. Let me carry that over, then I'll finish mine."

He lifted her pail and carried it to the sheet, Eden beside him. He loved the way she still managed to walk gracefully, how she held her proud head high. He loved the raven's wing gloss of her hair, the sapphire of her eyes. He loved everything about her.

Jesse finally stopped trying to fight admitting the realization that had come to him yesterday while he was cutting hay.

He loved *her*.

At noon dinner, Eden passed Cade the bowl of new potatoes and green beans, cooked with the last bit of bacon. "Eat all you want, there's plenty," she urged him. Cade's appetite had been poor since he'd been injured two days before.

Cade took the bowl, smiling at her. "That looks good," he said, giving himself a hearty portion, then handing the bowl to Jesse.

Willa's visit yesterday had done him good. Eden's gratified glance collided with Jesse's equally pleased gaze, then quickly moved away. She'd felt self-conscious with him ever since that moment of fantasy on the porch this morning.

Something seemed to have happened to him at that same time. Although they'd both tried to maintain the earlier casual atmosphere during the hour it had taken to finish the peaches, they hadn't succeeded very well. She'd felt tense and awkward, and Jesse had appeared to feel the same.

She lifted her head at the sound of the porch steps squeaking. That must be Willa, she thought, relieved. She'd been worried about the girl, hoping she'd come today.

But it wasn't Willa who loomed in the doorway a moment later. Mattie stood there, taking up almost the whole space. She gazed at the three people sitting at the table, then her eyes locked on Cade and her face hardened.

Eden's stomach knotted with tension. Oh, God, she hoped Mattie wasn't here to cause trouble.

"Good afternoon, Mattie," she said, forcing her voice to stay calm and even pleasant. "Won't you come in and eat with us?"

Mattie stood inside the doorway, folding her hands across her ample bosom. "I've done et, but I aim to talk with this young 'un," she said heavily, pointing at Cade.

"Why, Mattie, what in tarnation ails ye?" Hannah asked, her voice astonished. She laid the fork she held on her plate.

Mattie swung her head around to stare at Hannah. "Ain't nothin' ails me. It's my gal I'm a-wearied 'bout."

Hannah looked alarmed. She pushed her half-eaten tray of food away. "Willie? What's wrong with her?"

Mattie's lips pursed and she let out her breath in a whoosh. "I reckon you ort to ask *him,*" she said. Again she swung her head to stare at Cade.

Cade pushed back his chair and stood, his eyes wide and scared. "What are you talking about?" His young voice broke at the end. "What's wrong with Willa?"

Mattie's pale blue eyes narrowed. "You ort to know th' answer to thet," she said ominously.

This had gone far enough! Eden rose, too. "Cade, why don't you go outside for a few minutes," she said. "We'll get this straightened out."

Jesse got up, making way for Cade. "Go ahead," he urged the boy.

Cade stood his ground. "I'm not going anywhere until I find out what's happened to Willa!"

He was right, Eden realized belatedly. They could no longer protect him from Mattie's venomous tongue.

Now that Cade was standing, Mattie looked him over thoroughly. "You don't look like yore hurt bad to me. Don't see nothin' wrong with you."

"Yes, he is," Hannah said, her voice quavering. "That Toby Varden kicked him in the ribs. Might o' cracked one."

Mattie's mouth curved in a sly smile as she turned to Hannah again. "That's a right good yarn he's a-tellin', but it don't fool me none. My gal come home with her clothes tore offen her. That's what I know."

In spite of Jesse's account of what had happened at the Freemans' cabin, Eden couldn't believe Mattie was saying these things. "Mattie, I was there, too. Jesse told you the truth of what happened."

Ignoring Eden's words, Mattie uncrossed her arms and again pointed an accusing finger at Cade. "You taken advantage o' my gal and now you're a-goin' to have to marry up with her!"

The silence in the cabin after Mattie's announcement was total. All four of the other people stared at her in astounded disbelief.

"What in the world are you talking about?" Eden asked her. "I just told you I was there, too! Toby attacked all three of us!"

Again, Mattie ignored Eden's statements. She kept her eyes fixed on Cade, all the lines of her face hard. "Jist cause my Willie is a ridge gal, don't mean a fancy plantation owner's boy kin have his way with her."

Eden glanced quickly at Cade. The boy's face was drained of color, his eyes wide and staring.

She pressed her lips together. This had to be stopped. Eden walked across to the other woman. "Mattie, you go on home. You're upset. You don't know what you're saying."

"You're crazy!" Cade burst out, his voice breaking again. "I wouldn't ever do anything to hurt Willa!"

"Mrs. Freeman," Jesse said, his voice stern. "You'd better do as Mrs. Clayborne said."

Mattie planted a big hand on each hip. "I ain't a-goin' nowhere till that young 'un owns up to what he did and promises he'll do the right thing by my gal."

A sudden noise from Hannah's bed made everyone turn in that direction. Hannah flung her covers back, knocking the tray to the floor. She put her feet on the floor.

"Mattie Freeman, I've knowed ye fer nigh on fifty year. You've done a heap o' foolish things, but this piece o' foolishment does beat all."

Hannah put her hand on the bed to steady herself, then

straightened up. Her faded blue eyes flashed with anger. She glared at her neighbor.

"Ye know as well as I do that boy never done nothin' to Willie! If he hadn't o' come along, that Toby varmint might o' done what you're a-hintin' at. You should be down on yore knees a-thankin' Cade!"

Mattie's mouth hung open in amazement. "Hannie, you'd better git back in that bed," she said.

Eden hurried to Hannah's side, but the older woman ignored her. She still faced Mattie. "I ain't a-gittin' back in that bed till you tell Cade yo're sorry you said them mean things to him or git yoreself out o' my cabin!"

Mattie's mouth swung shut like a trap. "We been neighbors fer a long time, Hannie. I never thought I'd live to see the day when you'd ast me to git out o' yore cabin."

Hannah's gaze didn't leave the other woman's. "I never thought you'd make up sich lies and accuse as good a young 'un as ever lived o' sich things. I know yore a-wantin' to git Willie married off, but this shore ain't the way to go about it!"

Mattie took a deep breath and let it out in another *whoosh*. She looked at the other occupants of the cabin, all staring at her as if she'd taken leave of her senses. Mattie opened her mouth, then closed it again. She turned her bulk around and walked over the threshold, then turned back.

"There may come a time, Hannie, when you'll wish you never told me to leave." She walked outside and disappeared from view.

The four inside the cabin heard the porch boards and steps creak under her weight as she left. Finally, all was silent.

Hannah suddenly seemed to lose her determination. Her face crumpled and she swayed. Eden grabbed her, easing her down to a sitting position on the side of the bed.

Hannah looked up at her. "I reckon I hadn't ort to have told her that," she said, her voice quavering. She glanced over at Cade, who still stood as if turned to stone. "But I couldn't let her say them awful things about Cade!"

"No, you couldn't," Eden said firmly. "You were wonderful."

"You know Mattie'll never set foot in this cabin agin," Hannah went on. "She'll never let Willie come back, neither."

A sudden choked cry came from Cade. He pushed past Jesse and ran out the door and off the porch. Jesse hurried after him but came back in a minute, shaking his head. "We'd better leave him alone for a while," he said, his voice tight with suppressed anger.

"Yes, I suppose so," Eden agreed, her voice as tight as his. "This would have to happen just as he was beginning to feel better." She was so angry she wanted to go after Mattie and pull every hair out of the woman's head!

"I hadn't ort to o' told her them things," Hannah repeated. She looked up at Eden. "We won't have nobody on the ridge to hep us now, 'ceptin' the Lorimers. And they's so fur . . ."

Her voice died away, but Eden finished the sentence in her own mind. The Lorimers lived too far away to call on in an emergency.

Such as the birth of a baby.

The knot of tension in her stomach clenched. It didn't matter. She'd never wanted to ask Mattie for help anyway. She'd send Jesse down to Cherry Creek to bring back Fern Willard at the first sign of the onset of her labor. There would be plenty of time. Hadn't Hannah told her dozens of stories about how long first babies took to arrive?

She reached down inside herself and summoned courage and a smile for Hannah. "Come on, let's get you settled again," she said. "We'll be fine." she told her firmly. "Just fine."

Chapter Nineteen

From behind a big maple tree, Willa watched as Cade walked down the path leading to her family's cabin. For two weeks, he'd done this every evening, right before dark. The first day, she'd seen him by accident.

He'd go to the edge of the woods, and, keeping himself concealed, look over toward the cabin. He never went any farther. He'd stand there for half an hour or so, then head back down the path to the Claybornes' cabin.

Mattie had forbidden her ever to go there again. She'd told Willa in great and indignant detail what had happened the day Hannah had ordered her to leave. Willa was amazed at Hannah's actions and so appalled at her mother's that nothing could have persuaded her to approach Cade.

But most of those feelings had passed. Now she wanted to talk to Cade, but she didn't know how he'd react if she walked up to him here in the woods. He might be mad at her, but if he was, why would he apparently be looking for her? Still, she wasn't certain.

She watched, her brow furrowed, as Cade stood gazing out across the clearing. Finally, he turned and began walking back down the path. He had his hands in the pockets of his old brown pants, and the sleeves of his equally old white shirt were rolled up. The cloth Miz Eden had wrapped around his ribs for a while, making a bulkiness under his shirt, was gone now and he walked with no sign of pain.

Except the kind she had. The inside kind of pain you couldn't get a remedy for. He looked like he might be feeling as much of that as she was. Willa watched as he came even with her hiding place, holding her breath.

Before she had time to think, she stepped out from behind the tree and walked toward him, her bare feet noiseless on the covering of dead leaves and twigs on the forest floor. He stopped dead on the path when he saw her. For a minute, she thought she glimpsed a happy light in his yellow-brown eyes, but then it disappeared.

Her heart was beating very fast. "Hello, Cade."

He didn't say anything for a minute. Then he nodded stiffly. "Hello, Willa."

They stood there looking at each other. Cade felt his heart going a mile a minute inside his chest. He was so glad she was here. He'd come over every day but had never caught a glimpse of her. "I thought maybe they'd sent you away."

Willa dared a grin. "Ain't no place they could send me, 'cept one of the other cabins on the ridge where some of our kinfolks live."

She waited to see if Cade would grin back. He didn't. He just kept standing there, staring at her.

"I should get on back," he finally said, his voice tentative.

Did he want her to persuade him to stay? He looked like he'd lost weight, Willa noticed. Like he hadn't been eating much. "Are you mad at me?" she asked him bluntly. "Because of what Mam said to you?"

Cade shook his head. "No, of course not," he mumbled, turning his head away from her.

She could see the red creeping into his thin face, and fresh anger at her mother swept over her. "*I'm* still mad at her!" she said passionately. "Iffen—if I had a place to go, I *would* leave this ridge!"

He jerked his head up to stare at her. "Are you all right?" he asked her. "Is your mother hurting you?"

Willa shrugged. "Not much more'n usual. She switches me some, but she's allus done that."

Cade's face reddened even more. His eyes flashed. "I wish I could take you away from here!" he said, his voice as passionate as hers had been.

She stared at him in astonishment. Then she felt her own face flush. She backed up a little. "I'll be all right," she told him, forcing herself to sound calm and controlled. "Mam ain't allus—always like that. Sometimes she's right nice."

Cade was looking at her now in a different way—kind of like he did that other day they'd been in the woods together. When they'd sat on the moss and he'd told her about his Georgia home that had been burned.

Again, as it had that day, a funny feeling went over her. It felt partly good and partly scary. But she knew one thing— they were both too young to explore where those feelings might lead. Even if her mother thought differently. And most of the ridge folk, too.

"I reckon I'd better be gettin' back home," she told him, hearing the breathless tone in her voice. "I ain't supposed to go to Miz Eden's no more. But maybe we could meet each other here in the woods sometimes."

The minute she'd said the words, she wished them back. It hadn't come out like she meant. She'd sounded like she wanted something . . . she turned the thought off fast, ducking her head shyly.

Confusion swept over Cade at her words and actions. He liked Willa, really liked her, but every time he looked at her, his mind kept going back to the day when her mother had said those awful things to him. As if he'd tear Willa's dress! As if he'd try to . . . hurt her.

And her mother had wanted them to get married! His face reddened more. "I'm pretty busy," he said stiffly. "Jesse and I are cutting the winter wood. And we're putting new chinking between the logs in the cabin and barn."

Willa quickly nodded. "I'm busy, too. Mam sends me down in the holler to look for sang, but there ain't very good beds over by our place. Best ones are where Miz Eden and me always went."

The reminder of what Toby Varden had done made Cade's face flame. He wanted to forget the day he'd tried to act like a man and had failed so badly.

"Well, goodbye, Willa," he said.

"Goodbye, Cade," she answered.

She stood watching as he strode rapidly down the path, not looking back even once. Her heart was no longer beating fast, like it had been. Now it ached. She wanted to run after Cade, tell him not to let those bad things that had happened, things that had been said, spoil their friendship.

But she didn't. It wouldn't do any good. This was something he had to get over by himself. She didn't know if he could, though. And it wouldn't be too much longer now before he and Mister Jesse would leave. So it didn't matter. Once he left here, it wasn't likely she'd ever see him again.

Her thin shoulders drooping, Willa silently made her way down the path. As she reached the edge of the woods, she saw Mattie sitting on the cabin porch.

Willa sniffed and swiped at the tears running down her tanned face, trying to remember if there was anything her mother could be mad at her for.

She'd done all her chores for today and this morning she'd gathered some sang. Darcy was going to take it down to Cherry Creek and sell it when there was enough.

Like her mother said, she'd better forget all those foolish notions Miz Eden had been putting in her head. She was a ridge girl, and someday she'd marry one of the ridge boys and settle down and have a passel o' young 'uns like all the other women here.

She made her face blank and left the shelter of the woods, her spirit shrinking within her as she saw Mattie lift her head and stare in her direction.

Eden turned over in bed, trying to sleep. The baby was moving around too much, and her back still hurt. It had been hurting since afternoon. Usually, the pain went away when she went to bed, but tonight it hadn't.

It was also very hot. Most of the time, the nights were cool, but for the past week, the ridge had experienced a hot spell. And she'd gotten used to the loft bed, which was more comfortable than this one. Now, Cade was back in the barn with Jesse.

She thought briefly of climbing the ladder and sleeping up there anyway, but dismissed it. It would be even hotter than here. She turned over again and looked across at Hannah. Her mother-in-law slept deeply, restfully.

Eden smiled in the dark. Since the day Hannah had so unexpectedly risen from her bed and sent Mattie hightailing it out of the cabin, it seemed as if a miracle had occurred.

The next day Hannah got up and walked to the table for meals, still obviously weak. From then on, she took all her meals at the table and began walking around the cabin, staying on her feet a little longer each day.

That was two weeks ago, and now Hannah was on her feet a good hour or more a day. She also ate better, and her spirits were much brighter.

Except for her relapses. There were also times when her mother-in-law refused to get out of bed, or eat anything to speak of. Eden still wasn't sure the improvement would be permanent, but all she could do was encourage Hannah. And because Hannah had lain so long in bed, her muscles had weakened and had to be strengthened again.

Cade worried her greatly. Physically, he was fine now, but he hadn't regained his high spirits. He'd been getting over the incident with Toby until Mattie's outrageous behavior. He still had his nightly visit with Hannah, still smiled at her stories. But he seldom laughed, and he was very quiet.

If only Willa hadn't stopped coming to the cabin! The girl had made a flying trip here the day after her mother's outburst and told Eden that Mattie had forbidden any more visits.

Eden hadn't expected Mattie to admit what she'd done was a deliberate ploy to force Cade to marry Willa. But she'd hoped the breach between the households wouldn't be permanent. Heartsick, Eden hugged the girl and gave her the textbooks they'd used for Willa's lessons. Willa had made no effort to see Cade, and that was the last time she'd come.

And then there was Jesse.

Just thinking about him made her heart speed up, she realized.

trying to ignore that bodily symptom of how he affected her. These last two weeks, they'd gotten to know each other. He'd helped her in the garden, helped her dry more vegetables and fruits and cleaned out the root cellar under the porch to ready it for storing the fall vegetables.

Jesse talked freely of his home and family. He even told her how his former fiancée had fallen in love with a Yankee officer and married him. They'd grown up together, he said, and their love had been that of brother and sister. It had taken Annabelle's truly falling in love to make them realize that.

Eden tried to ignore the relief that swept over her. It should mean nothing to her that Jesse didn't pine over his lost love. That Annabelle hadn't even *been* a real love. But she knew it did.

In turn, she told Jesse how her love for Alston had changed over the years, turned into fondness, like the feelings he had for Annabelle. And the expression that had come into his amber eyes then had looked strangely like relief, too.

She and Jesse had talked, worked together, even laughed together. But they were never alone together, as they'd been that night under the walnut tree. Eden had relived those moments, the kiss they'd shared, more times than she wanted to admit. And just as often, she'd been appalled at her wayward thoughts and firmly pushed them into the deepest recesses of her mind . . . only to have them thrust themselves out again when she least expected it.

As they were doing now, while she lay here sleepless. The feel of Jesse's warm mouth moving over hers, his strong arms pulling her against his muscled body, was so easily and quickly summoned, she couldn't have banished the memories to a spot very deep inside. But just as swiftly, guilt followed.

If not for her actions and Jesse's, Alston might very well still be alive. She probably wouldn't be facing the prospect of bringing a fatherless baby into the world.

Eden sighed. She wasn't going to sleep any time soon. She got up, donned the now shabby dressing gown and slippers she'd brought with her from Connecticut, and quietly made her way to the door.

It opened silently under her hand and she went onto the

porch, thanking Jesse for oiling the hinges. She walked to the railing and stood looking out over the clearing. The moon was full, but it was a cloudy night, and at the moment, clouds hid the moon. She took deep breaths of the fresh mountain air, trying to relax her tense body and mind.

The clouds moved away from the moon, and the clearing was bathed in silvery light. This ridge truly was a lovely place, she thought. Her gaze traveled across the clearing, pausing a moment when it reached the walnut tree, standing like a tall sentinel.

At the edge of the woods, something moved.

Eden's tight muscles tensed even more as she tried to make out the shadowy shape. Was it Sadie? Several times since the night Jesse had returned, Eden had caught glimpses of the woods woman. But she'd never approached the cabin.

Clouds sailed across the moon again, bringing blackness. When they glided on, the shadowy shape was no longer visible. Relief relaxed her tautness. Whatever had been there was gone. Maybe she'd imagined it.

She'd better go back inside, try to get some sleep. As she started to turn back to the cabin, she caught a flash of movement and froze halfway into the arc. Her breath caught in her throat.

Its long, lithe body extended in a loping run, a panther flashed by her field of vision, heading toward the barnyard.

Eden opened the cabin door and hurried inside. She grabbed up the old musket rifle, always kept loaded, in the corner and threw a quick glance toward Hannah's bed as she headed for the door again. Moonbeams shining through the front window showed her an unmoving mound. Thank God Hannah hadn't awakened.

Reaching the door, she closed it quietly behind her. Hannah had told her a few times in years past that panthers had raided the chicken house, which was the main reason the chickens were now housed inside the sturdy log barn. A couple of families on the ridge had lost calves, too.

But Hannah had also said panthers were extremely fond of horseflesh. Jesse and Cade kept their horses in the barn at night, but she knew they'd been leaving the big main door open for air circulation during this hot spell.

What if the panther had Cade and Jesse trapped in the barn? Did Jesse sleep with his revolver handy? She supposed so but didn't know for sure.

Eden stepped off the porch and quietly made her way toward the barnyard. Clouds covered the moon again and she had to call on her knowledge of every inch of this homestead to guide her footsteps. Something seemed strange about the night. Then she realized what it was.

It was utterly silent. The katydids had stopped their singing in the trees. No mockingbird trilled a haunting night song. A shiver slid down Eden's spine. Cautiously, holding the gun carefully, she inched her way forward in the pitch dark.

She was past the privy now, she was sure, halfway to the barnyard. Careful, she told herself, don't make a misstep. The night was still silent as death.

A sudden thought occurred to her: maybe the panther hadn't been headed for the barnyard at all. It was quite possible he'd sped on past. But she still had to go on to the barn to make sure Cade and Jesse were all right.

Into the eerie silence a horse's excited, frightened whinny rang out, followed by an answering whinny from its neighbor. Instantly another sound rose out of the night, making the hair on Eden's nape stand up.

It was an incredible sound. Like a woman screaming, a child wailing, magnified a hundred times. The first time she'd heard that sound it had frozen the blood in her veins. Now, it sent a sharp thrill of fear racing through her body.

The panther hadn't raced on past. It was right here, and it was after the horses!

The moon reappeared. Eden stopped, dead, looking toward the barnyard, fearful of what she might see. In front of the barn, its tawny coat darkened by the moonlight, was the panther.

Crouched to spring.

Opposite the animal stood a figure holding what looked like a revolver. From this distance, by the moon's uncertain light, she couldn't tell if it was Jesse or Cade.

The panther screamed again, rose up, and sprang, and a shot rang out simultaneously.

Then the night was plunged into blackness once more and

Eden choked back the scream trying to escape her throat. Her backache was worse, she realized. She needed to sit down, but she ignored the pain and continued walking, forcing herself to keep her steps slow and careful as she neared the scene. She couldn't risk falling now.

She also couldn't risk calling out. If the animal hadn't been hit, that might excite it further. For what seemed an interminable time, she cautiously walked across the grass in the dark. She alternately prayed for the moon to reappear and dreaded what it might disclose.

When it finally did, she took a deep breath, then looked toward the barnyard. Her breath whooshed out of her in relief. The panther lay on its side, obviously dead.

Jesse and Cade stood side by side, looking down at the animal. She drew in her breath in surprise. Cade held a revolver in his hand. He must have been the indistinct figure she saw. He must have shot the animal.

Both seemed to hear her approach at the same time. Their heads jerked up and they stared in her direction. Then Jesse hurried to meet her, a worried frown on his face.

"What in hell are you doing out here?" he growled at her. "Give me that!" He took the musket from her.

"I saw the panther come this way. I was afraid he was after the horses."

"He was," Jesse said grimly. He nodded at Cade. "If Cade hadn't seen him and grabbed the gun, he'd have gotten one of them, too."

Eden turned to Cade. The boy had an awestruck, stunned look on his face as he stared down at the beautiful animal. Finally, he lifted his head and turned toward them. "I didn't want to kill it, but I had to," he said.

"Yes, you did," Jesse said firmly. "With one shot, too. I'm proud of you, Cade."

He turned back to Eden. "Cade had to, uh, go outside. He saw the panther coming as he got to the doorway. He ran in, grabbed my revolver, then went back out, and—"

Eden nodded. "I saw the panther spring, then Cade shot and the moon went behind a cloud. I was so afraid! I didn't know what had happened. I didn't even know which of you was out here."

She realized her knees were shaking, and she was trembling all over. Her backache was much worse, and now it had moved around to her abdominal region. She saw the big chopping block behind her and sat down on it.

"Are you all right?" Jesse asked sharply. Cade walked over beside Jesse, worry on his young face.

She nodded. "Of course. It's only the reaction from being so scared. I'll be fine after I rest a little." She gave them both a reassuring smile.

Then her eyes widened and a surprised look came over her face. Liquid was trickling down her legs. She knew what that meant, had to mean.

"What's wrong?" Jesse's voice was sharper. He laid down the gun and knelt beside her.

Eden lifted her head, the surprise still in her eyes, but something else had been added—fear. She swallowed, then her face contorted with pain, and she leaned forward.

"Eden, my God, what happened? Did you fall and hurt yourself?" Jesse asked frantically. His arms instinctively slid around her shoulders, supporting her.

When she lifted her head the second time, the surprise had left her eyes. But the fear hadn't. She swallowed again.

"Jesse, you'd better help me back to the cabin. I know it's a month too soon, but the baby's coming. And he seems to be in a terrible hurry."

She heard Jesse's sharp intake of breath, then he carefully lifted her and cradled her against his chest. "It'll be all right. I'll go for Fern Willard as soon as I get you back to bed," he told her, his voice tight with tension.

"I'll go," Cade said quickly from behind him. "I'll go right now."

Another pain contorted Eden's body. When it passed, she gasped out, "No! There isn't time."

She raised her head and looked at Jesse, her eyes deep and enormous in the moonlight.

"You'll have to help me," she told him. "There's no one else."

Chapter Twenty

Cade opened the cabin door and Jesse walked inside, then paused, carefully balancing Eden in his arms. The moon was back behind clouds, leaving the cabin in darkness again.

During the walk from the barnyard, Eden had twice more been convulsed with pains. As she'd said, this baby appeared to be in a hurry to be born.

Renewed fear for her and the infant coursed through Jesse's veins.

"Find the lamp and light it," he told Cade, trying to keep his voice low, then wondered why he was concerned about waking Hannah. She'd soon be awake in any case.

"Eden? What's wrong?" Hannah's anxious voice came out of the darkness.

The rasp of a match sounded, then light from the lamp on the table illuminated the room, revealing Hannah sitting up in bed, looking worried. Her expression changed to alarm when she saw Jesse holding Eden.

"The baby's coming, Mrs. Clayborne," he said, making his tone as positive as he could. "But don't worry, Eden's all right."

God, he hoped that was true.

He gave Hannah a reassuring smile as her eyes widened, the

alarm in them increasing at his words. He carried Eden across the room to her bed. The covers were thrown back as she'd left them. He carefully laid her down between the sheets, then pulled the covers over her.

Just as he did, he saw that another pain had her in its inexorable grip, and she turned on her side, doubled up with it. He desperately wanted to sit down on the bed beside her, take her into his arms, somehow try to comfort her.

But he couldn't do that; he had no right. The pain grew and crested, and after what seemed an interminable time, began to subside.

Jesse straightened, meeting Hannah's eyes. He tried to keep his anxiety from showing.

"Oh, my Lord, it ain't time fer the babe to come yit!"

"It's only a few weeks early," Jesse said, hoping his voice sounded reassuring, then turned back to Eden. The contraction over, she lay on her side, her eyes closed. While he watched, she opened them again and looked at him.

"You'll have to build up the fire and put on some water to heat and find some clean cloths. The baby's things are in the chest at the foot of my bed."

Her voice was shaky from the pain just past. Jesse's desperation increased. He swallowed. "All right. What else can I do?"

He'd never felt so helpless in his life. He'd never been around a woman giving birth. He didn't know any men who had. Men were supposed to make themselves scarce during this time, leave the women alone to handle it. He had no idea how long it usually took, or anything at all that would help Eden.

Eden looked at him, her face drawn and pale, showing the marks of the pain she'd already experienced. "I don't know," she said. She hesitated, then went on. "Ask Hannah. I think we need to send for Mattie."

"Do you want me to go get her?" Cade spoke up.

Jesse shot him a quick glance. He'd forgotten the boy was in the room. Cade was already at the stove, stirring up the embers of the evening fire, adding more wood.

The thought of Mattie here, helping with the birth, appalled Jesse. He remembered the slovenly state of her cabin, her soiled dress. No! He didn't want her anywhere near Eden.

But maybe he was wrong to feel that way. Any woman, even Mattie, would certainly be more prepared than he was.

He turned toward Hannah, ready to accept her decision on this, then stared at her. Hannah had thrown back her covers and stood beside her bed, unbuttoning her nightgown.

Her eyes met his. "Git me some clothes out of th' chest at th' foot of my bed," she commanded, her voice firm. "They's some things on top, I think."

"Mrs. Clayborne, what are you doing?" Jesse asked, the astonishment he felt apparent in his voice.

"What does it look like I'm a-doin'?" she said, her voice even firmer. "I'm goin' to git dressed and then birth my grandbaby."

"But you're still sick. You can't——"

"If you think I'm a-goin' to let Mattie Freeman in here after what she did, you are wrong," Hannah interrupted. She frowned at him. "I've birthed all the babes on this ridge fer twenty year. Now, hurry up and git my clothes," she commanded.

Not knowing whether to be relieved or even more anxious, Jesse obeyed, handing her the stack of clothing.

Hannah gave him a stern look. "Now, you and Cade turn yore heads whilst I git into these. Go ahead and build up the fire and then I'll tell you what else needs doin'."

Cade already had the fire-building done. Jesse glanced across at Eden to see that another pain had her in its grip. He felt perspiration breaking out on his forehead. Damn it! He couldn't stand to watch her suffer. Not looking toward Hannah, he hurried back to the bed.

He didn't care if he had the right or not, he was going to try to comfort her.

He reached one hand down to her clenched fists. "Take hold of my hand," he told her. "Squeeze as hard as you want."

She grasped his proffered hand with both of hers and did just that, her grip increasing until he saw her knuckles turning white.

He clenched his jaw. God, he'd never known women went through this much suffering when babies were born. He supposed the women took care not to let the men know. Finally, the pain eased and her grip on his hand gradually relaxed. She lay limp, her eyes closed.

Alarm gripped Jesse as he gazed down at her white face. She looked so pale and still. Was she all right? He shot a glance toward Hannah. The older woman was fully dressed, finishing the last button down the front of her dark cotton gown.

She looked up and met his gaze. A smile turned up the corners of her mouth, then she glanced across the room to Cade. "You go put some clean water in the washbasin and fetch it in here with some soap." Her voice was still that new, firm, commanding one.

Cade hurried to obey, putting the items on the table.

Hannah washed her hands thoroughly, then dried them on a clean towel. Finished, she smiled at Cade, standing by the table.

"Cade, honey, you might as well go out on the porch," she said. "They ain't a thing you kin do here. We jist got to wait now."

"All right."

Jesse heard the relieved note in Cade's voice, then the door opened and closed again as the boy let himself out.

Hannah walked back to Eden's bedside. "Now, you move fer a minute and let me have a look at her," she told Jesse. "Git them baby things out of the chest, like Eden said. Git a couple a sheets out o' there, too."

Again Jesse did as he was bidden, realizing that Hannah had pulled up Eden's gown and was examining her. He felt sweat trickling down his face. My God, was Hannah up to this? What if she collapsed right at the point when Eden needed the most help?

Then he would take over and finish the job. If Hannah showed signs of weakness, he'd ask her for instructions on how to proceed and send her back to bed. Between the two of them, Eden was going to be all right—and her baby, too, he vowed.

He kept his head bent to his task, his jaws clenched so tightly they ached. When he'd found the items needed, he still knelt by the chest, head bowed, waiting until Hannah finished.

"All right," Hannah finally said. "You kin come over and sit by her and let her grab yore hand when she needs to."

Jesse got up, throwing a quick glance at Eden. She still rested quietly. He brought his glance back up to Hannah, a question in it.

Hannah nodded, her voice calm and certain. "The babe is turned right, and ever'thin' looks fine. I'm a-goin' to give her some crampbark tea, and a glass of blackberry wine, but I think things has gone too fur to stop them now."

Jesse knew she meant the reassuring words and tone for Eden, too. But what if things weren't as she said? What if Hannah, too, had worries she wasn't revealing? He sat down beside the bed, reaching for Eden's hand. She grasped it with both of hers as another pain began and held on, as she had before, her grip gradually tightening.

The baby would be almost a month early. What did that mean? Only that it would be smaller? He searched his mind, but couldn't remember anyone of his family or acquaintances that this had happened to.

In a situation like this, a month was a long time.

What if the baby wasn't strong enough to survive?

Cade eased himself down on one of the porch rockers and tried to sit still and wait, but he couldn't. Tonight, the chair seemed the most uncomfortable thing he'd ever sat on. He squirmed some more, then finally got up and perched on the rail.

He hated being out here alone, but he knew Hannah was right. He sure as heck wasn't needed inside the cabin.

Maybe Jesse wasn't, either. He was certain his cousin had never before helped with a birthing. Men weren't even supposed to talk about such things. They were supposed to stay out of the way and wait until it was all over.

Waiting. That was the hardest thing in the world to do. He wished there were someone with him.

He wished Willa was here.

Cade hadn't seen her since that day in the woods a couple of weeks ago. He hadn't treated her very nicely, and he had been sorry later. But he'd been so embarrassed and angry over all the things that had happened. Letting Varden knock him down, so that he couldn't defend Eden and Willa. Then, letting Willa's mother say those things to him.

Why, he was almost a man! He should have beaten Varden

to a pulp. And he should have done something about Mattie's accusations, too, but he hadn't known what, except to deny them.

And as for him and Willa getting married . . .

Cade felt his face flame. The thought of marrying anyone at his age was ridiculous! And Willa was even younger than he was. But still, the whole mess had made him feel somehow ashamed, inadequate.

But now, after shooting the panther tonight, something had happened inside him. He hadn't wanted to shoot the beautiful big cat, but there'd been no choice. It would have killed him, because he stood between it and the horseflesh it was after. Even if he'd scared it off, it would probably have come back another night.

And if he hadn't been awake and seen it, it would have killed one of the horses. He'd had to do it, and knowing that, he felt no guilt or regret.

Instead, the act had had the opposite effect. He felt somehow restored to himself. No longer like an inept, fumbling boy.

He felt like a man.

Oh, he knew he still had quite a bit of growing up to do, but that would come in time.

Cade shifted on the rail again, then stood. He wanted to see Willa. Talk with her. Listen to her laugh.

Silently he left the porch and headed out toward the path through the woods leading to the Freemans' cabin. The moon came out from behind the clouds and he found the path easily enough. He almost knew it by heart anyway, all those times he'd walked it a couple of weeks ago.

Half an hour later, he moved out from the shelter of the woods into the Freeman clearing. His feelings had changed again. Now he felt like a fool. What had made him do this? Willa would be in bed asleep, probably up in the loft. There was no way he could attract her attention without waking up her whole family. And he sure as heck didn't intend to do that.

Cade glanced over toward the cabin, wondering why he bothered, then grew still.

Someone was sitting on the top porch step.

Willa? He thought so, but he couldn't tell for sure. If it was her father or one of her brothers and they saw him, they'd probably come after him with a gun.

Willa couldn't sleep. She'd brought her bedding out on the porch because it was such a hot night, but that hadn't helped.

Then, a little while ago, she'd heard a gunshot. She wouldn't have thought much about it, supposing it was one of the ridge men out hunting, except it had come from over toward the Claybornes' cabin. Could be Jesse and Cade were coon or possum hunting, but she'd never heard them mention doing such. They got squirrel or rabbit sometimes, but that was during the day.

So she'd gotten up and now sat on the steps, watching the moon play hide-and-seek with the clouds. She considered walking over to the Claybornes', but finally decided against it.

The moon came out again. Willa glimpsed movement at the edge of the woods and glanced that way.

Someone stood just into the clearing, looking in her direction. Her heart almost stopped, then began beating very fast.

Cade. It was Cade. The moonlight shone on his yellow-brown hair, and besides, she would know him anywhere. Without thinking, she walked down the steps and hurried across the clearing toward him.

The minute Cade saw the figure get up, he knew it was Willa. He felt his heart leap in his chest as he watched her start walking in his direction, and moved out to meet her.

They met halfway. As they came within a few feet of each other, the moon coyly hid itself again, and they were only indistinct shadows to each other.

For a few moments, neither of them said anything or moved. Willa spoke first. "Cade? Did you come over here to see me? Or is somethin' wrong?"

She heard his intake of breath. She saw his shadow move a little. "I came to see you, Willa. But there is something wrong. Miss Eden is . . ." He hesitated, then went on. "She's having her baby! And it's too early."

The moon showed itself again, revealing Willa's surprised eyes, her parted mouth.

And the fact that she wore only a long white nightgown. He swallowed, embarrassment making his face redden.

"Who's helpin' her?" Willa asked. "Did Mister Jesse git Fern Willard from the settlement?"

Cade decided Willa had forgotten she was in her nightclothes. She couldn't stand there so confidently otherwise, he was sure. Even if the gown covered her clear to her neck.

"No, she told Jesse there wasn't time. Miss Hannah and Jesse are helping her."

Willa's eyes widened even more. She couldn't believe what Cade had just said.

"Miz Hannah is up and able to do that?"

Cade sighed. "I don't know if she can or not. I think Jesse's worried about it. But Miss Hannah is sure acting like she can. She just took over and she's bossing Jesse around and told me to go outside."

"Do you think I need to go in and wake up Mam?" Willa asked, a little doubtfully. "She's still mad at Miz Hannah, but I believe she'd go over and help."

"No," Cade said hastily. "Don't do that. Miss Hannah said she could take care of everything." He hesitated, wondering if he should tell her Hannah had also said she didn't want Mattie.

Willa gave him a shrewd look. "I don't blame Miz Hannah fer not wantin' Mam." She frowned. "But I think I better go over. Maybe I could do somethin'."

Cade gulped. He hadn't considered this possibility. "Willa," he said, hesitantly, "that's probably a good idea, but you'd better . . . you'd better go get dressed first."

He saw her horrified look as she glanced down at herself, before, mercifully, the moon once again disappeared. Then he heard her soft gasp.

"I'll be right back," her disembodied voice said in the dark. He saw her outline go flying back toward the cabin.

Willa was more embarrassed than she'd ever been in her life, even more so than during these last few weeks when all these awful things had been happening. How could she have forgotten she was wearing her nightgown when she'd gone running out to meet Cade? Why, he must think she was shameless!

Reaching the porch, she tiptoed up on it, then inside, and up to the sleeping loft, thankful that her family all slept like the dead. Mam would be mad as fire that she'd left in the middle of the night—and to go to the Claybornes' cabin. But she was going anyway.

The loft was divided into two cubicles. Willa occupied one and Darcy the other. She jerked off her gown and got into her chemise and dress, then was outside again and running back across the clearing toward Cade in the space of five minutes.

"You jist keep on a-bearin' down, honey," Hannah told Eden, her voice low and full of compassion. "I know yore tired, but it's about over, now."

Eden gripped Jesse's hand with hers and squeezed tightly. His steadfast presence comforted her more than he'd ever know. He hadn't wavered for an instant.

He'd been there for her from the moment in the barnyard when she'd told him he'd have to help her, there was no one else.

She'd been wrong there. She was still amazed at how Hannah had risen from her bed and taken over. But when that happened, Jesse hadn't retreated to the porch with Cade. She knew most men probably would have. After all, males weren't supposed to be involved in birthings. The very idea was shocking.

But not to her—not now. She held fast to his hand, as to a lifeline. Her face contorted in a grimace as she followed Hannah's instructions.

A trickle of perspiration ran down the side of Eden's cheek. With his free hand, Jesse reached for the cloth in the basin of cool water, wrung it out, and gently wiped the moisture away.

Fear still had him in its grip, even though Hannah was handling the birthing so competently he found it hard to believe this was the same woman who, not long ago, had been bedfast.

He knew she was tired. Her fatigue showed in the slight trembling of her hands. And she'd sat down a few times when she'd looked as if she couldn't stand a moment longer. But he felt sure now that she'd be able to get through this ordeal with sheer determination.

But would Eden and the baby be all right? Would the baby be too small to survive? God, how he wanted this to be over!

"I see the babe's head!" Hannah's voice trembled with excitement. "Bear down harder when you git the next pain."

Eden nodded, not wasting any of her strength in answering. When the next pain gripped her, Jesse felt a shudder go through her and the tremendous effort she put forth.

The knot in his stomach doubled in size. The next few minutes would decide the outcome. He tried not to think of how many women died in childbirth, how many babies were born dead or didn't survive. He clenched his jaw even more tightly, wrung out the cloth again, and wiped Eden's face.

"Yore doin' good, honey!" Hannah encouraged her. "Jist one more hard push, now."

Eden grunted with effort.

Jesse felt his own muscles contracting as he watched her face.

"Oh, my land, here 'tis!" Hannah said, her voice tremulous with excitement. "Jesse, come here," Hannah commanded. "Quick!"

Eden released his hand and he moved back beside Hannah. He drew in his breath. Hannah held a tiny infant. Fear stabbed him. It wasn't breathing!

He saw Hannah's fear, too, as her body tensed. Then the infant made a choking, coughing sound and let out a lusty yell. Hannah's face lit up with a delighted, relieved smile.

Relief flooded through Eden as she heard the cry, making her muscles limp and weak. It was over. The baby was alive.

"Hand me them scissors," Hannah told Jesse.

He scooped up the scissors from the chest and gave them to her and watched with awe as she deftly cut and tied the umbilical cord. Then she gently washed the baby, who looked perfect in every way, as far as Jesse could see. True, it was small, but it certainly had good lungs!

"Jesse, let's wrap this young 'un up."

He picked up the small blanket on the chest and held it out. Hannah placed the baby in it and folded the blanket around it.

Jesse swallowed, an indescribable feeling flooding through

his body. Was this how a new father felt? As if truly there were miracles in this world and he'd just witnessed one?

Not only witnessed it . . . he'd been a part of this birthing from start to finish. A surge of love swept over him, almost as if this infant belonged to him. At once guilt took its place. How could he feel like that?

The true father of this newborn lay buried with dozens of his companions.

Because of decisions Jesse had made.

"Eden, honey," Hannah said, her voice full to bursting with joy. "Ye got yoreself a purty leetle gal babe."

Jesse turned to see Eden looking at the blanket-wrapped bundle he held. He caught his breath.

The pain and weariness were gone from her face. She smiled radiantly, her face luminous. She held out her arms.

"Give her to me," she said softly, surprise mixing with the intense rush of love she felt. A girl! She'd had a girl baby, not the boy she'd expected.

Jesse laid the baby in her arms, his heart turning over with tenderness as he watched her cuddle the infant close to her breast as if she'd done it a hundred times before. She would be a wonderful mother.

And incredibly, the guilt he'd felt only a few moments before had left him.

As if blinders had been lifted from his eyes, he felt that for the first time he was seeing the events of those last terrible days of the war as they'd actually happened.

It was true Clayborne had died at least partly because of decisions Jesse had made. But it was also true he'd chosen to go back to the fighting when he didn't have to. He was a sick man. He'd have been completely justified in staying home for weeks more.

He had *wanted* to fight in that last battle.

Even if Jesse had tried to send him home, forbidden him to fight, the man most probably would have ignored him and stayed.

Eden looked at Jesse over the top of the baby's blanket. Time seemed to stop as their glances met and held. Once again, she felt that sense of communion with Jesse's spirit.

Jesse couldn't move his gaze from Eden's. He felt as if their very souls were attuned, one with the other.

He'd already admitted, to himself at least, that he loved her. He'd also acknowledged that their love was hopeless because of the guilt that lay between them. He'd resigned himself to staying here as long as he could persuade Eden to let him, then returning to Georgia.

Now, suddenly, in the space of a few moments, everything had changed. Because of the birth of this tiny infant, the load of guilt he'd carried for months had left him.

Her birth could be a new beginning for them—including Hannah. A time to set aside the bitterness, all the terrible things that had happened.

In his heart and soul the barrier between Eden and him had crumbled as if made of sand instead of the granite he'd thought.

Then new doubts assailed him. There was no reason for him to believe Eden felt any differently than she ever had. The baby's birth might very well have worsened her guilt. It was quite possible she was, even now, in the midst of her joy, grieving over the fact that Clayborne would never see or know his daughter.

Eden smiled at him, another radiant smile. His spirits lifted. But he didn't know how she felt. And this was no time for gloomy thoughts. A new life had come into the world. It was a time for happiness and rejoicing.

He smiled back at Eden. "What are you going to name her?"

Cade and Willa didn't talk much during the hurried trip back through the woods. Willa forgot her embarrassment in the urgency of the situation. Cade must feel the same, she thought. They walked up on the porch, both a little out of breath.

The moon was out again. Willa gave Cade an uncertain look. Now that she was here, she wasn't so sure she should go barging into the cabin.

What if Miz Hannah's anger at Willa's mother included her? The older woman might tell her to go home and mind her own business. On the other hand, her help might be needed . . .

While she hesitated, a sound came from within the cabin.

She quickly turned to Cade and their eyes met. Wide, delighted smiles turned up the corners of their mouths.

It was a wonderful sound. A baby's cry.

Cade grabbed Willa and pulled her to him and hugged her. "It's all over! It's all right!" he said into her ear.

Willa hugged him back. "Oh, that's so good!" she said.

Cade suddenly became aware that his arms were tightly holding Willa. He let go of her and backed away. "I'm sorry," he mumbled. "I didn't mean . . ."

Willa smiled. "That's all right," she told him. "I know you were jist a-givin' me a friendly squeeze, 'cause we're both so tickled about the babe. Do you think we could go in now?".

Her words made Cade let out his breath in relief. After all the things Willa's mother had said, he didn't want Willa to think . . .

Well, he didn't know what he wanted her to think, but anyway, he was glad she understood what had prompted his unplanned hug.

He frowned a little, looking toward the door. "I don't know. Maybe we should wait until Jesse or Miss Hannah tells us to come in."

The door suddenly opened. Jesse stood framed in the doorway. He looked disheveled and a little dazed, but he was grinning widely as he looked at the two standing on the porch. He didn't even seem surprised to see Willa.

"Come on in," he said, his voice as delighted as his facial expression.

"And meet Miss Hannah Rosalind!"

Chapter Twenty-One

"I wrote down some things to try to find at the settlement store," Hannah said, handing the scrap of paper to Jesse. "Course, I don't reckon there'll be no flour. I'm a-gittin' a powerful cravin' fer a batch o' biscuits!" She smiled at him, her brown eyes twinkling.

Jesse smiled back, amazed every time he looked at Hannah. She'd gotten steadily better since the night more than two weeks ago when little Hannah Rosalind, her name soon shortened to Annie Rose, had arrived. To him, it still seemed a miraculous recovery.

"Yes, some of your biscuits would be wonderful," Eden agreed, smiling at them both from her bed, then returning to the letter she was writing.

It was also wonderful to be able to say that to her mother-in-law.

Only a short time ago, she'd never thought to see the older woman out of bed again, let alone to have her gradually taking over the household reins once more.

Of course, Jesse and Cade still did all the outside chores, as well as helping Hannah with many of the inside ones. After her long sojourn in bed, her strength still hadn't fully returned.

Eden glanced up again, warmth spreading through her as she looked at the back of Jesse's tawny head. Warmth mixed with uncertainty. Every time she thought of the night Annie Rose had come into the world, a chaotic blend of emotions spread through her. She hadn't sorted them all out yet.

Another of those moments out of time had happened between them, when she'd felt as one in every way with Jesse, more intense than ever before. And when Jesse had put the baby into her arms, when he'd looked at her, something different seemed to be in his eyes, his face.

She wasn't sure what it was, though. Or what it meant. Her stomach tensed and she quickly turned the thoughts aside. She had to finish this letter to her parents so Jesse could take it with him when he rode down to Cherry Creek. The letter hadn't been as difficult to write as she'd expected.

She'd recounted Alston's death and the baby's birth. Then she'd opened her heart and told her mother and father how sorry she was for the long alienation between them. She hoped they'd be pleased she'd named the baby for her mother as well as Hannah. And she'd ended by saying she also hoped, very much, they'd come to visit her and their granddaughter.

Eden signed her name, folded the sheets, put them into an envelope, and sealed it. She turned the envelope over and looked at it for a moment.

It had been four years since she'd had any contact with her parents. It was quite possible that one or even both of them might be ill or dead by this time. But surely she'd have been notified if that had happened.

She wouldn't think about that possibility. Her parents had always been healthy, vigorous people, so there was every reason to believe they still enjoyed good health. Eden took up her pen again, dipped it in the bottle of ink sitting on the chest by her bed, and addressed the envelope with firm, clear strokes.

As Eden addressed the envelope, Jesse watched her from across the room. He loved watching her, whatever she did. He marveled at how much she'd softened since the baby's birth. She looked like a madonna when she held Annie Rose.

But he didn't suppose this soft, dreamy mood would last

much longer. Soon she'd be up—back to her old direct, energetic self. Capable and strong.

And she'd be telling him it was time to leave.

He dreaded that day and was determined to postpone it as long as possible. But he wasn't sure how long that would be. He'd already stayed longer than they'd agreed.

And even though no one had seen a sign of Varden since that day he'd done so much damage, Jesse knew he was still a danger. Always would be, unless he decided to leave the ridge, which wasn't likely, or unless someone killed him. Jesse veered away from that reflection because every time he thought of Varden he wanted to hunt him down and beat him senseless.

The resolution of the guilt Jesse had felt for Clayborne's death the night Annie Rose was born had lasted. He still felt regret, but no longer the soul-searing blame which for months he'd heaped on himself.

But he had no idea how Eden felt about anything, except her deep love for her baby.

There had been no chance for them to be alone together. Hannah was always there. And he was probably the biggest fool the world had ever known to think that Eden's feelings might have changed because his own had.

But one thing he knew, he wasn't leaving this ridge until he talked to her. Until she told him herself everything was still the same, and a future between them was impossible.

Until she told him she didn't love him and never would.

"Here, I'm finished," Eden said, holding out the envelope. Their glances met, but he could see nothing in her eyes for him.

He walked across the room and took the envelope from her. *Mr. and Mrs. Norris Thornton.* Now that she'd finally written to her parents as he and Hannah had urged her to do, he realized he had mixed feelings.

Of course, he wanted her reconciled with them. Not only for her baby's sake, but also for her own. He'd told her she'd badly need their help. Now, he wondered what he'd meant by that.

If they answered the letter, if they came here to see her and the baby, wouldn't they try to persuade her to go back to

Connecticut with them? They certainly wouldn't stay here, and there was nothing to hold her in the South now, except Hannah.

And maybe, if he was very lucky, himself.

He'd cross that bridge when he came to it, he decided. Because he planned to try some persuasion of his own. He smiled at Eden. "Do you have anything to add to my list?"

She smiled back, shaking her head. "I don't think so. Hannah seems to have taken care of everything."

Annie Rose, snug in her cradle beside Eden's bed, began fussing, which in a moment turned to lusty cries.

"Here, let me get her," Jesse said, reaching into the cradle and lifting the baby into his arms.

His mouth turned up in a smile as he looked down into her face, now contorted with anger, her tiny fists flailing. He held her against his shoulder and patted her small back, but her cries only increased.

"She's hungry again," Eden said, fond indulgence in her voice. "Here, give her to me."

Jesse did as she asked, and during the transfer, his hand touched hers. Her honey-tanned hand was warm, and it was the first time he'd touched her since the night of Annie Rose's birth, when she'd held onto his hands for dear life.

He'd felt so close to her that night. Had she felt that way about him? Their glances met again, and he wondered if she was also remembering that time.

He couldn't tell. Eden's mouth curved into a doting smile as she looked down at the baby and cuddled her. Annie Rose stopped crying and began making small snuffling noises as she moved her head against her mother's breast.

"I'd better go," Jesse said, turning away. He knew Eden was waiting for him to leave so that she could nurse the infant.

A sudden vision of the baby suckling from Eden's full white breast filled his mind. It was strangely erotic. He tried to shut it out, but it persisted as he left the cabin and headed for the barn.

Eden watched him go. She loved the way Jesse walked, so straight and tall. The touch of his hand on hers had brought back vivid memories of the night of the baby's birth, and how she'd depended on him to help her get through it. How close she'd felt to him.

"He's a good man," Hannah said. "I jist don't know how we'd a-managed if he hadn't stayed here."

"Neither do I," Eden answered, her voice ringing with heartfelt conviction.

Annie Rose's snuffling turned into frustrated cries. Eden unbuttoned her gown and guided the baby's eager mouth to her breast. Happiness filled her to bursting as it always did when the baby nursed, and she marveled at it. She gave the baby another soft smile and smoothed back the dark hair from her forehead.

She glanced at Hannah again. The older woman, sitting at the table peeling potatoes, still looked at her, an odd, speculative expression on her face.

For some reason, it made Eden feel uncomfortable. "I never knew motherhood was so wonderful!" she said, smiling at the older woman.

Hannah smiled back, the pondering look leaving her face. "Yes, thar ain't nothin' like that first babe. Annie Rose is shore a growin' fast, too. I was plumb worried 'bout her when she come, she was so leetle, but she's a-goin' to be all right."

"Of course she is." Eden gave her child another besotted look. She was so beautiful. Then, without warning, a moment of sad regret hit her, as it had at intervals since the baby's birth. How she wished Alston could be here to see his baby. But the moment didn't last long.

Somehow, she felt that Alston *could* see Annie Rose. She'd felt at peace, her guilt dissipated since the birth. Alston had been a kind, forgiving man. He wouldn't have wanted her to let guilt ruin her life. Or his child's life.

Why hadn't she been able to see that before? And how did those new insights affect her feelings for Jesse? She quickly pushed the thoughts aside. She didn't know, and it was too soon to be thinking about such things.

But you'd better be thinking about them, another part of her mind insisted. *Jesse will soon be gone. You agreed to let him stay only until the birth. And that was over two weeks ago.*

Was he waiting for her to get on her feet again, be able to handle the additional work the baby would create? Of course, the situation had changed for the better since Hannah's recovery.

Or was Jesse waiting for her to tell him to go?

A sound came from the open doorway and a shadow fell across the sunlight streaming into the cabin. Eden lifted her head, expecting to see Cade, then her eyes widened. Cade wasn't standing in the doorway—Sadie was.

The woman stared straight at her. Eden felt her heart begin beating faster. She hadn't seen Sadie since that night in the clearing when Jesse had returned. The thought of that incident made uneasiness curl in her stomach. She told herself there was no reason to feel that way. Sadie was strange, true. But she'd never harmed anyone. There was no reason to feel threatened by her presence.

Hannah turned her head toward the door, then pushed her chair back and stood. "Why, Sadie, it's good to see ye," Hannah said. "Are ye hungry? We ain't got much cooked, 'cept pone. And we have some milk."

Sadie ignored Hannah as if she hadn't spoken. Her vacant brown eyes still looked straight at Eden. She walked over the threshold and made for Eden's bed. Her hands were clasped in front of her, carefully cupping some object. Eden couldn't tell what it was.

In spite of the fact she'd tried to convince herself of Sadie's harmlessness only a few moments ago, Eden's arms instinctively tightened their hold on the baby.

Hannah followed the woman across the room, frowning. "Sadie," she said, her voice louder and firmer. "Come on over to th' table and I'll fix ye a plate o' vittles."

Again the woman ignored her. She reached the bedside and stood there looking at the baby nestled against Eden's breast. Sadie's eyes were different now. A yearning hunger had replaced the vacant expression. Her hands unclasped and she extended them, a small object held in their curve.

Eden drew in her breath and shrank back farther.

Hannah reached the bedside, too, and looked down at Sadie's hands. "Why, that's right purty." She smiled at the woman.

Sadie moved a step closer to the bed, her hands still extended. "I made it fer the babe," she told Eden.

Eden forced her gaze away from Sadie's disturbing eyes and looked down at the woman's hands. Sadie held a small basket woven of pine straw. And as Hannah had said, it was intricately made, beautiful. Eden let out her breath in a relieved *whoosh*.

She felt ashamed of herself for her fears. The woman only wanted to give Annie Rose a gift. Of course, her eyes would hold yearning. No doubt the baby reminded her of her own lost little one. Eden felt tears behind her eyelids at that thought. "Thank you," she said.

"Well, that's right nice o' you," Hannah said warmly. "Here, give it to me and I'll put it away fer her till she grows some and it kin pleasure her."

Sadie didn't move or speak. Hannah plucked the tiny basket from her hands and took hold of the other woman's arm. Sadie let Hannah lead her across the room to the table.

"Now, you jist set down, and I'll fix you somethin' to eat." Hannah set the woven basket on the table, then pulled out one of the wooden chairs and motioned toward it.

"No, no, I cain't take th' time," Sadie said, backing toward the doorway.

"Wait!" Hannah said. "Iffen you cain't stay, I'll give you a pone to take along." She got one of the cornpones from a covered plate and gave it to the woman.

Sadie looked at the pone for a moment, bit into it hungrily, chewing and swallowing, then took another large bite as she turned and left the cabin.

Eden and Hannah watched her go. Hannah picked up the small basket from the table and turned it around in her hands. She glanced at Eden.

"I never heared tell o' Sadie a-doin' anythin' like this afore. But now that I'm thinkin' on it, I recollect she used to make baskets and her man carried them down to the settlement and bartered them. Course, thet were afore she went crazy and her man left the ridge."

Taking a deep breath and letting it out, Eden tried to relax. Sadie's unexpected visit had disturbed her more than she wanted

Hannah to guess. She supposed these overprotective feelings were only another part of being a new mother.

"I feel so sorry for her," Eden said. "Even more now that I have Annie Rose. I can't imagine anything happening to her. It might be enough to make a woman lose her mind."

Hannah nodded solemnly, a faraway expression coming into her eyes. "I lost five young 'uns, two o' them babes in arms."

Compunction smote Eden. And one of them in a useless, futile battle. "I'm sorry, Mother Clayborne," she said. "I didn't mean to make you remember." Was her mother-in-law also recalling Alston's death?

Annie Rose made a small, discontented sound, and Eden shifted her to the other breast. That accomplished, she looked up at Hannah to see the older woman gazing at the baby, a loving smile curving her mouth.

"You didn't, honey. That was a long time ago." She paused, lifting her head to look at Eden. "And I'm a-beginnin' to be able to think on Alston and recollect the good times. And not the bad endin'. Ever'time I look at this babe, it makes that easier."

Her gaze held Eden's for a long moment. "And you and the babe have got long lives ahead o' ye. You got to start thinkin' 'bout that. Dwellin' on the past ain't good fer a body." Her smile became wry. "I know I'm a fine 'un to talk about that, the way I laid up in the bed all them months."

"You couldn't help it," Eden said quickly, firmly. "You were truly sick." What was Hannah trying to tell her?

"I reckon so," she said, "but it seems like a quare thing, now I'm over it. I caused you a lot o' extry work, and you takened sich good keer o' me. Jist like my own gal."

Eden laid her hand on the other woman's arm. "That's how I feel, Mother Clayborne."

Hannah patted her hand. "Yore a fine woman, Eden. Alston was lucky to have you fer his own." Again she gave Eden a searching look. "But now, honey, ye got to make a new life fer yoreself and this leetle 'un. You cain't stay here on this ridge. It ain't fer a woman like you."

Shocked, Eden stared at her. "Are you trying to get rid of me?"

"Course not," Hannah declared. "But there ain't nothin' here fer ye."

"*You're* here," Eden said, her voice very firm, her gaze very straight. "If I go anywhere, you'll come along with me."

Shaking her head, Hannah laughed. "I've lived on this old ridge, in this cabin, ever since I married nigh on fifty year ago. It's home to me. I couldn't never leave it."

What were they talking about? Eden suddenly wondered. The possibility of her returning to Connecticut with her parents? If and when they answered her letter and came to visit?

Or was her mother-in-law trying to tell her something entirely different—that there might be another reason she would consider leaving this ridge? Another kind of new beginning for her and Annie Rose?

Would Hannah heartily approve of that choice, too?

Chapter Twenty-Two

Sitting at the table, Eden held Annie Rose against her shoulder and gently patted her back, loving the feel of the warm little body cuddled against her. The morning sun slanted through the doorway as Jesse came in.

He smiled at her, his glance lingering. "I can't believe how fast she's growing," he said.

Eden smiled back, feeling warmth come to her cheeks. "Neither can I."

She watched him set the bucket of milk on the small kitchen worktable, her gaze lingering. Her flush deepened as he half turned toward her. Quickly, she rose and walked to Annie Rose's cradle, placed the baby in it, then came back to where Jesse still stood.

She got out the straining cloth and held it tautly across one of the big bowls, not looking directly at him, while Jesse carefully poured the milk through it. "Bossy's still giving plenty of milk," she said into what was fast becoming an awkward silence.

"Yes," Jesse agreed, then was silent again.

The mornings and evenings were getting nippy, now that September was advancing, and he wore the butternut jacket he'd carried the first time she saw him. That time seemed so far away even though it had only been a few months. Now, he was such a part of their lives she couldn't imagine being without him.

But she'd better start imagining it.

Because Annie Rose was seven weeks old. It was long past the time when Jesse should be returning to his home in Georgia.

Her mind shied away from that thought. She set the bowl aside and got another one, and Jesse poured the remainder of the milk through the cloth. "Bossy's a good milk cow," he said. "We had several Guernseys, too."

"That's what Hannah always says," Eden answered. She could feel the tension building between them, knew Jesse felt it as strongly as she did. Whenever he was in the cabin, all her nerve ends seemed to be attuned to his presence, his voice, his every movement.

Why were they saying these trivial things when there was so much that needed to be talked out? Or was there? Maybe only she felt this way. Jesse could merely be waiting for her to release him so he could return home.

He and Cade had set them up well for the coming winter. All the wood they'd need for cooking and for the fireplace was cut and neatly stacked on the porch and against the cabin wall.

The root cellar was filled with the garden's bounty. Strings of green beans, which Hannah called leather britches, and many other dried foods hung from the rafters. Most of the corn was picked and in the corn crib.

Now that Hannah was well on her way to full recovery, they could manage fine. Her heart denied that, insisted she needed Jesse for far more than helping with the chores. She tried to ignore that, too, because she had no idea how he felt about her. That uncertainty no longer plagued her.

Eden knew how she felt—she loved Jesse Bainbridge.

She'd probably loved him from their first meeting, no matter how hard she'd tried to deny it. But Jesse had never given her any reason to think his feelings went any deeper than desire.

Oh? her mind asked. Or was it her heart? What about those special times when she'd felt as if they could see into each other's souls? What about when Annie Rose was born? There seemed to be something between them that night she'd never felt before.

Jesse turned toward her, his gaze meeting hers and holding. A shiver of even more intense awareness slid down her spine. Hannah was outside, at the privy. For the first time since the baby's birth, she and Jesse were alone together.

As he looked at her she felt almost mesmerized, not able to turn her head away, remembering those times when he'd held her in his arms . . .

"Eden, we have to talk." At last he had a moment alone with her. And if she agreed to his suggestion, they'd have more than that. Jesse was acutely conscious of her deep blue eyes, her gleaming black braids, her newly slim body. He tried to ignore all that and concentrate on what he had to say.

She hesitated, something he couldn't interpret coming into her eyes. Then she nodded. "Yes, we do."

There weren't too many places they could be alone. The cabin was out of the question. That left the barn or the spring. He wanted more privacy than the barnyard offered, and he couldn't see them perching up in the hayloft.

"Will you meet me at the spring in half an hour?" he asked.

"Yes, I'll meet you," Eden quickly agreed.

"Good." Jesse smiled at her and left the cabin.

Eden watched him go. As he walked down the porch steps, a beam of sunlight caught him, gilding his hair to gold, making her remember the first time she'd seen him that day, walking toward the cabin. Exhausted and hurt and sick, he'd still had some kind of inner strength left—strength she'd attributed to his southern aristocratic roots and disparaged.

He'd represented all the things she disliked about his class of people. And when he'd revealed his identity, his role in Alston's death, her dislike had become personal.

All that seemed far away and almost unreal to her now. Her feelings had changed radically. She hoped Jesse's had, too, but she couldn't be sure.

What she *was* sure of was the fact her life must soon change. Her parents were alive and well. They'd been overjoyed to get her letter, thrilled to learn they were grandparents, and were now somewhere between Connecticut and here.

"We can't wait to show off our granddaughter to everyone at home," her mother had written.

They were taking it for granted she'd return to Connecticut with them. After today's talk with Jesse, she might well do it, if she could persuade Hannah to come, too.

Bleakness hit her at that thought. Because today she and Jesse had to explore their feelings, honestly and openly, for the first time.

The thought scared her to death.

Cade, kneeling on the ground beside a ginseng bed, pulled up another root. The earthy smell was strong in his nostrils as he broke off the top and put the root into the burlap sack between him and Willa. He glanced up to find her grinning at him. "What's so funny?" he asked, grinning back.

"You look like you've been doin' this all yore—your life," Willa said. She sat back on her heels, sticking out her lower lip and blowing a wisp of flaxen hair away from her forehead. She wished they could stay here all day, in this shady ravine.

But they couldn't. She wasn't even supposed to be here with Cade. Ever since the day Mam had tried to make Cade marry her, she'd been forbidden to have anything to do with anyone at the Clayborne cabin. If Mam found out they'd been meeting here, she'd get the switching of her life.

"It's not a hard thing to learn." Cade sat back, too, for a little rest. They'd been working steadily the last two hours, and soon he'd have to go back to the Claybornes' cabin. And Willa would have to go to hers.

"I reckon not," she conceded. "You know how to do all kinds o' things I never thought you would."

Cade eyed her curiously. "Why? Because my family owned a plantation? I was taught to do about everything the workers did."

Willa nodded. "I can see that. And you know your family still does own a plantation."

He looked down at the ground, not wanting to think of all that again. "Only the land." When he looked back up at her, she was frowning at him.

"There you are, all down-hearted agin. I still say you ought to be happy that you do have the land!"

They hadn't talked about this since that other time when she'd made him feel a lot more hopeful about the possibility of rebuilding his family's home, starting over. Now, with the passage of time, that hopefulness had died.

He shrugged. "Land's not much good if you haven't the money to do anything with it."

He saw she was going to give him another talking-to. Today he didn't feel like it. It was time, past time, for him and Jesse to be leaving this ridge. And he'd be going back to Alabama. He wasn't looking forward to it.

"Let's not get started on that," he said quickly. "Let's talk about you today, Willa."

She looked surprised. "Me? There ain't nothin' interestin' about me."

Her voice was so flat and final. It disturbed Cade. He didn't want her to feel that way about herself. "Of course there is," he said. "Why, you're the most interesting girl I ever knew."

Her surprised expression deepening, she stared at him. A tinge of red appeared on her cheeks. She looked down at the skirt of her drab calico dress.

He'd embarrassed her, Cade realized, surprised at her reaction.

Lifting her head, she gave him a straight look. "You don't have to say things like that to me. I know I'm jist an ignorant hill girl. And that's all I'll ever be."

Anger filled Cade. He got up, standing over her. "You are not, Willa Freeman! You're one of the smartest girls I ever met. I already told you that. And I meant it."

She tilted her head up and looked at him. The pose accentuated the fine-boned lines of her face. Her eyes looked a deeper blue in the shadows of the trees surrounding them. Sorrow and resignation were in her eyes. Something else, too, that made him feel good and a little scared at the same time.

"Maybe so, but what difference does that make? The ridge women don't do nothin' but take keer o' th' cabins and have young 'uns."

His anger increased. "You make me so mad when you talk like that," he said fiercely.

She got up and stood facing him. "Why? That's how you were talkin' about yoreself and how bad off your family is, too."

He stared at her, shock driving out the anger. Finally, a smile curved his mouth upward. "You're right. I was. You need to give me a good kick and I need to shake you—like this!"

He put his hands on her shoulders and gave her a little teasing shake. "There, now I'll turn around and you can kick me."

He grinned at her, expecting her pert grin in return. But she only looked at him, her face tilted up toward his, that something in her eyes he couldn't identify growing stronger.

"Willa?" he asked, a strange tremor going down his spine. Her pink lips were slightly parted. She had such a pretty mouth. Slowly he lowered his head to hers, his mouth brushing against her own in an infinitely light kiss.

She stood there for a moment longer, then jerked away from him, her blue eyes wide. Now he could plainly read the expression in them: it was fear.

Silently, he cursed her mother for the poison she'd introduced into their friendship.

Friendship? Hadn't he begun to wish for more than that? But he also knew they were still too young for anything else.

And besides that, Willa was right, they were worlds apart in background. Not that he cared about that.

But *she* cared. And he didn't think she was going to change her mind.

So it was probably best for both of them that he and Jesse would soon be leaving the ridge.

Eden pushed aside the overhanging limb of the willow tree, letting herself into the small, private space by the spring.

Jesse was already here, sitting on the bench. She looked at the back of his head, feeling the familiar tension grip her, tightening her stomach muscles.

Why had she agreed to this meeting? Maybe he hadn't

heard her. Maybe she could quietly back out and return to the cabin . . .

Jesse turned his head and smiled at her. He moved over on the bench, patting the space beside him. "Come and sit down," he invited. He tried to make his voice casual, hoping it gave away none of the uncertainty he felt.

He'd caught her. She had to go through with this now. She smiled back, but her facial muscles felt stiff, reflecting the growing tension in her whole body. She moved to the bench and sat beside him.

It was chilly today, closed into this small, damp space. She shivered, pulling her shawl around her, remembering the other time they'd sat here, when he'd talked her into allowing him to stay for those two weeks . . .

How aware of him she'd been with every cell of her body, just like now. Then there was the other time, when he'd carried her to this bench, the day she'd tried to prove she didn't need him in any way. How wrong she'd been about that. She'd loved the feel of his arms around her, even though she'd tried not to admit it, even to herself.

Eden could admit it now, acknowledge she wanted his arms around her again. She shifted a little on the hard seat.

Jesse caught her slight movement, correctly assessing it. She was as unsettled as he. Now that he had her here alone with him, he didn't know where to start. He looked at her lovely profile. She'd be beautiful when she was eighty. He wanted to be beside her in all the years to come . . .

"I—we need to talk about Cade and me going back to Georgia," he said at last.

Damn it! He didn't want to talk about that at all. He wanted to tell her he loved her. He wanted to ask her if she loved him, too—if she'd go back to Georgia with him. But he couldn't spring that on her all at once. He had to feel her out, lead up to it gradually.

He saw her jaw tense at his words. Spots of color appeared on her cheekbones. Did that mean she didn't want him to leave?

She turned toward him, embarrassment making her voice stiff. "Yes, we do." His words had taken her by surprise. She'd expected him to say they had to talk about their feelings for each other.

Had she been completely wrong in her assessment of his feelings? Had he asked her to come here only so he could tell her he and Cade must leave? Had he stayed these weeks since Annie Rose's birth only because he thought she needed him and because she'd said no more about his going?

Now that Hannah was recovering so well, the baby flourishing, was he champing at the bit to be back home? It certainly seemed that way.

Those thoughts sent a tremor of almost unbearable loss through her, but she managed to give him what she hoped was a friendly smile, because she owed him so much.

"Of course you need to get back to your home," she said. "Hannah and I are very grateful for all you and Cade have done. I don't know how we could have gotten by without you, despite all my arguments to the contrary."

Dismay swept over Jesse at her prim, stiff expression of thanks. Were all the barriers on her side still firmly in place? Even worse, were all the tender feelings on his side alone? Had he been so wrong? Had she never felt more than passion for him? And now, maybe not even that?

There was no way to lead up to this gradually, he decided. He shouldn't even have tried. He had to tell her how he felt, bare his heart to her, and hope that she cared for him.

Her hands were folded in her lap. She was looking straight ahead again. But that muscle in her jaw was still tensed. She wasn't as much at ease as she wanted him to think.

He laid one of his big hands on both of hers, feeling her surprise as her hands jerked beneath his own. Her skin wasn't warm today. He rubbed his fingers across hers and felt her slight shiver.

"You're cold," he said, suddenly concerned for her. "We shouldn't have come here. We'd better go back—" Oh, hell! Why did he keep sabotaging his plans?

No more of this. He took a deep breath and let it out. She was still gazing straight ahead.

"Eden, look at me!" he commanded, more forcefully than he'd intended.

She turned startled eyes to him. Her heart skipped a beat as she saw the intent expression on his face. "All right, I'm looking," she said, striving for lightness in her tone.

Maybe she'd been cold a moment ago, but that was fast changing. His hand on hers, the way he looked at her, made heat begin to circulate through her body. She swallowed, trying to keep her composure.

Jesse saw her small movement, then his gaze fixed on her full, pink lips. God, how hungry he was for her. But they had to talk, he reminded himself desperately. He had to know how she felt. His hands tightened on hers.

Eden's lips parted a little in unconscious invitation, and she heard him draw in his breath. What did that look of his mean? That he wanted her as she wanted him?

"Eden," he said again, his voice hoarse. "I want to kiss you, hold you in my arms. But this time you must come to me freely. Will you—can you do that?"

Her heart leapt as she listened to his words. She understood what he meant by that question.

Could she go to him without the guilt that had been between them from that moment in the barn when he'd revealed his identity? She kept her gaze steady on his as she listened to what her heart and soul told her.

Yes, she could do that, because she no longer felt that guilt.

Was he telling her he, too, had shed that burden?

She had to know.

"What about you?" she asked. "Can you come to me freely?"

Again she heard his sharp intake of breath. His eyes seemed to see into the depths of her. "Yes, I can," he answered.

Finally she nodded. "So can I," she said clearly, her voice steady. The oddest feeling swept over her. In this hidden bower, they seemed to be pledging vows to each other—vows of the deepest, most sacred kind.

For another long moment they looked at each other, then Eden swayed toward Jesse and he leaned toward her. When their lips finally touched, she felt as if a long drought of her body, heart, and soul was ending.

It had been with her all her life, although until this moment, she'd not been aware of it. He trembled against her as the kiss deepened, intensifying her own desire, making her tremble, too.

Jesse slid his arms around her neck, drawing her close to him, as he had those other stolen times. But this was so different, he knew. This moment, the moments to come, weren't stolen. They were freely given.

All his senses seemed fully alive for the first time. He heard the gurgle of the stream, the rustle of the tree limbs as a passing breeze stirred them. He felt the rough wood of the bench beneath him, then the satin of Eden's soft lips beneath his own.

She sighed and her lips parted. He drew in his breath and his tongue slid into the velvet recesses of her mouth. She smelled of sunshine and fresh air and a fragrance that was all her own. She tasted sweeter than honeysuckle.

Eden moved her arms around Jesse's neck, her shawl sliding off her shoulders onto the bench. She no longer needed that, she noted; she was no longer cold. Heat spiraled through her body. Her fingers curved into the hair on his nape, her hands clenching and unclenching as she kneaded the hard muscles of his neck.

She moved closer still to him, wanting to be as close as it was possible for two separate people to be to each other. But it was awkward, sitting turned sideways on the bench. There was no way to get close enough. Without conscious thought she stood, and Jesse came up from the bench with her, their mouths still pressed tightly together.

And now their bodies were, too. She drew in her breath at the feel of his hard length pressed against her, the unmistakable evidence of his arousal. She felt his heart pounding against her own in an unmatched rhythm.

Against her mouth, Jesse drew a ragged breath, then took his lips away from hers. He picked her up in his arms as he'd done those other times and stood holding her, looking down into her uptilted face.

"I want to love you," he told her, his voice uneven and hoarse.

She looked into his golden eyes, heard the unspoken question in his voice, and nodded. "Yes. I want you to love me. I want to love you." Her own voice was remarkably steady, she thought. She felt no hesitation in her decision.

Slowly, tenderly, he knelt and laid her down on the soft, mossy ground beside the spring, then stayed on his knees beside her. "I've dreamed of this so many times," he told her. "But I was always afraid to hope it would ever come to pass."

Her hand reached up to gently stroke down his cheek, curve around his jawline. "So have I," she confessed. "I was beginning to fear you'd go back to Georgia without ever saying a word to me, without ever touching me again."

"I could never have done that." He stretched out beside her, pulling her against him again, reveling in the feel of her soft body so close to his own. Again their mouths found each other, and as the kiss deepened, hunger leapt between them like a fire too long banked.

The earthy smell of the grass pillowing her head filled her nostrils. Over them, the green leaves of the willow, now tinged with brown, swayed, enclosing them.

She felt his hands on the buttons down the front of her calico dress, and after a moment, gently pushed them aside and performed the operation herself, pulling the halves of her bodice apart to reveal the white cotton chemise underneath. Those buttons were quickly mastered, too.

She heard his indrawn breath as he looked at her full white breasts. Almost reverently, he cupped one in his hand, his thumb gently stroking the rosy brown nipple. Instantly it hardened.

He lowered his head and his tongue laved her nipple, his teeth gently nipping at it. Her hand slipped around his neck once more, pulling him closer to her.

"That feels so good," she said, her voice husky with desire. "So wonderfully good."

"You are so sweet," he answered, his voice unsteady.

Eden looked at his bent head. A smile curved her mouth, her other hand reached up to rake through the untamed strands of his tawny hair. As she'd expected, it felt coarse to her fingertips, yet at the same time, oddly erotic. Deep inside, at the very core of her, something began uncoiling, reaching out . . .

His mouth left her breast to close over her mouth once more. His tongue thrust possessively into her dark recesses, then withdrew and thrust again.

Heat swirled out from her core explosively, making her arch against him. She opened her mouth wider. Her tongue found his and curled around it and against it . . .

Jesse's hands slid under her back, pulling her up off the grassy carpet, closer to him. His body arched against hers, his manhood pressing hard against her softness. He felt himself trembling with hungry desire as he lowered her back down. Never, ever, had he needed a woman so badly.

"I want you so much, all of you," he whispered, his voice trembling, too. His hands slid out from under her. He moved away from her a few inches. "Do you understand what I mean—do you want me, too?"

In answer, she reached her hands, her arms, out toward him, a smile of piercing sweetness illuminating her face. "Yes," she whispered back. "Oh, yes!"

He drew her to him, flattening both their bodies together tightly, then he slid his hands under her again and rolled them both over, so that in a moment she was lying on her back and he was close against her.

They smiled at each other, loving smiles that soon turned to smoldering looks. "Kiss me," she begged, reaching up to pull his head down to hers.

Jesse complied gladly, his mouth closing over hers with that same possessiveness of a moment ago. Their tongues played with each other, but then Jesse's thrusts became harder, the rhythm mimicking that other rhythm their heated bodies urged them to begin.

His mouth still closed around hers, Jesse pushed her skirts up. Eden arched upward, undoing the drawstring that held her drawers, and helping him pull them down, her trembling movements as eager and urgent as his.

She felt him fumbling with his own clothes, and in a moment he lowered himself to her again. She closed her eyes and drew in her breath in startled delight, moving her thighs apart as his hard, throbbing manhood pressed against her softness.

He moved back a little and pressed against her again, demanding entry, and then she felt him slide inside her hot, wet sheath, and it closed around him convulsively.

"Jesse!" she gasped, curving her lower body closer to his— closer, yes, closer!

Jesse felt as if he was going to explode. He forced himself to stop, lie rigidly still, hold back. In a few moments he raised himself up over Eden and looked deeply into her sapphire eyes. "Am I hurting you?" he asked softly.

She gazed just as deeply into his golden eyes. "No," she answered. "No—oh, no!" She moved her body upward and heard him gasp with pleasure.

His mouth closed over hers again and he held her to him fiercely as the ageless rhythm drew them into its spell. Jesse's movements and Eden's answering ones became ever more frenzied. Finally, she felt the aching need in the most inner part of her gather itself together and gain its release in spasms of pleasure so intense that tears formed in her eyes. She felt Jesse find his own ecstasy, then collapse upon her breast, his breathing harsh and rasping.

She caressed his gold-streaked hair, sweet languidness stealing over her, her eyes closing drowsily. In a moment he slid off her to lie beside her and draw her close again. His hand stroked her disheveled hair back from her heated forehead.

"You feel so good. This feels so right," he murmured in her ear. He felt himself drowsing off. He hadn't been sleeping well. And it was heaven to have her in his arms like this. He could stay here forever.

Dimly he heard someone whistling a tune. Cade, he thought drowsily, coming back from wherever he'd gone . . .

Cade! Jesse's eyes opened wide. His head jerked up, and so did Eden's. They stared at each other, coming out of their love-induced spell. "We'd better get out of here," he said finally. He turned away from her, adjusting his clothing, then got to his feet.

Eden watched his movements. She felt a sense of letdown and wondered why, when only a few moments ago she'd been gloriously happy and content. She got up, too, pulling her skirts down, buttoning her chemise and dress.

They turned to each other at the same moment, almost colliding. "Oh, sorry," Jesse said, smiling at her.

But his smile didn't linger; it was almost perfunctory, Eden thought, watching him quickly rake his long fingers through his hair, then lean down to examine the grass where they'd been lying.

He wanted to be sure Cade didn't suspect what they'd done here, she thought, embarrassment sweeping through her, and anger as well. She didn't want to feel either negative emotion about what had happened between them. She wanted to keep her joyful happiness, hug it close to her, savor it.

She wanted them both to be proud of their love for each other, she realized. She hated for it to so quickly become a furtive, hidden thing, that they had to keep anyone from knowing.

A shock traveled through her nerve ends. Why was she calling it *love,* she asked herself. Jesse had said he wanted to love her, he hadn't said that he *did* love her.

Those two things weren't the same at all. She pressed her lips together and smoothed her hair back as best she could, then gave a frowning glance at her wrinkled skirt.

Jesse looked at her downcast head, felt her sudden withdrawal. Damn it! What had he done? He shouldn't have taken her here on the grass. He hadn't planned that at all when he'd asked her to meet him. He'd intended to have them talk everything out. What in hell had happened?

He knew he loved her. In his dreams the consummation of that love he hoped she also felt for him had taken place in a proper bed, after a proper marriage ceremony.

But the fire that always flamed between them whenever they were alone together had flared out of control today. And at the time it had seemed so right, so inevitable.

It was only now, in the aftermath, facing the ordinary world again, that it had taken on this sordid feel. Hell, it still hadn't for him, but look at her! Silently he swore again as Cade's whistle sounded closer. There was no time to talk things out, not now.

He glanced at her again to find her head up, that proud, almost haughty expression that he hadn't seen on her face for weeks once more firmly in place. He sighed inwardly.

"Are you ready?" he asked her.

She nodded, stepping up beside him as he moved the overhanging limbs of the willow aside and let them out.

"Eden, we have to talk," he said again, as he had earlier that day, in the cabin. He glanced at her, smiling tightly. "I mean, really talk."

She nodded, stiffly. "Yes." If he did love her, why didn't he say so? It was such a simple little three-word sentence: *I love you . . .*

Because he probably didn't. And now that she'd given herself to him so eagerly, so shamelessly, he no doubt only wanted to talk about returning to his home. That's what he'd said just a few minutes ago, right before she'd told him she was afraid he'd leave without ever touching her again.

He'd denied that, then at once proved it. Oh, he'd touched her, all right. Thoroughly and completely.

But love—the kind of love that led to marriage—was a different thing entirely. Especially to men.

Eden glanced at Jesse, watching the muscles of his strong legs move as he walked, remembered the sensual heights he'd taken her to only minutes before.

She was no longer unsure of her own feelings. She'd exchanged the shackles of guilt for other ones. Bonds of love that were just as binding.

But Jesse had given her no reason to believe he loved her in return. He'd only spoken of desire and wanting. He'd only said he needed to talk to her about him and Cade going back to Georgia.

Not once had he mentioned anything about her and Annie Rose being included in that journey. The barrier of guilt between them had been dissolved. But what difference did that make now?

Cade walked toward them, smiling. "Your parents are here!" he told Eden, his smile widening.

Her parents! The nervous anticipation she'd had for weeks

over this long-delayed reunion intensified, mixed with the new doubts and fears of the last few minutes.

Oh, why couldn't they have come tomorrow, giving her and Jesse time to talk this through?

Chapter Twenty-Three

"Oh, Eden, it's so wonderful to see you again!" Rosalind Thornton, standing on the cabin porch, hugged her daughter, tears in her eyes. Her husband stood by, a happy smile on his face as he waited his turn to greet Eden.

Tied to trees were the horses they'd hired in Cherry Creek and ridden up the trail from the valley. The livery stable worker who'd come with them to act as guide, and to bring their baggage, was already heading back down to the settlement.

Out of the corner of her eye Eden saw Jesse and Cade turn and walk back toward the barnyard. Shocked surprise hit her. She tried to tell herself Jesse was only showing sensitivity, not wanting to intrude on the reunion. But her doubts increased.

If Jesse loved her, he'd be standing here beside her, proudly letting her parents know he cared.

"It's been such a long time." Eden hugged her mother back just as fervently. She firmly pushed her doubts and fears aside. She owed it to her parents to present a smiling, happy face.

Her mother looked fit and healthy, hardly different from when Eden had last seen her, more than four years before. Rosalind's black hair had more gray streaks, but her fair skin was still unlined, her carriage upright, her figure slender.

She gave her mother another smile, then let her father enfold her in his still strong arms, press her against his robust chest.

"Papa," she said, lifting her head to kiss his cheek. His hairline had receded, but its auburn color showed no gray at all. His ruddy color was still fresh, his deep blue eyes were clear.

She saw tears in them, too, as he smoothed her hair back. "My little girl," he said, a catch in his voice.

"And where is Hannah Rosalind?" Eden's mother asked, turning toward the cabin door. "Oh, there she is."

Her mother's voice had softened, taken on the intonation of an indulgent grandmother, Eden thought, amazed as she, too, turned to see Hannah standing in the open doorway, the baby in her arms.

"May I hold her?" Rosalind asked, moving toward Hannah, her arms already outstretched.

"Ye shore kin." Hannah gave the other woman a wide smile as she handed her the baby. "We call her Annie Rose."

Eden saw her mother's eyes widen a bit at Hannah's speech, but she smiled back warmly. "Annie Rose, I like that." She looked down at the wide-awake, alert baby, her expression as softened as her voice.

Norris moved closer to his wife, gazing down at the baby. "Pretty little thing," he said. Eden saw his face held the masculine equivalent of his wife's doting gaze.

Rosalind glanced up at Eden, who was still giving her a somewhat bemused look. "She looks like you did at this age."

"You can still remember how I looked at seven weeks?" Eden asked, her voice teasing, relieved the reunion with her parents was going so well. If only she and Jesse . . . no, she wouldn't think about that now.

"Of course, I remember," her mother said, her voice now mock-indignant. "You were the most beautiful infant in the world." She glanced down at the baby again, her lips curving in another smile. "Just like Annie Rose."

Hannah laughed. "I reckon she is jist about the sightliest young 'un I ever seen," she agreed.

Eden forced a smile. It was wonderful to have her two mothers here together, she told herself firmly. And maybe Jesse was right to wait until later to introduce himself. Maybe that was the only reason he'd left. Desperately, Eden tried to hold onto this thought, not let the painful doubts creep back.

This *was* enough to deal with now, without having to introduce Jesse, explain why he and Cade were here on the ridge, sleeping in the barn. She had no doubt her parents would consider the whole arrangement distinctly odd. It was only a short while until noon dinner. The awkward task could be performed then.

At least there should be plenty of lively talk around the table. She wouldn't have to worry about catching Jesse's eye, or, worse than that, wondering if he was deliberately ignoring her if he didn't look at her—and what it meant.

"Gosh, Miss Eden's parents sure aren't like these hill people," Cade said, his voice showing his surprise. He lengthened his shorter stride to keep up with Jesse, who seemed to be in a big hurry to get back to the barnyard.

"Why did you expect them to be? You know Eden's from the North," Jesse answered, hearing the tightness in his voice.

"I know, but I didn't expect them to look like . . ." His voice trailed off, as if uncertain how to phrase what he meant.

"Like our families did before this damnable war changed everything," Jesse finished for him, the tightness in his voice increasing. His own surprise exceeded Cade's. No, he felt more than surprise.

Stunned shock would be more like it.

Why had he unconsciously assumed Eden's parents would be from some ordinary, middle-class family? Because she'd married a hill man, he assumed. But he'd known she was educated, cultured, from the first moment he'd seen her, heard her speak.

"I guess so," Cade agreed, giving his cousin an uneasy glance. Jesse sounded like he was mad at something—or someone. He and Miss Eden had acted funny ever since he'd found them by the spring. As if he'd interrupted something. His face reddened when he suddenly remembered Miss Eden's hair had been mussed. But they hadn't been angry.

Damn it! Jesse swore silently. He should have forced himself to resist that overwhelming physical pull between him and Eden. They should have talked everything out.

He relived the moments when he'd at last held her, loved her, as he'd burned to do for months. She wanted the loving as much as he. Hell, she'd *said* so! They'd fallen into each other's arms, but they'd done it with their eyes open, knowing exactly what they were doing.

What had gone wrong so soon afterward? Why had she avoided his eyes, acted as if she was ashamed of their loving? Was it only because Cade had so abruptly ended their special time together, startling her as he himself had been startled? Or was it more than that?

He knew that desire had swept her away as it had him. But maybe, unlike him, desire was *all* she felt.

Now, with her parents here, it would be almost impossible to talk to her privately. He didn't know how long they planned to stay. He didn't know anything about them, he realized. And he could have kicked himself for that, too.

Because when they left, Eden and Annie Rose might very well go with them. They *should* go . . .

It was clear to him, as it was to Cade, from the few moments when he'd stood there watching Eden's parents, hearing them talk, that they were well-to-do, and no doubt also socially prominent. He and his cousin had recognized that from their clothing, their speech, the air of assurance that clung to them like an invisible sign.

He and Cade had also belonged to that social group, once upon a time. Up until the war had changed the South forever.

For himself, he didn't care that much. If he had the money to start over, begin planting again in a small way, he'd be content. Farming was in his blood. He couldn't imagine any other kind of life.

But after her years of hardship on this ridge, Eden needed a different life for her and her baby. An easy, comfortable one— such as it was obvious her parents could offer her. He couldn't hope to do that for years to come, if ever.

He'd been a fool to think she'd marry him and go with him back to his ruined, impoverished plantation. And even if she was willing to do that, he had no right to ask it of her. He couldn't be that selfish.

He realized there was no need for them to talk, after all.

No amount of talking could change the facts. He loved Eden so much that leaving her would tear out his heart, but that was what he had to do.

"I guess we'll be leaving here soon, won't we?" Cade asked into the silence. He wondered again if his cousin and Miss Eden had been kissing each other at the spring. Like he had kissed Willa.

"Yes," Jesse said shortly, not looking at him. They'd reached the barn and he went inside and came out with some burlap sacks. He tossed a couple to Cade.

Cade gave him a surprised look. "What's this for? We're caught up on all the chores and it won't be long until dinner."

Dinner. He didn't want to think about that. He looked down at his old gray pants, the same ones he'd worn when he'd come to this ridge months ago. Eden had mended them and his spare pair several more times, put a patch on one knee, and also kept his two shirts in decent wearing condition.

He didn't want to sit across the table from her mother, who wore her elegant gray traveling suit—or her father, in his well-tailored coat and trousers. He didn't want to feel their disdain.

"We can pick quite a bit of corn in an hour," Jesse answered, turning away, heading for the cornfield.

Without arguing further, Cade followed him. His cousin was mighty upset about something, and he knew it had to do with Miss Eden and her parents. But he didn't know what it was.

Cade had known they would leave soon. They'd already stayed a lot longer than they'd planned. He also knew he'd have a big argument with Jesse when they left.

Because he intended to go back to Georgia with Jesse, back to his family's plantation, instead of letting Jesse ride with him to his aunt's house in Alabama, where his mother and sister still stayed.

He kept thinking about this afternoon, when he'd been with Willa. Like that other time, she'd made him ashamed of his complaining, his downheartedness, about what had happened to his family and his home. She'd again made him see that compared to many other people, they still had a great deal left.

No matter what Jesse said, he was going to go back and clean up his family's plantation. Maybe, with Jesse's help, plant a crop next spring. Only then would he go to Alabama, try to talk his mother into coming home.

He'd never see Willa again after they left here, he supposed. Sadness coursed through him at the thought. So it was probably a good thing they had kissed each other.

It was their goodbye kiss.

"Eden tells me your home is near Savannah?" Rosalind Thornton smiled at Jesse, handing him the platter of fried chicken.

"Yes, ma'am," Jesse answered, smiling back a little warily as he took the dish. He couldn't help responding to her warmth, in spite of his earlier negative thoughts. Eden's father was warm and friendly, too—another surprise. Since Eden had said they were abolitionists—hell, they'd broken with her because of their beliefs—he'd expected them to be cool and disapproving with him.

Of course, maybe they were merely using good manners to mask their true feelings.

"We've seen some terrible photographs in the papers about the destruction in that area," Norris Thornton said. He savored a bite of chicken, then shook his head. "This war was a terrible thing for the whole country. Take us years to recover from it."

"Yes," Jesse answered, feeling himself stiffen. So, he and his people, his country, were to get pity, instead of the disdain he'd expected. Resentment coursed through him, replacing the warmth he'd begun to feel. These two obviously affluent people hadn't suffered any losses. It was easy enough for them to sympathize with the South's plight.

He glanced across the table and met Eden's gaze. Her deep blue eyes, so like her father's, looked back at him with no expression. His resentment increased. She'd introduced him as simply her husband's commanding officer, who'd so generously offered to help them out. Now, the cool way she looked at him, no one would ever think that only a little while ago they'd lain on the mossy grass, locked in each other's arms.

He realized Eden's father looked at him expectantly, awaiting a comment about his last remarks. Jesse nodded. "Yes, the war was terrible. I don't know if the country will ever recover from it entirely. I know the South probably won't . . . what's left of it."

His words had been harsher, his tone more bitter, than he'd intended, and he saw everyone around the table looking at him, various kinds of surprised, even shocked, expressions on their faces.

Rosalind Thornton recovered first. She smiled at her daughter. "This chicken is wonderful. You certainly have become a good cook. You'll have to give me this recipe."

Eden laughed. "Well, Mother," she said, her voice light, "first you have to chase down your chicken and wring its neck."

Her mother's eyes widened, the shock back on her face. But she recovered swiftly. She shook her head. "I can't believe how much you've changed. Why, you were nothing but a girl when you left Connecticut."

"Eden shore is a good cook," Hannah put in. "And she's a real fast learner. She kin do ever'thin' I do, and mostly better than I kin." She gave her daughter-in-law a fond smile.

Eden returned it, then, seeing an almost envious look cross her mother's face, felt her conscience give her a twinge. She hadn't meant to make her mother aware of how much time she'd missed in Eden's life—the years when she'd grown from a girl to a woman.

She'd only wanted to get the conversation back on a lighter level after Jesse's almost angry remarks. She could understand how he felt, but she didn't want her parents' first meal here on the ridge to end up in a shouting match.

Not that she really thought it would. Her father was diplomatic enough to head that off. But Jesse was obviously on edge, ill-at-ease with her parents. And all his previous resentments toward the North seemed to be resurfacing.

Or was that the real reason for his discomfort? Maybe it was due to the fact that he was sitting at the table with two people whose daughter he'd made passionate love with only an hour or so before.

And to the fact that he'd seemed to want to get away from said daughter as fast as he could afterward.

Eden swallowed a lump in her throat. Why hadn't she and Jesse talked everything out before they'd let passion consume them? Or was there anything *to* talk out on his side, except the date of his departure?

When their glances had met a few moments before, it hadn't reassured her. Jesse's gaze had been cool and distant, freezing her own, wiping off the smile she'd planned for him. Annie Rose had begun fussing in her cradle. Eden had excused herself and tended to the infant, half an eye on the people around the dinner table.

Her mother and father were trying to make conversation with Hannah and Jesse and Cade, with mixed success. Hannah, as unself-conscious as always, was pleasant with everyone. Cade was quieter than usual, a little downcast looking, she thought. Had he and Willa had an argument? That the two had been seeing each other she had no doubt.

Jesse was more than quiet. He was withdrawn, answering only in monosyllables after the one bitter outburst.

"Oh, Eden," Rosalind's voice floated across the room. "All our friends were asking about you when we told them about your letter. Especially Clarice and Gorden. You remember them?"

"Of course, Mother," Eden answered warily. Her mother had emphasized *Gorden*. Clarice Wilson had been her best friend for years. But Gorden Hallett had been more than that—almost her fiancé, before she'd met and fallen in love with Alston.

"Gorden still hasn't married," Rosalind continued, her voice light. "Can you believe that—as handsome and eligible as he is? Of course, he was in the war, but he came back with a shoulder injury after one of the early battles."

Eden heard a chair scrape on the puncheon floor and glanced up to see Jesse standing behind his, pushing it back against the table. "If you'll excuse me, I have some work that needs to be done," he said politely but distantly, his voice cool.

"Why, Jesse, cain't you set and visit with us fer a while?" Hannah asked.

"No, I'm sorry. Mrs. Thornton, Mr. Thornton, I'm glad to have made your acquaintance."

"It was nice to meet you, Mr. Bainbridge," Rosaline answered. "I'm sorry you can't stay now, but I'm sure we'll have other opportunities during our visit."

Jesse took a deep breath, knowing now was the time. No use for Eden to think she owed him anything. He'd let her off the hook, so she and her parents could begin planning their future. Without him in it.

"Yes, ma'am," Jesse answered, with an effort of will keeping his voice steady. "But Cade and I must be heading back to Georgia within the next few days."

Pain pierced Eden's heart at his unexpected words. She moved a little, causing the baby to fuss and settle more firmly against her breast. In a moment, Eden realized she was staring after Jesse, her mouth open, and no doubt with a stricken look on her face.

She closed her mouth, turning her head sharply away from Jesse's and Cade's retreating forms, adjusting the blanket modestly shielding her and Annie Rose from the room's other occupants.

Jesse really did plan to leave here, leave *her*. All he'd wanted to discuss was his departure. And only that strange physical pull, between them from the beginning, had drawn them into those minutes of passion. He felt the pull, too. She was sure of it.

But unlike her, that was *all* he felt.

He could make love to her with tenderness and fire—as she had with him—and afterward, walk away without a backward look. *Ride* away within a few days. Never see her again.

Hot tears stung her eyelids and she fiercely blinked them back before her parents or Hannah could notice.

All right, then. She was strong and tough. She'd *had* to be, these last four years. She'd survive this.

And to hell with Jesse Bainbridge!

Chapter Twenty-Four

"Are we really going to leave in the next few days?" Cade asked.

"Yes," Jesse answered. He clamped his jaws so tightly a sharp pain shot up the side of his cheek.

Half his attention was back in the cabin they walked away from so rapidly. He strained to hear the sound of Eden's footsteps hurrying to catch up with him.

To tell him he couldn't leave without her.

A mirthless smile curved his mouth upward. Why was he trying to fool himself? Why was he prolonging the agony? She'd never do that. And even if she did, he couldn't allow her to make that kind of sacrifice. His brain accepted those bleak facts.

So why couldn't he convince his foolish heart?

When Eden's mother had made that reference to—what was his name? Gorden Hallett?—then made a point of saying the man had never married, that was the final proof he needed. Her parents wanted to take her back to Connecticut with them.

They could offer her the kind of life she'd been accustomed to before her ill-fated marriage to Clayborne, the kind of life she and Annie Rose should have. Eventually, she'd marry someone of her own type, maybe even the man her parents had mentioned. She'd be a fool not to go. And Eden was no fool. She was a sweet, beautiful woman he wanted so badly he could think of little else.

But he had to. As if to put Eden and all thoughts of her behind, he walked even faster.

Cade gave his cousin a wary sideways glance. Boy, was Jesse mad about something! He didn't quite know what though. Miss Eden's parents might be Yankees, but they'd been nice as could be. Yet Jesse had acted like they'd insulted him.

He guessed Jesse and Miss Eden really didn't like each other that much, after all . . . didn't *love* each other. The word felt strange. Another thought, even stranger, slid into his mind: would there ever come a time when he and Willa would feel like that about each other?

No, you idiot, he quickly told himself. Because once you leave here, you'll never be back. And as Willa had said, she was a ridge girl. She'd live, marry, have children, and die right here on this stony hillside.

The thought sent a bleak feeling of loss spreading through him. Resolutely he tried to forget it, push it deep into his mind. One of these days, a few years from now, he'd marry, too, he supposed. A girl he'd grown up with, no doubt. Maybe one of the Simmons girls. There were two pretty ones a few years younger than him.

That thought made him feel worse.

"I guess we'd better start getting our stuff together, then."

"Yes," Jesse said, his voice still tight and clipped. He'd told the people in the cabin he'd be leaving in a few days. Why wait? There was nothing for him here now.

He'd done the job he'd made the journey from Georgia to do . . . *more* than done it. He'd seen Eden through her pregnancy, the birth of Annie Rose, and her recovery. She was ready to begin a new life now, back in her old home in the North.

Without him.

He tried to block out his memories of the lovemaking they'd

shared so short a time ago. How right she'd felt in his arms, how right and wonderful they'd been together.

He clenched his jaw again and walked through the big barn doors, Cade behind him. He began collecting his few possessions from the loft. It wouldn't take long to get his things together.

And early tomorrow morning, they'd ride down off this ridge for the last time.

"Mister Bainbridge is certainly taking the South's loss of the war hard," Rosalind said, her voice thoughtful.

"He did fer a while," Hannah answered. "But lately, he seemed to be feelin' a heap better. I don't know what's ailin' him today."

Eden heard the surprise in Hannah's voice and glanced up to see the other woman's eyes on her.

"I didn't intend to bring up things he didn't want to talk about, but apparently I did," Norris said ruefully.

Eden gave Annie Rose one last pat and laid her back in her cradle, her heart raw and hurting. How could she carry on a conversation with her parents this afternoon, when she felt like an injured animal, wanting only to crawl into a cave somewhere to lick her wounds?

She delayed as much as she could, adjusting the baby's gown, her covers, but finally she had to get off the bed and return to the dinner table.

Everyone had finished the meal. "I'll clear the table, then we can have some herb tea," she said, relieved her voice didn't reveal her feelings.

Rosalind also at once got up. "I'll do it," she said firmly, waving Hannah back when the older woman started to rise. "No, you stay right there, Hannah. You and Eden cooked this wonderful meal. You shouldn't also have to clean up after it. Eden, make the tea, then sit back down," she said, her crisp northern voice commanding. Her gaze lingered on Eden's faded, worn calico dress, her work-roughened hands.

Despite her misery, Eden felt her pride rising. She straightened, lifting her chin as the other woman briskly set about scraping and stacking plates. "Mother, don't tell me you've learned how to do dishes!"

Rosalind gave her a lifted-eyebrow glance. "I've always known how to do household chores, dear," she said, gently.

Eden at once felt ashamed of herself. "I know," she answered. "I was only teasing." She hadn't been, though. Not entirely.

She'd seen the earlier glances Rosalind had given her and Hannah, and the cabin. Her mother had tried to hide her feelings, but she was obviously dismayed and shocked to discover how her daughter had been living these last four years.

Eden went to the stove and stirred up the glowing coals, then added a few more sticks of wood, wood Jesse had sawed and split for her. Another piercing pain struck her at that thought, and she quickly dipped water into the kettle and set it on to heat.

Just because her mother had always had household help didn't mean she spent her days in idleness. She'd worked with several charities while Eden was growing up, been involved in community affairs. And of course, during the war, she must have been even busier. She wasn't lazy, and she was no snob.

But just the same, Eden realized her mother had hurt her pride. She'd been raised to consider self-pity a weakness. She wanted no pity of any kind.

She heard the scrape of a chair behind her.

"No use me sitting here watching you women work," her father said jovially.

Surprised, Eden heard more sounds of cutlery and plates being moved around. When she was living at home, her father had never appeared even to notice how food got to the table and was cleared away afterward.

"Papa, for heaven's sake, sit and talk to Hannah. We can do this." She got cups and saucers from a cupboard and brought them to the table.

Norris Thornton was stubbornly and efficiently getting the last of the dishes stacked. "Don't try to boss me around, daughter," he said, grinning at her. He handed them to his wife, who in turn took them to the worktable.

"Wal, I swear, I feel like a old lazy body," Hannah protested, squirming uneasily in her chair.

Annie Rose began to make small, fretful noises. Hannah's face lightened, and she quickly got up. "I'll git th' babe back to sleep." She hurried across the room.

Eden attended to the tea-making while her parents did the dishes with dispatch. Soon, the three of them sat around the table again with their full cups. Hannah, lying on the bed, gently rocked the cradle. Good. She still needed these afternoon rests.

"We've missed you very much," Rosalind said, after a moment. She cleared her throat. "We're so sorry we took such a strong, unyielding stand when you left with Alston."

"We were wrong," Norris said. "You did the right thing to go with your husband. We shouldn't have let our political differences come between us and our only daughter." His voice was gruff with feeling.

"And we regretted it almost as soon as you left." Rosalind reached across the table and squeezed her daughter's hand. "But when you didn't answer our letters, we thought you'd never forgive us."

Eden stared at them. "I never received any letters."

Her parents stared back, their faces shocked. "We should have thought of that possibility, and kept on writing," Rosalind finally said. "But—"

"But your pride wouldn't let you," Eden finished. "I know. I wrote a letter to you soon after I arrived here. And never mailed it because I thought you wanted nothing more to do with me."

Tears filled her eyes. She tried to blink them away, but this time they wouldn't go. Instead, they overflowed and ran down her cheeks. She swiped at them. Not all the tears were for the years away from her family. She, too, deeply regretted them, but her deeper pain came from knowing Jesse now planned to leave her. He might be packing up his things this minute. How could she let him go?

But how could she keep him when he didn't want to stay? Even worse, he didn't want her to go with him.

"And I've regretted I didn't get in touch with you before now," she told her parents, smiling through her tears, touched to see tears in their eyes, too.

Rosalind smiled. "The important thing is that we're all together again." She paused and glanced at her husband.

He nodded. "Yes. And we must *stay* together. We want you to go back with us. Come home." His voice was pleading.

Eden drew in her breath. She'd expected this, but not so soon. She glanced across the room. Relieved, she saw that Hannah, her hand still on Annie Rose's cradle, had fallen asleep.

Her pain had subsided to a dull ache somewhere in the region of her heart. She suspected it would remain there for a long time. Maybe forever. But life must go on. And now she had Annie Rose's future to think about. There was nothing to keep her in the South any longer except Hannah.

Calling on all her willpower, she summoned a warm smile. "I'd like nothing better." Oh, that wasn't true! Even though she deeply loved her parents, returning to Connecticut with them wasn't her heart's desire.

But since she could never have that, she'd go back with them. She hesitated, then went on. "There's a problem, though. Mother Clayborne has no family, other than me, and I can't leave her here alone."

Her parents' smiles widened with relief. "Of course, she'll come, too," Rosalind said at once. "We'd love to have her live with us."

"Wouldn't think of anything else," Norris echoed.

Neither of them had hesitated a moment to reassure her on that point, and their voices sounded as if they meant what they said. Eden glanced across the room again. Hannah still slept deeply, her hand dropped from the cradle now.

"The trouble is, she won't go. She won't even consider leaving here."

Eden turned over on the featherbed for the dozenth time, trying to sleep. For a while, she'd heard restless sounds from the loft where her parents had retreated soon after supper, but finally all was quiet up there.

Hannah and the baby both slept soundly, too. Why couldn't she? She knew the answer: she wanted desperately to go to the barn, wake Jesse, admit her love, and beg him to take her and Annie Rose back to Georgia with him.

Her face burned with those thoughts, with her total loss of pride. No, not total, she guessed, or she *would* be out there. She could never do that, no matter how badly she wanted to.

Because Jesse obviously didn't love her.

If he did, he'd have told her when they'd made love so wonderfully and satisfyingly.

He'd have asked her to marry him and share his life.

Pain pierced her heart again. Her foolish thoughts by the spring had been so wrong. He'd *never* loved her. He'd only wanted her. And now that he'd had her, he was going to leave without another thought.

Oh, she *hated* him!

Eden pounded her pillow with frustrated fists, then stopped, appalled at her anger. She could stay here in this bed no longer. Quietly she slipped out from under the sheet and quilt, found her dressing gown and slippers, and made her way to the door.

Silently she opened the door, closed it behind her, and went to lean against the porch rail. The moon was almost full, its silvery light shining across the clearing like the night Jesse had come back to the ridge.

A mockingbird sang a few trills, then stopped. The night had an almost unearthly beauty, as it had that other night when she'd walked across the clearing. A sudden urge to do that again filled her. Maybe walking would relax her, help her get to sleep.

She went down the steps and across the yard, toward the line of trees and bushes marking the woods. Halfway across, she stopped abruptly, her heart banging against her ribs.

Something had moved at the edge of the woods.

Could it be another panther? Of course it could, she answered herself. It could be any number of animals—or people. *Toby?* That thought made her swallow. Encountering him out here tonight would be even more frightening than finding a wild animal.

Eden glanced back at the cabin, wondering whether to make a run for it. No, she decided. If it was another panther, flight might make it attack. And it certainly could outrun her.

She'd wait a moment, try to see what it was. If it *did* turn out to be Toby, she'd scream and flee. She thought she could probably outrun him.

Frozen in place, she waited, keeping her glance on the place where she'd seen the movement. After what seemed an eternity, the bushes moved again and a figure stepped out into the clearing.

Relief made her knees tremble.

It was only Sadie, as it had been that other night. The woods woman came steadily toward her, stopping a few feet away. Her vacant brown eyes stared at Eden. She coughed harshly, her thin body wracked with the spasms. Then the vacant look faded to be replaced by an indignant expression.

"Whar's the babe?" Sadie demanded, her voice indignant, too. "Did you leave her alone in the cabin?"

Eden shook her head, concerned with the raspy sound of the woman's cough. "No, of course not, Sadie," she said soothingly. "Hannah is with her, and also my parents. Are you ill?" she added.

"You hadn't orter left her by herself," Sadie said, as if Eden hadn't spoken. "She might git afeared. She might git sick."

There seemed to be no way to get through to her, but Eden tried again. "No, Sadie," she said slowly and clearly. "Annie Rose is fine. There are people with her."

Sadie's accusing eyes bored into Eden's. "Yore her Mam. Ye ort to be with her. Ye ort not to leave her alone atall!"

Eden nodded, giving up. "You're right, Sadie. And I'm going back to the cabin right now. Goodnight." She forced a smile, then turned and hurried away.

"Yore not a fittin' mam to that babe," Sadie called, her voice agitated. "Ye don't deserve to have her!" Again the harsh, rasping cough sounded.

Eden frowned, slowing her steps. Should she try to persuade the woman to come back to the cabin with her, attempt to give her some medicine for her cough? That wouldn't be an easy task, since Sadie seemed to comprehend very little of what anyone said to her.

But she'd have to try, Eden decided, stopping and turning around. Her eyes widened with surprise.

Sadie had already disappeared into the woods. Eden stood there for a few moments, then sighed and returned to the cabin, knowing there was nothing more she could do. Even if she went after Sadie, she'd never be able to find the woman in the shadowy woods.

When she got back to the cabin, she found Annie Rose was fussing. It was almost dawn, time for her early morning feeding. Silently Eden made her way to the cradle and lifted the baby into her arms.

Eden lay down on the bed and let the baby nurse, her eyelids growing heavy. By the time Annie Rose was satisfied, Eden was almost asleep.

She adjusted her clothing and snuggled the baby close for a moment, tempted to leave her in the bed. No, that wasn't a good idea. She'd better return her to the cradle.

Eden laid the infant down and covered her securely, love sweeping over her.

Oh, how she adored this child! If anything ever happened to Annie Rose, she might well go mad, like Sadie.

Now she'd go back to Connecticut and somehow build a satisfying life. She had loving parents, a beautiful daughter. That was enough.

It would *have* to be enough.

Chapter Twenty-Five

"Eden, honey, is Annie Rose in yore bed?"

Hannah's worried voice penetrated Eden's exhausted slumber. She stirred. Was the baby in her bed? No, even though she hadn't wanted to, she'd decided to put her back in her cradle . . .

Eden's eyes popped open. She came wide awake instantly. What did Hannah mean? She jerked upright in the bed, turning her head quickly toward the cradle.

The baby wasn't in it.

She glanced toward the sleeping loft. Her mother was descending the ladder, her father close behind. Neither of them held Annie Rose.

Hannah's face was full of puzzlement and worry. Her eyes met Eden's. She tried to smile. "I guess Jesse must o' come in and took her outside for a few minutes. I'll jist go see . . ."

"No, I will," Eden said.

Fighting down unreasoning panic, she got up and grabbed her dressing gown and slippers. Of course Jesse had to have taken the baby. She hurried to the door and outside, trying to ignore the voice inside her head telling her Jesse wouldn't have done such a thing this early in the morning, with everyone still in bed.

The sun was just coming up, a big red ball in the eastern sky. She hurried off the porch, and halfway to the barnyard, saw Jesse heading her way.

Alone.

She could fight the panic no longer. It swept over her, making her stagger for a moment. If Jesse didn't have the baby, only one other person could. She ran to meet Jesse.

"What's wrong?" He grabbed her, steadying her.

"Annie Rose is gone," she managed, trying to stop the shakes that had overtaken her.

Jesse pulled her close against him, his arms comfortingly around her. "What are you talking about?"

Eden lifted her head. "Sadie took her out of the cradle while we were all asleep. I saw Sadie out in the clearing, and she accused me of not being a good mother, of leaving the baby alone. I came back in and went to sleep! Oh, how could I have?"

Jesse stared at her. "How can you be sure that's what happened?"

"What else could have?" she demanded. "No other person on this ridge would come in and steal a baby!"

They stared at each other for a long moment, then Jesse nodded. "How long ago was that?" he asked.

"Right before daybreak. I couldn't sleep, and I went for a walk. Oh, Jesse, the woman isn't in her right mind! What will she do . . .?" Her voice breaking, she couldn't finish the sentence.

"Nothing. She loves babies." For Eden's sake, Jesse forced his voice to sound positive. He sure as hell didn't feel that way. There was no predicting the woman's actions. She could drop the baby, hide her somewhere . . . *anything*.

"I'll find her—don't worry." He summoned a reassuring smile. "Do you know the likeliest place she could be?"

"Willa and I saw her once when we were picking ginseng. Down in that hollow on the north side of the ridge. She sleeps in barns sometimes. She might have taken the baby somewhere like that. She might be any—"

"I'll find her," he said again, cutting off her voice with its rising panic. "Go back to the cabin." He pressed a quick, hard kiss on her lips and turned to go.

His touch, his kiss, couldn't comfort her now. "No!" Eden grasped at his arm. "I'm going, too!"

"You're not dressed. You'd slow me down," he objected.

"We *all* need to search," she insisted, her voice trembling.

Jesse nodded. "Of course, you're right, but I'm going ahead." He turned and strode across the clearing.

Eden met Cade halfway to the barn and quickly explained the situation, then both of them hurried to the cabin. Everyone was up and dressed, standing on the porch. Eden, her heart pounding, her voice filled with urgency, told them what she was sure had happened.

Hannah nodded, her face looking every day of its age. She held up a tiny basket similar to the one Sadie had brought for the baby those weeks ago when she'd come here. "I found this by Annie Rose's cradle."

Any remaining doubts Eden had crumbled at this evidence. "Oh, God." She fought against tears, against giving in to weakness. This was no time for that. She had to be strong.

She hurried inside and quickly dressed, trying not to think about the odds against finding the baby unhurt. They had no idea where to look for Sadie. The woman roamed at random, with no pattern to her journeys. She could be anywhere!

Annie Rose was only seven weeks old. And a month premature. She still needed to be fed every three or four hours. How long could she go without food?

Back on the porch, Eden made swift decisions. "Cade, go to the Freemans', get them to help. Mama, Papa, you go with Cade," she said, "since you don't know the ridge."

"I'm goin', too," Hannah said shakily. "I know the ridge like the back o' my hand."

"No, Mother Clayborne, you'd better not . . ." Eden's words trailed off as she saw the determined look on Hannah's face. There was no keeping her here. "All right," she finally agreed.

Without looking back, Eden hurried across the clearing. Jesse had disappeared by now, and she wouldn't try to find him. She'd look in the most likely places for her baby. With all of

hem and the Freemans searching, they had a better chance of
inding Annie Rose before . . .

Eden turned those thoughts off quickly and hurried toward
he hollow where the ginseng grew.

Jesse was cold and wet to his knees from the morning dew.
Ie didn't even notice as he made his way down the slope to
he bottom of the hollow. He'd look here first, since it was the
>nly place away from the cabin Eden had ever seen Sadie.

He found nothing except chattering squirrels and birds in
he little hollow, heard other small animals scurrying through
he underbrush. Jesse searched it thoroughly, then headed back
ip the gentle slope. Halfway up, he heard a noise, and a stone
olled down toward him. His heart leaped. Hope rising, he
quickly glanced upward.

Eden made her way down the slope. His stomach clenched
n disappointment as he hurried toward her. "They're not here,"
ie said gently.

She pushed down the resurgent fear and panic. "Then let's
get out of here," she said, fighting to keep her voice steady.

Looking at her beloved face, Jesse felt a sudden rush of love
io intense that it staggered him.

How could he ever have thought he could leave her? Or
Annie Rose? He could no more do that than he could stop
oreathing. If he lost them, he'd have no more reason to keep
on living.

But this was no time to tell her that, find out how she felt.
He nodded. "All right. I'm going to the Freemans' next. She
might be in their barn."

"I sent Cade and everyone else there," she said quickly. "We
should separate. I'll go to the Lorimers'. I'll show you the path
to one of the other Freeman cabins."

They hurried up the slope, then to the main trail. "I just
remembered something," Eden said, stopping at the fork in the
trail.

"Sadie has a bad cough. She sounded really sick. I thought
about trying to coax her inside and give her medicine—but I

was sure she wouldn't let me. If only I had!" Her voice rose filled with despair.

"Forget that," Jesse said. Her hand felt so right in his, she felt so right walking beside him. They'd find Annie Rose, he vowed silently. And then he'd fight for the woman and child he loved to share his life. "Stop blaming yourself for this," he ordered, squeezing her hand.

Strength radiated from his touch, into her, giving her courage and hope, along with a sharp pang of regret. Why couldn't he have truly loved her?

But none of that was important now. All that mattered was finding her baby daughter. Eden slid her hand away from his and hastened down the left fork, Jesse taking the right.

Two hours later, Eden hurried back along the path. The six of them had among them been to every cabin on the ridge. All the able-bodied ridge-dwellers were now out searching.

No one had seen Sadie recently, and a thorough search of every barn and outbuilding had turned up no sign of her.

Or of Annie Rose.

Fear swept over Eden again, knotting her stomach. She couldn't stand this!

Reaching the fork in the trail, she saw Jesse approaching from the other direction. She swiftly glanced at his face, her hopes rising. His worried frown brought them crashing down again.

He hurried to her, his mouth tightening at her despairing expression. "With all of us hunting, someone is bound to find them soon," he said quickly.

Eden swallowed past the huge lump in her throat. "Yes," she said, her voice sounding far away and strange to her ears. Her breasts felt heavy and full, reminding her of how long it had been since the baby had nursed. She was afraid to think about how swiftly time was flying by.

How much time was left for Annie Rose?

Jesse reached for Eden's hand as they hurried along the path. His fear for the baby's safety had made his feelings reach a peak of intensity. He could restrain them no longer.

"These last hours have been hell on earth," he told her, his voice tense. "Made me realize how meaningless my life would

without you and Annie Rose." He took a deep breath and
let it out. "I want to marry you and take both of you back to
Georgia with me."

His totally unexpected words pierced Eden's haze of despair
and fear. She stumbled and Jesse grasped her waist, pulling
her upright again. Jerking her head around, she stared at him,
her eyes wide with surprise and shock. "What are you talking
about?" she asked.

He met her startled gaze steadily. "I love you. I want to
marry you."

"Why are you saying this now?" she demanded, her shock
giving way to anger. "Why didn't you tell me before? At the
spring, when we made love?"

A muscle tensed in Jesse's jaw. "I meant to. Cade took me
by surprise. All I could think about was not having him find
us like that."

"You've had time since then!" she said fiercely. "I don't want
to discuss this now!" She jerked her hand away and increased
her speed, her set profile turned away from him.

He caught up to her. "I had no idea your parents were so
well off. That they could offer you so much more than I can
now. Maybe ever can."

She threw him a furious glance. He'd put her through hell
for reasons like that? She jerked her head around and walked
even faster.

Then her steps slowed as she saw someone approaching from
the other direction. It was Cade—alone. He was only searching,
just as they were. Her shoulders drooped, all the fire leaving
her.

Jesse frowned fiercely. He should have waited. He'd only
made things worse between them. Then he, too, saw Cade
sprinting toward them, a wide smile on his young face. Hope
sprang up inside Jesse, his frown dissolving as he stepped up
his pace.

When Eden saw Cade's smile, her heart quit beating for an
instant, then began pounding wildly. "Have they found my
baby?" she demanded as he stopped in front of her. "Is she all
right?"

Cade was breathing heavily from his run. But his smile was

still in place—and wider. "Annie Rose is fine," he said quickly "She's back at the cabin—screaming for you to come fee her."

Everything went black before Eden's eyes, and she woul have fallen if Jesse hadn't caught her and drawn her up agains his chest. When the darkness cleared, she looked up at him smiling through the tears streaming down her face.

The tremulous radiance of her smile took his breath away He smiled back. "It's all over," he told her, relief making him want to sit down somewhere, cradle her on his lap, kiss he deep and long. But that would have to wait.

Eden broke away from him, moving to Cade. She hugge the boy and kissed his cheek. "Bless you, Cade," she said, he voice unsteady. "Who found my baby?"

He looked abashed but pleased at her praise. "Why, no on found her, Miss Eden. Sadie brought her back. Said she wa crying and she couldn't get her to stop and she knew she wa hungry."

Eden and Jesse exchanged startled glances. "I'd never consid ered that possibility," she said in a moment. "Thank God sh still has some of her wits." She glanced at Cade again. "Wher is Sadie? Did they let her go?"

Cade shook his head. "No. She was burning up with feve and coughing something terrible, and she fainted on the porch I carried her in and put her in your bed."

Eden hadn't thought past finding Annie Rose unhurt. Afte what Sadie had done, she could no longer be allowed he freedom. But she *had* returned Annie Rose unharmed.

"Hannah's at the cabin, too. I'll run ahead and tell them found you two," Cade said. Eden nodded and the boy sprinte back down the trail.

Jesse moved up beside Eden. He took her hand and agai squeezed its slim length inside his own as they hurried dow the forest path. What a fool he'd been. If this hadn't happened he and Cade would be on their way back to Georgia now.

"I'm sorry I didn't tell you how I felt sooner," he said. " don't blame you for being angry with me."

Eden's hand stiffened in Jesse's. In the exquisite relief she' felt at learning her baby was safe, she'd pushed Jesse's sudde

nd stunning declaration of love from her mind. Now, he'd
rought it back with his words, his touch.

She gave him a quick glance and shook her head. "I'm not
ngry. I just don't want to think about anything right now except
etting back to Annie Rose," she told him, her voice trembling.

Anger at his own bad timing swept over Jesse. "I understand,"
e told her, holding his emotions in check. "We'll talk about
t later."

"Yes," she answered hastily, her relief evident.

Jesse let go of her hand and she didn't even seem to notice.
He frowned as he looked at her profile, the happy smile that
urved her mouth.

That smile was for Annie Rose, not him. He'd picked a hell
f a time to declare his love.

After what had happened to their granddaughter, Eden's par-
nts would want to whisk her off this ridge and back to Connect-
cut as soon as possible. He couldn't blame them.

Nothing had changed just because he'd told Eden he loved
her. The same problems were still between them.

Did he have the right to ask her to go with him back to
Georgia? To give up a life of comfort and affluence for one of
truggle? He had nothing to offer except his love. Would she
hink that enough?

He made himself face the final question.

Did she, in fact, love him at all?

Chapter Twenty-Six

"Lord, take this poor critter into yore lovin' arms and give her rest for her troubled soul."

Eden felt tears behind her eyelids as Hannah said the final words. Jesse, Cade, and several ridge men began shoveling dirt over the pine coffin that Hollis Freeman had made for Sadie's mortal remains.

The woods woman hadn't suffered long. Her frail, long neglected body couldn't fight off the pneumonia that had gained too strong a hold on her. When she'd collapsed after bringing back Annie Rose, it had already been too late. Now, three days later, Sadie was finally at peace, buried in the woods that for so long had been her only home.

All the ridge folk were here to see her laid to rest, including the Freemans. Ever since the ridge had turned out in force to search for Annie Rose, the rift between Hannah and Mattie, and therefore the entire Freeman clan, had been healed.

The women and children were beginning to drift away, leaving the filling in of the grave to the men. Eden let her glance rest on Jesse as he dipped another shovel of dirt from the mound behind him. Her heart turned over as she watched his blond

rown hair beginning to return to its natural shaggy state after
eing slicked down for Sadie's burial.

Since the day of Annie Rose's abduction, when he'd made
is completely unexpected declaration of love, Eden hadn't
een alone with Jesse for a moment. She'd been caught up in
e joy of being reunited with her baby, then helping Hannah
urse Sadie until her death last night.

Hannah was flanked by Eden's father on one side and by
Mattie on the other. She was glad the feud had ended, even
hough she knew, by the looks Mattie had given Cade and Willa
is morning, that Mattie hadn't given up on her wish to see
e two young people paired.

But Mattie's manner was warm and friendly toward Cade,
s if that horrible scene in the cabin had never occurred. On
is part, Cade was warily polite toward Mattie, but he tried to
void her.

"Here, let me have that sweet baby." Rosalind reached for
Annie Rose's quilt-wrapped little form.

Eden started, then, smiling, handed the baby over. Her glance
et her mother's.

Rosalind's doting grandmotherly smile faded. She gave Eden
straight, firm look. "If you don't hurry up and tell that won-
erful man how much you love him, I'm going to do it for
ou."

Surprise shot through Eden. Were her feelings for Jesse so
ansparent? After a moment, she nodded. "I intend to," she
aid, her words as firm as Rosalind's expression.

"Good," Rosalind answered crisply, as they walked together
ack toward the cabin. "I'd like nothing better than to have
ou come back to Connecticut with us, but not at the expense
f a happy future with the man you love."

"I wish I could be that sure of what my future holds," Eden
nswered, wry uncertainty in her voice.

"You should be," Rosalind answered dryly. "The way you
wo look at each other . . ."

Eden shot her another surprised glance. "But we don't, we
aven't . . ."

"I don't mean *exchange* looks," her mother said, patiently.

"It's those yearning glances you give Jesse when he isn't look-ing at you, and vice versa, I'm talking about."

A warm glow spread over Eden at her mother's words. "I'm glad to know I'm not the only one giving the yearning glances."

Rosalind rolled her eyes. "I'm available all afternoon to take care of this blessed child."

"Thank you, Mother. After dinner I'm going to take you up on that offer."

"See that you do," Rosalind said.

Eden walked toward the barnyard, her back straight, her head high. Even though Jesse had declared his love for her a few days ago—proposed, even, she guessed—he hadn't tried to get her alone since.

True, there hadn't been much opportunity, but he obviously planned to leave the next move up to her. She couldn't blame him. She hadn't been very receptive to him. In fact, she'd been almost hostile.

But he'd taken her so much by surprise, angered her, when he'd told her the reasons why he hadn't declared his love. Then, later, all she'd wanted was to be reunited with Annie Rose.

Sudden doubt hit her. Or was that the real reason he hadn't tried to approach her since that day? What if he'd only been caught up in the same terror as she that day the baby had been taken, his emotions at such a fever pitch he'd said things he didn't mean?

What if he didn't love her, after all, didn't want to marry her? What if she was getting ready to make a complete fool out of herself?

It took every ounce of courage she possessed to make her feet keep walking toward the barnyard.

Jesse and Cade were grooming their horses by the barn. They both glanced up as she approached, then smiled.

She nodded in greeting, deciding to wade right in before her courage failed her. "Jesse, I have to talk to you," she said, her northern voice firm and brisk.

"I'm through with Duke," Cade said quickly. "I'll finish Ranger."

"All right." Jesse gave Eden a wary glance. He'd been tensely awaiting this moment for three days, but he didn't like the cool, no-nonsense tone of her voice, or how she wasn't looking directly at him.

Eden swallowed. "Shall we walk over by the spring?" she suggested.

Remembering the last time they'd been at the spring together, Jesse felt his heart thump. A dozen times a day he relived the lovemaking they'd shared there. But then his gaze became even more wary. The spring was about the only place on this entire homestead where people could go for privacy.

It was also the spot where Eden had turned down Darcy's marriage proposal.

"Fine," he answered, making his own voice even and non-committal.

He fell into step with her. She was walking fast, he noticed. Was she nervous, or only wanting to get this over with? He glanced at her profile to find it closed and unreadable.

As they approached the willow-surrounded spot, Eden's pace slowed. Belatedly she realized this might not be such a good idea. The last time they'd come here to talk, not much had been said, nothing had been decided.

Already, as Jesse pushed back the overhanging willow branches so she could precede him into the enclosure, she felt breathless, the pull of his nearness beginning to affect her as it always did.

He gestured to the bench, but she shook her head, quickly turning to face him. Their glances met and held. She felt herself being drawn to him. She took a step nearer, then another, until they were only a foot apart.

"Jesse, I accept your proposal," she said rapidly, while she still could. "I love you and want to go with you back to Georgia." She held her breath, watching for his reaction, waiting to hear his answer.

He stared at her, not able to believe he'd heard her correctly. Then, joy leaped in him, and a wide smile curved his mouth upward. He clasped her shoulders and pulled her to him for a long, deep kiss.

"I don't have much to offer you," he told her, pulling back

a little and giving her a serious look. "An empty, damaged house. Practically no money. Years of hard work. And I'm stubborn. I intend to stay there, on my plantation, and start over."

Deep relief spread through her. He *did* love her, after all. He'd meant every word he'd said that day. The look she gave him was equally serious, even though it was all she could do to keep from moving deep into his arms again and leave the talking for later.

"*Our* plantation," she corrected him, her voice firm and steady. "I'm not afraid of hard work. And I know you're stubborn. I've had ample proof of that. I couldn't get rid of you no matter how I tried, could I?"

He felt another smile tugging at his mouth, but he had to finish this. He had to make her see what she'd be getting into and give her a chance to refuse, even now, after she'd already accepted him.

"If you go home with your parents to Connecticut, you and Annie Rose will have a much more secure, comfortable life."

"I don't care about that. Neither would Annie Rose, if she was old enough to choose. And Connecticut isn't my home," she answered, her voice trembling. "My home is wherever you are."

He drew in his breath at her last words, then pulled her close against him, swooping down to claim her parted lips with his own. "I love you," he whispered against her mouth.

"I love you," she whispered back, parting her lips more, her tongue seeking his own.

He pulled her as close against him as he could. As the kiss deepened, he picked her up in his arms and then laid her down on the soft, mossy grass where they'd lain before, coming down beside her.

"Is anyone going to come looking for us for a while?" he asked, as he unbuttoned her bodice.

"No," Eden said, her mouth curving in a smile. Her mother would see to that. "We have hours before I have to tend the baby."

"Good." He finished unbuttoning her bodice and chemise while her fingers were busy with his buttons. His touch on her exposed breasts made her tremble, heightening his anticipation. "Because what I have in mind will take hours."

Tracing tiny circles around her nipples, he felt her shiver, saw her nipples contract, and felt himself harden instantly, completely. He followed the path his fingers had taken with his mouth and tongue. "Do you like this?" he asked her, his voice thick.

For answer, she pulled him down against her, reveling in the feel of her soft breasts against his hard chest. She felt his hands pushing up her skirts and at the drawstring of her drawers. She lifted her hips to help him along. "Do you suppose we'll ever make love in a bed?" she asked him.

"I wish we were in a bed now," he told her, his voice thick with passion. "I want to kiss every lovely inch of you."

"Then you shall." She quickly finished undressing, and when he saw what she was about, he shed the rest of his clothes.

He drew in his breath as he looked at her lying on the bed of soft grass. Her breasts were full, tipped with rosy-brown nipples. Below them, her lustrous, satiny skin tapered to a slender waist, then curved out again into rounded hips. His glance traveled to the apex of her thighs, to the triangle of silken black curls nestled there.

"You are so beautiful," he whispered, his voice trembling with desire. "So very beautiful."

Her eyes roamed over his strong body, frankly unashamed. Fire grew in her as she caressed his hirsute, muscled chest with her glance, moving lower to his flat stomach, ridged with muscle, and lower still, to where his manhood, in its nest of tawny hair, thrust proudly outward.

She thrilled to that evidence of his desire for her. And smiled at him, sweetly, hotly.

Jesse smiled back, trembling with his fierce need. His hunger for her was so great he didn't know how he could wait to satisfy it. But at the same time, he wanted to savor this time, prolong it, make it last forever.

He gazed so deeply into her eyes that Eden felt herself trembling, melting with heat before he'd even touched her. She held up her arms to him. "Come to me," she told him softly.

He drew in his breath at her words, barely restraining himself from lowering to her, plunging into her. Instead, he lay down beside her, pulling her against the hot length of his body, letting her feel his swelling manhood against her softness.

Eden gloried in the feel of him, the hard, muscled strength of him. How could she ever have doubted that he loved her? She pressed herself against him, moving her thighs apart, adjusting her body so that the hard, throbbing part of him was pressing against her softness.

She shuddered, sensations she'd never felt before, never even dreamed of feeling, washing over her heated body. Her arms went around Jesse's neck. She lifted her head, seeking the fire of his mouth.

His mouth closed over hers and she felt his answering shudder. She opened to him and his tongue eagerly accepted the riches she offered, demanding the same from her. Their tongues circled, thrust, and parried, and all the while she felt the heat steadily building between them.

She was lost, no longer conscious of time or place, only of their two bodies pressed together, their hearts thundering in their chests, their mouths hot and seeking. She opened her mouth wider, thrust her tongue deeply into Jesse's mouth, arched herself against him.

Jesse gasped, pulling away from her a little. And then his fingers pushed her willing thighs apart and slid inside her hot, welcoming body.

She tightened herself around his hand, savoring the feel of him, wanting this, yet wanting more, too. Slowly his fingers moved inside her, then slid out and thrust again, deeper this time.

"I don't believe I can wait for hours," she told him, her voice little more than a breathless gasp.

"Neither can I," he said huskily. Gently he rolled her over, onto her back, and rose above her. Then she felt him against the lower part of her again, hot and throbbing.

Each seeking mouth found the other, their kisses frenzied and feverish as their bodies clung together, moved together as if they were one flesh. Still as one, they found their final joy in a blinding moment of shared delight that shivered through them, then left them clinging together as if they'd never be apart again.

Jesse moved restlessly on the blanket covering the hay that made up his bed. His wide-open eyes gazed at the blackness around him. He couldn't sleep tonight for remembering the lovemaking he'd shared with Eden this afternoon. Just thinking about her soft, warm body close against his own made him achingly hard.

Damn it! How in hell was he going to wait until they were properly married and back in Georgia to have her in his arms again? They'd have to wait, though. He couldn't keep taking her on a bed of moss as if she were some tavern wench.

He moved again and Cade complained sleepily. Hell, he might as well get up and walk around outside. Maybe he'd even go back to the damn spring and cool off! He quietly slipped on his trousers and boots and climbed down the ladder.

The night was dark as Hades, not a sign of a moon or stars. A chilly gust of wind hit him, making him shiver. It would storm before morning. Restlessly he walked around the barnyard, then decided he needed to go to the privy.

Leaving the small building, he knew he wanted to walk to the cabin. He wanted to be as close to Eden as he could get. Smiling at his lovesick fancies, he nevertheless found his steps heading that direction.

Damn, but it was dark! If he hadn't walked this path a hundred times before, he'd have no idea where he was. As he finally neared the side of the porch, he heard a small noise, like someone colliding with an unseen object, then a muffled grunt of pain.

Instantly, Jesse stopped, alert and wary. Four years of war had made that reaction automatic. He wouldn't still be alive, otherwise.

War had made his senses unusually acute, too, and that ability hadn't left him, either. The sound had come from the front of the cabin. Silently, he lowered himself to his hands and knees and crept in that direction.

As he rounded the side of the porch, he heard more stealthy

noises, then saw a fiery torch arc toward the roof. It landed with a thump and flames swiftly moved along the old, dry cedar shakes.

It had to be Varden! Jesse didn't wait for any confirmation. "Get out of here, you rotten bastard!" he shouted, running for the porch.

Another flaming torch slammed directly at him, narrowly missing his head. There was no time to go after Varden now. He had to get everyone out of the burning cabin.

His heart racing, Jesse sprinted for the door and jerked down the latch. Thank God these ridge people never locked their doors! He flung the door open and ran inside. If possible, it was even darker in here.

"Wake up! The cabin's on fire!" he shouted, heading for Eden's bed and Annie Rose's cradle.

"Oh, my Lord!" Hannah said, her voice trembling. He heard the bed creak as she rose, and a sharp cry from Eden's mother in the sleeping loft as he hurried across the room.

Eden awoke instantly at the sound of Jesse's urgent voice. She heard the flames crackling on the roof. Her heart pounding, she scooped Annie Rose from the cradle, quilts and all, and hurried toward the open doorway. She and Jesse collided in the middle of the room. He reached for the baby.

"Give her here," he said, "and follow me."

As he took the baby, an evil chuckle sounded from the porch and the cabin door slammed shut. The blackness inside the room seemed intensified, almost palpable.

"God damn it!" Jesse swore. "I'll kill that Varden bastard."

Eden stifled a scream, fear sweeping over her as the acrid odor of smoke and burning wood began filling the closed-up cabin. "Hannah, Mama, Papa, where are you?" she cried.

"We're here," her father's calm voice answered from nearby. "Get outside. We're right behind you."

"I'm here, too," Hannah said, her voice shaky but also close by.

Eden fumbled for Hannah's hand, closing her strong fingers around it.

Jesse found the door, and after tugging hard at it, swung it wide. They filed outside quickly, coughing as the smoke billowed in from the roof, now engulfed in flames.

"Here, take the baby," Jesse told Eden, when they were at a safe distance. The night was still pitch dark and the people were only darker shadows. "We'll never be able to put the fire out, but I'll try to get some things from the cabin."

"I'll go with you," Norris's disembodied voice added.

"No!" Eden hugged Annie Rose close to her. "It's too dangerous!"

"Don't go back in there," Rosalind pleaded.

"We'll be all right," Jesse reassured them, and both men ran back inside.

"Oh, dear Lord, don't let anything happen to them," Hannah prayed, as they waited in tense silence for the men to reappear.

The women heaved sighs of relief when, a few moments later, the men reappeared, Jesse with the cradle and a bundle of the baby's things, and Norris with the chest at the foot of the bed containing Hannah's and Eden's clothes.

Another trip and they'd brought out the Thornton's traveling bags and the other, smaller cedar chest.

As they started for the third trip, Eden stepped in front of Jesse, clutching at his shirt sleeve. "No!" she said, her voice high and frightened, but firm. "You can't go back! I won't let you."

The flaming roof suddenly burned all the way through. Burning pieces of wood and shingles fell into the cabin, instantly starting small blazes that flared into larger ones.

Huddled together, for a few moments they watched in silence. A shout of alarm came from the barnyard and the sounds of frightened, panicked animals.

"God, what a fool I am! I should have known he'd burn the barn, too!" Jesse headed for the barnyard at a run, stumbling over obstacles and almost falling a couple of times. Behind him he heard Eden's father's footsteps, then a heavy thud, and he knew the man had fallen.

There was no time to aid him now. "Stay there," Jesse called and sprinted on. Nearing the barn, he saw the whole structure in flames. The son-of-a-bitch had set the hay on fire!

Fear slammed into him. God damn, was Cade still inside?

Jesse's boot struck something and he went sprawling, hitting his head on a rock. He scrambled to his feet and ran on impatiently swiping at the blood trickling down his face.

"Cade," Jesse yelled when he got close to the burning barn. "Where are you?"

"Here, Jesse!" the boy's voice answered, close by.

Relief so great he felt giddy swept through Jesse. Mingled sounds of fear and panic came from the animals, and Jesse realized they were all safely outside.

"Thank God you woke up, Cade. And kept your head."

"Smart boy," Norris said approvingly from beside him.

A flash of white moved at the corner of the barn. Jesse's muscles tensed; fury seized him. Varden! Damn the man! He'd not get away this time.

No time for stealth now. Jesse ran toward the barn, seeing the flash of white again. Jesse made a running tackle just as Varden reached the barn door, and they both fell inside the doorway.

The two men grappled with each other, rolling over and over. Too close, Jesse felt the heat of the flames as he landed a solid blow to Varden's jaw, making him grunt with pain. Before Jesse could hit him again, he'd somehow slid out from under Jesse's pinning arms, coughing as he staggered to his feet.

The flames behind Varden illumined him, revealing the feral snarl on his bearded face. With Jesse blocking the exit and coming toward him, Varden had two choices: charge, or retreat.

He retreated.

Jesse, smoke stinging his eyes, making him cough, advanced, his fists clenched.

Varden, backing up, stumbled on something, staggered again and fell, landing heavily on his back.

The entire barn was engulfed in flames now as the hay burned like tinder. One of the big center supports blazed white hot. Jesse knew if he didn't get out now, he'd never get out. He ran for the door and fell through it, and then the beam collapsed into the middle of the inferno.

A scream of fear and agony ripped through the night.

The hair on Jesse's neck stood up. He felt Cade gripping his arm.

"My God!" Norris muttered from beside him, his voice horri-
ed.

Jesse felt a certain grim pity himself that Varden had to die
ke this. But the pity was overshadowed by relief.

No one on the ridge would ever again have to worry about
hat the man might do to them or theirs.

While the three of them stood there, the sky opened and the
in began to fall in torrents.

"I'll miss this old place," Eden said to Jesse, as they stood
y the spring filling canteens and jugs from the sparkling water.

She gently touched the side of his head where a bandage
overed the cut he'd gotten during the fire two nights before.
he winced. "I can't stand to think of what would have happened
' you hadn't been wakeful," she told him. "Or if you hadn't
otten out of the barn in time."

He squeezed her hand. "Neither can I. So I don't think about
. We're all safe, and that's all that matters."

"Yes."

Finished with their task, Jesse moved the willow branches
way for the last time and looked back at the place that had
een their private heaven. "I'll miss this, too," he told her, a
icked grin curving his mouth. "A bed just won't be the same."

Eden gave him a mock frown and walked under the branch
e held up for her. She winced again as the burned-out barn
nd then the cabin came into view.

"It's terrible Hannah's cabin burned," she said. "But at least
e rain put out the fire and we saved some of her things. And
' it hadn't burned, I don't think there was any other way on
arth I could have talked her into coming with us."

"Probably not," Jesse conceded. "Thank God Mattie agreed
) let Willa come and live with us. Do you think she really
elieves you need help with the baby?"

Eden shrugged. "I doubt that's what persuaded her. More
kely it's because Hannah gave Mattie and Hollis all her stock
nd is letting them farm the land."

"You know Mattie pretty well, don't you?" He grinned at
er.

Eden raised her brows at him. "Yes. And of course, she st
has hopes of Willa and Cade making a match of it someday

He shook his head. "That's an outcome I wouldn't want
put my money on. They've got a lot of strikes against them

"Yes," she agreed. "I had almost as hard a time talking Wil
into leaving this ridge as I did Hannah. She's convinced sl
can never be anything but a hill girl—and woman. I do
know if she'll ever consider herself good enough for Cade.'

"Aunt Viola probably won't agree—she's a bit of a snob-
but Willa's good enough for anyone," Jesse answered. "She
sweet and smart, and in a couple of years, she'll have bea
swarming around her."

Eden gave him a rueful smile. "Are you up to that?"

"No, but I guess I'd better get in practice for when the san
thing happens with Annie Rose."

"You have a few years to wait," she assured him. "I thi
what surprises me the most," she went on thoughtfully, "is n
parents' decision to spend the winters with us." She smiled
him. "It was so nice of you to ask them. Now all the people
love will be together at least some of the time."

"I like your parents." Jesse reached out his hand a
smoothed it across her smiling mouth.

"Don't do that, or I'll take you back to the spring," she moc
threatened. "And we do have to get out of here this morning

"Do we?" he asked. "Going back to the spring sounds lil
a fine idea to me."

Laughing, she pushed his warm hand away. "I shouldn't ha
mentioned it." Then she sobered, giving him a serious look

"What truly amazes me is that you're willing to let n
parents lend you money to get started again in planting. I gue
you've finally gotten completely over your dislike of Yankees

"I got over that a long time ago," he told her huskily. "Wh
a certain black-haired, blue-eyed Yankee woman stole my he
the first time I looked at her."

"It took you a while to admit it!" she challenged.

"No longer than it took you to concede there was some go
in a southern man," he counterchallenged.

"There are more likenesses than differences between us

he told him, suddenly serious again. "I hope this country can
someday realize that."

"So do I," he said, his own voice serious. "That's another
reason I could never leave Georgia. I want to have a part in
that healing, if I can."

"I'm still nervous about meeting the rest of your family. Are
they going to hate me because I'm a Yankee?"

He looked at her for a long moment, then a wry smile turned
up his mouth. "Aunt Viola is too wrapped up in herself and
her aches and pains to worry about anyone else. Cade loves
you already—and I'm sure Belinda will, too."

"What about your neighbors?"

The smile faded and he gave her a completely serious look.
"I don't know. Some of them can probably never accept you.
Others will, in time. Can you live with that?"

Eden looked back at him, soberly. Then her face lightened
as she looked deeply into his golden eyes.

"Yes. I told you before, my home is with you. We'll make
it work."

She lifted her face to him, waiting, her smiling face radiant.

And his mouth claimed hers in a kiss that promised a lifetime
of shared love and laughter.

Dear Reader,

I hope you enjoyed COURTING EDEN.

My next book will be MY DARLING KATE. Nicholas Talbot, owner of a plantation in the Maryland Colony, eagerly anticipates his fiancée's arrival from England. He's waited five long years for her.

But to his shock and dismay, her red-haired older sister Kate gets off the ship—announcing *she's* to be his bride!

Won't you join Kate and Nicholas in their stormy journey as these two strong-willed people search for lasting love?

Look for MY DARLING KATE in July, '97.

I enjoy hearing from my readers. You can write to me at P. O. Box 63021, Pensacola, FL 32526. If you'd like a bookmark, please include a self-addressed, stamped envelope.

Elizabeth Graham

Please turn the page for
an exciting sneak preview of
Elizabeth Graham's
next wonderful historical romance,
MY DARLING KATE,
coming from Zebra Books
in July 1997.

Chapter 1

Maryland Colony, 1759

"Ah! Sweet, sweet Alyssa! At last you're here!" The two workers standing beside Nicholas Talbot on the wharf gave him curious glances, but his anticipation and excitement were so great he didn't even notice.

His heart pounded in his chest as he watched the *Rosalynde* come ever closer. A vision of Alyssa's blond curls and sky-blue eyes filled his mind's eye. Then a frown drew his dark brows together. Blue eyes and yellow curls, yes—but what did she really look like?

He firmly pushed down the doubts trying to surface, doubts that had plagued him on and off for months, ever since he'd sent the letter and passage money to his fiancée. After all, he told himself as he had a dozen times before, it had been five years. No wonder he couldn't remember the shape of her face, the way her features were arranged.

It didn't matter. In a few minutes now she'd be here in person, no longer the dream woman he'd worked so hard and so long to bring over from England to be his bride.

Nicholas pulled his dark blue cloak closer against the chilly wind sweeping across the wharf. It was an unusually cold day on the Tidewater, and dark, lowering clouds filled the sky.

He hoped it didn't storm. Alyssa had probably had a rough passage. Late November was a bad time to sail the cold Atlantic, but when Henry Aldon had told him his ship would make a late crossing this year, Nicholas hadn't been able to wait until spring.

He needed Alyssa now. Both for himself and . . . he pushed these thoughts aside, too. He wouldn't dwell on his recent problems. Time enough for that later, when he had to explain to her.

But maybe he should have sent another letter, after all, telling her that considering his changed circumstances, they must wait for yet another year. His tumbling thoughts reversed themselves again. No, they'd waited far too long already. His darling wouldn't care. Of course she wouldn't.

She loved him—as he loved her. And that was all that mattered.

The square-rigged ship came alongside the wharf. The deck-hands, aided by the two men on the pier, made the vessel fast, then put the plank walkway in place.

Nicholas erased the frown and summoned a smile as he eagerly studied the people on the deck, searching for a head of golden curls, a sweet smile, and blue eyes.

Recognizing a familiar face, he lifted his hand in greeting to Morgan Lockwood, the *Rosalynde's* personable young captain. Lockwood, pushing a lock of black hair off his forehead, smiled and waved back.

Two women dressed in coarse garb, obviously bond servants, made their way across the planks. One of them gave him a smile full of invitation as she passed.

A new frown drew his brows together. Where was Alyssa? Was he to be disappointed, after all the years he'd waited? Had she fallen ill? Or had something happened to keep her from sailing?

He peered at the only woman left, his heart sinking. That couldn't be the girl he'd fallen instantly in love with the first moment he'd seen her in her father's greengrocer shop.

No, this woman was too tall. As she made her way across

he planks, she clutched her hood around her face with a slender,
ong-fingered hand, obscuring her features. But the errant curls
ossed about by the wind were most definitely not blond. They
were red. An uneasy feeling stirred inside him. No, she couldn't
oossibly be Alyssa. His sweetheart was small and cuddly. Born
o warm a man's bed during the long winter nights.

"Careful, now," Nicholas warned.

Automatically, he took the woman's hand, surprised by the
irmness of her grip. She was even taller than he'd thought.

And something about her seemed familiar. Had they perhaps
met at one of the Tidewater gatherings? Could she be a daughter
of a local landowner, returned from a visit to England? Again
hat uneasy ripple went through him.

Wind gusted across the wharf, flipping back the woman's
nood, revealing her face. Nicholas drew his breath in sharply,
lropping her hand as if seared.

"Kate! What in God's name are you doing here? Where is
Alyssa? Has something happened to her?"

Katherine Shaw felt her throat tighten at Nicholas's question,
nis anxious and dismayed expression.

She clutched her gray cloak tighter against the biting wind,
nearing a protest from the kitten in its left pocket.

"My sister was in perfect health when last I saw her," she
assured him. Postponing her answer to Nicholas's other ques-
ions, she slipped her hand into the pocket, smoothing the
unseen tiger-striped head, and was rewarded with a vibrating
ourr.

She glanced quickly around. Formal gardens, frost-blighted
now, made their way almost to the creek's edge to left and
right of the oystershell lane.

Far up the lane she glimpsed an imposing manor house.
She'd seen several others as the ship had stopped at various
ooints to pick up cargo and unload people and supplies, but
this one looked far grander than the rest.

As Nicholas had written, his plantation was truly prosperous
and beautiful.

And despite the gulls and the sea smells, this Maryland
Colony was very unlike her home in England! Overriding her
nervous exhaustion, excitement filled her. She'd made the long,

uncomfortable voyage in search of a new life, completely different from the one she'd left behind in Devon.

Finally, she let her gaze fully meet Nicholas's and felt a pulse leap in her throat.

She would have recognized him anywhere, too.

His richly colored chestnut hair was as unruly as ever, his thick-lashed eyes dark brown. His wide-legged stance still held a touch of arrogance.

But his face looked different—older, hardbitten, as if he'd gone through some bad times. A scar now slashed across his forehead. A few lines had etched themselves around his eyes and mouth. His voice had sounded harder and deeper, too.

But none of this detracted from the potent male attractiveness that had stunned her from their first meeting.

Kate pulled her hood back around her face and pushed straying wisps of hair under it, delaying a moment longer.

But there was no way to break the news to him gently.

She lifted her head and met his frowning gaze again.

"Alyssa can't marry you. She's betrothed to John Latton."

The anxiety left Nicholas's eyes, his expression changing to one of incredulity. "What are you talking about?" he demanded. "Alyssa's been *my* betrothed for five years!"

Kate nodded, her throat tightening again. He wasn't going to take this well. Dread for what she still had to tell him swept over her.

"I know. But Alyssa was so young when you left—hardly more than a child. You couldn't expect—"

"I couldn't expect her to wait for me as she promised?" Nicholas interrupted. "Why not? Her letters never hinted that she tired of the waiting, that she had found another man."

Kate hadn't read her sister's letters to Nicholas, but she didn't doubt he spoke the truth. "You know Alyssa can't bear to hurt anyone. She just couldn't bring herself to tell you."

Even as she said the words, Kate knew she didn't fully believe them. True, Alyssa hadn't wanted to inflict pain on Nicholas, but her overriding concern was to keep unpleasantness away from herself. Kate realized some of this was her fault. She'd spoiled her younger sister since their mother's death seven years before.

Nicholas's brown eyes narrowed. "So she sent *you* to tell me? Wasn't that a rather extravagant gesture? Didn't she perhaps think it more sensible to write me a letter and return the coin I sent her instead of spending it on *your* passage? Or have you suddenly come into a windfall?"

Kate swallowed with difficulty. Her throat felt very dry. Why had she let her sister talk her into this plan?

Then her innate honesty resurfaced. Alyssa hadn't had that hard a time convincing her. She'd gently reminded Kate of her meager options. One was marriage to Cecil Oglethorpe. Seventy if he was a day, he'd already buried three wives and was panting to make her the fourth. Two or three other would-be swains were little better, even if younger.

And well she knew her person wasn't the big attraction. Once she married, the greengrocer shop she and Alyssa had jointly inherited would no longer be half hers, but her husband's.

The other choice was remaining single and running the shop until she dropped dead behind the counter as her father had done a year ago.

Both were bleak alternatives.

Was it any wonder the plan Alyssa suggested had sounded so attractive, had seemed to settle all their difficulties? Kate coming here, for an exciting future in the New World, leaving the shop for Alyssa and John to run . . .

She shook her head. "No, no windfall. I used your money for my passage. You see, Alyssa and I thought . . ."

Embarrassed dismay hit her as at last she fully realized the sheer audacity of the plan they'd concocted.

But she *wouldn't* stand here stammering like a ninny! She'd done this of her own free will, and now she'd face up to Nicholas Talbot and tell him the whole of it.

She lifted her head and looked him straight in the eye. "I've come to take my sister's place. I've come to be your wife."

Kate held his gaze, watching as his expression changed to dumbfounded amazement—then true and intense anger.

"Woman, you have lost your wits," he said, biting the words out. "Why would you think I'd want to take *you* to wife?"

Kate felt her fair skin warm, her embarrassment deepen at his scornful words and tone. Her left hand curled around the kitten in her pocket as much for her own comfort as for the animal's.

"Because you want a wife, and it's common knowledge that women are scarce in the Colonies," she told him, forcing her voice to remain cool.

She noticed that more people had come to the dock and were boarding the ship, giving an occasional curious glance toward her and Nicholas. They were simply dressed and some of them were dark skinned—African slaves, she assumed. She hated the idea of one person owning another.

Confusion swept over her. Then why had she come here, prepared to live under such a system? She brushed the thoughts aside. It was too late now for regrets.

"I'm strong and in excellent health. I'm skilled at running a household and a shop and not afraid of hard work." She paused, feeling her flush returning, then continued. "I am prepared to make you a good, faithful wife, and to bear you children."

Nicholas's expression didn't soften. "Are you trying to sell yourself to me for a workhorse or a brood sow? Surely you don't think those are my only reasons for marrying Alyssa! I *love* her. I love her blond beauty and grace. Her sweetness. Everything about her!"

The words he left unsaid hurt more than if he'd spoken them. *And you're not beautiful, Kate Shaw. Not particularly graceful or sweet. You're tall and red-haired, and I never gave you a second look.*

She wanted to fling his unsaid words back in his face, declare that nothing about *him* appealed to *her,* either. But that wasn't true. Something had stirred inside her the first time he'd come into the shop.

But he'd been instantly captivated by Alyssa's deceptively sweet smile and her beauty.

Suddenly, Kate's anger surfaced. He had every right to be furious with her and Alyssa, but just the same, she couldn't humbly accept his open scorn.

Sell herself to him, indeed! Maybe she wasn't beautiful, but everything she'd told him was true. She'd been ready to make Nicholas a good wife. She shot another glance at him. He looked black as the stormclouds swirling above them, ready to continue his diatribe.

She took a deep breath, drawing herself up and gathering the shreds of her pride about her. She'd give him no chance to do that. She kept her gaze steady on his, raised her chin a bit.

"You have no cause for concern, Nicholas Talbot. I wouldn't marry you now if you were the last man left alive on God's green earth!"

A dark-skinned woman stopped and stared their way, her mouth open. Kate pressed her lips together, wishing she'd kept her voice down. She didn't want Nicholas's servants to hear them quarreling.

Nicholas blinked and backed up a step. "That is indeed a swift change of mind, mistress," he said coolly. "Only a moment ago you were begging me to wed and bed you."

Kate barely restrained herself from stamping his booted foot with her own. "I was *not* begging you. I merely explained the situation and offered you another choice—which I have now withdrawn."

He lifted an arrogant brow. "Oh? So you have passage money for your return to Devon?"

Kate opened her mouth to tell him that of course she did, then common sense won out over her temper and she closed it again. She shook her head. "No. I will not go back to England. I'm not a fool. I can take care of myself. I will find work."

She also had a second plan that she had no intention of revealing to him. Maybe she wasn't a beauty like her sister, but she was sure she could find another man to wed here in the Maryland Colony. A better choice than she would have back in Plymouth. But that was a last resort, to be used only if all else failed.

Nicholas glanced around him deliberately, slowly. In spite of her anger, Kate's glance followed his as the strangeness of these new surroundings swept over her again.

But this time the realization didn't fill her with excitement. She'd imagined the ship docking at a city, with her pick of shops in which to find work if Nicholas rejected her.

But instead, it had sailed down the huge bay called the

Chesapeake, then entered a wide river with deep-water creeks running off it. No sun warmed the wintry day, and the lowering sky hung over a dark wood that grew close beside the gardens stretching away to the left as far as she could see.

Across the creek, there were nothing but more trees with bare black limbs, only an occasional tall green tree towering over the shrubs.

Never mind. It couldn't be too far from some town or city. She lifted her chin a little higher. "I'm sure I can find employment in the city of Baltimore."

He laughed shortly and with no amusement. "Baltimore consists of a few houses and taverns. There are no towns or cities close by. Do you plan to seek employment as a tavern wench or doxy?"

Kate's temper flared again at his words and tone. Before she could stop herself, she stepped forward and slapped him hard across the face.

Nicholas grasped her hand with his own before she could withdraw it. For a moment he held it pressed tightly against his reddening cheek.

With a jolt, Kate realized they were standing close together and Nicholas had a most appealing masculine smell about him. His hand, even through her glove, felt hard and strong, the heat of his touch radiating up her arm. The old attraction she'd felt for him resurfaced with a rush of warmth that left her breathless.

Despite his arrogant attitude, despite her own repudiation of him only a few moments ago, it wouldn't be wholly a bad thing to be married to, bedded with, this man.

Mortified at her thoughts, knowing how he felt about her, she stepped back and Nicholas moved her hand very slowly away from him.

"Don't ever do that again," he warned, his eyes gleaming.

"Since I have no intention of seeing you after today, that shouldn't be hard to manage," she answered in kind, glad the servants had gone aboard the ship and no one seemed to have witnessed the scene just past.

"Are you planning to stow away on the *Rosalynde* for your return voyage to Plymouth, then? That might be a long wait as this is her last trip until spring."

His eyes raked her from the top of her head to her damp
slippered feet. "Also difficult to manage, since you're consider-
ably more than a slip of a lass."

Even while her mind accepted his statements as true, her
palm tingled with a renewed urge to slap him—on the other
cheek, this time! She half-lifted it, and Nicholas instantly
reached out and pinned her hand to the side of her cloak.

"What did I just tell you about that?"

Again, against her will, she was very much aware of his
touch, his warm, hard strength. Humiliation flooded her face
with heat. She'd been a fool to come here! She'd done a stupid,
ridiculous thing, leaving herself open to his contempt.

She had to get away from him.

"Oh, you wretch!" Kate jerked her hand loose from his.
Lifting her cloak, she whirled about and half-ran up the
oystershell road. In a moment she heard Nicholas's steps behind,
closing in fast. Irrational fear swept over her. She *wouldn't* let
him lay hands on her again!

Wildly, she turned left, leaving the lane and zigzagging across
the gardens. She heard a muttered curse and a thud and realized
Nicholas must have stumbled and fallen, giving her a short
reprieve.

Kate increased her pace until finally she reached the wood,
with its tangled growth of underbrush as far as she could see.
A path loomed ahead and she took it. A short way into the
wood, the path forked. She took the right, then moved off the
path and blindly pushed her way through the mass of growth
as fast as possible.

Behind, she heard Nicholas crashing through the underbrush,
and more curses. Then the sounds faded away. Triumph filled
her. He must have taken the left turning! He'd lost her! But a
few minutes later, the triumph turned to uneasiness.

She was the one who was lost.

There were no paths in the wood surrounding her. She'd
never had much sense of direction, and she had no idea how
to find the path she'd left behind.

She'd been born in Plymouth and lived there all her life.
Her family were thoroughgoing town dwellers. She hadn't even

walked alone in a wood before. And never one without well
marked paths.

Her uneasiness increased. She might wander for days and
not find a house or people. And what about wild animals? Or
possibly hostile Indians?

Kate stopped where she was before panic could claim her.
She took a few deep breaths to calm herself. All right, she'd
done another supremely foolish thing, just because she'd let
Nicholas provoke her. Now, the sensible thing to do was to
stay put.

In a few minutes he'd be bound to realize she'd taken the
other fork. He'd retrace his steps and take the left path and
find her. Oh, but how he'd gloat and scold!

Kate took a step forward before she could stop herself, then
ordered her feet to quit walking.

She knew her personality was an odd blend of quick-tempered impulsiveness and practicality. Most of the time, common
sense curbed her temper, ruled her behavior. Only sometimes
did the other side of her nature take over—usually, when she'd
been goaded past thinking into anger.

As had happened now. How could she have forgotten she and
Nicholas had angered each other so easily when he'd courted
Alyssa? How could she have believed for a minute that they
could marry, live together in peace?

Again she berated herself for not seeing what a harebrained
plan she and Alyssa had concocted. But her younger sister had
never truly loved Nicholas, Kate thought. She'd been too young
to understand what love meant. Now, with John Latton, it
seemed she did.

Nicholas's letter and passage money had taken Alyssa by
surprise. It had been so long, she'd thought Nicholas would
never send for her, she'd wailed to Kate. She didn't even
remember Nicholas's face!

So, since Alyssa had no intention of giving John up, the plan
hadn't seemed completely unreasonable. Men in the Colonies
married women they'd never seen all the time to have a helpmate and mother for the children they wanted and needed. On
the *Rosalynde* alone there had been half a dozen women coming
to meet and marry equally unknown men.

And Kate and Nicholas weren't strangers by any means. ince he couldn't have *her,* Alyssa had said, he would no doubt ccept Kate as a substitute with good grace.

Of course, he'd be broken-hearted about losing her, Alyssa ad gone on, not without a certain amount of satisfaction in hat thought, Kate remembered. But he'd get over it, and he nd Kate would get along just fine.

Ha! *Why* had she listened and believed her sister's specious rgument? Kate scowled and kicked at an inoffensive rock by er foot. *Why* hadn't she found out more about opportunities or employment in the Maryland Colony? *Why* had she assumed verything would work out?

She knew why. She'd turned a deaf ear to her doubts because he'd wanted so passionately to get away from Plymouth, from he shop, from everything about her dull, predictable life. There as no promise of it ever getting any better. Nicholas wanted nd needed a wife, and she wanted and needed a chance at a ew life.

Look where her wishes had gotten her . . .

Not yet half an hour off the ship, she and Nicholas had rgued violently, and he'd insulted her in every way possible nd refused even to consider having her as his wife. She'd ound there was no work to be had. And she was penniless. uring the voyage, the small amount of coin she'd brought ad been stolen from her cabin.

She'd given up the security she'd had in England for nothing. low, she was cold, hopelessly lost in a thicket, and forced to ait for Nicholas to rescue her.

A new, worse thought invaded her mind.

What if he couldn't find her? What if she'd strayed farther om the path than she'd thought? What if he didn't even try? fter all, he was *very* angry.

That possibility didn't even bear thinking about, so she uickly dismissed it. Of course he would. No matter how angry, e was a good, decent man.

Wasn't he?

The kitten in her pocket mewed plaintively, and she again omforted it with strokes and soft murmurs. For the first time a her adult life, she felt helpless, with no way to turn. It was a feeling she hated with every bone in her body, every breath she took.

A large, cold drop of water plopped on her nose, then ran down her face, followed in a moment by another. On top of everything else, it was raining. Kate shivered, fear and despair sweeping over her.

What was she going to do?

ABOUT THE AUTHOR

Elizabeth Graham lives with her family in Pensacola, Florida. COURTING EDEN is her second Zebra historical romance. Her first Zebra historical romance, SWEET ENCHANTMENT, was published last year. Elizabeth is currently working on her next historical romance, MY DARLING KATE, which will be published in July 1997. She will also have a short story in Zebra's historical romance angel collection, ANGEL LOVE, to be published in August 1996.

FROM AWARD-WINNING AUTHOR
JO BEVERLEY

ROMANCES BY BEST-SELLING AUTHOR COLLEEN FAULKNER!

O'BRIAN'S BRIDE   (0-8217-4895-5, $4.9⬛

Elizabeth Lawrence left her pampered English childhoo⬛ behind to journey to the far-off Colonies . . . and mar⬛ a man she'd never met. But her dreams turned to du⬛ when an explosion killed her new husband at his powd⬛ mill, leaving her alone to run his business . . . and fa⬛ a perilous life on the untamed frontier. After a despera⬛ engagement to her husband's brother, yet another ma⬛ strong, sensual and secretive Michael Patrick O'Bria⬛ enters her life and it will never be the same.

CAPTIVE   (0-8217-4683-1, $4.9⬛

Tess Morgan had journeyed across the sea to Marylа⬛ colony in search of a better life. Instead, the brave Britiⵙ innocent finds a battle-torn land . . . and passion in tⵀ arms of Raven, the gentle Lenape warrior who saves h⬛ from a savage fate. But Tess is bound by another. Aⵀ Raven dares not trust this woman whose touch has eⵀ slaved him, yet whose blood vow to his people has ⵙ him on a path of rage and vengeance. Now, as cru⬛ destiny forces her to become Raven's prisoner, Tess mⵀ make a choice: to fight for her freedom . . . or for tⵀ tender captor she has come to cherish with a love thⵀ will hold her forever.

Available wherever paperbacks are sold, or order direct from ⬛ Publisher. Send cover price plus 50¢ per copy for mailing and ha⬛ dling to Penguin USA, P.O. Box 999, c/o Dept. 17109, Berge⬛ field, NJ 07621. Residents of New York and Tennessee mⵀ include sales tax. DO NOT SEND CASH.